THE AMATEURS

John Niven was born in Irvine, Ayrshire. He read English Literature at Glasgow University and spent the next ten years working in the UK music industry. He has written for *The Sunday Times*, *The Times*, *Scotland on Sunday*, *Esquire* and many other publications. He is also the author of the novella *Music from Big Pink* and the novel *Kill Your Friends*. He lives in Buckinghamshire.

ALSO BY JOHN NIVEN

Music from Big Pink

Kill Your Friends

The Second Coming

JOHN NIVEN

The Amateurs

VINTAGE BOOKS
London

Published by Vintage 2010

4 6 8 10 9 7 5

First published in Great Britain in 2009 by William Heinemann

Vintage
Random House, 20 Vauxhall Bridge Road,
London SW1V 2SA

www.vintage-books.co.uk

Addresses for companies within The Random House Group Limited can be found at: www.randomhouse.co.uk/offices.htm

The Random House Group Limited Reg. No. 954009

A CIP catalogue record for this book is available from the British Library

ISBN 9780099516668

The Random House Group Limited supports The Forest Stewardship Council (FSC®), the leading international forest certification organisation. Our books carrying the FSC label are printed on FSC® certified paper. FSC is the only forest certification scheme endorsed by the leading environmental organisations, including Greenpeace. Our paper procurement policy can be found at: www.randomhouse.co.uk/environment

Printed and bound by CPI Group (UK) Ltd, Croydon, CR0 4YY

For my father, John Jeffrey Niven, and my son,
Robin John Niven. Golfers who never met.

Here, in Scotland, golf was not an accessory to life, drawing upon one's marginal energy; it *was* life, played out of the centre of one's being.

John Updike, 'Farrell's Caddie'

He rallied, my tears being in unsurpassably bad taste, and said, 'Look here, it's *only* a game.'

Trying to speak softly so the children wouldn't hear, I said, *'Fuck you!'*

Frederick Exley, *A Fan's Notes*

PART ONE

They dream in courtship, but in wedlock wake.
Alexander Pope

1

IT WAS THE MOST HUMILIATING START TO A BIRTHDAY Gary Irvine could remember.

There had been more painful – his twelfth, when his parents had been unable to afford the skateboard he'd wanted. His dad had fashioned him one by gluing a piece of rubber tread to one side of a short plank and fixing the wheels from an old pair of roller skates to the other. Lacking any steering capabilities he'd barrelled down Castleglen Bridge and straight into the bus shelter, losing his front teeth in the process.

There had been more outrageous – his eighteenth, when he had been woken by his mum's shrieking after she found him unconscious in the downstairs hall, the cold trail of vomit marking his wobbly progress from the front door, the cock and balls inked on his forehead starkly proclaiming that he was now of legal drinking age.

And there had been more confrontational – last year for instance, when Pauline had accused him of being selfish because he'd suggested derailing her plans to go shopping in Glasgow so that he could play golf.

But this was definitely the most humiliating. It happened like this . . .

Pauline had to be up early, to get to a school over near Cumnock where she had a show to put on for some Year One kids. Even though it was *his* birthday he got up before her, as he always did, and made her breakfast.

At 6.30 he slipped from the warm pocket of the bed, the golf dream he was having (ball flying straight and true under a clear sky) evaporating around him as he yawned and scratched his way downstairs. It was the second week of April and the spring dawn was already under way on the west coast of Scotland, squares of weak sunlight forming on the walls.

Opening the kitchen door he saw Ben's lifeless form slumped in the corner – his snout buried deep inside a training shoe, like he was wearing an oxygen mask – and for a second Gary entertained the usual delicious thought: the monster had finally died in the night. But when he leaned in to investigate he saw that the dog's flank was rhythmically rising and falling as his ancient, tattered lungs emptied and refilled, his back legs trembling and twitching as Ben pursued his own dreams into the dawn. (Terrible Ben-dreams – rivers of human blood. Turds the size of cities.)

Ben scented him and rolled over, not completely awake yet but already composing his features into a snarl of hateful greeting, the growl rising within him his instinctive response to any human presence bar Pauline's. As he stretched himself fully awake Ben's growl sharpened in pitch, quickly reaching the level of ultra-hate reserved solely for Gary – defiler of his mistress – before resolving into a series of short barks.

'Oh, *please* shut up, Ben.'

Ben stopped barking. Not, of course, through any impulse towards obedience, but simply to allow himself to concentrate fully on glaring at Gary; his lips pulled back, black and pink gums and caramel teeth exposed in a furious scowl. Gary and Ben eyeballed each other silently, each seeing what the other saw.

Gary saw a seventeen-year-old mongrel, the issue of the congress between a corgi and a Border collie; this unholy union the crucible in which Ben's unique 'personality' had been formed. Predominately black with white and tan patches, most notably on his face, which was half-white and half-black (the colours erroneously suggesting a yin and yang of the soul, a light side and a dark side. There was no yin; Ben's soul was all yang). Ben was short – like a regular collie that had been cruelly sawn off at the knees. His eyes, once jet-black pools, were cracked and fissured with milky cataracts, and in those eyes Gary saw a Scotsman – thirty-three years old that very morning – with a thick, boyish thatch of reddish-brown hair and rust-coloured patches in his stubble. (A 'hawf' or 'semi' ginger they'd called him at school.) Gary's eyes were blue and clear, the eyes of a man who ran three miles most mornings and who rarely drank spirits. His complexion was youthful, although lately he'd been finding, in the hollows beside his nostrils, in the pouches beneath his eyes, the odd open pore that contained deep reserves of waxy pus: a posthumous inheritance from his dad, a two-handicap golfer in his prime and thirteen years dead this summer.

Man and beast remained locked in the stare a moment longer – old adversaries acknowledging that fresh hostilities were about to commence – before Gary opened the back door and, with some difficulty, hustled the dog into the garden. Ben, of course, didn't even make it as far as the grass, gleefully urinating on the patio three feet from the door, his panting face wreathed in steaming urine.

Now the ritual of Pauline's porridge.

Pauline's porridge was the product of much ingenuity and toil. It was made with milk and nuked in the microwave for exactly three and a half minutes. This specific timing produced exactly the right consistency of gruel and had been arrived at after much research and development early in their marriage, after Pauline had rejected many a bowl of too-loose or too-solid porridge.

Gary stood in the warming kitchen in boxer shorts and ancient Stone Roses T-shirt, listening to the hum of the microwave and the rumble of the kettle. Had he been standing in this exact spot a year ago he would have been in the garden. The extended kitchen/dining room – Pauline's project – had only recently been completed, long over-schedule and much over-budget.

They had moved into the small development five years ago. ('Spam Valley' his brother Lee had called it, a piece of indigenous abuse meaning that the fools who bought such houses had to live on tinned meat in order to make the mortgage payments.) The house was brand new. Their arguments were the first its walls had contained, their lovemaking the first its oatmeal carpets had borne. (And when had *that* last happened?)

The microwave pinged brightly. He removed the blistering bowl and added chopped banana, blueberries and slices of strawberry. As the fruit sank into the grey quicksand he added a drizzle of maple syrup. (Just a drizzle, mind. Pauline wanted the echo of sweetness. She did not – emphatically *not* – want to get fat. Much of her reading, her ferocious scanning of *Babe!*, or *Hot!*, or the women's section of the *Daily Standard* – 'Scotland's brightest family paper!' – was devoted to the subject of avoiding fatness.)

While he prepared the porridge Pauline's tea was brewing. Again the methodology here was chillingly specific. The tea bag had to be left in the cup for a minimum of three minutes and a maximum of five. The bag then had to be lifted cleanly out of the mug. It was not to be squashed against the side as this could result in a 'bruising' of the tea.

Gary Irvine performed these tasks with the assiduity, the attention to detail, of a man in a long-term relationship who very much hoped he would soon be having sex.

Before he took the tray up he went out into the garden to fetch Ben. From the kitchen door to the back of the garden was no more than fifty yards. A half sand wedge from where he stood. (But probably better to pitch-and-run it with the seven-iron. Percentage shot.) There was no point in calling Ben, for the dog's deafness was now almost total. (Or, Gary suspected, selective: the rustle of a biscuit wrapper, or a styrofoam tray of meat squeaking on the kitchen counter, could bring the fiend running from half a mile away. But if Ben were engaged in an activity he enjoyed – eating, sleeping, probing the delicate rainbow of scents in another dog's quivering anus – you could scream his name from three feet and he heard nothing.) The grass was cold under his bare feet as he looked around at the two neighbouring gardens, both of which had brightly coloured children's toys scattered around them; tractors and trikes and big water pistols – more like bazookas these days – in orange and yellow and pink plastic. There were no toys in their garden.

This year she'd promised.

He came up behind the dog and discovered – as the beast turned to greet him and black chunks of the succulent turd he was munching on fell from the corners of his mouth – that Ben had indeed been engaged in an activity he enjoyed.

'Oh Jesus!' Gary said, gagging. 'Oh you . . . you *animal*!'

He hurried back towards the house, Ben barking angrily after him, saying to him in broad Scottish dog: *'Hey, whit's your problem, bawbag? Do ye no fancy a wee bit o' breakfast jobby? Naw? Well, get tae fuck then!'*

Pauline was already at her dressing table, wrapped in a beige towel, busy with the straightening tongs and the hairbrush. She had already showered and her milk-chocolate hair was slicked back, giving her a sleek, otter-ish look. He set the tray down next to her and leaned in to kiss her cheek, smelling apple and vanilla and tea tree and blackberry and gingseng and lime and whatever other scents were in the oils, unguents, conditioners and gels Pauline spent a small fortune on. (*'By Christ,'* his mother had said once when balefully inspecting the rows of tubs, tubes and jars in their bathroom, *'is that lassie wanting tae open a bloody chemist's?'*) As he gazed down at his wife's heavy breasts, tightly contained by the towel, Gary was conscious of the return of the erection that had woken him in the night.

'Happy birthday,' Pauline cooed, pecking him back and handing him a purple envelope. His full name was written on it in her girlish hand (the little balloon over the second 'i' in his surname) and Gary dimly recalled the thrill that had run through him when he first saw her handwriting – on a valentine card, fifteen years ago. (The thrill he'd experienced the first time he saw her too – coming out of school assembly arm in arm with two of her friends. Pauline Shaw. The May Day Queen. Just fourteen years old and already the cause of much creative self-abuse among Gary's fellow fifth-formers.)

'Aw, thanks, doll. What time you got to be at the school?' he said, making it sound casual, jumping back into bed, jamming a slice of toast into his mouth and working a thumb into the seal of the envelope.

'Half eight. *Please* be careful with that toast. I don't want butter all over those sheets.' The new sheets, from that designer place in Glasgow she liked.

'Sorry.' He set he toast down on top of the dog-eared copy of Dr Ted Alabaster's *Putting: the Secret Game* that lived on his bedside cabinet and checked the time: 7.02. Thirty/forty-minute drive to Cumnock, she'd already showered . . . plenty of time.

He took the card out: a photograph, black and white, 1950s Gary guessed, of a couple kissing on an iron bridge in some European city. The kind of card Pauline normally chose – classy, a wee bit arty. Inside was a handwritten message ('Happy 33rd! All my love Pauline xxx') and his present – one hundred pounds of gift vouchers for Oklahoma Dan's Discount Golf World, the new golf superstore up by the bypass.

'You can get yourself something nice for your golf, can't you? I wouldn't have a clue.'

'Aye, great, that's brilliant. C'mere –' He reached out towards her as she crossed the room. Pauline kissed him primly on the forehead, but, before he could pull the towel off, she twirled away out of reach, across the landing towards the bathroom.

Calm. Keep calm. Don't paw.

He slipped his T-shirt off, lifted the duvet with one hand and the elastic waistband of his boxer shorts with the other. Fuck sake – look at the state of that. A cat couldnae scratch it. Suddenly he sneezed, the starburst of the sneeze falling tingling and sparkling over the length of his near-naked body.

Take your mind off it for a minute.

He grabbed the remote control and thumbed through the

channels until the screen turned a familiar comforting green and he heard the swish and clank of metal driver hitting ball: the Golf Network, a preview of the Masters, which started the following week. The camera roved over the lush green fairways and rich forestry of Augusta National in Georgia (arguably the most photogenic golf course in the world) with stirring, dramatic music playing and an American voice saying '*where the greatest players in the world will be teeing it up to compete in the first major championship of the year*'. Now a quick compilation clip of some of the greats – Brett Spafford, Torsten Lathe, James Honeydew III, Drew Keel – before the commentator's voice shifted down a gear dramatically and he said, '*including, looking for his tenth major title*,' and then the screen was filled with the image of a man.

A man? *The* Man. The Big Man. The Don.

'*The world number one . . . Calvin Linklater.*'

Calvin Fucking Linklater.

A shot of Linklater slashing an iron from thick rough at St Andrews the previous summer, on his way to winning his second consecutive Open. Gary had been in the crowd, managing at one point to get close enough to the ropes to shout 'Go on yerself, big man!' as Linklater passed. Gary felt the familiar ripple of awe he always felt when he watched his hero at work. For Linklater was not just a man to Gary. He was a god.

They were the same age.

They had both taken up the sport when they were five years old, taught by their fathers.

They both played Spaxon balls.

They were both golfers. (Indeed, Gary had even been named after a golfer – the great South African pro Gary Player. His father had been much taken with Player's compelling victory in the 1974 Open at Royal Lytham & St Anne's, where the black-clad dynamo had led the tournament from the first day.)

Actually, to say that Linklater and Gary were both golfers was a little misleading. Like saying that Jimi Hendrix and a busker cranking out the three chords of 'All Along the Watchtower' on an out-of-tune acoustic guitar were both musicians. Linklater was a *golfing machine.* The youngest major winner in history. Arguably the greatest putter in the history of the sport. Owner of the smoothest, most faultless swing since Ben Hogan; a swing that had brought him over fifty million dollars in career earnings (and many times that in ancillary income) and nine major titles.

Gary's handicap was eighteen. He was capable of routinely whiffing two-foot putts and he could always, always, be counted on to choke in a crunch situation. (If he had ten pence for every time he had uttered the words 'Sorry, partner' he would be richer than Linklater.) Gary's swing was so terrible that many golfers at the club refused to watch it in case they became contaminated by its uncountable faults. It had, as they say, more moving parts than *Terms of Endearment* and it had brought him a pen and a single golf ball in career earnings (both token prizes given to any junior member who had finished the Junior Medal in a terrible rainstorm twenty years ago) and more heartbreak than any man should have to endure. Linklater was one of the very few whom the Golf Gods chose at birth to bestow incredible talent upon. Gary was one of the very many whom the Golf Gods devoted their immortality to tormenting.

As he lay in bed listening to the punditry – who was on form, who wasn't, who was struggling around the greens and so forth – Gary became aware that he had been stealthily massaging his cock and that his erection was now of torturous proportions. Suddenly a thrill of panic shot through him – what if she . . . ?

No. No way, man. It was his *birthday*! She wouldn't . . .

Still, he could hear the blast of the hairdryer being usurped now by the drilling of her electric toothbrush – the morning symphony of Pauline's machines – and he thought, *Best not leave it too late*.

Pauline came back into the bedroom, humming to herself, turned to the chest of drawers in the corner, and dropped the towel. As they always did at such moments Gary's thoughts went something like – *How the fuck did I pull this off?*

Pauline was tall – a couple of inches taller than Gary – and dark-skinned for someone from the west coast of Scotland. (Italian grandmother on her mother's side.) Her nose flicked up at the end – forming a little button that Gary delighted in but which its owner regarded as an imperfection – and her hazel eyes were flecked with tiny mint-green shards. Moving down, the breasts – larger and heavier than her slender body would lead you to expect – were capped with glossy mahogany nipples. Down over the stomach – flat and fluted from hours at the gym, or in the spare bedroom with the cycling machine and the weights – and onto the long, tapering legs that were permanently slick from their monthly waxing. But it was Pauline's bum that stole the show. It jutted out so prominently it bordered on comic. *'Christ,'* Gary once overheard a guy in the Annick saying to his mate as Pauline sashayed by them on her way to the Ladies, *'ye could sit yer pint oan that.'* Gary possessed a clean soul, a decent soul, and was not given to jealousy. So he felt no anger, only mild pride, when strangers ogled and commented on his wife's body.

He watched her shimmying into a pair of translucent

champagne-coloured knickers. 'Are you still having lunch with your mum?' Pauline asked, her back to him.

'Yeah. We're going to the Pepper Pot.'

'Nice.'

'Errr, Pauline . . .' Gary said huskily.

'Mmmm?' she said without turning.

'Pauline?'

She turned round, topless, her thumbs snapping out of the band of her knickers, as Gary patted the space beside him on the bed, grinning shyly.

'Oh,' Pauline said.

Oh? Fucking *oh?*

'Look,' she said, fishing a bra out of the drawer, 'I haven't got time.'

'But . . . it's only half seven! It's not going to take you –'

Don't say 'it's my birthday', don't say 'it's my birthday' . . .

'It won't take long,' he said instead.

'Great,' Pauline said flatly. Her green sparkly tights were on now and she was pulling up the green sparkly tutu.

'But –'

'Listen, tonight we'll –'

'But . . . it's my birthday!'

Pauline gave him the look – a disappointed headmistress staring down a hopeless miscreant after yet another transgression – and said, 'I knew you were going to say that,' as she pushed her feet into the green felt slippers. She was now dressed head to foot as Tinkerbell.

'Fine,' Gary said.

'Oh, don't sulk. Tonight. I promise.'

A scuttle of paws across wooden boards, a low growling, and Ben shouldered his way into the bedroom. 'Aww, hello, boy! Hello!' Pauline said, kneeling to greet him. 'Come here!

Come here!' She buried her face in Ben's neck, nuzzling him and shrieking delightedly as his tongue basted her face.

Gary loved his wife, he really did. However, right at this moment, lying there in bed, abandoned and bereft on his birthday, with an aching erection pressing into his belly and sick lust running uselessly through his veins, he was certainly enjoying watching her French-kiss a dog who had just eaten a huge pile of shite.

'Christ, I'm late,' Pauline said. 'See you tonight. Have a good day.' Then her feet on the stairs, Ben pounding after her, the front door closing, her feet on gravel, the car door slamming, and she was gone.

Gary leapt out of bed. He scampered naked through to the spare bedroom (*'home gym' ma fucking baws*) and opened the third drawer of the metal filing cabinet. Halfway down the stack of golf magazines he found the crackly copy of *Spunk Sluts*. Back into bed, on autopilot now, flip straight to page 32 – a blonde in riding gear reclining on a hay bale, her jodhpurs pulled down and her blouse ripped open, one hand tugging an enormous breast greedily towards her mouth – and heigh-ho let's go.

Actually, he was so worked up that the pornography was a totally unnecessary addition. Approximately twenty seconds in and already his balls were tickling his lungs and trying for further north. His toes began curling as he felt the semen – and it felt like deep-core stuff, heavy sediment dredged up from the testicular floor – beginning to pump into the base of the shaft. Heigh-ho, let's g—

Fuck! The new sheets!

He feverishly scanned the bed for something, anything, within arm's reach that could be pressed into service, his hand now clamped around his twitching prick like it was an unstable nuclear device. Nothing. Not a tissue or a sock or a pair of underpants. He looked through the open bedroom door and across the landing into the bathroom: the open, willing mouth of the toilet bowl.

Carefully inching out of the bed – if a butterfly beat its wings within three inches of the tip of his penis right now it would all be over – he crept towards the door. He began crossing the landing. To his right a short staircase led straight down to the small hall and the front door. As he came shuffling across – naked, bone-hard cock in hand – he heard the letter box clank and looked down.

There, looking up the stairs through the glass panel that ran down the side of the front door, was the postman. Gary stopped in his tracks as they made perfect eye contact.

Gary's fist jerked involuntarily.

A butterfly beat its wings.

Gary closed his eyes and shuddered as he felt the warm drops spattering onto his right foot.

Caught wanking by the postman? No, scratch that, caught *ejaculating* by the postman.

Definitely the most humiliating start to a birthday Gary Irvine could remember.

As Gary wiped and dabbed, the golf ball that would soon change his life beyond all recognition was on its way up the M42 in the back of an articulated goods lorry. The ball – a Spaxon V – was in a sleeve of three, packaged in a box of twelve, which was in a crate along with 199 other boxes of Spaxon Vs, which, along with various other bits of golf equipment, were being freighted from Oklahoma Dan's Discount Golf World warehouse in London to the branch in Glasgow.

2

PAULINE DROVE FAST THROUGH THE STREETS OF Ardgirvan, heading for the bypass that ran around the town centre and then south towards the larger town of Kilmarnock. She shifted down from fourth to third to overtake a dawdling pensioner and, as she experienced the minimal acceleration of the jeep's feeble engine – the increase in noise easily outweighing the increase in speed – she thought to herself, *Christ, I hate this car.*

Pauline was first-generation Ardgirvan. She was born here shortly after her parents moved to the town in the mid-seventies. (Unlike Gary, who could probably trace his roots right back to the first peasant who ever tilled this miserable soil, Pauline thought.)

Historians of Ardgirvan – a rare and unlikely breed – could slice the town's development into two distinct phases: pre and post New Town. The oldest streets and buildings dated back to the thirteenth century, when the town was a bustling port, serving Glasgow, thirty or so miles up the coast. Later, as

Glasgow prospered under the Victorians – those canny old tobacco barons, sugar lords and spice dons – so did Ardgirvan.

Handsome sandstone villas went up along the main roads into town and shops thrived on the high street. A fine wrought-iron bridge spanned the River Ardgirvan in the town centre and tall, ornate street lamps threw orange-yellow pools of gaslight across the broad avenues and cobbled streets. Great shipments of coal and lumber from the local mines and sawmills were loaded at the harbour and sent up the water to help build the great ships on Clydeside.

The first half of the twentieth century was harder all round – as it was for pretty much everybody – but the place chugged along well enough. Plentiful council housing sprung up after the war – brown pebble-dash terraces with little squares of garden behind them for the veterans to grow carrots. Then, in 1966, it was decided that Ardgirvan was to become Scotland's last New Town: one of the poured-concrete paradises designed to help ease overpopulation in the big cities. Hundreds of acres of woodland vanished under the steel treads of diggers as roads were improved, roundabouts and bypasses were built, and fresh estates of council houses – these ones white as Polo mints – went up around what had been the outskirts of the town. Government money was used to build factory units to house the companies that – drawn by sweet rental deals and cheap local labour and about to be surfing the mid-seventies economic boom – would surely flock to the town. Glasgow was invited to send its poor huddled masses down the coast for a better life.

Well, the Glasgow people came all right. But the mid-seventies economic boom was more reluctant to show its face. In fact, it decided to skip the party altogether. Instead of reverberating with the bustling sound of small companies growing bigger, the huge prefabricated units were soon echoing to the tinkle of glass, the crinkle of the glue bag and the snake-hiss of the aerosol can as the vandals delighted in their new-found playgrounds. What did come along at the end of the seventies, when Pauline was taking her first steps, was something entirely different. Gary – two years older than Pauline – could dimly remember his mum saying that it might be a 'nice wee change' to have a lady prime minister.

She didn't think that for very long.

Gary's mum's potted history of the town went something like this: Ardgirvan was an idyllic coastal community filled with happy Hobbits who knew and trusted each other, a place where you left your doors and windows open when you went away on holiday (presumably, Pauline thought, so that your neighbours could pop in and water your flowering money trees) and where there was no poverty or violence. After a hard week digging coal or sawing timber the men would drink two pints of beer on a Friday night before going home to dutiful wives and happy children, children who ran laughing through sunlit woodland glades and whose rare bouts of apple-scrumping were the only crimes in this unfallen Eden.

Then the Glasgow people came.

And they brought knives and guns and drug-dealing and gangs and prostitution and devil dogs and Aids and gambling and ram-raiding and graffiti and mugging and Indian restaurants and video nasties and greenhouse gases and power cuts and the three-day week and unemployment and paedophilia.

How could the Hobbits survive these savages?

Although it stemmed from very different reasons, Pauline's dislike of Ardgirvan New Town was the only thing she had in common with her mother-in-law. (Gary, of course, loved living here, in this golf-studded stretch of Ayrshire that ran from Largs in the north to Ayr in the south.) Pauline – impatient at the lights now – had been the May Day Queen. Her family's house had been festooned with ribbons and streamers. There had been stories about her in the local paper. On the big day itself she had travelled at the head of the great procession in a horse-drawn carriage, waving at the throngs who turned out to cheer her royal progress and take her photograph. As the flashbulbs crackled against the spring sky, for one glorious afternoon, the fourteen-year-old Pauline had felt like she was at the centre of the universe, exactly where she was meant to be, her future glittering ahead of her like a diamond path lit by fireworks.

This was not the way she had been feeling lately.

Lately, as she thumbed through the pages of *Babe!* or *Hot!*, seeing these women – women no more attractive than she was, no brighter, no more driven – wearing dresses that cost more than her car (her stupid bloody car), with their own perfumes and fitness videos, their four-figure handbags, their first-class flights and their silicone cleavages, Pauline had begun to feel an odd sensation, not exactly jealously or avarice, but something closer to *terror*.

How were these things going to happen for her now? Here? In Ardgirvan?

As she turned onto the dual carriageway a removal lorry shuddered past her. Removal lorries caused Pauline to feel vaguely uneasy. The first time she'd seen one she'd been ten years old. It had pulled up in front of their house and the men had started taking things out to it. But they weren't moving anywhere. Pauline remembered her mum crying and trying to stop the men. It had all been something to do with her dad's business. It was years later before Pauline heard the full story. Before she heard the word 'bankrupt'.

She couldn't really remember Gary from school. He was just one of the older boys whose nervy gaze flittered over her as she walked along the corridor. She'd really noticed him for the first time a year or so later, in Annabel's, the disco in town. He'd already left the school and was working at Henderson's. He wasn't drinking. He was *driving*. It was the first time that a boy had given her a lift home *in his own car*. She'd blinked and now here she was – thirty-one, with no marketable skills and married to a man who was unlikely to be making six figures any time soon. She had been the May Day Queen and she was going to end up living in an ugly little house, driving second-hand cars and maybe going on holiday twice a year.

So Pauline set up Kiddiewinks – 'North Ayrshire's Premier Children's Entertainment Service', as her Yellow Pages ad proudly proclaimed. She had been at a friend's party for their five-year-old and happened to find out what they were paying the idiot who came along and made balloon animals and told stories to the kids. It sounded like a lot. Pauline's original vision had been to establish the company and then take a purely managerial role as the cash poured in. Sadly this hadn't quite happened yet – children's entertainers were thin on the ground and paying them was severely cutting into Pauline's profit margin. So, for now, it was just her and her seventeen-year-old assistant, Derek, and long hours and lots of driving.

Pauline's mobile trilled. She pulled it from her handbag and read the text message. Slowing down and pulling into the left-hand lane, she began thumbing a reply. One, two, four, six words, the longest ('later') not more than five letters. Not more than thirty characters then in the sentence that would have sliced her husband's heart into bloody pieces. She hit 'Send', tossed the phone onto the passenger seat and crunched the accelerator all the way down to the floor. Nothing much happened.

3

GARY WALKED ACROSS THE FACTORY FLOOR ON HIS WAY to the office. A huge, loud space – many thousands of square feet filled with the sound of machinery; the rumble of the overhead tracks as they whirred large parts from one place to another, the heavy clank of metal on concrete, the hammering of rivet guns. You could comfortably hit a five-wood the length of the place. Plenty of height – the corrugated-iron roof in darkness over a hundred feet above him, pale sunlight coming through the filthy plastic skylights. The smells of the factory too – oil, spray paint and the smoky aroma of hot metal. He kept within the yellow lines and returned the 'Mornings' that came his way from the canteen area, an island of Formica tables and orange plastic chairs lit softly by the red, white and orange lights of the vending machines that guarded it. He knew some of the boys down here well, he'd gone to school with many of them, indeed – if it hadn't been for his three Highers (History, Geography and Maths) – he might well have been one of them.

Henderson's Forklift Trucks was one of the very few companies that *had* come to Ardgirvan in the 1970s. It had weathered the recession of the early 1980s, the redundancies caused later by technological advances (the jerkily moving robot-welders Gary was passing now, their steel limbs oblivious to the blue sparks), and the market erosion caused by cheaper foreign competition. They had offered Gary a job in administration a few days after his seventeenth birthday.

He returned an increasing number of 'Mornings' and two 'Happy birthdays!' (Big Sue from Accounts, wee Marion from Export) as he passed through the grey warren of cubicles towards his desk. There had been a moment, a long time ago, a year or two after he'd been here, when he'd thought about quitting. About going to college, or the uni, to study . . . something. But Pauline hadn't been keen. Three or four years as a penniless student? What was the point of that exactly?

With a sigh he sat down and began rearranging the piles on his desk: pink, yellow and green forms, bills of lading, customs documentation, invoices to be assigned purchase order numbers, the huge amount of paperwork that was created whenever a forklift truck rolled out of the factory below and was freighted somewhere in the world. He nudged his mouse and his screen lit up – his screen saver was a photograph of the famous eighteenth at St Andrews, the Swilcan Bridge a jut of grey stone in a sea of green grass. The clock in the corner of the screen told him it was 9.13, but before he got to work on the PO numbers he looked out of the window.

The office overlooked the scarred brick wall of an old warehousing building, unused since the late 1980s. At the far corner of the wall, low down, faded but still clearly visible, someone had used silver spray paint to daub a five-foot-high matchstick man. Or rather, matchstick woman, for the figure had two gigantic, misshapen breasts jutting from its frame. The nipples – clearly an afterthought, or possibly rushed by the approach of a nightwatchman – were just quick dashes. A demented tangle of hair covered the pubic region. Next to her, crudely sprayed in the same silver paint and still perfectly legible despite several attempts to remove it, was the legend:

TEGS BEGS AND HAIRY FEGS

Sixteen years and it was still a rare day that it did not make Gary Irvine smile: the fact that someone among the youth of Ardgirvan, their veins fizzing with Merrydown or Buckfast, their synapses popping and expanding with glue or hashish, had so felt the biting need to share their love of tits, bums and hairy fannies with the rest of the population that they were forced to come here under cover of darkness and create their enduring masterpiece. He smiled, his reaction reminding him of one of Stevie's sayings – 'Never trust a man who can't raise a smile at the sight of a crudely drawn cock and balls.' Yes, Gary smiled, but it sometimes troubled him that he'd been smiling at it for sixteen years now.

A couple of hundred miles to the south the lorry climbed the off-ramp to Knutsford services. On a wooden pallet deep in the vehicle's bowels the gleaming white Spaxons rolled backwards in their cardboard sleeves.

4

CATHY IRVINE NERVOUSLY FLATTENED HER NAPKIN ON the table and wondered if it was too soon to go back outside for another cigarette. Bloody smoking ban. Cathy had never been a political woman – when she saw *Braveheart* she briefly regretted not voting SNP back in '78 – but the smoking ban had definitely radicalised her. 'This is jist how Hitler started,' she told Gary shortly after the ban came in, her finger jabbing the kitchen counter for emphasis.

She tried to look as though she was thinking about something important and, in doing so, she actually did start thinking about something important. For Cathy that usually meant thinking about her eldest son. Lee. That boy. Two hundred pounds he'd borrowed last week. Three hundred the month before. Loans he had to pay off. Said he'd pay her back soon, that he had some job coming up. But doing what? If he . . . she'd talk to Gary about it, see what he said.

Cathy didn't like being in restaurants by herself. Scary. Especially somewhere like the Pepper Pot, Ardgirvan's swankiest Italian. Well, Ardgirvan's *only* Italian. Their father, Cathy thought dreamily, her mind sepia-tinted by half a glass of the house red, would never have left her sitting alone in a restaurant.

Death had elevated her husband from a mere deity into something closer to all the gods of Greek mythology rolled into one: handsome as Apollo, as merry as Dionysus, wise as Zeus. Thirteen years gone and how often did he cross her mind? It would be far easier to ask how often he left it, for his memory occupied by far the largest part of Cathy's consciousness. When she woke in the morning, from her dreams of when they were young and together, her stretching leg still registered the other side of the bed as being empty. Every night she fell asleep communing with him, whispering to his ghost, telling him what had happened that day, of her tiny triumphs and disasters, fancying she could feel him beside her in the dark – the nightly transubstantiation in which the pillow became his body. Thirteen years gone and she could no more see herself taking a lover than she could picture herself piloting a space shuttle. Thirteen years gone and, when faced with any decision, from serious financial ones to what to put in her weekly shopping trolley, Cathy's first question was invariably *'What would he have done?'*

What he *wouldn't* have done, she thought, was leave her sitting on her own in the bloody Pepper Pot. But, Cathy reminded herself, her younger son had an important job. Office. Management. Three Highers. Could have gone tae the uni. Brains from his father. And, just as she thought this, as her dead husband was conjoined in her mind with her living son, here he was coming through the door, both of them coming through the door, the father's echo in the face of the child, an apology already forming on his lips as she rose to greet him, her face exploding into the kind of terrifying super-happy smile Cathy used only on very special occasions.

'Happy birthday, son!' she beamed, kissing him on the cheek and pressing her face into his neck as she hugged him, savouring the smell of his hair as fiercely as she used to when he was little, when, freshly scrubbed from the bath, he would sit in her lap and she would read him *Harry by the Sea*, his tiny mouth quickly learning its way around the slippery vowels as they followed the wee dog's adventures on the beach. Thirty years ago. It felt like yesterday afternoon to Cathy.

'Aye, same to you, Mum.'

Gary had been born on the morning of his mother's twenty-fifth birthday. When he was younger he wondered what this might mean. He didn't wonder any more, although Cathy was still convinced that this serendipity had marked him out for some great and special destiny. Events had proved her right so far, she thought. Gary definitely represented progress for the Irvine clan: he was the first member of their family to earn a living indoors, to earn it without tearing and bloodying his hands. He was the first to live in a private house, who had a mortgage rather than rent to pay, and the first who didn't smoke like a laboratory beagle.

'Sorry ah'm late, meeting dragged on. You look nice, Mum.'

Cathy was thoroughly made up and wearing one of her best dresses. Her reddish-brown hair, a victim of constant experimentation, had recently been streaked with yellowish highlights, the net result making her look as though something had frightened her half to death. 'And what did Pauline get ye for yer birthday?' As always when she used Gary's wife's name, Cathy experienced a tremor of anxiety, as though just saying it might be enough to summon up Pauline herself. Cathy feared her daughter-in-law, feared that she considered

Gary's family – meaning her and Lee – beneath her, unworthy to play a part in the kind of life Pauline was trying to create.

'Gift vouchers for that new golf place up at the driving range.'

'Oh, very nice,' Cathy said, thinking, *Vouchers? She couldn't be bothered to get her arse in gear and buy her husband a proper bloody present?*

They fell to studying their menus and Cathy did her thing – reading out every single item in her 'doesn't-that-sound-yummy?' voice, with special emphasis being placed illogically on certain words ('with a cream and *mushroom* sauce'), any foreign words being agonisingly mangled ('pancheetah') and random 'oohs', and 'mmmms' being inserted here and there. (The 'doesn't-that-sound-yummy?' voice had its opposite – Cathy's 'doesn't-that-sound-revolting?' voice, last used when Pauline had dragged them to that sushi place in Glasgow. 'Sa . . . sash-mee? *Raw slices of salmon? Pickled ginger*?' an incredulous Cathy had said, everything coming out in italics as she scanned the demented menu. The sushi idea had been a non-starter from the get-go – like many women of her time and place Cathy didn't 'take' fish.) At some point, Gary was sure, probably when they were choosing dessert, he would hear the gratuitous use of the expression 'tae die for', an Americanism his mother and aunts had bafflingly picked up on over the last few years.

They ordered – steak and chips for Gary, bolognese for Cathy – and sipped their wine and he caught the distant, cloudy look in her eyes. 'OK, what's wrong, Mum?'

'Nothing.'

'Come on.'

'I . . . och, I'm just worried about your brother, so ah am.' (An interesting aspect of the type of deep Ayrshirese Cathy spoke: the double qualification, following the proclamation you have just made with an additional affirmative. The same technique also had a negative application – 'Ah didnae bother going down the town, so ah didnae.' Its effect was to confirm the veracity of the original statement – even though it was usually appended to a statement no sane person would have ever doubted the veracity of, i.e. 'Ah don't like the cold, so ah don't.')

'Christ, what's he done now?'

'Och, nothing . . . I just wonder what's going to become of that boy sometimes. He's no nearer finding a job. He's those three weans tae feed. I couldnae take it if he ended up in wi a bad crowd again. If he ended up . . . going away again.'

'Going away', Cathy's euphemism for prison.

Lee Irvine. Hard man. Madman. Gary's elder brother had served three years in Saughton for his part in the bungled armed robbery of an Edinburgh jeweller's. Since his release seven years ago he'd managed to largely avoid the world of gainful, regular employment. He did 'bits and pieces'; building sites, scrap-metal dealing, second-hand goods of questionable origin. Within a town of no more than 20,000 inhabitants Gary and Lee managed to lead very different lives and, apart from when Lee wanted to borrow a little money ('thanks, bro'), Gary didn't see a lot of him. The idea of going into one of the pubs Lee frequented – the Boot, the Cross, the Bam – made Gary feel faint. He tried not to spend too much time thinking about where whatever income his brother did have came from but there was one aspect of his brother's life Gary did covet. True, his nephews and niece – Delta, Styx and Amazon – were appallingly raised and demonically behaved, but there they were all the same.

'He does OK, Mum. He seems to manage.'

'Aye, it's *how* he manages I'm worried about, son.'

'Oh stop it. Come on, how was your trip to Glasgow with Aunt Sadie?'

'Och! She drives ye up the bloody wall so she does!' Cathy was grateful for the diversion. Her tone brightened, her smile returning. 'She goes oan like a book needing battered. She said she would pick me up at hawf nine, so that we'd miss the rush-hour traffick going intae Glasgow, ken?'

With his mum safely onto recounting an anecdote Gary was free to stop listening. He could switch to AutoAye and plan the rest of his day off.

'... because ye know there's aw they roadworks oan the Kingston Bridge the noo?'

'Aye.'

Finish lunch in about an hour ... go home and get changed.

'So, anyway, ah'm still sitting there drinking ma cawfee and waiting for her tae show up at hawf past ten. If she's much later it's gonnae be lunchtime by the time we get up there and then we'll huv tae eat before we go shopping – cause ye know whit yer Aunt Sadie's like if she disnae eat ...'

'Aye.'

Get up to the driving range about three ...

'... So she finally shows up and, my God, she's up tae high dough. Ah couldnae believe it – she's late because she'd decided at seeven o'clock that morning tae defrost her freezer. Ye ken they've the big freezer oot the back?'

'Aye?'

Work on that shoulder turn, practise my wedges, get to the golf course for half four ...

'... so she's goat aw this meat she'd forgotten wis in there scattered aw over the kitchen flair – she disnae think for a minute tae call ye and tell ye she's gonnae be late, naw, no oor

Sadie – she's goat aw this newspaper doon tae soak up the water, I says tae her, Sadie, whit the bloody hell ur ye daeing defrosting yer freezer when ye know we're gauin up tae Glasgow? Och, she says, ah didnae think it'd take long! Is she no aff her suffering heed?'

'Aye.'

Get a quick nine holes in before Pauline gets home . . .

Gary drifted back into the conversation and realised his Mum had finished the story and was looking at him expectantly, that an actual question was being posed. That a rejoinder beyond 'Aye' or 'Aye?' was required of him.

'Sorry, Mum?'

'Ah said – how are things wi you and Pauline?'

'Och, fine. Fine.'

'Have you talked any more about . . . ?'

'A wee bit. She says she wants tae wait until her business is a bit more settled.'

'Her business!' Cathy snorted. 'Whit, running aboot dressed as a bloody chicken or whitever? It's no like you're no making good money.'

'It's important tae Pauline, Mum.'

'Aye, but having a family's important tae you.'

'Aye.' Gary sighed.

'Och, Gary son,' Cathy said, squeezing his hand.

Don't say it, Gary thought. *Please don't say it.*

'Whit's fur ye won't go by ye,' Cathy said.

What-is-meant-for-you-will-not-pass-you-by: the haiku used by Cathy to cover everything from career frustration to National Lottery disappointments. Gary thought it possible she might even use it were they ever to find themselves in an antiseptic waiting room, keenly anticipating the results of his cancer test.

'Aye,' he said, managing a smile and sitting up in his chair as their steaming plates approached.

'C'mon and we'll enjoy oor lunch,' Cathy said, spreading her napkin in her lap. 'Ah'm gonnae have some pudding. That Death by Chocolate is tae die fur so it is . . .'

As Gary cut into his steak, the motorway twisted and uncoiled before the speeding lorry, the concrete spools of the M74 bleeding into the concrete spools of the M8. There in the distance, glowering and hulking beneath low, cloud-filled skies, was Glasgow. Just the one delivery to make, in the city centre. Should be finished by four o'clock, the driver thought.

5

LEE IRVINE HAD BEEN NAMED AFTER THE GREAT Mexican golfer Lee Trevino, his father having being much enamoured with Supermex in 1972 – the year Trevino won his second Open at Muirfield. (Cathy remembered well the cold nights in a damp wee caravan, the East Lothian wind rattling the thin walls. Hardly a wink of sleep and then up at the crack of dawn to go and watch her husband watch golfers all day. Some holiday.) Trevino had been famed for his sense of humour on the course, his ability to stay calm and crack jokes under pressure. Alas, Lee Irvine was displaying none of his namesake's traits as he tried to cope with a high-pressure situation of his own.

'Fur fuck sake!' he shouted to the empty house. 'Is that it?'

Lee was on his hands and knees on the living-room floor, kneeling in front of the dismembered sofa, its cushions scattered around him like the hacked-off chunks of some monster he had bested in combat. He'd been right through the fucking thing, even cutting into the lining with a kitchen knife in the hope that a few pound coins had somehow made their way into the interior. But no – the sofa had yielded him two ten-pence pieces, a twenty, and a few coppers. Forty-four pence to be added to his haul from the wee ceramic pot on the bedroom windowsill (eighteen pence), the pockets of various trousers (eleven pence), and the bottom drawer of his bedside cabinet (jackpot! – *two* twenty-pence pieces and a few more coppers). Breathing hard from the exertion he counted the money in his hand, moving the change around his palm with a trembling forefinger.

£1.22.

The net worth of Lee Irvine, thirty-five.

Two pints in the Bam, even at the lunchtime happy-hour rate, would still be three quid. With a sick lurch he realised there was nothing else for it.

He sprinted out the living room, up the stairs and into the tiny bedroom shared by his sons Delta and Styx, the journey from one corner of their council house to the other taking six seconds. On entering this room most people would have assumed it had been the site of a recent dirty protest, a violent burglary at the very least, but Lee tuned out the mess as he waded through a pile of video games and reached up onto the shelf beside the bunk beds.

Styx's piggy bank was a plastic model of Darth Vader that spoke to you and waved its glowing light sabre when you put money in it. *'Impressive . . . most impressive,'* Vader would say as the coins went in. The rubber stopper in the bottom came off with a sucking sound and Lee carefully spilled the contents onto the Rangers bedspread and began sifting through the tangy-smelling pile of nickel and copper, hoping, praying, to feel the chunky heft of a thick pound coin under his fingers.

No such luck, but he did quickly find four fifty-pence

pieces, the silver heptagons emerging dazzling from the brown slush. Half a dozen twenty-pence pieces and a few tens followed. Fine. Say four quid he owed Styx. (Or was it a bit more? There had been that time the week before when he'd needed fags . . .) Anyway, he'd slip it back before the boy knew it was gone. Even stick a bit more in. As he slammed the piggy bank back onto the shelf he triggered the mechanism buried in the base of the plastic casing.

'Impressive . . . most impressive,' Vader rumbled at the man stealing his child's savings.

'Shut yer mooth, ya fucking prick,' Lee growled back.

He hurried out of the bedroom and stopped to check his reflection in the mirror on the landing. He was wearing jeans, trainers and a frayed Armani sweatshirt. His hair was short, with the fringe plastered across his forehead in a succession of kiss curls. There was a thin gold chain around his neck, a chunky fake Tag Heuer sports watch on his right wrist and two gleaming sovereign rings on the pinkie and third finger of his right hand. Lee was tall, close to six foot, and thin, wiry, having never put the weight he'd lost in prison back on. He checked his fingernails (he'd just about got all the dirt out of them after another useless morning digging in the woods), made a minute adjustment to his fringe, taking care not to meet his own eyes, the eyes of a man who'd just stolen money from a six-year-old boy, and was coming down the stairs when he heard the front door opening and then Lisa and Amazon were in the hall.

'Daddy! Ah found a dolly at the swings!' His daughter, his youngest, was brandishing a filthy, naked plastic doll.

'Fuck sake!' Lee said, ignoring Amazon and turning to his wife. 'Whit ye letting the fucking wean pick up shite in the fucking street fur?!'

'Ah fucking tried tae take it aff her, right?' Lisa said, lifting her dirty-blonde hair from her face. She was still a good-looking woman – despite having had three kids by the age of thirty. Three kids by Lee Irvine. 'She was greeting her fucking face aff. Ah'm gonnae fucking gie it a wash in a minute!'

'Don't play wi that, hen,' Lee said, snatching it from Amazon. His children were all named after rivers. Lisa's idea. Delta, their eldest boy, and Amazon were named after rivers Lee had heard of. (The Delta: in America. Something tae dae wi Mississippi and aw that. The Amazon: wi aw they mad darkies that nae cunt hud ever seen.) He'd never heard of the Styx but Lisa had assured him that she'd read somewhere that there was definitely a river called that. Maybe in Australia or somewhere.

Amazon burst into tears.

'Ah fucking told ye!' Lisa said.

'Well, fucking wash it then!' Lee said, tossing her the doll and moving around them to open the front door.

'Where are you going?' Lisa asked.

'Ah telt ye. Ah've goat a meeting.'

'Meeting?' Lisa said witheringly. 'Meeting ma fucking erse.'

'Fur fuck sake, Lisa, gie's peace. Ah'm late.'

'Who're ye meeting?'

'Nane o' your fucking business, right?'

'Aw, fuck off then.'

'You fuck off!'

Lee slammed the door and hurried down the path. Fucking Lisa – whit happened tae that lassie? Non-stop moaning. She's a short memory too, Lee thought, fishing in his pockets for cigarettes. Wisnae that long ago – just before Christmas, when ah did that wee job over in Ardrossan – ah was walking in the door wi a couple o' grand oan ma hip. Hang on though.

That was the Christmas *before* last. Truth be told things had been tight for a while. Lisa kept asking him when he was going to get a job. Shite like that. Turning into his fucking mother so she was.

Realising he had no cigarettes he checked the comedy Tag – 1.15. Wouldn't be that late to meet Sammy if he hurried. He could buy one round, Sammy the other, and then Lee would make his excuses. (Or maybe better to try and get Sammy to buy the first round, then he could buy the second and he might get a third pint out of Sammy.) Part of Lee resented going along to spend the last four pounds he (or rather, his son) had in the world until the broo cheque arrived next week, just to listen to someone moan, but he needed to reassure Sammy that – despite his frustrating morning in the woods – everything would be OK.

Anyway, Lee reasoned, you had to speculate to accumulate.

6

DRIVING RANGES; FLOODLIT CITADELS OF CONCENTRATED torment where the damned gather to toil in collective silence, the only sounds the swish and clang of metal drivers meeting chunks of balata, the swish and crump of irons chunking into AstroTurf mats, the occasional agonised moan or growled curse, the even rarer whistle of appreciation as the Golf Gods throw the suckers a sweet connection, just enough hope to keep them coming back.

The range Gary used was up at Stone Cairn, just off the bypass, and had been built four years ago to cater to the unstoppable flood of amateur golfers desperate for new means to inflict pain upon themselves. Eighteen floodlit bays looked out onto a green strip of land 150 yards wide and just under 300 yards long, the far end marked by a metal sign, red paint on white saying '250 YARDS'. There were more distance signs at 200, 150 and 100 yards, then, about fifty yards out, the little nets, about the size of a car bonnet, for hitting practice chips into. The rusting hulk of an old Land Rover sat smack in the middle of the field: a comedy target that would occasionally reverberate as a ball clattered off its roof or doors. Thousands of golf balls lay dotted all across the range, almost every one representing the fallen hopes of a madman.

Gary wanted to work on his long irons, the three and four, for most amateur players the hardest clubs in the bag to hit well. He fed five pound coins into the squat metal monster that sprayed out the balls. There was an ominous rumbling from the depths of its steel guts and then thunder as it unleashed a torrent of balls into Gary's green plastic bucket. He walked to the far end of the near-empty range, choosing the very last bay, the one furthest away from his fellow players. He lifted the chequered metal lid on the floor of the bay and poured the balls in. There was the faint grinding of underground machinery and – magically, comically – a white ball rose up out of the ground, trembling on its rubber tee peg. Gary slipped his golf glove on, took off his sweater and pulled the four-iron from his bag. He threaded the club through the crook of his left elbow, across the small of his back, and then through the crook of his right elbow. He rotated left and right, loosening up the muscles, and then repeated the exercise with the club across his shoulder blades and his arms hanging over the ends – a parody of crucifixion. In his head he ran his new swing thought over and over, 'Relax and release, relax and release, relax and release . . .'

The swing thought – a simple key phrase that golfers mantra to themselves as they make the swing – is designed to calm the mind and to simplify the many variables of the swing down into a single essential. Gary had read widely of the swing thoughts of the professionals: *'No stop at the top'* reminded you that, although there is a slight lag, or pause, at the top of the backswing, there should be no definite stop.

But Gary didn't like the negative connotations of the word 'no'. He'd read an interview with the huge-hitting American tour pro Cyrus Cheeks where Cheeks said his swing thought was: 'Let the clubhead be the first thing to move away from the ball.' What a mouthful! By the time Gary got all that out his ball was often already well on its way. *'Back and through'* was simpler, but a wee bit dull. When he was playing particularly badly the swing thought would sometimes morph into 'You. Fucking. Cunt.' Or – on truly terrible occasions – 'I. Am. A. Cunt.' But, again, this really was very negative and, having recently frowned his way through top golf psychologist Dr Emil Koresh's new book *Banish Negativity*, Gary was trying to, well, banish negativity. Koresh recommended 'relax' on the backswing and 'release' on the downswing.

A warm, clear afternoon, a fresh ball on the tee, the afternoon off work, shirtsleeves. Could there be a finer feeling in the world? Gary was glad to be alive, almost smiling as he stepped up to the ball, waggled the clubhead and settled his breathing.

Relax and release.

He brutally shanked fifty-six balls in a row.

They bulleted diagonally rightwards across the range – the last one ricocheting off the wooden frame of his bay and nearly killing the astonished schoolboy a few bays along. Gary bit his left hand until his teeth went through the glove and drew blood and then ran to the car fighting tears, leaving the remaining balls unspent in the underfloor chamber. He'd gone from glad-to-be-alive to a gnashing, weeping madman in a little over twenty minutes.

Only golf can do this.

As Gary ran for his car (ignoring the stares and chuckles of his fellow players), high above him, above the clouds, above the vaporised jet trails, above the sky itself, the Golf Gods roared with helpless laughter as they tossed another shrieking corpse onto the blazing pyre. The pyre was fashioned from the wretched souls of the fools they had damned to live as golf spastics. It was a thousand miles high and hotter than the sun.

The shank – the amateur's biggest nightmare, golf cancer – is caused by the ball being struck not with the clubface, but with the hosel of the club: the point where the blade joins the shaft. This type of misstrike causes the ball to fly off to the right (for a right-handed golfer) at the most violent angle imaginable. The shanks come in bouts, striking the weak, the tired, the feeble-minded, the careless. Like the hiccups, once in the grip of a bout it is impossible for the afflicted to do anything else: no matter what modifications are made to the swing the end result remains the same – the sickening misconnection followed by the ball rocketing off diagonally to the right.

It is said that the insane asylums of the world are filled with men – good men, men who had careers, wives and families – who were taken down with the shanks. They cry all day and rend the night air with their dreadful screaming. They struggle against their bonds, wriggling in hot straitjackets and clawing at the cool walls of their padded chambers with their toenails. An enormous percentage take their own lives, gratefully placing their spittle-drenched lips around the smoking exhaust pipe or oiled gun barrel that will deliver them to the green fairways of heaven, where never a shank was struck.

You will sometimes hear people saying that the difference between hitting a shank and hitting a perfect shot is a matter of millimetres. This is like telling a man with a three-inch penis that the difference between him and King Dong is less than a foot. Of course, Gary Irvine, sitting weeping in his car now, knew all this. How well he remembered his father's bout of the shanks back in '82.

One summer evening his father stormed into the house from the course, dragging his golf bag behind him like a policeman might drag a howling anarchist towards the Black Maria. He marched straight through the hall and out to the back garden. He fetched a hacksaw from the garage and he sawed the head off of every club in the bag while Gary, Lee and Cathy looked on in mute horror. There were thirteen clubs. It took quite a while. When he was finished he began digging a hole and the whole family – and a couple of the neighbours – watched, darkness falling now, as their dad hurled the severed clubheads in and leapt up and down on the makeshift grave. He came into the kitchen, washed his hands with the viscous green-black Swarfega he kept by the kitchen door, and went to bed.

Two weeks later he bought himself new clubs and the incident was never spoken of.

The golf swing, the single most complex action in sport, was once described by Valentine Stent – 1920s tour pro and one of the sport's most respected early theorists – as 'a miracle, a physical wonder'. Almost every muscle and fibre in the human body is used at the same time – some twisting and pulling in opposite directions – to deliver a metal blade, with a sweet spot smaller than a penny, to a ball a little over four centimeters wide, administering enough force to launch the ball at speeds approaching two hundred miles an hour at a target which often lies perhaps a quarter of a mile away. There are as many different golf swings as there are golfers, but the

King, the key thing, the absolute priority, is repeatability: if you can make the same swing every time, if you can keep delivering the clubface to the ball the same way no matter the external pressures, you will win golf tournaments.

Gary's swing was indeed a 'miracle' – a miracle of bad engineering, wasted energy and poor physics. It was composed of four separate parts, beginning with the takeaway, where Gary started to move the clubhead away from the ball. This part was slow and careful, very slow and careful, as though Gary was trying not to disturb a caterpillar which had crawled onto his clubface and fallen asleep. The next section of the backswing saw a dramatic increase in speed, as if trying to suddenly compensate for the laziness of the takeaway. Then, stage three, he stopped at the top of the backswing. Not a pause, not the graceful, power-gathering lag you saw some of the top players incorporate. No. Gary just kind of stopped swinging for a few seconds, as though he'd changed his mind, as if he'd come to his senses and realised that swinging this golf club was a bad idea, possibly the worst idea he'd ever had in his life. Stage four – the downswing – really had to be seen to be believed. It was as though Gary had suddenly realised that the ball was not an innocent sphere, but that it was, in fact, a hand grenade minus the pin. He had to get it out of here. NOW! Consequently, stage four was just an insane blur, a demented lunge, as Gary swung so hard he generated almost as much clubhead speed as Calvin Linklater himself.

However, there the similarities with Linklater ended. Linklater's swing brought the clubface back to the ball exactly where it had left it, right on the sweet spot, pinching off a neat postage stamp of turf and sending the ball rocketing off on a true line. Gary wasn't so sure where the clubhead would land because he would often have his eyes closed by this point.

Golf, it has often been pointed out, is like sex. You don't have to be good at it to enjoy it. But when you were as bad at it as Gary was . . . then why? Why keep coming back? The truth was that Gary – like millions of other unfortunates around the globe – had hit just enough good shots to facilitate a lifelong, soul-destroying addiction. Like the monkey-typewriter-works-of-Shakespeare principle, if an amateur plays enough golf he will, at some point, hit one like Calvin Linklater or Gram Novotell. Gary told himself what all the poor, deranged fools told themselves: 'If I can do it once, surely, with enough practice, I can do it all the time?' Alas, while it is one probability that, if you leave your regiment of monkeys alone for a few millennia with a bank of word processors and unlimited recourse to coffee and doughnuts, then eventually one of them might come excitedly screeching and hopping up to you, grinning its chimp-grin and holding a few badly chimp-typed sentences from *King Lear*, it is another probability altogether that they will ever produce the complete works.

He needed a drink, some comfort. Respite from the heartbreak. He dried his eyes, started the car, and went to see Stevie.

7

IN ROOM 411 OF THE HOSPITALITY INN NEAR THE harbour, more heartbreak was unfolding.

The green, sparkly Tinkerbell tights were balled on the floor while, on the bed, Pauline enveloped a scrotum in her mouth and circled her tongue around the bursting balls within it. She came up, tracing the tip of her tongue up the length of the cock, and took it in her mouth, causing him to cry out, 'Oh doll, oh fuck, that's fucking magic so it is!'

Fearing it might all be over too soon, he looked around the room, trying to take his mind off things. He took in the nondescript hotel furniture and fabrics – soft oranges and muted reds – and briefly wondered who supplied their carpeting. Big contract that. Then he looked back down at Pauline – her eyes closed as he slid in and out of her mouth, the tips of her heavy breasts visible below her face.

Findlay Masterson thought to himself: Result.

About three months ago was it? Sometime in mid-January, just after Rangers lost at home to . . . anyway, whenever, they'd had a birthday party at the house for wee Jake, his wife's sister's boy. (Leanne was always throwing parties for her friends and family: none of them had a house for entertaining like the Mastersons had.) Leanne had booked some company to do the entertainment for the weans and Masterson had been surprised when he opened the door to find Pauline on the doorstep, beaming and dressed as Minnie Mouse. He'd been expecting some fat clown, some sad old alky-paedo. Even so, he hadn't taken much notice of her until later that afternoon. Several bottles of wine had been drunk, the spirits had been cracked open, and the party had definitively swung towards the adults. Masterson had been in the kitchen mixing drinks when she'd come in and said, 'I think your TV adverts are really funny.'

'Oh aye? Making an arse of maself is mair like it,' Masterson said, although really he was flattered. The TV ads hadn't run for a couple of years, but a surprising number of people still recognised him from them. He'd been dressed up in a robe and crown for them – *'the Carpet King of Scotland'*. Stupid idea. Dreamed up by a couple o' benders from that ad agency in Glasgow he'd hired. Still, folk seemed to have liked it.

'And you have a lovely home,' Pauline added.

'Aye, it's no bad fur a boy from Wilton Terrace.'

This was true: a big house like this up in the bloody Meadows for a boy from the hardest street in the town? A boy who left school at fifteen without an O level to his name? Findlay Masterson had taken his dad's wee carpet firm and built it into the west coast of Scotland's biggest carpet-clearance business, making himself a millionaire by the time he turned forty.

She had been sweating a little from whatever she'd been doing to entertain the kids, her brown hair sticking to her forehead. She was a fucking wee honey right enough. Stonking. And the arse on it? Ye could sit yer pint oan it, so ye could.

'Ye look parched, hen,' he said. 'Are ye wanting a wee drink?'

They'd talked for a while in the kitchen while her assistant loaded all their stuff back into the silly wee jeep they'd parked next to his Mercedes. From a distance, with kids running around and having their hair ruffled, and guests coming in and out, it would have looked innocent enough. But, in Masterson's experience, the experience of a wealthy, robustly priapic man, it never was. Sure enough, after a while – with him on his third vodka and Coke and her on her second bowl-sized glass of Chardonnay – she was laughing a little too hard at his jokes and holding his gaze a little too long. He'd been talking about how he had taken Masterson's Carpets from eleven people in a small industrial unit to a turnover of eighteen million last year. She was talking about her own experience as a small businesswoman. It was perfectly logical that she accepted his offer – given sotto voce, when he could hear Leanne's voice coming from far away in the house – of lunch. To discuss, in her words, 'marketing techniques'. Ways to 'grow the brand'.

Aye, 'grow the brand'. She still came out wi' shite like that now and again. But, on the other hand, here she was now in room 411, letting his prick spring out of her mouth and turning away from him, getting on all fours and pushing that incredible arse towards him, a strip of late-afternoon sunshine not quite blocked by the drawn curtains burning across her bare back.

Afterwards they lay breathing in the rented room, listening to the sounds the hotel made around them. Masterson scratched his thick moustache and sneaked a peek at his Rolex – just gone four. Did they have Sky Sports here? They did. Probably some football on the go, but would it piss her off if he turned the TV on? Birds could be funny like that. She was bound to go to the bathroom soon enough. Natural window.

He'd told Leanne he was driving over to the Ayr showroom. Stock problem. Back in time for dinner. He was starving now right enough. Could really go a toastie or something. The beasting always gave him the munchies. She pressed back against him. Surely she couldn't, not already. But no, she was just stretching, her back was wet from where he'd . . . she'd said she was on the pill, mentioned it twice now, but he wasn't taking any chances. Not Findlay Masterson. Big FM? No way, man. Negatori. No fucken danger. He'd be getting off at Paisley as usual and nae mistake. Right wee fiend for the boabby this one. Then again, Masterson reflected, weren't they all at first? Look at his Leanne. When they first started seeing each other? Daft for cock so she was: swallowing, touching herself up while they were doing it, even, that one time, in that hotel in Edinburgh, offering to let him . . . But nowadays? Ye'd need tae coat the thing wi' sugar-covered fucken diamonds just tae get it intae the cow's mouth.

A tremor ran through his arm as Pauline's jaw tightened into a yawn. What was she thinking about? Not about ham-and-cheese toasties and Rangers–Aberdeen, that's for sure. Probably about her husband, the poor cunt. Ah well, Masterson thought – *if he was taking care o' business, ah'd be oot o' business*. Right, when she goes to the toilet, double whammy: room service and Sky Sports. Magic.

Such were the thoughts of carpet millionaire Findlay Masterson – a man who had never cooked a meal, read a book, relished an aspect of nature or knowingly enjoyed a piece of music in his life.

Pauline looked at the green digital numbers below the TV screen. Plenty of time – he wasn't expecting her back until eight. An image of Gary, patting the bed shyly that morning, came back to her. Guilt. When she thought about Gary's nature – his grinning decency, his total lack of guile – guilt was still capable of running through her. Then she thought of the extent of his ambition; to fill a house slightly bigger than the one they had now with children. The past couple of years with Kiddiewinks – with the stumbling, drunken toddlers and the screaming primary-school kids – had brought something forcefully home to Pauline. She *hated* children. A part of her, she thought, still loved him. And the cliché was on the money because it really did feel like a *part*. A component. One that was becoming increasingly redundant in the new person Pauline was setting about becoming.

She untangled herself from Masterson. In the shower she could hear the TV – football – and Masterson's voice, him saying 'cheese and ham'. Not his wife then. Pauline looked down and watched as warm soapy water containing tiny pearled globules of semen cascaded across her feet, between her toes and gurgled down the plughole: her adultery washed away and quickly gone, swallowed up as though it had never existed, like raindrops falling far out in the middle of the ocean.

Around the same time as Pauline stepped out of the shower, the manager of the Glasgow Argyll Street branch of Oklahoma Dan's Discount Golf World signed for his delivery. He checked the pallets of boxes – now being loaded by two employees onto a forklift truck (inevitably a Henderson's forklift truck) – against his inventory of ordered items and slapped a hand down on a crate just as the warehousemen went to lift it. 'Haud on,' he said, 'put those over there. The Ardgirvan shop is needing baws.' Deep within the case as it was roughly hauled from the pallet the Spaxon rolled forward in its cardboard sleeve.

It was a number 3.

8

'SO AH SAID TAE HIM – "HO, CUNT, AH'LL BREAK YOUR fucking jaw if you speak tae me like that again. Ah don't gie a fuck if you ur a fucking doctor." Ah'm no kidding, Lee, ah wis raging so ah wis.'

'Aye, he's a fucking wank that Dr Murray,' Lee replied with authority. Lee, a prolific and creative benefit cheat, was on intimate terms with most of the members of Ardgirvan's medical profession. Lee suffered from facial tics, insomnia, ME and chronic fatigue syndrome. He endured bouts of migraine and disabling, non-specific fevers. He was also incontinent – a ruse that brought in an extra twenty-odd pounds a month in laundry payments.

Lee and Sammy were in a dark corner of the Bam, swapping stories. Hard men, swapping hard stories: jaws that had been/should have been/were going to be tanned. Jobs that were going to be pulled. Who was doing what to whom in the world of Ardgirvan's underclass. Lee cast an eye around the place as Sammy talked on about the latest threat to his incapacity benefit. A couple of minor villains looked up from their pints and their tabloids and nodded respectfully to Lee, who returned the nods with a barely perceptible inclination of the head, enjoying feeling like a tuna or a barracuda amongst a shoal of sprats. Lee was afforded this measure of respect in the Bam because he was widely rumoured to have murdered the Kilwinning speed dealer Tits McGee. It was rare for someone to be tactless enough to bring the subject up but, when they did, Lee remained tight-lipped, perhaps, if it was some young bam, going as far as to say, 'Shut yer fucking mooth. Are ye wantin' tae get me the jile?'

Maddeningly, he'd arrived at the bar just before Sammy, so convention had dictated that Lee bought the first round. 'Go and grab that table, wee man,' Lee had said. The boy kind of looked up to Lee, he felt. It wouldn't have done to let Sammy see him picking through a pile of shrapnel to buy the drinks. They were onto the second pint now and Lee was feeling the golden glow of the lager, but with an undercurrent of sadness – this might well be the last pint until the broo cheque arrived.

'Listen, Lee,' Sammy said, leaning forward, moving his pint closer, indicating that the small talk was over with. 'The boys are getting a bit fucking anxious. Ye said a key was no bother.'

'It is nae bother, Sammy. Fur fuck sake, whit's the fucking rush aw o' a sudden?'

'They've got that big rave through in Edinburgh coming up. They've got tae get it aw weighed out and cut and bagged up an aw that. It's a fucking kilo, that's . . .' Sammy thought for a second, 'a thousand grams.' Sammy pictured his Glasgow pals, wee Flakey and Alan Trodden, sitting in their flat folding a thousand speed wraps. Lot of fucking work that. 'It's a lot of fucking work that,' Sammy said.

'Aye, aye. Tell them we'll have it next week.'

'It's just . . . it's a good score for us this. Ah don't want them tae go tae someone else if we cannae deliver.'

'Fuck sake, Sammy! Whit did ah just fucking say?'

'A'right! Fucking hell. Whit's wrang wi you?'

'Ah've just got a lot oan ma fucking plate the now, OK?'

'You and me both, pal.'

The pub doors opened, a brief flash of sunlight spilling across the filthy tiled floor, and Alec Campbell walked in with Frank 'the Beast' Barton.

Shite, Lee thought.

There was nothing as obvious as an intake of breath, but the rhythm of the pub changed suddenly, like the collective flick of the tail a shoal of tiny fish makes when a large predator enters their lagoon.

Alec Campbell was in his early thirties and wiry, about the same build as Lee. There the similarities ended. Alec was casually, expensively dressed. Ralph Lauren. His trainers looked like they'd come straight out of the shop. He cocked a crisp twenty at the barman, who stopped serving someone else in the middle of their order to attend to Alec. The Beast leaned on the bar, the deep scar down his face visible even in the half-light, looking like he was listening to whatever joke Alec was telling the barman, but really, Lee knew, he was scanning the room, evaluating, categorising, grading threats. Not that there was anything in the Bam that would have posed much of a threat to Alec and Frank – two great whites in this lagoon.

Alec Campbell – the heir apparent. Only one man in Ardgirvan more powerful than Alec: his father.

Ranta Campbell.

Gangster No. 1.

If Alec and Frank were great whites, what was Ranta? He was a mythical beast, a deep-sea terror that rose up once a century from dreadful depths – depths few creatures could live at – to remind men that he existed and that they should fear him.

Ranta was the Kraken.

Lee quickly weighed up his options: skulk against the wall and nurse the last of his pint with his back to the door, hoping the pair would have a quick drink and leave, or brass it out?

'Your shout. Get them in,' Sammy was saying, shaking his empty pint glass at Lee like a collection tin. Fuck, it was his round. Impossible to stay now.

'Naw, Sammy, ah've got tae be somewhere,' Lee said, getting up. Brass it out. Brass fucking baws.

'A'right, pal. Give me a call when we're sorted, eh?'

'Aye. See ye, Sammy.'

Lee walked towards the door, composing his features into a normal hard-man expression – something approaching a relaxed scowl. Alec Campbell turned as Lee approached and their eyes met. Alec's were dark and saying nothing.

'A'right, Alec?' Lee nodded.

'Lee! The very man! How's it going?'

'Aye, good, Alec, good. Ah wis going tae call ye.'

'Is that right? Ye hear that, Frank? Boy was gauin tae call us. Whit did ah tell ye? Lee's a'right. Ah don't care what you say.'

Frank the Beast Barton smiled. A truly terrifying sight.

'Aye, it's aw sorted. Ah wis just having a wee meeting there.'

'That's magic, Lee.' Alec took a sip of his pint. 'Cause as you know, our sale-or-return terms are very strict – we require either the money or the return of the goods within thirty days.'

'Aye, Monday, Alec. Nae bother. Ah'll see yese.' Lee went to move past them, towards the door.

'Ye no stay for a pint?' Alec said.

'Naw, Alec. Ah promised Lisa ah'd be hame early.'

'Oh aye. Ah know how that goes. How is the lovely Lisa?'

'She's fine, Alec. Brand new.'

'Tell her ah said hello.'

'Aye. Cheers. See ye, Frank.'

The Beast didn't reply.

'Ye wouldnae think he had it in him, would ye?' Alec said to Frank after the door had shut behind Lee.

'The Tits McGee thing?' the Beast said, casting a baleful glare around the flyblown interior of the Bam, at the hushed conversations taking place in the shadows, at the crackpot get-rich-now schemes being hatched and fermented. 'Who knows? There's a lot of pish talked in this toon.' He drained his glass. 'C'mon, drink up. We've that cunt lying in the boot.'

Outside on the sunny street Lee checked the time on his fake Tag. It was 1.18. Piece of shit. He checked his mobile. (Pay as you go, all credit long exhausted, it served basically as a timepiece and a way to receive calls.) Nearly five o'clock. Baws. By the time he got home, collected his spade and got up to the woods he wouldn't have any digging time left tonight. Have to leave it till tomorrow morning. The Beast's smile was fresh in his head as he turned and headed up the high street, quickening his pace.

Less than a mile from the Bam, in a small pebble-dash council house, Billy Douglas was celebrating his sixtieth birthday. 'Happy birthday, Papa!' seven-year-old Anna said self-consciously as she handed her grandfather an envelope.

'Aww, thanks, doll! Here, give yer papa a kiss.' Anna did so and ran away while Billy balanced his whisky and lemonade on the arm of the sofa and tore open the envelope. He pulled out a £20 voucher for Oklahoma Dan's Discount Golf World, the new golf place up by the new bypass. (Billy had lived in Ardgirvan all his life – everything was new to him.) 'Aww, thanks, son,' Billy said to his son, Billy Jr, the actual buyer of the voucher. 'Ah'm needing some new golf baws . . .'

9

GARY WENT TO SEE STEVIE FOR SOME COMFORT. As ever Stevie served it up ultra cold.

'Your problem, pal, is that the beginning, middle and end of your existence is defined by the level of your performance at a middle-class indulgence. You have no concept of political reality. If you –' He broke off, keeping a pudgy forefinger levelled at Gary, and turned to a young couple who had approached the counter, box in hand. 'Sorry, that's out,' Stevie said. They went back to browsing the shelves and Stevie turned back to/on Gary. 'If you woke up for even a minute to think you'd realise that, like cocaine, mini-breaks and training shoes, your silly wee game is just another of the many features of late-period capitalism which is built entirely on the blood of the poor.' Stevie was small, fat and without a visible neck. In his own words 'a pudding, a fucking cannonball'.

'I think –' Gary began, but he was interrupted by the couple approaching again with another DVD box.

'Naw,' Stevie said, barely looking, 'our copy of that's

scratched. That box shouldnae be oot. Sorry.' He took the box from them, the man sighing as they headed back to the shelves again. 'I mean,' Stevie continued, 'do you know that when golf was first established a single ball cost more than twice what the average St Andrews farm worker earned in a week? Think about that.' The couple approached the counter for the third time and the man handed Stevie a third DVD box. Stevie looked at it.

'Is this,' he asked the guy slowly, holding the box up like a barrister might show a murder weapon to a jury, 'how you're going to spend your Friday night?' The film was called *Love Again*, and the cover showed a handsome middle-aged man in a pinstriped suit and an attractive younger girl in a short skirt eyeing each other seductively across a desk.

'Is it no any good?' the man, about their age and nervous now, asked.

Stevie sighed. 'Without ever having seen it let me summarise the plot for you, pal. Some lanky streak o' faux upper-class pish plays an Oxbridge Professor of Medieval History-cum-research scientist who meets a kooky working-class toilet cleaner played by some blundering hoor of a soap actress. Against all the odds they fall in love and together they find a cure for Aids. With a soundtrack by Wet Wet fucking Wet or some other shower o' Thatcherite bampots.'

'The *Daily Standard* said it was quite good,' the girl offered timidly.

'The *Daily Standard*?' Stevie spat the words like a curse. 'The *Daily Standard?* And what do you turn to for your literary criticism? The fucking *Beano*? Look, I've got the complete works of David Mamet in here. Every film David Lynch has ever made. Films that will shake and unsettle your entire belief system. And yet you want to watch *Love Again*? I wouldnae force a convicted murderer tae watch this as punishment. I'd rather go for a pint *with* a convicted murderer than watch this fucking pish,' he concluded, tossing the box onto the counter.

The man shrugged and turned to his girlfriend. 'C'mon, let's go up tae Silver Screen.' The couple left.

'See what I'm saying?' Stevie continued. 'That pair have made a terrible political decision. They think they're just renting a wee film to watch on a Friday night, curled up on the sofa with a bottle of some Chilean Cabernet pish water and a bag o' sweeties. But, the minute they walk up the road and hand their money to those right-wing, fear-mongering, family-values, Christian fundamentalist bastards at Silver Screen, they're rubber-stamping censorship, repression and artistic strangulation. They're rubber-stamping nothing less than a return to the Inquisition.'

'I think I'm over-swinging.'

'Could be,' Stevie said, lifting the hatch in the counter and stepping through. 'And ye've a tendency tae swing from in to out. C'mon and we'll go for a pint. Bernie, hold the fort. And keep this fucking pish –' he held up the box for *Love Again* – 'aff the shelf.'

Bernie appeared from the horror section with an armful of glossy slashers. 'Nae bother, boss.'

'And stop calling me boss, ya toadying wee bam.'

Stevie's father had opened Target Video in the early 1980s – at the height of the video-nasty boom, the days of the big V2000 boxes and the Betamax/VHS battle. The days when most video shops had floor-to-ceiling gore apocalypses surrounding a single copy of *On Golden Pond*. He'd made a small fortune, at one point having three shops scattered across northern Ayrshire. As the years passed the competition all gradually sold out to chains like Silver Screen. Stevie had inherited the shop – with its prime, high street location – from his father, but how he managed to stay in business was beyond Gary. His goal, his reason for getting up in the morning, seemed to be to insult and berate anyone foolish enough to approach the counter with a film that didn't feature in Stevie's personal top 100.

'Thirty-three. Thirty-fucken-three, ya auld bastard, ye!' Stevie said, raising his frothing lager. It had just gone five and they had the snug of the Annick to themselves. In 1990 they had sipped their first illegal pints in here – hiding behind big Tank MacIntyre, who'd got the round in, their tiny, childish hands struggling to grip the huge tumblers. Gary had been drunk before half of the lager had gone down, someone had put 'Hallelujah' by the Mondays on the jukebox and, for a moment, the snug of the Annick bar on the corner of Ardgirvan High Street had felt like the epicentre of the world. Over the last two decades its stone walls and dark wood had contained Gary, Stevie and their friends as they celebrated Christmases, birthdays and – more recently – the arrival of children. Its faux-leather seating had supported and comforted them as they mourned deaths and football disasters, its truncheon-handled pumps dispensing lager which served as champagne or hemlock, depending on the occasion.

'Come tae fuck, it's no that old . . .'

'Same age as Christ on the cross,' Stevie said, tearing open a pack of cheese and onion and spreading the contents on the table before them. 'Jim Morrison, Byron, James Dean, Jimi Hendrix, Kurt Cobain, Ian Curtis, Bill Hicks, Edie Sedgwick, John Belushi, Nick Drake, Otis Redding, Sid Vicious, Kenny

Dalglish, William Wallace . . . aw deed by the time they were your age.'

'Kenny Dalglish isn't dead.'

'That bastard died the day he went tae Anfield!' Stevie spluttered, spraying a film of crisps across the table. He had never forgiven King Kenny for leaving Celtic and transferring to Liverpool back in '77. 'Anyway, whit's the problem wi' yer swing?'

'Ah'm shanking everything again.'

'Och, yer probably jist standing too close tae the ball.'

'I'd been trying that new tip but –'

'This is the thing, Gary. You're always looking fur a quick fix: this new tip, that new club, this new book . . .'

Stevie shook his head and took a great slurp of his pint at the same time. 'You've got tae take care o' the fundamentals: grip, stance, ball position. Besides, you're too nice to be a real sportsman. Look at Linklater. A perfect organism. Unclouded by conscience, remorse or delusions of morality.'

'Ian Holm in *Alien*,' Gary said automatically.

Stevie had been a decent golfer in his youth, certainly a more naturally gifted player than Gary. He just chose not to play any more. Consequently he had indeed been granted the kind of deep peace, the serenity that only comes to those who have given up golf.

'And I've got the Medal tomorrow,' Gary said.

The Medal: Ravenscroft Golf Club's monthly competition. Gary entered every month with the hope that a combination of an unexpectedly decent round and his ridiculously high handicap would somehow propel him into . . . well, not the top three, the prizewinning slots, but at least the upper half of the field. Maybe get a couple of strokes shaved off his handicap. Actually *winning* a Medal? This had never crossed his mind in daylight. It existed only in his most elaborate fantasies, the ornately constructed kind he used to get himself to sleep on restless nights. 'It's just, every spring I start off with these high hopes and I . . .' Gary paused, looking into his glass, into the swirling amber bubbles, '. . . I never seem to get any better, Stevie.'

Stevie looked at Gary sadly. They had known each other for over a quarter of a century – since they had bonded over a rare *Star Wars* trading card in the violent melee of the playground of Castle Glen Primary School – and he felt his friend's pain. What could he say? The truth – 'you are a very poor golfer who is unlikely to ever get much better' – was unthinkable. Stevie said the only thing he could. 'Slow down and take a wee bit aff yer backswing. And don't go up that driving range so much. All you're doing is practising yer faults. Ah told ye – book a couple of lessons wi the pro up at the club.'

'Aye. You're probably right enough,' Gary sighed.

'Fucking hell, it's no that bad, is it? Whit's wrang?'

'Ach, it's no just that. It's Pauline. We're no, we haven't, y'know . . . for a while.' Gary looked up at Stevie, sad and ashamed.

Stevie nodded, using his back molars to grind the last mouthful of cheese-and-onion crisps into a tangy, grainy paste. He would have to tread carefully here. It happened to all men sooner or later: one of your friends will decide to spend the rest of their lives with someone who is patently the Antichrist.

When Gary had started going out with Pauline, Stevie had thought soothingly, *it'll never last*. She was way out of his league. All the sixteen-year-old Pauline saw in the eighteen-year-old Gary was the fact that he had a job, a car and some money in his pocket. As opposed to the other boys around her, with their school books, their acne and their wanking.

What did Gary see in Pauline? Beyond her face, breasts, belly and much-worshipped bum? (And Stevie, despite his unwavering commitment to socialist principles, was no prude or killjoy. He enjoyed a quality bum as much as the next Marxist and he could see that Pauline's bum was unquestionably A Good Thing. But you don't decide to spend the rest of your life with a pair of cheeks, do you?) Stevie could overlook the fact that she was obsessive about status and possessions. That when she met someone you could see her taking in their shoes, their watch, the type of credit card they produced, like she was feeding all this into a computer program: WindowsNetWorthCalculator 10.9. That she had no interest in much of anything beyond celebrity and fashion. Ultimately, what doomed Pauline for Stevie was this: she had no sense of humour. None. Nothing. Not. A. Flicker. She was the kind of person who, when confronted with something genuinely funny would actually utter the words, 'That's funny.'

Stevie looked at Gary, staring into the inch or so left in his glass. He had, Stevie thought, the kind of life that was great if you were happy, terrible if you weren't. Hence distractions like improving your golf handicap. How do you address this? What do you say when your best friend tremblingly confides their darkest fears?

'Same again?' Stevie said.

'Aye, cheers, wee boy.'

As Stevie shouldered his way in at the bar the grey van's orange indicator began winking as it left the bypass via the Stone Cairn roundabout, taking the third exit towards Ayr, towards Oklahoma Dan's Discount Golf World, its final destination.

10

THE KRAKEN RISING.

Alec Campbell pulled into the car park of a small industrial estate on the northern edge of Ardgirvan – a cluster of a dozen nondescript breeze-block units. Only four were occupied; a garage, a company called Ayrshire Ceramics that made fancy tiles, a double-glazing company and the unit owned by Ranta and used primarily for storing certain things he wouldn't want in the house. There was only one other car in the car park, a big grey Audi, parked in front of Ranta's unit. They pulled up beside it and Alec turned the ignition off, the loss of the air conditioning immediately noticeable. 'Some day, eh?' Ranta said, popping his seat belt. He was sweating.

As always when he found himself in a confined space with his father Alec was aware of the sheer bulk of the man – eighteen stone plus and a little over six feet tall, he'd turned fifty last year but his hair was still the same thick, gypsy black as Alec's, although here and there Ranta's was showing fine strands of silver. Just visible at the neck of his polo shirt was the faint pink welt of a scar, some bam's bladework from back in the day, when the old boy still had to get involved in the more run-of-the-mill violence that kept the business on the rails.

'Are yer clubs in the boot?' Ranta asked.

'Aye, Da.'

'Bring us yer driver and some baws.'

Out of the warm spring sunshine and into the cool darkness of the unit, into the smell of engine oil on cement, where, under the fizzing glare of three fluorescent strip lights, a man was tied to a chair. He had a bag, a cloth sack, over his head and he was making strange noises.

The Beast and two other men were playing cards at a table against the wall, seemingly oblivious to the tethered, hooded man. The Beast looked up from cutting the deck as Ranta walked over. 'How ye doing, boss?'

'Ach, fine, Frank. Ye see it aw.'

'Fucking luck oan this prick here,' Frank said, indicating Davy, one of the other card players, a young lad in his early twenties. 'A hundred-odd pound the cunt's taken aff us.'

'Is that right?' Ranta said. 'Good for you, Davy son. As well you taking it aff him as William Hill, eh?'

Ranta walked across to the middle of the room and gently pulled the sack off the man's head. He had a strip of silver electrical tape across his mouth and his face was bruised and cut, slick with sweat and blood. He blinked into the cold fluorescent light, his eyes adjusting, the pupils shrinking, as he looked up into the face of Ranta Campbell.

The man started to cry.

'Shhh, Charlie, c'mon, son.' Ranta spoke soothingly, in the tones he used when one of his children fell and skinned their knees. 'Nae need fur that. Ah just want a wee chat.' Ranta ripped the strip of duct tape from Charlie's mouth, tearing off a good portion of skin from Charlie's upper lip in the process. Charlie hardly seemed to notice. A torrent of speech instantly poured out of him:

'FucksakeRantafucksake!Ahdidnaeknowwhitwasgoin goanaahsweartaefuckahdidnaeah'llgetyethemoneybacksoah-fuckingwillplease –'

'Charlie, Charlie, shhh. Ah don't care about the money. It's trust we're talking about here. Now, come tae fuck, we all know you couldnae huv thought of this on your own. Christ son, you've no the brains you were born with. Who was the bright spark who had the idea?'

'Ah swear, Ranta, oan ma wean's life, ah didnae know anything aboot it.'

Ranta sighed and thought for a moment. 'Strip him off and haud him doon,' he said.

Davy and Frank ripped Charlie's clothes off and, with Alec helping, they pinned him naked and wriggling on the cement floor.

'Open yer mouth, Charlie,' Ranta said, picking Alec's driver up from the table. He already had a golf ball and tee in his hand.

'Naw, Ranta, please.'

Ranta knelt down and forced a wooden tee peg between Charlie's teeth. 'Now, ah've been struggling a wee bit wi' the driver lately so, ah'd recommend keeping yer heed very still.' Ranta tried to place a golf ball on the tee, but it kept falling off because Charlie was struggling so much. 'Here, Davy, hold his head.'

Davy roughly got hold of Charlie's head and Ranta managed to tee his ball up, the ball standing a couple of inches clear of Charlie's nose on its long wooden tee peg. He addressed the ball and all his men pressed their heads closer to the ground.

'Ah've been trying to shorten ma backswing a wee bit, Charlie,' Ranta said, taking a few preparatory waggles with the club, 'mair accuracy . . .'

Suddenly Ranta swung the club and Charlie – hyperventilating now – felt the cool breath of air on his face as the driver thundered by, millimetres from his face, picking the ball cleanly off the tee and sending it rattling off the grey breeze-block walls and bouncing around the unit. Ranta teed up another ball. Davy, Alec and Frank, really fighting to hold Charlie still.

'But ah don't like sacrificing ma power . . .'

Ranta addressed the fresh ball. Charlie was really trying to say something. Ranta nodded to Davy, who released his jaw. Charlie spat the tee and ball out and, panting, said, 'Bobby Hamilton . . . it was Boab's idea.'

'Ah fucken knew it!' Alec said. 'That wee prick.'

'Good boy, Charlie,' Ranta said. 'You know, ah wis thinking o' maybe changing ma balls.' He was moving down Charlie now, waggling the driver above his groin. 'They say these new Spaxons have a really soft feel. Ah don't know. It's a big decision, whit brand o' baws ye play with.' Ranta nuzzled the cold titanium of the clubface up to Charlie's bare testicles. 'Whit dae you think?'

'Ranta –' Charlie began, but the word 'Ranta' quickly modulated into a shrill scream as Ranta whipped the club back. Using his old swing, the full swing, Ranta smashed the metal driver into Charlie's balls: like hitting a pair of soft-boiled eggs with a cricket bat. Charlie's scrotum burst open, covering wee Davy and Frank with blood and viscera. Davy leapt up, wiping at his face as Charlie's screams echoed off the bare walls. 'Gads! Gads o'fuck! Fuck sake, boss!'

Had this been necessary?

Ranta had no extreme feelings about Charlie Douglas. He was just a daft boy who had tried to rip Ranta off. It was one of the dangers of running the kind of business where you entrusted large sums of cash and quantities of expensive narcotics to shady bams. However, Ranta understood the PR value of a certain type of violence. Wee Davy here, he'll be in the pub tonight, he'll have had a few pints and he'll say to some fanny he's trying to impress, 'You'll no believe whit the boss did tae this cunt the day . . .' and the fanny will go off and repeat the story and after a few days it'll be all round the whole bam community: Ranta Campbell battered Charlie Douglas's baws aff wi' a fucking gowf club.

Some wouldn't believe it, but enough would for the message to be writ large: *NAE CUNT MESSES*. It would help keep people in line for a while. You had to feed your rep every now and then. Even at Ranta's age.

'Right,' Ranta said, tossing the bloody club to Alec, finding he had to raise his voice considerably to be heard over Charlie's inhuman screaming, 'come on, Alec. Ye can run me by the butcher's. Ah've tae pick up some steak fur yer mother. We've got half the fucking toon coming fur their dinner the night . . .' Charlie was rolling around on the floor, clutching at the ruins of his groin. He pulled his hand away and found to his horror that he was holding one of his own testicles, still attached to his body by some stringy tendrils that ran into the ragged wound where his scrotum had been. 'Davy,' Ranta continued over Charlie's screams, 'take whoever ye need and go and get Bobby Hamilton. Frank, for fuck sake do the boy a favour.' Ranta nodded towards Charlie. 'That'd burst yer heed so it wid.'

Ranta turned and walked off towards the door, Alec

following him. Davy wiped blood from his face and watched his boss go, deeply impressed that he could be thinking about eating red meat right now.

The Beast took his kit from the table – a black, plastic toolbox. He knelt beside Charlie and opened it to reveal a neatly arranged collection of stainless-steel knives, packed in custom-cut foam. He selected an eight-inch butcher's knife and leaned in over the bloody, squawking Charlie. He ran a thumb up his ribcage, first rib, second rib, third rib: about the only thing Frank had learned in the paratroopers that he still used. He pressed the point of the knife between the third and fourth rib, just breaking the skin. Charlie tensed.

'Maw . . .' Charlie said, crying, clutching uselessly at his wet, bloody groin.

'Yer maw's no here, son,' the Beast said pleasantly. 'She's away getting rode by a big fucking darkie.' The last word pronounced in the full Ayrshire – 'dorr-kay'. As he said this he pushed the blade in and up, through Charlie's heart. Charlie gasped, the expression on his face one of surprise more than pain, very much like someone who has plunged into an unexpectedly freezing sea.

11

SUNNY SATURDAY MORNING AS GARY PULLED INTO THE car park, popped the boot open, and lifted out his clubs.

Ravenscroft Golf Club (founded 1907) was a public course. Anyone was welcome to come along and play, but there was a membership of some two hundred golfers: full members who used the humble locker room (an extension to the original Edwardian building, built just after the Second World War, with cinder-block walls and chipped stone floors), who ate in the little dining room and who had access to the clubhouse.

The clubhouse had been added in the early 1960s. It was a long rectangular room with a bar in the middle, a parquet dance floor and a pool table at one end, whose blue baize was overlooked by the gold-lettered honours boards listing all the club champions. The name 'Irvine' was proudly etched there not once but twice – 1976 and 1981. (Gary could only remember the second triumph: his father coming in the front door, flushed and holding the big silver cup as he hugged them all to him, the smell of success, whisky and tobacco strong on him and Cathy whooping delightedly as he broke open the thick envelope stuffed with the sweepstake cash. Gary and Lee's jaws dropping as his father handed each of them a banknote, a strange banknote, a brown note: a *ten-pound note!*)

A couple of fruit machines stood near the pool table. The opposite end of the long, low-ceilinged room was composed of a floor-to-ceiling glass window that overlooked the eighteenth green, where members would gather to watch the outcome of any crucial matches.

Beyond the clubhouse the golf course stretched over several square miles, bounded on the north by a development of large private homes, to the east by Ravenscroft Academy, the secondary school, and to the west by Ravenscroft Geriatric Hospital: the loony bin. The mento home. (Gary sometimes thought the geography here was convenient: you tumbled out of school, joined the golf club, and, forty or fifty years later when golf had done its work and you had been driven completely insane, you were shipped back across the road to the mento home, where you saw out your days drooling through the glass at the golf course, the very cause of your madness.)

The southern perimeter of the course ran along the right-hand side of the tenth fairway – a treacherous dogleg right, uphill par five – and formed the dividing wall between the golf course and the gyppo camp. The whole right-hand side of the fairway was out of bounds: any ball flying into the gyppo camp was never coming back. And a good few balls that landed squarely on the fairway too. For the gypsies were bold. Many a Ravenscroft golfer had stood on the tenth tee, posing in his finishing position, elegantly cocked like a proud stag as he watched a perfect drive sail high in the air and land softly on the fairway, only to see a filthy figure streak from the undergrowth, snatch the ball and disappear back into the wilds of the camp. Under an unwritten local by-law called the Gyppo Rule, the unfortunate golfer was allowed to play a new ball from the tee without penalty. Everyone was very happy with this ruling. Alas, in recent years some of the younger gyppos had grown more experimental in their tortures. They would run out onto the fairway and you could only watch helplessly from a few hundred yards away as they straddled your ball, pulled down their trousers (trousers, some of the more bigoted members conjectured, that had probably been freshly stolen from a neighbourhood washing line) and repeatedly and theatrically inserted your pure white Titelist or Spaxon into their anus before replacing it exactly where it was. In this instance there was much debate among players as to what the exact ruling should be. Some argued that the ball, complete with its brown film of gyppo bum residue, had to be played exactly as it lay, but could of course be changed after the hole had been completed. Others argued that the soiled ball should simply fall under the general Gyppo Rule and that a new ball should be dropped without penalty. Often players would try and argue the grey area to their advantage: a gyppo-arse-wiped ball in a bad lie would often be deemed unplayable while one with a perfect lie would mysteriously be found acceptable. Where there was usually complete agreement was in a refusal to pick your gyppo-arse-wiped ball out of the hole when your final putt dropped; on hot summer days you would often come to the tenth green to find the cup filled to the brim with abandoned golf balls, which would have to be fished out by Auld Basil, the long-suffering head greenkeeper.

No, it is safe to say that Ravenscroft Golf Club was not a world-class facility. It is unlikely that the walnut-panelled walls of the locker room at, for instance, Augusta National, ever bore witness to an exchange like this:

'Fucking gyppo stuck ma baw up his erse at the tenth!'

'Black bastard! Ah hope ye played it.'

'Did ah fuck. Dropped wan. Gyppo Rule.'

'Ya fucking wide-o ye . . .'

Not a world-class course, but it was Gary's course.

It had been since 1980, when, as a besotted five-year-old, he first scampered down its fairways after his dad, too small to carry his clubs yet, but eagerly holding the flagstick while they putted (his dad showed him how to hold it so that the flag didn't flap in the breeze and put people off their putting stroke) and joining in the hunt for lost balls. His dad liked Gary to hold his clubs for him between shots, because his wee hands were sweaty and his dad liked the stickiness this imparted to the rubber grips. So Gary held the clubs and watched as his father smashed the ball distances that were incredible, inconceivable to a child, the ball seeming to vanish into the next county, his father's five-foot-seven frame looking to him like a rippling powerhouse of muscle. He held the clubs and listened as the men talked about things he didn't understand, feeling privileged to be there with the grown-ups, among the talk of football and work and wives and the smell of aftershave and cigarettes and foosty sweaters pulled from golf bags when the wind got up. Gary knew every blade of grass on this course (thanks to his errant driving he knew some of its more obscure byways better than most players) and – despite his shanking, despite never having won a medal, despite his maddening inability to progress at the game at all – he loved it here.

He shouldered his bag and headed towards the locker room, to see who his playing partners for the Monthly Medal would be.

* * *

Meanwhile, Billy Douglas moved quickly along the aisles of Oklahoma Dan's Discount Golf World, past the racks of putters, golf bags, woods and irons. (A cardboard cut-out behind the irons section featured a grinning, thumbs-up Oklahoma Dan – six foot three of furious Republican – with a speech bubble saying 'I LOVE IRONS'. Some of his advisers had considered telling the great man that this expression might not play in the UK due to confusion with something called cockney rhyming slang, but they decided against it. It would have meant discussing homosexuality, something the boss refused to believe existed.)

Billy surveyed the stacks of gleaming cartons: Titelists, Top Flites, Callaway, Nike. 5.99 for a sleeve of three brand-new Spaxons? They were 7.99 at the Ravenscroft pro shop! Billy picked up three cartons and made his way to the tills, feeling in his inside jacket pocket for the voucher as he went.

The number 3 ball was in the first tube he picked up.

'Anything else for you today, sir?' The beaming wee lassie in the baseball cap behind the till was asking him.

'Naw, jist these thanks, hen. Jist the balls.'

They would be enough.

The first tee: a fresh start with all previous sins absolved. Every time a golfer steps onto the first tee they are stepping into opportunity; the opportunity to commence a new love affair, this one not like all the other ones, free from bickering and squabbling. This one holy and sacred and . . . well, not perfect, perfection would be stretching it a little in Gary's case, but there was always the hope of improvement.

The first tee at Ravenscroft held particular meaning for Gary as it was along this fairway, the fairway he now looked down as the match ahead began to move out of range, that they had scattered his father's ashes. Thirteen summers ago now, Gary and Lee, both a little drunk, running down the hill, throwing handfuls of the man who had made them into the air, clouds of him catching on the breeze and blowing into their faces, into their mouths, the two of them laughing until they realised they were crying, their father disappearing in silver-grey skeins into the Ayrshire skies above them, the cancer reduced to dust and carbon along with the rest of him. Like many Protestants, Gary only thought of the dead watching over him when he was doing something that he imagined would have pleased them. So, on the rare occasions he drove the ball straight and long, or when a snaking putt clicked into the cup, he would sometimes look up, picturing his father's face rippling through the clouds and thinking – *Were you watching? Did you see that?*

Gary's four ball stood on the tee. When the match ahead of them was past the second bunker on the left-hand side of the fairway – a little over two hundred yards away – they decided that Auld Tam, the shortest hitter, was safe to play. Like a lot of the old boys, Tam didn't mess about: tee up and a quick wee practice swing to get the rhythm. With a punchy half-swing he sent the ball safely up the middle of the fairway, just short and right of the bunker.

'Shot, Tam,' his partners chorused.

Tommy Wilson played next, but he teed too high and came under the ball, sending it sky-high and short, the ball plopping back down to earth like a sand wedge rather than a drive, finishing short of Tam's ball.

'Bastard,' Tommy said simply.

Rab Forest, a four-handicapper, the best player in the group, stepped up. He prowled the tee, searching for just the right spot, finally choosing to tee up on the left-hand side of the tee box, aiming out to the right, looking to hit a draw, moving the ball from right to left in the air, following the curve of the fairway and making best use of the slight tailwind they had. It was a difficult shot for the amateur player to hit on demand. Get it wrong and you could end up with a duck hook, the ball jerking violently off to the left, towards the telegraph poles and thick rough that separated the first and fifth fairways. Forest was good right enough, but this was a ballsy opening shot.

He took a couple of easy practice swings, sighted down the shaft of his driver and addressed the ball. He shuffled down into his stance, waggling the clubhead four, five, six times. Suddenly he stopped, looked up and stepped back.

'Sorry, lads,' Forest said. 'I'd better wait a minute. Make sure they're out of range.'

Gary squinted down the fairway. The match ahead were passing the far right-hand bunker – nearly three hundred yards away – and Forest still thought he should wait? *Aye*, Gary thought, *yer fucking maw*. (A curious Ayrshire-ism – meaning literally 'Yes, your mother' – its only living relative in the slang world of mother-abuse is the American expression 'Yo moma'. Like that expression it is used sarcastically to cast doubt. For instance: 'I had sex with five women last night.' 'Aye, yer maw.')

Forest waited. Auld Tam raised an eyebrow at Gary – both of them thinkng 'fucking show-off prick' as Forest ran through his pre-shot routine again. He stepped up to the ball, shuffled down into his stance, and *creamed* the fucking thing: a beautiful draw, catching the wind and a good bounce, the ball trundling up to just thirty or forty yards short of the green, and just a few yards behind the group in front. Over three hundred yards, easily. The audience behind them burst into soft, sincere applause and Forest gave a little nod as he reholstered his driver.

'Beauty,' Gary said, feeling faint.

'Ah'll take it,' Forest said. Smug cunt.

The crowd – nearly thirty strong now – fell silent as Gary settled the clubhead behind the ball. It was a new driver, a Titan Pro XIII, with a huge, sleek metal head of sparkling titanium the size of a cat's head and it had cost nearly three hundred quid – three hundred quid he hadn't quite got round to telling Pauline about yet. Gary took an exploratory waggle, settled his breathing and pulled the trigger.

The dreadful clang of metal misconnecting with ball and he was looking up to see the shot rocketing off crazily towards Auld Basil's tractor, which was safely parked about fifty yards to the right of the tee box. The ball whanged into the metal frame of the machine and – with a slapstick 'KA-PING!' noise – flew a hundred feet straight into the air before it dropped down, clanged once off the tin roof of Auld Basil's maintenance hut and came to rest on the gravel path that led from the tee to the fairway. There was a two-second pause, almost scripted in its comic perfection, before Auld Basil's puzzled face appeared at the door.

Then everyone burst out laughing.

Head down, Gary stumbled back towards his bag, his face humming with shame.

'Ho, Irvine!' someone shouted. 'Ah'll gie ye a hunner poun' if ye can dae that again!'

Nodding and smiling good-naturedly at the abuse, while dying inside, Gary shouldered his bag and set off on the horrifically short walk to his ball. 'Don't worry, son,' Auld Tam said, clapping him on the arm, 'it can only get better, eh?'

Thank fuck Dad's dead, Gary thought.

12

LEE SLUMPED BACK AGAINST THE TREE AND SLID DOWN onto the ground, his feet dangling into the hole he'd just finished digging. Fighting tears, he looked around the woods – green sunlight filtering through the treetops and the busy chatter of birds filling the air. Lee had loved the woods when he was a kid; finding skud mags, reading skud mags, finding frogs, torturing frogs. But now it was hard for him to imagine a more hateful sight. He looked around the clearing, at all the other holes he'd dug in the past few days, seven or eight of them, all about three feet wide and two to three feet deep. This was the third clearing he'd tried. How could he have been so stupid?

It happened like this . . .

Sammy mentioned to Lee that a couple of his mates – Alan somebody and wee something-or-other, a couple of Glasgow fannies Lee had met once or twice – were looking to move their speed-dealing operation up a gear or two. They wanted to buy a kilo of decent, uncut gear they could then turn into two kilos of undecent, very cut gear. Lee thought about it (2,000 grams at a tenner a bag = 20 grand) and told Sammy to tell them he could get them a key of pure rocket fuel for five grand.

Lee called Alec Campbell and asked what price he could sell him a kilo of amphetamine sulphate for. Alec said two grand. Lee said 'Come tae fuck' and began negotiating. They settled on two grand.

The only problem (other than the fact that the entire enterprise was a cluster-fuck of bams) was that Lee did not have two grand. Would Alec be willing to extend him a (very short) line of credit?

He would, with the usual caveats of course: 4 per cent weekly interest and 'Your life is at risk if you do not keep up with your repayments.'

Fair enough, Lee thought. He'd only have the gear in the house a few days, a week at the most, so, even with the interest and Sammy's finder's fee, he'd still clear nearly two and a half grand profit. No bad for a week's work.

Lee collected the gear and stowed it in the bottom of his wardrobe. Sammy said the Glasgow boys were just getting the last of the cash together. Be a few days. 'Tell those boys tae get their fucking arses in gear,' Lee said, feeling very much the kingpin. Business taken care of Lee went back to his regular daily routine – that is to say he smoked cannabis and watched daytime television.

He was sitting stupefied watching an obese single mother being physically restrained from assaulting a thirty-five-year-old grandmother who was sleeping with her teenage boyfriend when Lisa waved the front page of the *Daily Standard* at him – 'DEALER SCUM GETS TEN YEARS'. Lee read the story; a Glasgow boy had indeed been given ten years for possession of 0.5 of a kilo of amphetamine sulphate. 'A class-B drug,' the article pointed out. *'This will send a strong message,'* a policeman was quoted as saying. *'Drug dealers can expect zero tolerance in Scottish courts.'*

It certainly sent a strong message to Lee: ten years for a wee bit o' billy? *Ten fucking years?* Cunt would probably only do five but still . . .

Driven by hashish-fuelled paranoia, he'd leapt from the couch, grabbed the bag-of-sugar-sized package from the bottom of the wardrobe, a shovel from the shed, and drove to Annick woods, where, by torchlight, he buried the speed in a shallow grave. Lee paced out the route he had taken into the woods and drew a careful map, 'X' marking the spot.

Then Lee lost the map.

Still, no danger, he thought. He could find the place easy enough. In a clearing, just next to the roots of a big tree of some kind.

Fucking trees, he thought, lighting a cigarette and looking around. Fucking woods were full of them. And the clearings all looked the same. Why hadn't he thought to mark the tree with spray paint or something? (*Because you were stoned tae fuck*, a quiet voice told him.)

Anyway, here he was. He owed Alec Campbell (and by extension Ranta Campbell, a thought that turned his blood to icy urine) two grand and counting and the Glasgow fuds wanted their speed pronto or they were going to go somewhere else. What was the worst-case scenario here? He didn't find the speed in time, the deal was off, and he'd have to tell Alec that he'd pay him back when he could. No big deal.

Aye – *yer maw.*

Lee wiped the sweat from his forehead with the back of his hand. He thought about his mum's poem – 'Don't Quit'.

It was stuck on her fridge along with a load of other magnets emblazoned with amusing or motivational nonsense: *'If I'd known grandchildren were so much fun I'd have had them first!' 'TODAY IS YOUR DAY!' 'A moment on the lips, a lifetime on the hips . . .'* The penultimate couplet of 'Don't Quit' always troubled Lee.

Success is failure turned inside out,
The silver tint in the clouds of doubt.

'Clouds,' the doctor had said, looking at the X-rays of his dad's lungs. Dark shadows on the milk-grey celluloid plates. The Regal. Forty a day. Smoked – pounded – right into the filter. Into the wood. Game over.

Lee picked up the spade and got to his feet.

Auld Tam had been wrong. It hadn't got better. It got worse. Much worse. Gary snap-hooked drives, he thinned wedges, he foozled putts and he shanked any iron that came his way until, a little over four hours later, he watched in horror as his four-foot putt for triple-bogey seven lipped out of the eighteenth hole. The four men shook hands on the green and then walked to the car park to tot up the scorecards – Forest and Gary marking one another's, Auld Tam and Tommy doing the same.

With a trembling hand Gary moved the pencil down the little column of boxes on the card; box after box containing neat 4s, the occasional incredible 3, a smattering of enviable (to Gary) 5s and one rogue 6, at the fourteenth, where Forest had pushed his drive out of bounds, incurring two penalty strokes. Numbly Gary wrote the total at the bottom.

Rab Forest had shot 75, less his four handicap, for a net

score of 71 – one under par and 15 shots better than Gary's best ever performance on a golf course.

Gary passed the card to Forest for him to check and sign. Forest took it and stuffed it in his back pocket. He was still frowning over Gary's scorecard. It looked like he was doing long division. Come tae fuck, Gary thought. It can't be that . . .

'Ye might want tae check that,' Forest said, finally passing him the card. 'I'm not sure if it was 11 or 12 you had back at the eighth . . .'

Gary looked at the scorecard, at the tumbling columns of 7s and 8s, the sickening 10, the terrible twin down strokes of the 11, the 15 he'd taken at the eleventh hole; where he'd put two drives out of bounds, and then, for good measure, flown his approach shot over the green and into some thick rough. A 7 at the par-three fifteenth? Could that be right? Surely he, no, it was right. His eyes kept trying to scan down to the bottom of the card, towards the final score, like someone reading a horror novel, knowing that some appalling atrocity is about to take place down the page, seeing out the corner of the eye some awful sentence standing alone between two fat paragraphs, something like:

'The creature was in the house.'

Gary gave in. His eyes surged to the bottom.

117.

He had shot 117.

Calmly he walked away from his playing partners into the middle of the car park, his putter cradled under his arm. Less calmly he hoisted the putter above his head, gripping it with both hands like a sabre. Very uncalmly indeed he began repeatedly smashing the metal head of the club down into the asphalt while really, really uncalmly screaming 'BASTARD!

BASTARD! BASTARD!', each expletive timed to explode with a fresh crack of the putter off the hot concrete.

The fine and noble tradition of golf club destruction dates back centuries and extends to even the upper reaches of the game. The legendary 1950s Texan tour pro and three times Masters runner-up Dirk Munter Jr once became so enraged with his driver during a practice round that he dropped the club on the tee box and ran to the boot of his car, returning a few moments later with a pump-action shotgun which he proceeded to empty repeatedly into the honeyed persimmon head of the driver, reducing it to smoking matchwood. Finally, all energy and cartridges spent, Munter leaned over the blackened corpse of metal and wood and whispered, 'Who's sorry now, motherfucker?'

Or the burly Irish Ryder Cup regular Kevin McKerrick who, upon ferociously pulling a five-wood into thick rough at the seventeenth hole of the 2003 US Open, effectively taking himself out of the competition, simply bent the offending club into a U shape and wordlessly handed it to an open-mouthed spectator before continuing on his way as though nothing untoward had happened.

Even Calvin Linklater, the world number one, a golfing machine, the Terminator, a man so eerily cool he is said to be able to suck down boiling water and urinate a thick plume of crushed ice, was once seen stamping up and down on a disobedient lob wedge while quietly chanting the mantra 'I am a spastic, I am a spastic, I am a spastic'.

Like many a golfer before him, Gary had learned the ways of club destruction from his father, a man whose talent at the dark art was still talked of in hushed tones around the clubhouse. It was Gary's father who had caused the Ardgirvan power cut of 1976. At the tenth, having already fallen foul of the Gyppo Rule, he had feathered his recovery shot out of bounds, terminally wrecking his scorecard. His playing partners had watched in awe as he launched the offending five-iron over a hundred feet into the air, where it connected with the overhead power lines, the head of the club and part of the shaft forming a freakish and perfect connection between two separate cables. Then the stunning blue-white flash-crackle, the frazzled club landing at his feet and all over town kettles switching off, lights going out and television screens fading to black.

Gary could clearly recall the moment he took his own first step into this larger universe. Indeed he only had to run his tongue over his teeth for the event to come rushing back. The summer of 1985, *'Baybee, I'm your ma-han!'* drifting on the warm breeze from a passing car radio and the ten-year-old Gary, putting *off* the twelfth green and back into the bunker he had just taken six shots to get out of. In the grip of pain and anguish that were beyond his capacity to understand he placed the shaft of the putter – his new putter, mallet-headed just like his dad's, bought for him by his dad only weeks before – in his mouth and bit down with all his might. After a few seconds of intense effort there was a horrible crunch as his upper right-hand incisor splintered and then warm blood was pouring down his face and intense pain was kicking in. Enraged at what the putter had done to him, Gary brought the club hard down into the turf at his feet. There must have been a rock beneath the surface, because a second later, he was just holding a shaft, the head of the club remaining in the earth.

Then the long walk to the clubhouse, crying all the way. He found his father ensconced with his cronies, warm with the Grouse that was famous and still glowing from the scratch

75 he had shot that morning. Father looked at son – at the tears, at the blood that had dried on his chin and flecked on his blue Adidas polo shirt, at the shaft he held in one hand and the putter head he held in the other – and understood in a moment what had happened. He burst into throaty laughter, hugged the broken boy to him, and exclaimed theatrically, 'THAT'S MA BOY!' There had been no censure, no anger at the destruction of the new club, only the understanding that his child now knew the pain, that he was now one of us. There had only been – Gary now realised, decades later – love.

He had read that there were tribes, in the Amazon or somewhere, who lived a remote and idyllic existence so cut off from realities like war and aggression that they would tattoo and pierce their offspring to make the children understand that pain and torment existed in the universe. Perhaps, far from the rainforests, far from the half-mile-high trees standing silent since before the birth of Christ, perhaps right here, amid the bypasses and all-night petrol stations of towns like Ardgirvan, golf was performing the same function.

But this was no comfort to Gary now as – with a final 'BASTARD!' – he brought the club down onto the concrete for the eighth or ninth time, the head of the putter incredibly still attached to the shaft but now reduced to a white-hot nub of metal.

It was Auld Tam who laid a gentle hand on Gary's arm. 'Come on, son. That's enough now. Ye'll break yer bloody wrists.'

13

GIVEN GARY'S GOLF ROUTINE, SATURDAY MORNINGS had become a regular time for Pauline and Masterson. Usually he'd book a hotel room although sometimes, like today, they met at the warehouse – sex in the office, or, once or twice, out in the middle of the huge warehouse itself, in a pile of offcuts, the new carpet smell sweet and plastic and strong all around them, reminding Pauline of when she and Gary had first moved into the house. Masterson had started to look forward to Saturday mornings like the last day of school. (Leanne thought he was out visiting the showrooms.)

However, this Saturday morning was developing differently from how he had hoped. He looked at Pauline again, sitting on the sofa in his office, still fully clothed and legs primly crossed. Her skirt was short and he could see a good length of brown thigh.

'Eh?' Masterson repeated.

'I'm sorry, Findlay. I just can't let myself get into this any deeper . . .'

He tried to think of something to say, something persuasive and romantic but at the same time not too pleading. Something suave, something assured and reassuring.

'Come tae fuck, hen,' he said.

'Look, I . . . oh God, I promised myself I wouldn't cry.' Pauline sat forward and exhaled. 'It was fine when it was just, you know, sex. But the longer we go on seeing each other the harder it gets for me not to be able to see you all the time. So –'

'Aye,' Masterson said, getting up and coming round the desk towards her, sitting down beside her. Christ, he already had a semi. 'But we've got something good going on here, doll. Ah've no felt like this since . . . fuck knows when.'

Pauline took his hand and stroked it. 'Me too,' she smiled sadly. 'But, we're both married. Let's be honest, where's this going to go?' He could see taut cleavage straining beneath thin cotton. Semi? There was a fucking four-bedroom detached wi ample parking going up down there.

'It's probably best if we don't speak for a while,' Pauline said. Her hand brushed against the crotch of his trousers. Jesus. 'Oh,' she said, putting her hand to her mouth childishly. Masterson swallowed thickly. 'OK,' Pauline said, sliding down from the sofa onto her knees on the scratchy, carpet-tiled floor. 'I suppose I owe you a going-away present . . .'

Masterson closed his eyes and savoured the cool relief of the air. Pauline watched his face, his jaw tightening, his apple bobbing, and thought to herself, *No risk, no reward,* as she opened her mouth.

Bert Thompson whistled his way through the locker room carrying his toilet bag and towel. His whistle – 'Spread a Little Happiness' – echoed off the stone walls and around the empty room. It was nearly lunchtime and everyone was either out on the course, or finished and in the bar, or off home. The younger lads all spent more time with their families, the young lassies today just didn't tolerate the old-school behaviour: straight to the course after work on a Friday night, a quick round and then propping the bar up till midnight? Then straight out again for the Medal on Saturday morning and rolling home half-cut at five for your dinner? Dream on, as his granddaughter liked to say.

Bert whistled the whistle of a man with an 81 under his belt – not bad for an old boy, at seventy-seven he could still come close to shooting his age on a good day – and a dark pint of heavy waiting for him in the clubhouse. He plopped his toilet bag and towel up on the window ledge and pulled his polo shirt over his head. Quick hoor's bath. Pits and pus. He was reaching for the hot tap when he heard it – a sucking intake of breath, then a whimper. His hand stopped on the tap and he listened for a moment. Nothing, just the sound of cold water trickling down the porcelain face of the long urinal. And then, as he reached for the tap again, another muffled sound, this time like someone trying not to sneeze, the sound of tremendous force being checked. Bert wandered cautiously around from the washbasin and through the archway, into the adjoining room, where he faced a row of three toilet cubicles and two shower stalls at the end.

'Hello?' Bert said.

Again the sucking intake of breath, the sense of something being stoppered up, and silence. Bert walked softly towards the one closed cubicle door. 'Everything all right in there?'

A sniffle. Then a whispered 'Aye.'

'Who's in there?' Bert asked.

There was a long pause, then the metal clack of the bolt going back and the door swung open. Bert's first thought was, Who's died?

Because Gary was a *wreck*: his face slick with tears, the front of his pale blue golf shirt too. His eyes were red puffy slits. He looked like one of Bert's grandchildren when they fell and hurt themselves, the floodgates uncloseable once they were opened.

'Gary son,' Bert said, an edge in his voice, genuinely afraid now, 'whit's happened? It's no yer mother, is –'

He placed a hand on Gary's shoulder. That did it. Something in the simple warmth of the human touch sent Gary over the edge and he convulsed again into racking sobs.

'Wh-why c-can't I do it, Bert?'

'Do what, son?'

'I ca-can't . . . d-d-do . . .' He could hardly get it out.

And Bert realised.

There was only one thing outside bereavement that could reduce a grown man to this state.

'Here.' Bert passed Gary a small pewter hip flask. Gary took a sip, gagging on the whisky, and the two men sat in silence on the wooden bench that overlooked the fifth green and the sixth tee.

It really had turned into an incredible afternoon; a cloudless sky, blue as tropical water, the slightest breeze wavering through the leaves of the silver birch trees which guarded the big gorge to the right of the sixth tee and ruffling the tattered yellow flag on the fifth green. Bert sipped the whisky and they watched the players moving along the distant fairways, dots of red, white and yellow in an emerald sea.

'Sorry, Bert,' Gary said finally, just remembering to say

'Bert' and not 'Mr Thompson'. He had known Bert since he was a baby. He had golfed with Gary's dad.

'Och, wheesht, son,' Bert said pleasantly, screwing the cap back on the little flask. 'By Christ, yer no the first man that's been in that state over a round o' gowf. And damn sure ye'll no be the last.'

'I don't seem to get any better. I practise, I read everything I can, I understand in my head what you need to do. All the shots, I know what I should be doing, I just can't . . .'

Bert had been a golfer for nearly seventy years. He had heard all this before: high-handicap players weeping with rage and despair over what was essentially the gulf, the chasm, between thought and expression. It was a commonplace problem in art and – make no mistake – Bert Thompson considered golf to be art. What some people found in museums or galleries, or in the pages of books, Bert found in the arc of a good drive.

'Do you know what the golf swing is, son?' he said.

Gary looked at him.

'It's *muscle memory*. You're talking about hundreds of individual movements all taking place within a couple of seconds. This –' he tapped Gary's forehead – 'doesn't have time to think about any of that. It just triggers the sequence and hopefully, like an engine if it's firing properly, everything falls into place.'

'But I keep shanking it, Bert.'

Bert stopped just short of crossing himself and thought for a moment before he continued.

'Well, ye know, son, some o' the greatest players ever born have shanked a ball. Ah remember, the summer o' '62, doon the road. Big Arnie.' Bert looked off into the distance, down over the golf course, over the gyppo camp and out towards

Ardeer and the sea, the present dissolving and falling away as he performed the very ordinary miracle of time travel: in half a second there were Austins and Ford Zephyrs in the car park behind him rather than Mondeos and Cavaliers, there were no mobile phones chirruping, John F. Kennedy was in the White House, the Beatles had yet to release a single, and Bert was walking these same fairways with men long dead.

Bert was talking about Arnold Palmer, at the Open in Troon in 1962, when the great man bested one of the hardest links courses in the world. The Open was coming back to Troon this summer. Just six miles away. The greatest championship in the game. Gary had already booked the time off work.

'Me and your father,' Bert carried on, 'we went over for the whole thing. Hot. Course was dry and running fast. We followed Arnie for four days. By Christ, whit that man could do tae a gowf ball. Hitting the driver aff the fairway like it was a seven-iron. Anyway, it's the third day and we're pressed right up the ropes at the eleventh, the long par five that runs along beside the railway. Massive crowd. Like your boy Linklater gets nowadays . . .' As Gary listened he was there with them too – the Irish Sea sparkling, the sun on his face, the cream-and-burgundy trains running by on their way to Glasgow, and his father alive, young and healthy in this story about golf. 'Arnie's playing his second shot, three-iron it was.'

Bert Thompson had regularly forgotten his wife's birthday over the years. He could not tell you any of his children's home phone numbers. There were men around the town who he had known his whole life whose surnames he could not remember. But he could tell you shot by shot how Arnold Palmer put together a 67 at Royal Troon on a summer Saturday nearly half a century ago.

'He gets the ball well back in his stance, trying tae punch it low, like, brings the club doon and – by Christ – does he no shank it!'

'Palmer?'

'Shanks it? He nearly puts it oan the railway line!'

'What did he do?'

'Well, first he hauds the club up and looks at it as if it had just called him a prick, pardon my French, son. Then he stamps his divot back in and, just as he goes tae walk off, your father leans over the rope and says tae him, sympathetically like, "It happens to the best of us, Mr Palmer."'

'What did he say?'

'Palmer looks up at yer dad, looks him right in the eye, and he says, "Fuck off."'

They both took this in for a moment, Bert shaking his head in silent wonder. '*Arnold Palmer.* Telling *your* dad tae fuck off. It was one of the proudest moments of yer faither's life.'

Bert took another swallow of whisky, the sun glinting off the silver flask. 'The point is, *anybody* can get the shanks. It's all up here. This –' again he tapped Gary's forehead – 'is the most important muscle in golf. Ah mean, you don't have what anybody would call a beautiful golf swing,' (this was the understatement of the millennium) 'but that doesn't matter. Look at the American fella, Drew . . .'

'Keel.'

'Drew Keel. Look at his swing. Steep? The boy looks like he's trying to chop one of his own feet aff wi' an axe. But he's winning tournaments. He's making the money. It doesn't matter how ugly it is if you can do it the same way every time.'

'Aye, ah know all that, Bert, ah just –'

'Look, tell ye what, the course is quiet now. Come on and

we'll go over tae the second fairway wi' a bag of balls and we'll see if we can crack this shanking carry-on.'

'Really? Thanks, Bert. I know I'm a hopeless case but –'

'Och, wheesht. God loves a trier, son. Get your clubs.'

Bert watched Gary walk back towards the locker room, then he turned at the sound of a car door slamming to his left. Billy Douglas was hurrying round to his boot. 'Afternoon, Billy,' Bert said. 'Running a bit late, are ye?'

'Aye, Bert,' Billy said. 'Ma sixtieth last night. Cannae take the drink like ah used tae.'

'Ah know whit ye mean, pal. Have a good game.'

'Aye, cheers, Bert. Ah'll see ye later.'

Bert leaned back on the bench and looked down over the golf course – players splayed and crucified, clubs dangling in one hand, necks craning after doomed balls. The finishing positions of the amateurs – physical apologies for the outrages they were performing in the name of golf.

Lee's mobile rang. Sammy. Again. Lee jabbed the button and uttered a brusque 'Ho?', trying for a tone of voice that suggested he was a very busy man. He was, in fact, rolling a joint and watching the Shopping Channel.

'They've cancelled,' Sammy said.

'Whit?'

'Alan and wee Flakey. Said they couldnae wait any longer.'

'Hey, you tell those pricks a deal's a fucking d—'

'Fuck sake, Lee! Ah telt ye the other week! They're no gonnae sit ab—'

'AH'LL FUCKING GO UP THERE AND CUT THEIR FUCKING THROATS!'

As he often did when he was completely in the wrong, Lee went for the attack-as-defence approach. Sammy let him shout and scream. 'Aye, Lee, fair enough. You go and dae aw that. It disnae change anything. They've got sorted fae somebody else.'

'Whit the fuck am ah meant tae dae with a fucking key o' billy?'

'Fuck knows. Ah'll speak tae ye later.'

'Hey, don't you hang up oan me, ya pr—'

Click.

'DON'T FUCKING HANG UP OAN ME YA FUCKING PRIIIIIIIICK!' Lee screamed into the empty phone, in the empty house. Then he hurled the mobile into the wall and watched it smash into several pieces.

Gary whistled appreciatively as Bert's ball soared high and dropped softly onto the back of the green – about ten yards past the pin.

'Naw,' Bert said, 'caught it a bit thin.'

They were stood in the light rough along the left-hand side of the second fairway, about 150 yards away from the green; a good green to practise approach shots to – big and welcoming and slightly downhill from them. There was a carrier bag full of old golf balls at their feet: fifty for a tenner, purchased by Gary down at the entrance to the gyppo camp that very morning. It was a nice additional income stream for the gyppos: selling mishit golf balls back to the people who mishit them.

'Not a pure golf shot,' Bert was saying, pulling a fresh ball towards him with the toe of the club. 'Ye know whit it feels like when ye catch it right, don't ye?'

Even a golfer as terrible as Gary knew this: the feeling of energy perfectly released into the centre of the universe.

Bert teed the ball up on a tuft of blonde grass. 'Now what you're not doing is getting a full shoulder turn. You're freezing up because you're already scared something bad is going to happen. You can't play golf like that, son. Ye need tae . . .'

Bert swung again, simple and elegant, effortlessly pinching the ball cleanly off the ground and sending it arcing towards the green, fading slightly from left to right as it came down. 'Ye see what ah mean?' Bert said, still watching his shot as he stepped back and motioned for Gary to try. Gary reached into his golf bag.

'Whit ye got there?'

'Seven.'

'Naw, son, try the nine.'

'Eh? I can't hit the nine-iron 150 yards.'

'Whit?' Bert said. 'Away and don't talk rubbish. Look at ye! Look at the muscles oan yer forearms. Yer like bloody Popeye! Ah'm an auld man and ah can hit a soft seven-iron *through* the green fae here. You're telling me you cannae get there wi the nine? C'mon now.'

With a shrug Gary let the seven-iron fall back and pulled out the nine.

Nearly three hundred yards away, to their right and uphill from them, Billy Douglas and his playing partners walked onto the first tee.

Gary addressed the ball. He flexed his knees. *Sit down into it.* He swung back carefully, his left shoulder dipping down and pointing at the ball, but, as he began to bring the club down, the thought proved impossible to resist – *never get there with a nine*. He accelerated crazily and, in trying to hit the ball far too hard, succeeded only in topping it, sending it skittering off along the ground and coming to rest a miserable fifty-odd yards away.

'Christ, sorry, Bert –

'Shhh, come on now.' Bert was already placing another ball

at his feet. 'Don't swing so hard. Find the rhythm. You've plenty club there.'

Billy Douglas reached into the pocket of his golf bag. He took out the silver-and-orange cardboard sleeve containing three new Spaxons. He opened the tube and the number 3 saw the light of day for the first time.

Gary swung again. This time he buried the clubhead into the turf two inches behind the ball, the force of the thwarted energy vibrating up his arms horribly, the ball skittering forward a few inches.

'FUCK IT!' Gary screamed, his voice carrying far over the crabgrass and trees.

Billy Douglas and his playing partners looked up into the distance. 'Who's that?' one of them asked, looking across to their right, towards the tiny figures over on the far side of the next fairway across. 'Somebody practising,' Billy said, teeing up the Spaxon.

Bert laid a hand on Gary's shoulder. 'Calm down, son. It's no the Open. We're just out here hitting a few balls. Don't take it so seriously.' Bert knew this was ridiculous advice. Golf was indeed like a love affair: if you took it seriously, it would break your heart. If you didn't take it seriously – what was the point? 'Just try and empty your mind. Ye want a bit of a draw here.' A draw: moving the ball right to left in the air. Gary understood how this was done. He had read countless articles on the subject. He just couldn't make his body do what his head understood. He set up his stance again anyway, aiming slightly right of the green. He regripped the club. He was breathing hard.

Bert's hand was on his shoulder now and the old man's face was close to his. 'Come on now, son.'

Gary looked up into Bert's eyes. The irises were pale blue, the whites rheumy and flecked with crimson. 'Breathe easy,'

Bert said. There was something hypnotic in his voice now and the green world around them seemed to be shimmering and softening. 'Loosen up your grip. Like you're holding a bird.' Gary hadn't realised he'd been gripping the club so hard, like a madman. He let go. Bert felt the tension drain from his arms. 'Good boy,' he said.

Up on the first tee Billy Douglas completed his practice swings and addressed the ball properly. New ball. First tee. Billy told himself – *Ah'm gonnae smash this intae next week.*

'Just relax.' Bert was almost whispering now. Gary felt a strange serenity descend as he looked towards the green – the pin was exactly 148 yards from where he stood. 'See the shot.'

Professional golfers have the ability to see *exactly* the shot they are intending to hit *before* they hit it. Gary often tried to do this, but he knew his efforts were poor – crude line drawings, a child's sketch, rather than the detailed blueprints the pros see in their heads. But now, with Bert whispering to him and the whiff of whisky washing gently across him, reminding him of his father, he looked up towards the green and he *could* see the ball in flight – a high, penetrating arc, drawing slightly into the gentle breeze. Bert sensed that Gary wasn't there any more. He'd gone somewhere in his head. He stepped back and Gary's world was peace and silence as he drew the club back.

On the first tee Billy Douglas brought the driver down with all the fury of golf. The Spaxon rocketed off the tee and for a split second it looked as though the shot might be good. Then the ball started to veer offline, slicing violently to the right, the crazed trajectory a combination of the slice Billy had hit and the tiny flaw in the ball's unevenly weighted core. One in a thousand. One in a million. 'Christ,' one of his partners said.

Gary uncoiled, bringing the club down, elegant and muscular, looking like a different golfer. He didn't even feel the contact. It was like the ball wasn't there.

A perfect connection.

He looked up to see the ball silhouetted against the sky, seeming to pause at the top of its trajectory and turning now, drawing right to left, just as he'd visualised, and beginning to drop towards the green.

'Gowf shot.' Bert whispered the greatest compliment in the sport.

'Fuck me,' Gary said, holding his finishing position, the club cocked elegantly around him and his jaw dropping.

'FORE!!' Billy Douglas screamed. He was 280 yards away. Downwind. Inaudible.

Gary's ball dropped onto the green twelve feet short and right of the flagstick. It bounced once and began to roll left towards the hole. Six feet, four feet . . .

'By Christ, that's close,' Bert said.

'GO ON, YOU F—' Gary began.

The viciously sliced Spaxon sizzled by Bert's right ear, missing him by two inches, and smashed into Gary's right temple at 186 miles per hour. Everything went black and the ground came rushing up to meet him.

He couldn't see Billy Douglas running down the gentle slope of the first fairway towards them.

He couldn't hear Bert shouting his name over and over.

He couldn't see his ball falling into the hole.

Nothing.

PART TWO

The brain is the ultimate organ of adaptation. It takes in information and orchestrates complex behavioural repertoires that allow human beings to act in sometimes marvelous, sometimes terrible ways.

From Neurons to Neighborhoods, Jack P. Shonkoff and Deborah A. Phillips (eds)

I know why we try to keep the dead alive: we try to keep them alive in order to keep them with us.

The Year of Magical Thinking, Joan Didion

14

NORTH AYRSHIRE GENERAL HOSPITAL, BUILT IN THE early 1980s, is a sprawling structure of white and chocolate that sits less than ten miles to the east of Ardgirvan, just on the outskirts of the larger town of Kilmarnock. NADGE, as the locals call it, was not a place of fond memories for Cathy Irvine.

Here, in the gift shop, when the hospital was sparkling and new, she had bought sweets and bright plastic toys to entertain her young boys while her father died upstairs. Here, in the cafeteria, she had drunk endless cups of sour black coffee – occasionally going out through the automatic doors to supplement these with fiercely smoked cigarettes – while her husband had his chemotherapy. Here, sitting on a hard plastic chair in a white corridor surrounded by the bitter hospital smells and the squeak and rattle of trolleys, she had looked up from the paper tissue she was tremblingly shredding as the doctor approached, his face already telling Cathy that they were done with the chemotherapy now.

Cathy's mind effortlessly replayed all these terrible memories as she walked along and turned a corner. Several private rooms lay to her right and she glanced in as she passed them, catching little snapshots of the very ordinary hells old age and random calamity lead us to: an old man sleeping, silently watched by an old woman with a fat, unread thriller on her lap. Another man watching television, a game show, as blood and urine dangled around him in plastic pouches. A younger man with his head in some kind of metal cage – bolts and studs actually going into his forehead – but still managing to joke with his friends. 'Hi, boys,' Cathy said, returning their waves. They were nice boys. Car crash one of them had been in.

Cathy reached the fourth room along and entered with her coffee and muffin. 'Hi, son!' she said brightly. 'Sorry I took so long. I bumped into Margaret from up the road. Ye know Margaret? She's in here with . . .'

Cathy talked on, her enthusiasm unmarred by the fact that her son had been unconscious for three days now.

Gary lay on the bed, his head near-mummified by white bandages. Clear tubing – no, not quite clear, a bluish tint to it – ran into his nose, into his arms and the corner of his mouth. A little dried blood was visible at the seam of the bandages, above his right eye, and his face around the same eye was iridescent with bruising – green and purple and yellow and blue.

When Cathy had first walked into this room three days ago, when she first saw Gary like this, she had automatically flashed on another image of him: six years old and dressed up for Halloween as the Amber Gambler, the man from the TV adverts who drove through yellow lights. She remembered his wee face smiling through the hole in the middle of the ketchup-stained bandages and him saying, 'But do I look *scary*, Mummy?' As Cathy moved closer to her sixties her mind increasingly had a mind of its own. It kept replaying memories from twenty, thirty, forty years ago, like it was asking her to rate them: Is this important? Do we want to keep this one? It was like someone preparing to move house, clearing out all the junk and trying to decide what was worth taking on to the next place. Cathy's mind clearly thought that Halloween 1981 might be important – for she could see Gary in the living room that night as clearly as she was seeing him now in this hospital bed.

Cathy settled down in a chair next to the bed – as close as she could get given the phalanx of warm machines guarding him – and started to read the evening paper to him, providing her own commentary on the news stories as she went. The reports themselves were read out in the slightly hesitant, formal voice Cathy used when reading aloud and then her commentary on the events followed in her own natural voice.

'"*Three men were sentenced to a total of fourteen years in prison at Glasgow Sheriff Court yesterday after it was revealed they had masterminded a heroin deal worth an estimated three million pounds.*" Och, ah hope they throw away the bloody key! The scum o' the bloody earth so they are!' She turned the page. '"*My life is hell, claims Hollywood actress.*"' Cathy snorted. 'Aye, hen, see, if ah'd yer bloody money sure ye'd no hear me complaining!' She turned the page.

There was no self-consciousness on Cathy's part. The doctor had said it might help if they talked to Gary, that coma patients had been known to respond to voices they recognised. So Cathy, being of a generation that listened to doctors, talked to him. Indeed, if the consultant had told her that there was a one in two billion chance that it might help Gary if she stripped off, stood on a chair and punched herself repeatedly in the face all day then right at this moment she would have been perched on a stool, buck naked and punching away until either her face or her knuckles gave out.

It was true: Cathy could only express her feelings in Hallmark-card poetry, in fridge-magnet philosophy, in platitudes and commonplaces; but her feelings were no less real for having been expressed as clichés. The grade, the quality of love she felt for the boy was something the childless, unconscious Gary was still many emotional miles from understanding. As she dabbed with a wet wipe at the dried saliva crusted at the corner of his mouth, his three-day stubble scratching the underside of her wrist, Cathy reflected on how gladly she would have taken his place, for her love for the boy was fathomless and her will for him to live weighed more than her own soul. So Cathy talked, leaving his bedside only to fulfil the bare essentials of her existence: toilet, nicotine, caffeine.

She put the paper down and looked at her watch. The consultant, Dr Robertson, should be in soon. They'd been operating on him again this morning, to drain some fluid or something. Where the hell was P—

'Hi, Cathy. Sorry I'm a wee bit late.'

'Hi, Pauline hen,' Cathy said, standing to embrace her daughter-in-law.

'How is he?'

'He's fine. Still sleeping.' Sleeping. Cathy had never said the word 'coma'. Like when Lee had simply been 'away', Pauline thought.

Pauline nearly hadn't answered when the call came on Saturday afternoon. She'd been in the house, alone, on her mobile, mid-sentence with the pleading Masterson, and the phone had just kept on ringing and ringing. Finally she'd leaned over the bed and picked it up, recognising the golf club number (Gary had it on speed dial) and then some old guy was telling her about an accident, a golf ball, an ambulance. The explosion of guilt she'd felt when she'd first seen him in here had surprised her.

'Hi, Mrs Irvine, Mrs Irvine.' Dr Robertson was in the doorway. A friendly man, tall and thin. Clever-looking, Cathy thought. A golfer too, as he'd told them when they'd first met.

'Hello, Doctor,' Pauline and Cathy chorused.

'How is he this evening?' Robertson asked, picking up the chart. The question was rhetorical and he only half listened as Cathy started talking about reading the paper to Gary. You had to give them something to do. You told cancer patients to drink plenty of fruit juice – like trying to ward off a Pershing missile with an umbrella. But you had to give people some raw material from which to fashion hope. 'Good, good,' Robertson said. 'Have a seat please, ladies.' He gestured for them to sit down and took his position leaning against the window, a Manila file clasped to his chest and a beautiful spring evening through the glass behind him.

How to explain? A large part of Robertson's job involved explaining the intricacies of complex medical traumas to people who struggled to understand the plotlines of Hollywood blockbusters. He scanned the file – *'pterygoid . . . torn middle meningeal artery . . . extradural haemorrhaging . . . GCS of 10 . . . raised intracranial pressure . . . temporal lobe . . . burr hole . . .'* – then reached down for the language as he held a blue-white X-ray of Gary's skull up against the window. 'So, the operation went very well,' he began.

Cathy sighed with relief.

'Unfortunately –'

Her blood, refreezing.

'– the golf ball hit Gary on the temple, where the skull is thinnest, and it damaged the artery that runs beneath the temple, causing bleeding into this area between the brain and the skull. Which is this dark spot you can see here . . .' He used his fountain pen to point out the area to them.

'Aww my God,' Cathy said, starting to cry.

Pauline awkwardly put an arm around her mother-in-law and shushed her. Robertson gave them a moment before continuing, tapping the pen against his teeth.

'Now, we performed a craniotomy and –'

'Sorry, Doctor, what is that?' Pauline asked, slowly recrossing her long legs.

'We opened up the skull –'

'*Aww my God!*' Cathy wailed. Her beautiful son, his brain all exposed to the world. She was really starting to get on Pauline's tits.

'– and drained off the blood.'

'Is . . . is it fixed?' Cathy asked, sniffling through a tissue.

'Well, it's too early to say really. I think we caught the worst of it. If the bleeding had continued, it would have put more pressure on the temporal lobe and would eventually have affected other areas of the brain. If it hasn't done so already.' He hadn't meant to say this last part. Got away from him. Maybe neither of them would . . .

'What do you mean?' Pauline asked, looking him straight in the eye.

'I . . . it's possible areas of the brain may already have been . . .' *don't say damaged, don't say damaged, don't say damaged*, '. . . affected.'

Cathy blinked, not comprehending.

'You mean damaged?' Pauline said.

'Possibly.'

'*Brain-damaged?* AWW MA GOD!!' Cathy unleashed a fresh peal of tears. A golf ball. A stupid wee golf ball. How the hell could something that size cause . . .

Robertson gave her a moment, waiting until she tapered off to a steady sob. 'But there is some good news. His score on the Glasgow Coma Scale, which is what we use to measure the severity of comas, is relatively mild. Ten. And with head injuries we really know so little. If he wakes up, there might be absolutely nothing wrong with him. On the other hand –'

Even through her grief Cathy lasered in on the word. '*If* he wakes up?'

'Yes.'

'B-but wasn't this operation going to make sure he wakes up?'

'Ah, the operation was to repair and to try and prevent further damage to the brain. There's no guarantee it'll bring him out of the coma.'

Cathy kept right on crying.

'How long,' Pauline asked, nodding towards the bed, 'can he stay like that without . . . ?'

'Again, it's hard to say. Some coma patients are out for weeks and regain completely normal lives. Others are . . . less fortunate. We just have to be positive.'

Robertson looked up as a nurse appeared in the doorway. 'Dr Robertson, you –'

'I know.'

He turned back to the Irvine women. 'I'm very sorry, I must see to another patient. Please, have a think about what I've said and Mr Cobham, the surgeon who performed the operation, can answer any further questions you might have about the procedure itself. You're in good hands, Mrs Irvine.'

Robertson placed a hand on Cathy's shoulder. 'He's one of the best neurosurgeons in Scotland.'

'Thank you, Doctor,' Pauline said, shaking his hand. Soft hands. No wedding ring. In her inside pocket, next to her left breast, she felt her mobile phone vibrate softly as *another* text arrived.

'Not at all,' Robertson said as he followed the nurse out of the room and down the corridor.

Pauline stood at the foot of the bed and looked at her husband for a long time before she softly whispered 'Jesus' to herself. She sensed Cathy's approach and let her put her arm around her. The two women stood there. Cathy was already getting her head around various scenarios: her wheeling Gary around the park. Liquidising his food. Feeding him. Cleaning him up down there. These were bad-case scenarios to be sure, but Cathy felt more than able to cope with all of them. The worst-case scenario – the headstone, the coffin – was something she was unable to picture. The boy was going to live and that was that. Whatever state he was in was something they'd just have to deal with as best they could. She patted Pauline's hand. 'Come on, hen. Ye heard what the doctor said, we have to stay positive.'

'I know,' Pauline said softly.

Pauline was positive.

She wouldn't be staying married to some drooling mongo. She was one hundred and ten fucking per cent positive about that.

15

MASTERSON THUMBED INTO 'MESSAGES' AND SWIFTLY deleted Pauline's most recent text before crossing the patio and going through the open French windows into the kitchen. It was a huge room – the cooking end was separated from the dining area by a black marble island that incorporated twin sinks and a battery of gadgets. Leanne was at one of the sinks washing an apple. 'I'm just making some fruit salad, do ye want some?'

'Naw, ah'm awright thanks, doll.'

Aye, right. Fucking fruit salad? Soon as ah'm oot that door the biscuit jar'll be getting a right fucking panelling . . .

He watched her waddling towards the huge, stainless-steel fridge-freezer, the loose grey material of her sweatpants flapping from monstrous cheek to monstrous cheek, each buttock easily weighing in around the same as a newborn baby, and thought to himself – *How the fuck did it get tae this?*

He had loved her once, this monster.

Her weight gain had been stealthy enough through her

thirties and early forties, but the last few years, now the kids were out of the house, now she literally had nothing to do, had seen a mammoth escalation. Every few months a new diet was launched – protein shakes, low-carb, no-carb, soup-and-salad, steamed food only – and then quietly decommissioned.

A few months back he'd gone over to Ayr to have lunch with Simon Murphy at Murphy, Mills & Harrington. Divorce – what was the worst-case scenario? Over expensive pasta Murphy laid it out for him: they'd been married for nearly twenty-five years. Raised two children together. Leanne had been there since before the business was worth anything. Forget her getting half of everything he'd made in the last two decades – she might get all that *and* be able to make a case against any of his *future* income.

'*Fucking whit?*' Masterson growled through gnashed teeth.

'Well, they could argue that by taking care of raising your children and running the household, Leanne enabled you to focus on making the business a success, which in turn led you to the financial position you're in today, where you have the capital to take advantage of further opportunities. Listen, Findlay, I've got a client in Glasgow, TV writer, about your age. He got divorced and she's getting a piece of everything he makes for the next ten years on the grounds that he *might* have had some of his ideas while he was married to her! The cunt's working his nuts off just to break even.'

'You mean,' Masterson said, 'if some hoor puts your dinner on the fucking table every now and then, and slaps a tit intae the mouth of a crying wean here and there, then she gets a chunk of your fucking dosh for the rest of her life?'

'Just cheat,' Murphy had said, pouring them more Rioja. 'Because, you're what, fifty-one?'

'Fifty.'

'Whatever. Listen.' He leaned in, lowering his voice. 'There's a girl I use over in Prestwick. Two hundred quid for the hour. Twenty-two years old and she could suck the chrome off a bumper. You could do that every other night for the rest of your life and it'd *still* work out cheaper than divorcing Leanne. I'll give you her number.'

Masterson didn't take the number.

He met Pauline shortly afterwards.

16

'DELTA! STYX! AH'M NO FUCKING KIDDING YE, IF YOU TWO DON'T FUCKING BEHAVE AH'M GONNAE LEATHER THE FUCKING PAIR OF YE! RIGHT? AMAZON! FUCKING STOP THAT! LISA – WHERE'S MA FUCKING CAR KEYS? FOR FUCK'S SAKE!'

A normal evening chez Lee and Lisa: Delta was smashing his younger brother's face off the wall. Amazon was grinding a crayon into the living-room carpet. Lisa was in the kitchen, surrounded by an Everest of ironing, and Lee was late. Lee hated hospitals. Had she said visiting was six till eight? Or eight till ten? Or . . . maybe he shouldn't have had that last joint.

Lee couldn't believe the timing. He'd been lying on the sofa all day, heroically smoking hash to try and get himself into the right frame of mind to call his little brother and ask him if he could borrow a lot of money. By late afternoon he was just about there – stupefied to the point where he didn't really care what he was doing, not quite stupefied enough to be unable to speak. (He had to watch his temper too. Gary was always nice and usually lent him the money but sometimes he could get a bit cheeky. Asking Lee what it was for and stuff like that. Lecturing him. Lee had once rung Gary intending to borrow money and had somehow wound up offering to cut his throat. The fucking temper on him. Like his old boy, Lee thought.) Lee had actually been reaching for his new mobile when it rang. He'd looked at the caller ID: 'BAWBAG'. It was Gary, calling him from home. Unbelievable. For a second Lee entertained the thought that Gary was calling just to offer to lend him some money. Out of the blue. No strings attached. It was this thought that made Lee realise how very stoned he was. But it hadn't been Gary. It had been his mum in tears, calling from Gary and Pauline's with the news about the accident.

'LISA! WH—' As he went to shout (all communication in their tiny house was conducted by shouting, it was almost unthinkable that someone would enter the same room as the person they were conversing with) he spotted his car keys on the mantelpiece.

'Da! Da!' Something tugging at the hem of his jacket. He turned and looked down to see Styx's crying face. 'He keeps calling me a fucking poof!'

'Naw ah don't, ya lying prick!' Delta shouted from the hall.

'You two watch yer fucking language!' Lisa shouted from the kitchen.

'Fuck!' Amazon shouted squeakily from the living room.

'SEE!' Lisa shouted.

'If he does it again,' Lee said to Styx, 'just lamp him wan.'

'LEE!' Lisa shouted.

'Ah'm away up the hospital tae see ma brother!' Lee shouted.

The breeze and the silence were blessed relief as he slammed the front door behind him. Then he looked up.

Alec Campbell and the Beast were walking up the garden path.

'Alec,' Lee began, 'I was just coming to –'

The Beast punched Lee hard in the stomach, his thumb jutting stiffly between his index and middle finger, and Lee went down. Alec lounged against Lee's ancient, battered Nova while Lee fought for breath. After a moment he said, 'Ye want tae try again?'

Lee got unsteadily to his feet, his legs trembling. 'Ah . . . ah just had a wee bit of a delay offloading the gear. Ah just need a few more days, Alec.'

'See? That wisnae so hard, was it?' Alec said. 'A *dialogue* is what we're having here. As a responsible borrower you need to inform your lender if you're having difficulty meeting your obligations. Then we can decide on the necessary course of action, eh?'

'Aye, aye, ah'm sorry, Alec. I just, ma brother –'

'Here's the deal – you've got two weeks. If ah don't have the money or the gear by then you'll just be dealing wi Frank, OK?' Alec slapped a hand on the Beast's massive shoulder, having to reach up half a foot to do so. The Beast wasn't even looking at Lee, like it was beneath him. 'And Frank doesn't do dialogue.'

'Aye, Alec. Two weeks. Fine. Ah swear oan ma wean's life.'

Finally the Beast spoke to Lee. 'Are ye sure about that, son?' he said.

17

THE SMELL OF THE PLACE WAS INCREDIBLE. SO MANY SCENTS dusting the warm air – pine, camellia, crab apple, jasmine, juniper, flowering peach, white dogwood, azalea and, of course, magnolia. Magnolia everywhere. In a daze Gary followed the gravel path through the groves of eucalyptus trees towards a beautiful building – a two-storey, whitewood structure with a veranda and balcony capped with a grey slate roof.

Heaven certainly looked a lot like Augusta National, Bobby Jones's immortal masterpiece, the most photogenic golf course in the world.

And there was Bobby Jones himself, standing on the first tee and waving Gary over. Jones was talking to someone, another golfer, who had his back to Gary. The man had a driver threaded through his arms and was stretching from side to side, warming up, and Bobby Jones was laughing at something he was saying. A third man stood at the back of the tee, slightly apart, taking graceful, precise practice swings with an old-fashioned persimmon-headed driver. His swing was picture-perfect. Of course it was. It was Ben Hogan.

The Georgia sun was warm on Gary's face and bright in his eyes and he had to shield himself against it with his hand as the man with his back to him began to turn round. He knew those shoulders and the thick, seamy sunburned neck. He knew who this golfing legend was before he saw his face.

'Hello, Dad,' Gary said.

'Hullo, son,' his dad said pleasantly, casually, as though he had only seen him the day before. 'Yer cutting it fine, are ye no? This is Boab.' Bobby Jones extended a hand and a warm smile,

'Pleased to meet you, Gary,' Jones said in his buttery Southern twang, 'I kinda feel like I know you already, your dad talks so much about you.'

'And this –' his dad turned as Ben Hogan strolled towards them extending his hand – 'is Ben.'

'Mr Hogan,' Gary said, shaking hands, his throat dry.

'You can call me Ben, son. Now, are you boys ready to play some golf?'

'Mugs away,' Gary's dad said, gesturing to the tee box. Hogan strode onto the tee, ball in hand, and Gary turned and looked down the first fairway at Augusta – its woods and waterways glittering green and silver in the morning sun.

'Now,' Gary's dad whispered, leaning in close to Gary's ear, 'ye huv tae watch Ben. Total bandit. Always trying tae do ye on the handicaps. He's just after trying to tell me and big Boab here he reckons he's aff plus 1 these days. Aye, his erse in parsley. Mair like plus 3.'

Gary nodded and looked at his father. His hair had not yet gone grey, it was the thick black it had been when Gary was a little boy. 'Dad, your hair, it –'

'Shhh.' His father pressed a finger to his lips as Hogan unleashed a ferocious drive, almost splitting the fairway but running too far, catching the thick right-hand side rough.

'Oooh, nae luck,' Gary's dad said. 'Heavy in there.'

Gary could hear music, faint but distant, some words about your heart being black and broken . . . seeming to come from nowhere, from the cloudless sky above them, as Bobby Jones drilled a three-wood up the middle – safe as houses, but he'd left himself a longish approach shot. 'You're up, son,' Gary's dad was saying, and now Gary was walking towards the tee, taking a ball he couldn't remember putting there from his pocket and recognising the music now. 'Can anyone hear the Stone Roses?' he said.

'Son,' Ben Hogan said, 'what the hell is the Stone Roses?'

'I'm sorry, you'll need to turn that down a wee bit.'

It was the elderly nurse with red hair, the one who Stevie liked, who'd asked him if she could bring him a cup of coffee the first night he was here.

'Sorry, Nurse. I was just . . .'

Stevie reached over and twirled his finger around the luminous dial of his milk-white iPod, wheeling the volume down, the track fading down to background level. The little speakers were set up on the bedside tables on either side of Gary's head. Fucking Apple, fucking Steve Jobs, Stevie thought. Self-aggrandising, hippy-face-of-corporate mother-fucker. Still, yer whole CD collection oan yer hip 24/7? Cannae be arguing with that. 'Was that one of his favourite songs?' the nurse was asking.

'Actually, no,' Stevie said, standing and stretching. 'I'm trying to wind him up. Annoy him awake.'

'Christ, friends like you . . .' The nurse laughed as she walked off.

The Stone Roses second LP had been responsible for one of the few serious fallings-out they'd ever had: Gary taking the party line that it was a disappointment on a par with finding out that Miss Kirk, their twenty-three-year-old, blonde third-year English teacher, was a Tory, while Stevie (perversely, always a big fan of raising his hand and saying 'Hang on a minute' when a consensus was forming) decided there was much to enjoy on the record. This track, for instance, 'Ten Storey Love Song', was as good as anything on the first album. 'Baws,' Gary had said. Nearly fifteen years ago now and today, after three or four pints, they could still get into it. One of those arguments that helps to define a friendship, that neither party wants resolved because it was too much fun to keep on having.

Stevie looked around the empty hospital room (Cathy had finally been persuaded to go home and get some sleep) and closed the door. He came back to the bed and looked down at his best friend, his chest rising and falling in the heavy, rhythmic pattern of someone in a deep sleep. There wasn't so much as a flicker beneath the eyelids. Stevie ran a hand down Gary's arm, along the plastic tube feeding him glucose, and swallowed. Not easy this: Stevie believed in no God and was not much given to Cathy-like displays of emotion. The only time he'd cried in the last ten years was when Celtic got beaten 3–2 in extra time in Seville.

'Um . . . listen, Gary, ah, uh, Christ, ah feel like a total fud.' Humour paving the way, leading him towards what he needed to say. 'I know you can't hear me by the way, but, anyway. I . . .' But he was already realising that he was talking to himself, that there were things he needed to hear himself say about his friend. 'I was just thinking, maybe you're right. *Second Coming* . . . it's no all that, is it? Well, maybe 'Tears' and 'Love Spreads' and 'Tightrope', but a lot of it's just Led Zep knock-off, isn't it? And . . . och,' Gary's hand warm in his now, the plastic valve jutting out the big vein feeling horribly alien and intrusive. 'This is –' Stevie tried to laugh, but it was the other thing that was on the way now, his bottom lip curling back into his mouth and his top teeth sinking down into it. 'Just wake up for fuck's sake, pal.'

And here they came, Stevie's tears, making their first appearance since that terrible night in the Estadio Olimpico.

They were parked in a remote spot, a small car park between the dunes at the back of the beach. The wind was up, the first bad weather for a couple of weeks, and the Irish Sea was fairly whipping against itself, a frothing slate-grey mass tipped with white breakers. Gulls struggled to hold their positions, or were thrown hard at dramatic angles across the dark afternoon sky.

'I mean, Jesus Christ, whit's the chances?' Masterson was saying, 'Wan in a million. Tae hit a wee baw nearly, whit, three hunner yards ye said? And huv it hit someone oan the heed? Wan in a million. Stupid bloody game anyway if ye ask me.' Masterson, having no soul, did not care for golf.

Pauline pressed her cheek against the cream leather of the passenger seat of the Mercedes and fixed her gaze on the cigarette lighter set into the walnut facia. She wasn't really listening to him. She was thinking about when she was little and they had had to sell Harriet, her pony, after her dad went bankrupt. *'Bye-bye, Harriet. Bye-bye,'* Pauline had said, crying and looking out the back window as the car pulled off down the long driveway from the stables. 'Ah wis glad ye called, doll,' Masterson went on. 'Ah've been going aff ma fucking nut this past week, so ah have. Ah miss ye like fuck.'

'I miss you too,' Pauline sighed. 'I just wish . . . I know it sounds terrible, with him in the hospital and everything, but I wish we could be together properly.'

'Ah know, hen. Ah want that too. Do ye think ah don't? But . . . if ah divorce Leanne she'll take me tae the cleaners so she will. Ah know her. She's a vindictive bitch so she is. Maybe in a few years when the kids are older, then it wouldnae, y'know, be so bad.'

Pauline nodded, still fixed on the cigarette lighter when suddenly another image came to her, not of a past reality but of a possible future: her and Gary old together in a small council home; him in a wheelchair while she spoon-fed him some sort of gruel. In Pauline's vision she was badly dressed and she had no credit cards.

She burst into tears.

'Aww, come on, hen. It'll be all right.' Masterson embraced her and felt the pulse in his groin. Would it be out of order to . . . ? Naw. Come tae fuck. Play the white man. That would be *totally* out of order.

'I know it's terrible and I'll probably, I don't know, burn in fucking hell or something,' Pauline spoke through her tears, 'but . . . but . . . I just keep wishing that Leanne wasn't, wasn't . . .'

'Wasn't what?'

She pulled her wet face away from his chest and got her breathing under control.

'Around,' Pauline said.

They looked at each other.

Pauline threw herself at him and they started kissing feverishly, his dark, bristly moustache tickling her nose.

This is bad, some part of Masterson was thinking. *Fuck sake. Man lying in the hospital an aw that.* But this voice was very small and feeble and he wasn't really listening to it as Pauline clawed at his belt buckle with trembling fingers.

18

GARY WAS PLAYING LIKE A DREAM. IN HEAVEN HIS SWING WAS smooth and rhythmic and grooved, his irons boring straight and true. His drives booming and accurate. By the time they walked off the ninth green he and his dad were two holes up on Hogan and Jones.

They were taking a quick break on the tenth tee: Hogan and his dad were lighting up, Bobby Jones was buying drinks and snacks from a man in a little cart while Gary stood a little way off from the group, staring into one of the deep, dark pools that dotted Augusta. He turned to see Bobby Jones approaching, holding something out. 'Soda?' Jones said.

'Thanks, Bob.' Gary took the green can. Something called 'Mountain Dew'. It was cold. 'It's something, this course of yours.'

'Why thank you. Yeah, I like it here.'

'Bob,' Gary said hesitantly, fiddling with the ring pull, not looking at Jones, 'are . . . are you God?'

Jones laughed and tilted his head back. 'Oh Lord no. But he's a member. Good player. Helluva temper sometimes. You know when you get thunderstorms down there? He's missing four-footers up here.'

'It can do that to you, can't it?' Gary looked over towards his father, laughing on the tee box with Hogan.

'It can, son. It surely can.'

The two men stood there quietly for a moment, looking down into the pool. Something flashed through the black water, something grey-white and huge. Gary thought he saw an eye. Teeth. He turned to Bobby Jones.

'Did . . . did you just see a shark in there?

Bobby Jones looked at him oddly.

'The *shark* isn't called Jaws, is it?' Stevie said to Lee. They were sitting on plastic chairs at the foot of Gary's hospital bed. Pauline, Cathy and Gary's Aunt Sadie, Cathy's sister, were in the comfier seats by the window. Sadie was wearing a powder-blue velour leisure suit. Cathy sported a similar number in black. 'I mean,' Stevie went on, 'no one in the film says, "Jaws is coming to get us!" do they?'

'Aye, awright, fuck sake!' Lee said.

'The shark doesn't say, "Hi, I'm Jaws by the way." Does it?'

Cheeky fat bastard, Lee thought. If it wisnae for his wee brother lying there in that bed he'd tan his fucking jaw. 'Ye ken whit ah fucking mean but,' Lee said.

'Jaws is the name of the *film*.'

'Jesus, who cares?' Pauline said, reaching for her handbag. 'You're giving me a bloody headache.'

'Aye, shut it, ya fucking sac,' Lee said, grateful for the support.

'Touché,' Stevie said.

'Boys! That's enough!' Cathy said, looking up from her

book – a bulky potboiler called, appropriately, *A Mother's Strength*.

'Aye,' Sadie agreed, 'gie's peace, the pair o' ye!'

Lee and Stevie shut up. They were all getting a little cabin-feverish, cooped up in this room night after night for nearly a week now, drinking endless cups of plastic coffee. Eating boiled sweets and grapes.

Pauline took out a packet of painkillers and began popping a couple from the foil. Sadie eyed the packet suspiciously. 'Pauline hen, how much did ye pay for thon tablets?'

Pauline looked at the pack. 'Umm . . .' Christ, here we go.

'Cause ah'll tell ye,' Sadie said, levelling a sovereign-ringed finger at her, 'see they paracetamol?' She took great care over the word, stringing the full five syllables out on a rack: *par-ah-sea-tah-moll*. 'It's the biggest rip-aff ever. Two pound eighty-nine they're wanting fur a packet o' twelve at the chemist's shop. Ah can get twenty-four o' Toler's own brand fur *ninety-nine pee*!' For Aunt Sadie the opening of the new no-frills, ultra-budget, ultra-basics Toler's hypermarket on the outskirts of town at the beginning of the year had been a moment of epiphany as intense and powerful as anything religion had to offer. Standing in the freezer aisle that glorious morning, hefting a one-kilo pack of minced beef priced at £1.34 in one heavily ringed fist and a box of twelve choc ices for 99p in the other, she had felt the light of God streaming upon her as radiantly as it had shone upon Moses on Sinai. From that day forward she had gone forth into this world to spread the gospel according to Toler's.

'Uh, really?' Pauline would as soon have shopped at Oxfam as Toler's.

'Aye, hen. It's aw packaging an that.'

Cathy went over to the bed and mopped Gary's brow. She

ran a finger along the seam of his fresh bandages. There'd be a small scar just below the hairline.

Someone coughed in the doorway and they all looked up. Auld Bert Thompson was standing there. Billy Douglas was behind him, twisting his bunnet nervously in his hands.

'Hullo, Cathy hen,' Bert said. 'Ah, Billy here wanted to come and –'

'Ah'm so sorry, Mrs Irvine,' Billy began, advancing slowly into the room. 'I didnae . . .' Now Billy saw Gary – the tubes, the monitors, the bandages – and he started to cry. 'Aw God. Whit have ah done?' Cathy was crying too as she embraced him. She had known him vaguely for years. Nice wee buddy. No a bad bone in him.

'Naw, Billy, c'mon. It's no your fault. It was just wan o' those things.'

Billy took a seat in the corner, where he sat quietly, dabbing his eyes and shaking his head while Bert stood in the middle of the room, his hands in his pockets. 'How did the operation go, Cathy?' he asked.

'Aw, the doctors seemed happy enough, Bert,' Cathy said, managing a smile. 'We've just tae wait and see now.'

Gary looked back down into the pool and, as he turned his head, he thought he caught a glimpse of a great tail sweeping away into the depths. Why would they have sharks in the water hazards here? The course was difficult enough. He turned as his dad approached. 'Hi, Dad,' he said. 'Are we ready to finish these guys off?'

'Not today. We'll have to play on as a three ball.'

'How come? Who's leaving?'

'You are, son,' his dad said, placing a hand on his shoulder. 'Time to go.'

'But . . .' Gary looked into his father's eyes, the same blue as his. Suddenly he realised that his lip was trembling. Here he was trying to talk his father into letting him stay out on the golf course with the grown-ups. He felt eight years old again. 'I want to stay here with you.'

'I know. Ah'd like that too. But not yet.' Gary nodded miserably, a child accepting its fate handed down by a higher power. 'It'll be a while before you're a member here.'

His father embraced him – Old Spice, the sandpapery rasp of silvery stubble, Embassy Regal and the Grouse that was famous – and suddenly it was getting colder here under the Georgia sun. More than anything, he did not want to leave this delicious dream.

'Say hello to your mum for me. And try and keep an eye on that brother o' yours . . .'

'When will I see you again?'

'Not for a wee while, pal. But I'll be watching ye.' His dad smiled. 'Now remember,' Jones and Hogan were waving goodbye from the tee box, 'keep your head still and get through that shoulder turn. You listen to whit Bert's telling ye now.'

Bert. The practice session. Six feet, four feet . . .

'Cheery-bye, son.'

Suddenly Gary remembered how he got here. And, in the instant of memory, he was leaving, everything – his father, Jones and Hogan, the magnolia and eucalyptus of Augusta – swirling and dissolving as, with the sensation of rushing upwards, rising very fast from deep black water into warm blue shallows and then exploding through the surface, he was back on the second hole at Ravenscroft with Bert Thompson, the nine-iron coiled around him, holding his finishing position and watching his perfectly struck ball rolling towards the hole, oblivious to the Spaxon coming towards his head at 280 feet per second. His ball rolling closer, closer . . .

Gary shot bolt upright in the hospital bed, pulling a monitor over and sending it crashing onto the floor.

'YA FUCKEN BEAUTY!' he roared in a hoarse, desiccated voice that no one had heard in six days.

Pauline and Sadie screamed.

Cathy fainted.

Lee instinctively reached for his chib.

Billy Douglas clutched at his heart.

Bert jumped two feet off the ground.

Stevie dropped his coffee and came very close to shitting in his pants, but it was he who spoke first.

He looked his friend right in the eye – Gary was sitting upright now, panting, eyes wide open, arms raised above his head in classic scoring-winning-goal-in-Cup-Final fashion – and said, 'Look who's up!'

19

THE OCHILPARK ARMS, SITUATED AT A CROSSROADS ON the Barrhead Road, the old Ardgirvan to Glasgow road, was quiet. Since the motorway had been extended, taking all the passing trade away, it was about the most out of the way pub in the whole county. Masterson, at a table by the window with his *Daily Standard* and his lager top. He looked around the place: a couple of old farmer boys with pints of heavy at the bar with the landlord, a massive red-faced guy in his fifties cleaning glasses, their talk of Glasgow Rangers and the horse racing on the telly above the bar drifting over. He looked down at his glass and realised it was almost half-empty already. He was nervous, drinking too fast. Better slow down.

When had he last seen the big man? Properly sat down with him that is, not just seeing him from a distance down the town, going into the bookies, or emerging from the Bam or the Boabby? Seven or eight years ago was it? At someone's wedding?

There had been a time, the 1970s, when they were teenagers,

living a few houses away from each other on Wilton Terrace, when they saw each other every day. They stole the same cars, they fought the same gangs – exchanging beatings with the Cumbie and the Young Apache – and they broke into the same schools, factories and houses. Then, as friends sometimes do over the years, their tastes started to move in different directions: Masterson, shifting cheap offcuts of carpet bought down south from the back of a van, discovered that he had a talent for selling and that he could make money without the worrying possibility of jail. Similarly, somewhere in his mid-twenties, his friend realised that his real talent lay in violence. Not the random, amateur-hour violence of their teenage years, but in controlled, strategic displays of astonishing force and power.

And, think of the devil, here he was now, the floor shaking and the old boys at the bar turning from the horse racing.

Christ, Masterson thought, he's *bigger.*

'A'right, ya fucking auld prick?' Ranta said cheerfully, the time-honoured greeting of Ayrshire men who have not sat down together in nearly a decade.

'Ranta. Fucking hell, ye look well.'

'Aye, yer maw, ya cunt. Whit ye drinking there?'

'Er, lager top.'

'Top? Away tae fuck. Ah'll gie ye top, ya cunt. The top o' ma boabby up yer fucking night-fighter.'

'Aye, a'right, fuck sake. Make it a lager then.'

'Haud oan a minute.' Ranta checked his watch and walked over to the bar, looking up at the TV where the next race was about to start. 'Ho, auld yin, do us a favour and turn that tae Sky Sports 2 fur a minute.'

'Away tae fu—' the landlord began to say. Then he turned round. He didn't know who Ranta was, but he could tell *what* he was. '. . . we're watching the racing.' The sentence had come in like a storm trooper and gone out like a cripple.

Ranta looked at the man and said simply, 'The gowf's oan.'

'Oh,' the landlord said, taking a sudden deep interest, 'is it?' He thumbed the remote and the screen lit up green: Torsten Lathe, lining up a putt.

'Ye been watching any of this?' Ranta shouted over to Masterson. 'Yer boy Linklater's going well – ah've got a fucken grand oan him tae win it – but this Nazi bam here might just dae it. No a British player anywhere oan the leader board of course, useless pack o' bastards so they ur.'

Like most people who caught the golf bug late in life the results for Ranta had been serious. He'd played a bit as a kid – everybody did around here – but it was only a few years ago, when he went out to play a few holes with one of his boys, that he hit *the* shot, the one that made a bell ring in his chest: a sweetly fading six-iron that came right out of the socket and flew nearly 170 yards before curling up near the pin. Ranta felt as though God had spoken to him.

They watched as Lathe's putt – a snaking fifty-foot monster that would tie him for the lead – dribbled downhill, turning closer and closer to the hole. 'Ooh, hello . . .' the American commentator cooed from the TV.

'Get tae fuck, get tae fuck,' said Ranta, trying to will Lathe's putt out of the hole. The ball crept nearer and nearer, but always looking like it would never get there. The crowd began to moan.

'Has he hit it?' the commentator asked. The ball paused on the edge of the hole for a split second and then dropped into the cup. 'Yes he has!'

'YA FUCKEN BLOND-HAIRED NAZI WEAN-RIDING BASTARD YE!' Ranta screamed, then, turning to

Masterson, completely calm again, he added, 'Sorry, Fin, was it a lager ye wanted?'

They drank and caught up on the last ten years: two lads from the wrong side of the tracks made good. Two successful independent businessmen swapping stories, bitching about manpower issues, supply costs and the like. And their problems were not so different: errant, ungrateful employees, aggressive competitors, shrinking profit margins. However, Masterson's commercial difficulties were rarely resolved by throwing people off bridges, or burning them alive in the boot of a car or – on one occasion – inserting a greased shotgun into a man's rectum and pulling the trigger.

Finally, somewhere into the third pint, Ranta asked the question Masterson had been waiting for: 'And how's the wife? What's her name again?'

'Leanne.'

'Aye, Leanne. That's right. Sorry, pal. Fucking memory oan me sometimes.'

'Well, tae be honest, Ranta, that's no so good.'

'Naw?'

'Naw. We've just, ye know, drifted apart.'

'Och, ah'm sorry tae hear that, Fin,' Ranta said, eyeing his pint, regretting asking now.

'Aye. In fact, ah've been seeing somebody else. Young bird.' He was surprised at how quickly it was all coming out.

'Aye?' Ranta himself had been happily married for over thirty years. But he passed no judgement on Masterson. He only wondered if they were drawing close to whatever they were really here to talk about. People rarely called up someone like Ranta out of the blue just to swap stories about old times. And it couldn't be for a loan – one of Ranta's other key business activities – because Findlay was minted.

'Aye. Ah want a divorce but Leanne would take me tae the fucken cleaners so she wid.'

'Fuck. Bad wan.'

'Aye, fucking bad wan is right. So ah've been thinking . . .' He looked at the carpet. 'Ah know this sounds bad, but . . .'

'Whit?' Ranta said, setting his pint down.

Masterson came right out and said it.

Ranta took a long swallow of lager and looked around.

'Fucking hell, Fin,' he said finally.

20

'AYE, BUT WAS THAT NO THAT SAME WEE MAN THAT used tae work fur Donaldson the electrician's? Mind?'

'Naw, you're thinking o' Robert *Fraser*, he was engaged tae that wee lassie fae Saltcoats. Nice wee lassie that was kilt in thon explosion at Ardeer. Ah'm meaning Robert Ferguson. Anyway, oor Hugh sees him outside the wee Paki shop at Calder Road, eleven o'clock oan, wis it Tuesday, Danny?'

'Aye.'

'Tuesday morning and he's drunk oot his mind so he is. In buying the carry-oot. By Christ, oor Hugh thought, wid ye look at the state o' that. I –' Aunt Sadie suddenly broke off, distracted by a glittering bauble on Pauline's dresser. 'Sorry, hen, dae ye know where your Pauline got thon wee jewellery box?'

'Och, somewhere in Glasgow ah think, Sadie.'

In the bed Gary drifted up from sleep. He recognised the three voices – his mum, Aunt Sadie and Uncle Danny.

'It's lovely so it is,' Sadie said. 'Ah could do wi wan o' them fur oor Margaret's birthday. Anyway, whit wis I saying?'

'Aboot Robert Ferguson?'

'Naw, before that.'

'Oh, thae beans?'

Gary lay there listening with his eyes closed. Voices he'd been hearing all his life, as comforting, as meaningless, as the gentle burble of a mountain stream.

'So then ah says tae her,' Sadie continued, 'but hen, Toler's ain brand are the same thing, jist cheaper. But ye ken her, Cathy, she'd argue wi ye till yer blue in the face. Mind you, her mother was the same. She disnae take it aff a stane dyke. Anyway, ah makes them and diz oor wee Sam no eat the lot and say "That wiz lovely, Nana!"? Ah!' She cackled delightedly, 'It wiz aw ah could dae no tae say tae her "Ah bloody telt ye, madam", away spending money at Saintsbury's thinking yer the bee's knees. Don't get me wrang now, Cathy.' Here Sadie laid a dramatic hand on her sister's arm, as though Cathy had been about to get Sadie very, very wrong. 'There's some things ah don't mind spending the money oan. The likes o' yer, oh whits that ice cream ah like, Danny? That H . . . Hogan-Daaz?'

'Aye,' Danny said.

'Aw God, that's tae die fur so it is. See, ah'll pay the money for the likes o' that but for yer basics? Naw. She's trying tae tell me that a wean kin tell the difference between two cans o' beans? Aye, pull the other wan, it's got bells on it. The wean jist sat doon quite the thing and ate the lot o' it. Did he no, Danny?'

'Aye.'

Uncle Danny had been hearing this story, or ones very like it, for over forty years now. His AutoAye facility was superhuman, as sharpened and attuned as the senses of a tiger in the dark, wet heart of the jungle. Just by faintly monitoring

Sadie's conversations (or rather, monologues) he could sense when a response was required from him, the depth of sincerity, curiosity or surprise his 'Aye' would have to convey ('Aye' or 'Aye?' or 'Aye!'), and – most crucially – whether the situation was so severe he would actually have to look up from the paper or away from the TV set.

'Mind you, wee Sam'll eat anything. Like his faither. Oor Hugh?' Sadie looked off dreamily into the mid-distance, her eyes misting and her chest swelling with motherly pride for her staunchly stomached elder son. '. . . Oor Hugh would eat shite.'

Gary yawned and stretched in the bed.

'Oh, Gary son, huv we wakened ye up?' Aunt Sadie said.

'No, it's OK, Sadie.'

'You've been sleeping a while, son,' his mum said, coming over to him. 'How are ye feeling?'

'No bad.'

'Ye were making some noise in yer sleep. Whit were ye dreaming about?'

'Putting, I think. Baws,' Gary said.

'You an yer bloody golf,' Cathy said, smiling.

'Aye, just like his faither,' Uncle Danny said.

'Are ye hungry? It's near teatime. We were just going tae have a cawfee and a wee craw sant . . .'

'I'm starving. I quite fancy a Chinese. I think there's a – fuck – menu by the phone in the kitchen, Mum. Fucking slut.'

Cathy flinched, but did not respond to the insult. 'Aye, the doctor said your appetite would be coming back. What would ye like, son?'

'Ah, chop suey? Maybe some spare ribs? Hoor. Sorry!'

'Chop suey and spare ribs. No bother. We'll away doonstairs.

You shout if ye need anything, son. Pauline's away oot working. She said she'd be back tonight.'

'Aye, thanks, Mum. Tits. Fuck. Sorry, sorry, Mum.'

'That's OK, son. Ye cannae help it.'

Cathy, Sadie and Danny went downstairs, to their coffee and croissants. Gary listened to Ben's barking sharpen as they neared the kitchen, exploding into full pitch as they entered it. He lay back and regarded the bedroom ceiling.

It had taken them a few days to notice how bad the swearing was. Tourette's syndrome, Dr Robertson said. A side effect of the neurological damage he'd suffered. 'Post-traumatic. It's quite rare, but not unheard of.' It manifested itself in several ways. Sometimes Gary seemed to use random single-word swearing as punctuation in sentences – 'So if I have to – fuck – stay in bed for the next . . .' Other times whole phrases would be rapidly jammed in there, almost as stand-alone asides. 'Could you pass me the – cuntyafuckinghoorye – water please?' Sometimes the swearing had sexual overtones: a large-breasted nurse they had passed in the hospital corridor on the way down to the coffee shop one morning had been greeted with 'Ooh, jugs, ya spunky boot! Big tits fuck.' Occasionally it had been chillingly specific: two maintenance men – one Indian and one very overweight – had arrived in his hospital room one morning to fix a radiator to be greeted with 'Fuck. Fucking Paki fat bastard ya fat cunt and Paki ye.' Stevie had taken the astonished janitors outside. Sometimes the swearing was also accompanied by animalistic grunts, barks and yelps.

Robertson explained to Cathy and Pauline that all of it was involuntary, a spasmic reaction not dissimilar to hiccups, and that often he would be completely unaware that he was doing it; although they noticed that sometimes Gary would insert a hurried apology into the outrage, or would swear consciously, through frustration at the condition. A sentence like this might go something like 'Hi, Mum, I was just – OW! Ya nuddy boot, fuck – Sorry! – fucking cow, sook ma – FUCK! – sook ma dook. SHIT! SORRY! Grrrr!'

Upsetting though Cathy found all this, she took it as a small price to pay for having her son delivered back to her from the dead. Whenever a string of obscenities flurried from Gary's mouth she simply chose to hear hiccups.

Pauline was less stoic. 'How long will he be like this?' she'd asked immediately.

'It's hard to say,' Robertson said. 'Hopefully, it'll gradually fade as the brain recovers from the trauma.'

Jesus, Pauline thought. *Jesus fucking wept*. Another sick hand life had dealt her.

Stevie thought it a strangely appropriate affliction for a golfer to suffer from. Stand on any busy golf course when the wind was blowing in the right direction and you would be forgiven for thinking that half the population suffered from Tourette's syndrome.

They'd kept him in for observation for a week before sending him home: two weeks minimum of absolute bed rest.

Gary took a grape and rolled it around his mouth, testing its thin skin with his teeth, making his mouth water, while he listened to the house noises around and below him: a door creaking, water rushing in copper pipes, a faint ping from a radiator, his mum and Sadie talking in the kitchen, the scrape and scuttle of Ben's talons on the wooden floors as the monster lurched from room to room, his perma-growling routinely breaking into a series of sharp barks. (Gary sometimes pictured the dog doing this when he and Pauline were both out: Ben eyeballing a door, or staring out a cushion – literally trying to pick a fight in an empty house.)

The enormity of his boredom struck him when he realised he was counting the number of DVDs they had in the rack next to the TV. (Sixty-eight, but did you just count box sets as one?)

Another week of this?

He crossed the bedroom and looked at himself in the full-length mirror inside Pauline's wardrobe. He lifted the corner of the turban of bandages a little and gingerly pressed the tip of his pinkie into the indent on his right temple: a concave hollow about the diameter of a ten-pence piece, with tiny dimples. The exact impression of Billy Douglas's golf ball. The bruising was still a vivid purple at the centre, fading into a deep green, into a funky yellow as it reached the hairline.

Gary had a little notebook next to the bed in which Dr Robertson had asked him to record the occurrence, frequency and severity of a number of symptoms, from headaches, to butterflies in his stomach, to experiences of déjà vu, to unusually intense perceptions of smells. There had been the odd headache, but none of the others. Oh, there was one thing, but Robertson hadn't mentioned it and Gary was in no rush to share it with anyone so it hadn't made it into the notebook yet.

The erections.

There was the run-of-the-mill Morning Glory that greeted him warmly every single day. There was the sudden and vicious Afternoon Delight that appeared out of nowhere, the Ferrari of erections, taking his penis from plasticine to the kind of metal they use in space in 3.2 seconds. There was the more gradual Slow Burner, a mild pulse in his groin, followed by a lazy, yawning semi, followed by a kind of three-quarter erect twanginess that could last for several hours.

Then there was the Fury, an agonising madman of a

hard-on that arrived during sleep and had the power to drag him from the bed and send him groaning and stumbling to the cold-water tap. It felt like mad cock-scientists had grafted a concrete tube with a titanium core onto his crotch while he slept. There had even been a couple of terrifying occasions where the Fury had lasted *all* night, finally colliding with the arrival of Morning Glory somewhere around dawn, the two joining forces in a hands-across-the-ocean deal to create the perfect storm of erections, an unassailable super-hard-on. Unwankable. The kind of boner that would take a wanking and just keep smiling right at you. Most erections, Gary reasoned, saw the jettisoning of semen as the end result. Not the Fury. Even *after* you had ejaculated, it just stayed there, trying to suck your testicles up into your stomach.

But maybe, he thought, this was all just a side effect of being in bed all the time, yawning and scratching, his hands forever absent-mindedly scampering down the front of his pyjamas. Nothing to trouble the doctors about.

God, he was bored.

In the corner of the bedroom, leaning up against the wardrobe, was one of his old putters. He got out of bed and crossed the room. On the floor of the wardrobe he found his putting practice machine – a plastic horseshoe with a green faux-felt cup that fired the ball back to you – and a few stray golf balls. He set the putting machine on the beige carpet at one end of the bedroom and walked to the other. One, two, three, four, five paces. Five yards. Fifteen feet. He lined up the first ball. Open stance, wrists forward, and commentator Rowland Daventry's voice in his head – *Here he is now, a tricky fifteen-footer to clinch the Open. Downhill. Gentle touch needed here.* Gary made a smooth pendulum stroke and the ball trickled across the carpet and rolled neatly into the cup. Click.

Rrrrrrp. Ting: the machine spat the ball straight back to him.

He set up again. *Final of the World Match Play Championship. He needs this to stay in the game. This is a must make* . . . Click. Rrrrrrp. Ting.

A chance here to secure the Ryder Cup for Europe . . .

Click. Rrrrrrp. Ting.

This for birdie –

Click. Rrrrrrp. Ting.

A long eagle putt –

Click. Rrrrrrp. Ting.

Can he possibly –

Click. Rrrrrrp. Ting.

Gary made fourteen putts in a row. He was oblivious to the doorbell, to the bedroom door opening, until he looked up and saw Stevie was standing there. 'Aye aye,' Stevie said. 'Shouldn't you be in bed?'

'I'm making putts. This is for fifteen on the bounce.'

'Fiver ye miss it.'

Click. Rrrrrrp. Ting.

'Impressive,' Stevie said, 'most impressive. But –' Stevie paused.

Gary looked at him. 'But what?'

'But you?'

'Eh?'

'But you are not a Jedi yet! Fucking hell, what's wrong with you?' Stevie said, handing the fiver over.

'What films did you bring?'

Stevie produced a pair of DVDs from his carrier bag. 'We have two Michaels – the new Haneke or the director's cut of *Heat*. What do we think?' He held one up in each hand. 'Challenging new cinema or mindless old school?'

Gary tapped the copy of *Heat*. Stevie sighed.

'You, my friend, have no interest in broadening your horizons.'

'Aww, come on – baws – ow! – I'm ill!' Gary said pleadingly, jumping back into bed.

'Aye, ma erse, ya malingering bam.'

The doorbell rang.

'Oh, here.' Gary handed Stevie back his fiver. 'Give this tae ma mum. Fuck. I ordered a Chinese. Grab a plate and ah'll cut ye in. Fud. Fat fud. Fuck!'

'Right, er . . .' Stevie tossed Gary the DVD. 'Set that mother up.'

Stevie started down the stairs in time to see Cathy round the corner below him and open the front door. A smiling Chinese lad of about nineteen stood on the doorstep holding up a blue plastic carrier bag. *'Gary!'* Cathy called out in her cheery sing-song voice. *'That's yer Chinky!'*

Stevie watched as she sang it – literally sang the word 'Chinky' – right into the guy's face. He and Stevie looked at each other; a look that said 'I'm so sorry' on Stevie's part and 'I know' on the delivery boy's.

'Thanks, son, keep the change,' Cathy said, smiling, as she handed over the money and closed the door.

Stevie numbly held out the fiver as he took the bag from Cathy. 'That's OK, son. I'll get it,' she said. 'You keep yer money.' Stevie stood there, warm carrier in hand, and watched Cathy bustle off towards the kitchen with something approaching awe.

21

RANTA WAS IN THE LOFT, PLAYING SCALEXTRIC WITH Andy and Tommy, the two youngest of his six children. Andy, seven, had just sent his little silver Lotus Elan flying off the end of the track for the umpteenth time.

'Naw, son, look, ye need tae slow doon fur the bends,' Ranta patiently explained again.

'He's a mutant, Da!' Tommy, nine, said.

'Naw – you're a mutant!' Andy shot back.

'Hey,' Ranta said, 'nobody's a bloody mutant! Here, son,' Ranta folded his massive fist gently around Andy's tiny hand and demonstrated how to ease the pressure off on the trigger of the pistol grip, slowing the car down into the bend.

Lately, with Alec increasingly helping run the business – not too much, the boy still had a lot to learn, but you had to let them make some decisions on their own, give them their head – Ranta was getting a wee taste of retirement. Ranta liked the look of retirement very much indeed: sleeping late, a wee bit of golf here and there, playing with his children and grandchildren every day . . . Alison often joked that the reason he liked spending so much time with the kids was because he was just a big wean himself. Whatever the reason, Ranta was a good father and a solid provider. Alison had long ago learned not to ask in too much detail about the finer points of the providing.

Wee Andy, his face a perfect study in concentration, slowed the car down now to a ludicrous degree, barely crawling around the bend, but keeping it on the track.

'Ah did it, Da!'

'That's the stuff!' Ranta furiously ruffled Andy's hair, the boy squealing with delight.

'Pile on!' Tommy shouted as he leapt on his father, the three of them rolling around on the floor in a frenzy of ticklish play-fighting.

'Hey! Will you three stop that carry-on!' Alison's head appeared through the hatch at the far end of the loft. She was far from angry; pleased as always at the delight her husband took in their children. 'Andy, Tommy, come and get your dinner.'

'Go on with yer mum, boys,' Ranta said, sending Tommy on his way with a playful smack on the arse.

'And that's number-one son here,' Alison said.

'Aye, good, tell him tae come up, hen.'

Father and son sat in the den, the TV on, showing the golf – the Schitzbaul Invitational Trophy, live from Benders Creek Golf Club, North Carolina – with the sound down as they talked business.

'Do ye want Frank tae dae it?' Alec was asking.

Ranta thought. A woman. Not a difficult job. 'Naw. Don't use one of the boys. Farm it oot tae someone. But make sure they're reliable, Alec. Someone wi a track record in doing the business, and who understands whit would fucking happen tae them if something went wrong and they chose tae mention us by name. Five should be plenty, eh?'

'Fuck, aye, Da. Half the bams in this toon would do themselves fur five grand.'

Ranta opened his desk drawer and took out the Manila envelope Masterson had given him the night before: fifteen thousand pounds in new, waxy fifty-pound notes. Ten grand profit for a couple of phone calls. No bad. Quickly, professionally, with a licked thumb, Ranta counted out a hundred of them and handed them to Alec.

'Cheers, Da.' Alec stuffed the notes into his inside pocket. 'Hey,' he said, nodding towards the TV, a shot of Drew Keel, biting his lip as he watched a drive sail into the sky, dangerously close to the tree line. 'Did ye see thon shot yer man there hit at that par five yesterday?

'Did ah fucken see it? Ah near shat maself watching it. Two-hundred-and-ten-yard carry over water wi a six-iron? No real.' Ranta slurped his tea and, without taking his eyes off the screen, said, 'Have ye someone in mind then?'

Alec nodded. He did indeed have someone in mind.

Two birds one stone.

Gary propped himself up in bed, a plateful of toast in front of him, a mug of tea in his hand, the curtains drawn against the sunshine and the golf on TV. Ben lay on the floor, his snout moving carefully from left to right and back again as he monitored the progress of each piece of toast from plate to mouth, strands of saliva hanging from his jaws. He looked like he was watching a very delicious tennis match – two stuffed, basted turkeys playing each other in ultra-slow motion.

Gary tossed the fiend a crust – snuffled up in a nanosecond – and turned up the volume.

Benders Creek was one of the toughest courses on the US circuit, with miles of jungly rough and greens cut tight against deep water. The Schitzbaul Trophy ('the Shit' the players called it) had one of the richest purses in golf: over a million dollars for the winner. The guy who came in *last* would get something like fifty grand. Consequently the tournament always attracted a star-studded line-up: Keel, Spafford, Honeydew III, Novotell, Lathe, Von Strapple and, of course, Linklater himself, were all playing, and Gary – golf-starved to the point of insanity – had wanted to catch every second.

But, Christ, lying in bed as the camera panned down a fairway – a gorgeous dogleg, velvety green grass, the sand in the bunkers smooth and golden, almost inviting – it was like watching golf pornography. Torture.

He got up and walked over to the window. It was a beautiful early-May morning. Not a cloud in the sky. When had he last gone nearly a month without swinging a golf club? He looked at the clock. Pauline gone all day, hours until his mum would look in . . .

Complete bed rest for at least a fortnight.

Well, it had *nearly* been a fortnight. He felt fine for fuck's sake. Just the driving range for an hour or so, hit a few wedges and whatnot – nothing too strenuous. Just get into the groove of swinging the club again.

Who's to know?

22

GARY HAD THE DRIVING RANGE TO HIMSELF.

He propped his golf bag up on its metal legs and ran a hand over the clubheads. What to hit? He knew he shouldn't really be doing this at all, so probably best not to overdo it. No trying to smash the driver, nothing more than, say, an easy nine. Nine-iron – the last club he had swung before the accident.

He pressed the button on the plastic panel set into the wooden wall of his bay and, with a faint hum of machinery, the white ball rose up on its rubber tee peg. After a couple of practice swings, his body feeling stiff and rusty, he sighted down the range and picked out a target: the old rusted-out Land Rover just short of the 150-yard marker.

He settled the clubhead behind the ball. Something felt different as he began his backswing, the club coming back smoothly, his left arm straight, his left shoulder pointing straight down at the ball. There was the slightest lag, a barely perceptible pause at the top of the swing, as his weight began to transfer from his right side to his left, and then the clubhead was whipping down, faster than he had ever swung it before, faster than he could ever have controlled before.

The clubhead whipped through the ball in a perfect transfer of energy and Gary was turning, his upper body coming round so that he was standing square to the target. He couldn't see the ball for a second. He had to look up. And then up again. He had never hit a golf ball that high in his life. The ball was pausing now, over a hundred feet in the air, and beginning its descent, falling right for the tractor. Gary watched as it fell to earth – maybe ten yards *beyond* the Land Rover but right on line with its rusted metal roof, whumping into the turf and hopping forward a couple of yards before coming to rest. Gary looked at the number engraved on the sole of the club: '9'. He thought for a second he might have pulled out the six, but no. He slipped it back into the bag and pulled out the pitching wedge, a club he should hit ten to fifteen yards shorter than the nine. Another smooth swing and again the ball flying straight and high. He watched, holding his finishing position, posing, as the ball came falling down.

'P-TANG!' – the hollow sound of the ball clanging off rusted metal reverberated around the empty range as Gary's wedge found its target: the roof of the Land Rover, a piece of metal not much more than five foot square.

He did it again.

And again. And again.

After he'd hit the thing six times he sat down heavily.

What was going on here? Maybe just the break, the time away from the game. Sometimes you played really well when you hadn't hit the ball for a while. You swung the club freely and unselfconsciously and you had no expectations and the tensions they created. That was probably it.

Aye, yer maw, a voice said to him.

Also, he reasoned, he was hitting with the wedge, one of the easier clubs in the bag. How would he get on with a club he was on less than speaking terms with? A club he routinely thinned, skulled and shanked? A club he had pulled from his bag maybe three times in the last year?

A club like the two-iron, say?

He pulled the two out of the bag, took his stance and sighted towards the 200-yard marker: 200 yards, about his best ever distance with the two-iron, and that on only a handful of occasions. He didn't hold back, really bringing the club down hard.

For a split second he thought he might have completely misswung and missed the ball altogether, for there had been no resistance, barely any sensation of the club hitting anything at all. Then he saw his ball dotted against the horizon and travelling in an absolutely straight line, sailing towards the battered metal sign saying '200 yards'.

He kept watching the 200-yard sign.

He was still watching it when he heard a 'KA-LANG' and, looking further down the range, saw his ball rattling off another sign.

The 250-yard sign.

These markers are wrong, was his first thought. Because this was ridiculous. He couldn't *carry* a bloody two-iron 250 yards. No human being could.

Only a professional golfer could do that.

Hit a few more, he thought. *You'll start fucking them up and with that will come the reassurance that everything is still the same.*

He creamed a dozen two-irons down the middle, catching one or two a bit thin, one off the toe of the club, but all of them landing soft and true in the patch of ground between the 200- and the 250-yard markers, four of them clanging right off the 250-yard sign itself, leaving deep dents in the metal.

It was with a dry throat and a slightly trembling hand that Gary pulled the driver from the bag.

The heavy artillery. The lumber. The Big Dog.

In something like a trance now – pumped up and confident and swinging free and hard – he pulled the club so far back on his backswing that its fat head actually touched his left buttock. He unloaded and the sound as metal ate ball was deafening. It seemed to take three minutes for the shot to begin falling to earth, to come whistling down and embed itself in one of the holes in the wire mesh at the very end of the range – about 270 yards away.

The second drive didn't touch the fence – it sailed straight *over* it, coming to rest among the blooming rows of potatoes in the farmer's field behind the range, a good 310 yards away from where Gary stood.

He sat down again. His hands were shaking. This was crazy. He'd never hit the ball this well in his life. Maybe a few dozen times in over twenty years. Not a few dozen in twenty minutes. Just a fluke, he told himself. Probably never hit it like this on the actual golf course.

No, something has happened to you, the other voice said.

Well, only one way to find out.

The Monthly Medal this Saturday . . .

23

LEE IRVINE WALKED INTO THE TINY KITCHEN. AMAZON was sat on the floor – patiently pulling arms and heads off of a pile of dolls and throwing the severed limbs all over the place. Styx hurtled screaming through the room en route to the 'garden' (twelve square feet of concrete, Lee had paved it over as soon as they moved in. Grass was just too much bother) closely followed by Delta, the latter screaming, *'Ah'm gauny kill ye, ya wee prick!'* Lisa, smouldering Club in one hand and tea mug in the other, was watching something slowly revolving in the microwave that didn't quite work properly – you had to give it a bang every now and then to keep the turntable rotating – while listlessly repeating her tired, half-hearted mantra: *'Stop that, you two, don't dae that, Amazon, gie's peace . . .'* Biscuit wrappers, crisp packets and empty three-litre plastic bottles of supermarket own-brand super-strength cola were strewn all over the floor, their sugary contents now barrelling through the veins of the children.

Normally Lee might have gone mental. But tonight he was

in a fine mood. Expansive even, with three double vodkas in his veins, cocaine still humming in his nose and close to one and a half thousand pounds in his jacket pocket.

'A'right?' Lisa said to him.

'Fine, hen.'

The microwave pinged cheerfully. Lisa popped the door open and the kitchen was flooded with the smell of melting plastic. 'Ah was just getting oor tea ready,' Lisa said, shoving a pile of dirty washing along the counter to make room for the bubbling platter of nuked chicken-and-pineapple frozen pizza. 'And, Styx, you need tae eat yer pizza, ye hear me?' Turning from son to husband she added, 'Ah don't know whit's wrong wi' that boy. He willnae eat a thing. He's even aff his crisps and ginger –'

'Fuck that. Ye can gie that shite tae the dug,' Lee said, nodding at the pizza. 'We're all going oot fur dinner. Tae the China Garden.'

'Really, Da?' Delta said.

'Aye.'

'Whit . . . sit in?' Lisa said uncertainly. The China Garden was the good Chinky, the dear one up the top of the high street.

'Aye. Only the best fur the best.'

'Magic!' the children chorused.

'Here . . .' Lee said, handing his wife the carrier bag he was holding. She looked inside: a bottle of Smirnoff – a whole bottle – and a bottle of Coke. 'You make us a couple of wee voddy and Cokes. Ah'm away fur a shower.' He kissed her on the cheek, Lisa looking at him in awe and wonder.

'Da,' little Amazon was saying, 'can we get starters? Can we get spring rolls?'

'You can get anything ye want, doll,' Lee said, ruffling his daughter's hair. He headed upstairs, the sound of familial celebration – excited children's chatter, glasses clattering from the cupboard – sounding good in his ears.

Lee could still not quite believe the change in his fortunes the day had wrought. When Alec Campbell's car had pulled up beside him this afternoon he'd thought he might be limping in the door tonight in a very different state.

He turned the shower on – it took ages to get warm. Maybe he'd buy a new one – and then crossed the landing to the bedroom, pulling his T-shirt over his head.

It's a woman, Alec had said. *Is that a problem?*

'No if the price is right, Alec,' Lee had said suavely, sipping his second double (Alec was buying) in the shadows of the Boot. And, by Christ, was the price right. Five grand? Obviously Alec was taking the two and a bit Lee owed him for the speed plus interest out of this. It still left nearly three thousand quid. 'Half now,' Alec said, slipping an envelope under the table, 'and half when we're done.'

Taking his jeans off Lee remembered the wrap in his back pocket. *You finish it. Call it a wee signing-on bonus.* Nearly a gram in there. Good gear too. With an ear cocked to the kitchen, Lee quickly racked out another wee line on the dressing table. Put one out for Lisa? Naw, put her aff her dinner. He'd surprise her later, after the kids were in bed. It'd been a while. He honked the line up and licked the bitter residue off the edge of his Silver Screen Video card. The coke and the booze were proving excellent help in preventing him thinking too far ahead, which was good news because when he did think ahead he kept coming up against a pretty big problem: contrary to what Alec Campbell believed, Lee had never killed anyone in his life.

Tits McGee? It happened like this . . .

Lee had met Tits to buy an ounce of speed which Lee was going to cut with some novocaine he'd got from Archie Boyd, who had got it from some boys that broke into the chemist's on Calder Road. Lee was then going to sell the speed/ novocaine mixture as cocaine down at the Southport Weekender, offloading it at about three in the morning when every cunt was too cunted to tell the cunting difference. Deal done, Tits had been driving Lee to the bus stop when he got a call on his mobile and said he had to make a quick diversion, some boys from Glasgow he had a bit of business with. They pulled into a lay-by up near the Annick woods and Tits walked off to a car parked nearby. Lee had watched Tits stick his head in the window and start talking to someone. Then a white flash in the night, a bang, and Tits falling backwards with half his face missing. Lee had felt the quick hot spurt in the trough of his pants and then, before he knew what he was doing, he was out the car, jumping the fence behind the lay-by and running headlong through the pitch-black woods, the dreadful sensation of cooling, viscous diarrhoea spilling down the back of his legs.

Lee had lain low for a few weeks, terrified that whoever had killed Tits would realise they had left a witness to the crime. In the meantime, the point-blank 'gangland'-style execution became a big story: a brief report on the evening news, the *Daily Standard* running a faintly celebratory piece along the lines of 'one less drug dealer in Scotland'. Wee Audrey Harrison had seen Lee and Tits driving through Kilwinning a few hours before the shooting and gradually the Chinese whispers escalated – Lee and Tits had gone off to do a deal, they'd got into an argument and Lee had shot Tits in the head at close range. Lee was pulled in for questioning but they had nothing really.

Suddenly he found he was afforded respectable elbow room at the bar in the Bam. Sly nods and hushed whispers in his direction. As the police seemed to have little interest in bringing the killer of Tits McGee (drug dealer and rumoured beaster of girls a little under the legal age of consent) to justice, Lee decided it would do his rep no harm at all to let the story grow. The truth – that he had soiled his pants and ran off through the woods – would have been far less flattering.

Are ye carrying anything these days? Alec had asked him.

Naw, Alec. Ah'm no daft, Lee said, shaking his head.

OK, Alec said. *We'll get ye a piece.*

Lee Irvine had done some bad things. He'd sold drugs to teenagers – bad drugs, drugs cut with laxative and baby powder and brick dust and grit. He'd broken into homes and taken people's property, creeping through dark gardens with video recorders and jewellery boxes under his arms. He'd stolen cars and been involved in low-level fraud, money laundering and passport theft. Yes, some bad things. But, kill a woman? Some poor woman he didn't even know?

When Lee pictured his father in heaven he thought of him as reclining on a big, fluffy king-size cloud watching television and reading the paper. He thought of him now, watching his eldest son taking an envelope stuffed with fifty-pound notes out of his jacket, peeling off four of them and hiding the envelope deep in his sock drawer. Then he thought of his father – someone who had worked hard all his life in return for very little – realising where the money had come from. What it was for. Lee had never seen his father cry and was unable to picture it now. Instead, he saw his father glowering and angry, the way he had seen him many times in the last years, after Lee's life had begun to go off-track: the wrong friends, the first arrests. The image helped: it was easier to defy the angry than it was to defy the sad, the heartbroken. Something else was helping too – Lee snorted, pulling a thick string of numbing cocaine down his throat, and the vision of his father popped and evaporated, like bursting a plump, soapy bubble when you were a kid, that faint sting on your face as it sparkled away into nothingness.

In his boxers now, tingling from the cocaine, he roamed the upstairs of his house. Well, it was the council's house. And it wasn't much of a roam: bathroom and three tiny bedrooms. Delta's school trousers were hanging over the back of a chair – the knees long worn through and stitched up. One of Styx's trainers, the sole flapping away from the bottom, gaping at him like a fish's mouth. Amazon's broken pink bicycle in the hall downstairs. The DVD player that no longer worked. The last two loan payments they'd missed. The holidays they never took. Aye, things were fraying at the edges of his little kingdom and no mistaking. Still borrowing money off his mum and his wee brother all the time? At his age? Jesus fuck, it was bad news.

So, kill a woman? Some poor woman he didn't even know?

Absolutely.

24

'NEXT MATCH . . . PRENTICE, ALEXANDER, IRVINE AND Mason,' the starter's voice trebly and sibilant through the ancient tannoy, drifting over the heads of the usual Saturday-morning crowd, thirty-odd members milling around the first tee. Bert stood double-fisting bacon roll and coffee in a square of sunshine by the door to the locker room.

As Gary took to the tee there was the usual murmur through the waiting players, the usual bets being laid off: *a pound he slices it out of bounds, a pound he shanks it, a pound he misses the ball altogether.* As he pushed the wooden two-and-three-quarter-inch tee peg into the turf Gary was aware of a strange sensation. Or rather, an absence of sensation. Because the emotions which usually trilled through his body when he teed off in the Monthly Medal – quivering nausea, fear, light sweating, the chest-crushing panic which had almost induced semi-blindness on a few occasions – were all gone. His head – usually a blare of noise, of layered voices, of half a dozen caffeine-jacked coaches all screaming contradictory advice (*Keep your head still! Turn your shoulders! Let the left heel rise! Just hit the fucking thing!*) – was as still and quiet as a winter field at dawn.

He stepped back and stood behind the ball. In the distance, 350 yards away, the yellow flag was flapping gently to the left. So, slight breeze coming off the right. He could just make out a copper-coloured patch of grass fifty-odd yards in front of the green.

Roll it over that.

In his head he saw the trajectory of the shot: a very slight draw, the ball just curling left, bouncing in front of the discoloured patch and rolling left. He addressed the ball and had one final coherent thought before he began his backswing: *I'm going to melt this.*

Rab Forest was whispering to Wullie Ellis, a ferret-faced seven-handicapper, 'Bet ye a pound he –' when Gary connected with the ball, the KEEERACK! so loud that Bert spilled his coffee.

'Fuck me,' said Wullie Ellis.

'Jesus wept,' said Forest.

'Where did it go?' someone else said.

'Intae bloody orbit,' Bert said.

Gary's ball landed just to the right of the patch of grass he'd been aiming at, bounced twice and rolled, curling left and finishing up against the fringe of grass ringing the green. Three hundred and ten yards if it was an inch.

The stunned silence lasted three or four seconds.

It was Bert who started the clapping.

Ravenscroft is a very decent municipal golf course. But a municipal course nonetheless, designed with the average mid-handicapper in mind. The golf courses that normal human beings play on are gentle affairs of motorway-wide fairways, light rough and small, slow greens. They bear about as much resemblance to the fearsome layouts played on the professional circuit as the drunken pub brawler bears to the heavyweight champion of the world. For golfers at the very top of their game a course like Ravenscroft is, in all honesty, a glorified pitch-and-putt.

It was in exactly this manner – driver, wedge, putter – that Gary birdied the first three holes straight, just missing an eagle at the second when his fifty-yard sand wedge lipped out, drawing a gasp from his tiny gallery – his playing partners, plus Bert and another pair of old boys from the club who'd watched him tee off and decided to tag along for a few holes.

He'd had to stretch himself a little at the longer third hole – a 420-yard par four – when he pushed his drive out to the right and had to hit a full-blooded eight-iron into the green. By the time the match reached the fourth tee he'd loosened up properly. The fourth: a short par three; 148 yards to the middle of the green, hitting over a water-filled ditch that ran across the front, a ditch that, in his previous life, Gary had skulled and thinned many a seven-iron into. Pin at the front today, just over the left-hand side bunker.

Gary reached into his bag and pulled out the sand wedge.

'Aye, yer maw,' Prentice muttered as Gary teed up.

Gary smiled, miles away, his head dancing with the beautiful maths and physics of the game: about 130 to the cup, the shoulder of the front bunker feeding down towards the flagstick. Land the ball on top of that and it should roll nicely down to the hole. Underhit it and you'd be in the bunker, or – worse – plopping into the ditch. These were negative thoughts that the old Gary would have been all too ready to entertain. Entertain? He'd have laid on a buffet and performed a one-man show for them. Not any more.

Need some height on this. Stop it dead.

WHUMP! – a clod of turf the size of a child's shoe flying forward through the air, the ball rocketing up in a great inverted U shape, seven heads following it into the air.

'Cuntfuckbaws,' Gary said, tongue between his teeth now, holding his finishing position, his eyes flipping between the descending ball and the shoulder of the bunker. (*Shoulder, lip, hole*: the human body referenced all over the golf course.)

The ball landed just two inches over the edge of the bunker and seemed to stop dead. Then it started to roll. Rolling downhill and to the right, very slowly at first, but gathering momentum, trundling through the fine powdery sand that had been blasted out of the bunker by previous matches, trundling down towards the hole.

'Tae fuck, that's close,' Prentice said, awed.

'Go on!' Bert urged.

The ball caught the right-hand edge of the hole, circled 180 degrees around, and plopped into the cup on the left-hand side.

They heard the cheer back at the clubhouse.

'SMOKE MA FUCKEN DOBBER!' Gary was yelling, dropping to his knees in the still-damp grass, his arms extended rigid in front of him and his partners engulfing him in a torrent of high fives. Gary looked up into the sky.

Did you see that? Were you watching me?

The fifth hole ran back uphill, with the green adjacent to the first tee and clubhouse. As they came up over the brow of the hill towards their drives they saw the crowd gathered behind the green: maybe a dozen people.

'Aye aye,' Bert said.

As they walked up to the green Derek Forbes detached himself from the group and approached Bert. 'We heard yese shouting yer heeds aff doon there,' he said.

'Hole in wan at the fourth,' Bert said.

'Big John?' Forbes whispered, nodding towards the green, where they were marking their balls.

Bert shook his head, smiling. 'Young Gary.'

Forbes looked at him.

'Boy's five under par after four holes,' Bert said.

'*Gary Irvine?* Away tae fuck.'

'Ah'm telling ye.'

Forbes stumbled back, almost falling over as he ran off towards his cronies to break the unbelievable news. By the time the group had putted out – Gary's ball stopping right on the lip, leaving him a tap-in for par, his worst hole of the day so far – and were making their way to the sixth tee, their gallery had doubled.

Bert and Gary fell into step with each other. 'Whit the hell's going on, son?' Bert said.

'Hoor. I don't know, Bert. Hoor,' Gary said.

'Well, whatever it is, just keep doing it. Right, ah'd better leave ye alone. Ah don't want tae break your concentration.'

I don't think you can, Gary thought to himself as Bert walked over to join his friends behind the tee box.

Word went round.

A dozen or so members were drinking in the bar when Forbes – red-faced from running for the first time in a decade – burst in through the double doors that led to the locker room.

'Derek!' said Senga the barmaid. 'Whit the hell's the matter?'

'It's, he's . . .' Forbes spluttered, fighting for breath.

'Christ, take it easy, bud. Here, huv a whisky . . .'

'He's just eagled the tenth! Ten under par now!'

'Who?'

Forbes took a gulp of whisky. 'Gary Irvine!'

A split second before the laughter started. 'Away and don't talk pish!' someone said.

'Hey, that's no the first drink you've hud the day!'

'Ah'm telling yese!'

They saw he was serious.

'He eagled the tenth?'

'Aye!'

'*Ten under par?*' someone repeated.

'Christ,' Senga said. 'He's gonnae win the Medal!'

'Win the Medal?' Forbes said, knocking back the rest of his drink. 'He's gonnae break the bloody course record!' With that he was off, running back towards the course. A clattering of pint pots and whisky glasses onto wooden tabletops, the whisper of jackets and sweaters coming off the backs of chairs, and everyone was following him.

Ardgirvan is a small town. it has often been said that if you farted on your way out the Bam, then the story that you'd shat yourself would be doing the rounds by the time you passed the the Annick. Stevie got a call from a mate of Prentice's saying that Gary was playing like Calvin Fucking Linklater and was going to smash the course record. He shut up shop and drove up to Ravenscroft, catching up with the match on the twelfth tee, where he joined the gallery of maybe fifty spectators as Gary's group prepared to tee off.

At 466 yards the twelfth hole was the longest par four on the course. The right-hand side of the fairway gave the best line into the green, but it was a dangerous route: out of bounds all the way. A rusted wire fence divided the golf course from the main road and, across the road, the mento home. Today, as every day, its saliva-flecked windows were thronged with the twitching, vibrating faces of those who had proved too much for their children.

Gary stepped onto the tee. There was a decent breeze blowing into his face, coming from the right.

Hit it down the right and have the wind keep it in play.

KEERACK!

Just at the moment the ball left the tee – struck well, flying on the line he had intended – the wind abruptly changed direction, suddenly, crazily, blowing from the left, pushing his ball right, sending it drifting over the right-hand edge of the fairway, over the right-hand rough, towards the road . . .

'Fuck,' Stevie said.

The ball struck the edge of one of the concrete posts marking the Out of Bounds line and ricocheted off across the road towards the mento home.

The mentos all turned their heads skywards as Gary's ball bounced three times down the roof above them.

'Shite,' Bert whispered to Stevie. 'Three aff the tee,' meaning that with the penalty strokes Gary's next shot would be his third.

Understandably shaken, Gary pulled it left into thick rough – the first drive he had mishit all day. He hacked out and overhit his approach shot into the deep bunker behind the green. He got the ball out of the bunker and then made his first three putt of the morning, chalking up a horrific quintuple bogey nine and tumbling back to five under par in the process.

'Well,' someone said, 'so much for the course record.' A few people began to drift away.

'What is the course record?' Stevie asked Bert as they set off towards the next tee.

'Sixty-two,' Bert said. 'Ten under par. He'll need to birdie every hole from here on in if he's gonnae beat it.'

'Sixty-two?' Stevie whistled. 'Who set that?'

Bert was laughing as he said: 'I bloody did!'

Five under par on the thirteenth tee. The old, pre-accident, Gary Irvine would have allowed one of his testicles to be surgically removed – sans anaesthetic – in return for such a score. The new Gary Irvine wanted more. And in golf wanting it too much can often translate into trying too hard; a fatal error in a sport which asks its greatest exponents simply to perform their very best with an attitude of complete indifference. This is the Zone, where the professional golfer must live when he is playing at full stretch: in his own little world where nothing exists except putting the club sweetly through the ball – not the munching, coughing, farting, camera-phone-waving spectators, not the swivelling, trundling black-eyed TV cameras, not the other players. Nothing. The fine art of being there and not being there. Gary had heard about the Zone, of course, but he had never been there for more than a few seconds at a time. Now, the trauma of the last hole behind him, he felt himself slipping back into it; his mind pleasantly vacant apart from a gentle fizzing sensation in his skull, like bubbling lemonade, his body loose apart from the usual nagging semi-erection in his pants.

He was there and he wasn't there when he drove the green at the thirteenth and then made the twenty-foot putt for his second eagle of the day.

He was there and he wasn't there when he made a perfect

connection with his approach on the fourteenth, sending the ball straight and high, pumping the eight-iron higher than most players can send the sand wedge, and nailing the six-foot putt it left him.

He was there and he wasn't there as he birdied the sixteenth and seventeenth (an unlucky roll of the green had denied him his birdie at the fifteenth; he'd tapped in for par) and walked towards the last tee with a crowd of sixty people following him, back to ten under par now and needing one last birdie to break the course record, a record set by the man walking beside him before he was even born. Bert smiled over at him, but Gary didn't see it.

'Come on, Gary!'

'Go on yerself, son!'

'Come on, big man!'

'Get in there!'

Gary drove first, bombing one just under three hundred yards up the middle. Prentice, Mason and Alexander, long reduced to walk-on parts and their confidence shredded by having to play in front of an audience, all missed the fairway, finding trees, gorse and – in Prentice's case – the driveway, which wound up the right-hand side of the fairway, connecting the golf club with the main road.

As they came up the hill the eighteenth green came into sight. It was completely surrounded. Every member was out from the bar. Members who hadn't been playing that day had been alerted that the course record that had stood for thirty-seven years was in danger of being broken. They had driven up to the course, abandoning lunches and families to witness this momentous occasion.

Gary's ball was about twenty yards behind the red-and-white post that indicated there was 150 yards to the centre of the green. Pin at the back left, tucked in behind the bunker. Sucker pin position, trying to lure you into the bunker. Ignore it and aim for the heart of the green? But that would leave him a long putt for birdie, with all those people watching . . . it'd be better to be close.

Hit a draw? Land the ball on the middle of the apron of the green, moving a little right-to-left and cosying up to the flag? A little under 170 yards to the hole: about a five-iron for the old Gary. The new one took a deep breath and pulled out the seven.

Don't hold back now.

That blissful sensation of weightlessness as he came through the ball, catching it right out of the middle, right out of the sweet spot, like there was nothing there at all, and Gary letting the club wrap around him, falling against the back of his neck, conscious of cold steel against his skin.

The ball bounced once in front of the green, a second time three yards onto it, and began to roll left, out of sight. A second passed, then two, and people behind the green were hopping up and down and beginning to emit a strange noise, a tortured whine, like a jet engine powering up for take-off. Another second, the whine powering up then resolving into a massed *'Ooooohhh . . .'*.

As he walked onto the green, into all the clapping and cheering, Gary saw that his ball was nestled just inches from the cup. He became aware of three things.

1) He had the simplest of tap-ins to break the course record.
2) The fizzing sensation in his skull was intensifying, like the lemonade in there was beginning to boil.
3) The erection in his pants was reaching a scarcely believable pitch of rigidity.

Dreamlike now – the sound of the crowd just a distant wash as he watched their mouths opening and closing but heard nothing – he walked into the middle of the green. Someone's hand on his shoulder, Gary turning to see Auld Bert saying something, indicating that Gary should tap in and take his place in Ravenscroft history right now, rather than waiting until his partners had hit their putts. Everything in slow motion. Numbly Gary settled the putter behind the ball and tapped it. It dropped into the cup with a 'clink' he did not hear and he was engulfed in a sea of backslapping, handshaking, smiling and laughing. A whoosing in his head. The hard-on. Jesus.

Senga the barmaid kissing him on the cheek.

His vision dimming at the edges now as he broke away from everyone, their expressions turning to concern as Gary began staggering, scrabbling at his belt buckle with jittery urgency, a strange moan coming from him.

His belt slithering open and his trousers falling down.

Jaws falling too as Gary's hand disappeared down the front of his boxers, reappearing a split second later, clutching his . . .

Senga the barmaid screamed.

Everything went black as his legs folded beneath him.

He woke up in a pile of sweaters still in their thin polythene wrappers. Looking up, Gary saw that Stevie and Bert were standing over him. They looked very worried.

'Where am I?'

'You're in the pro shop, son,' Bert said softly.

'Why? What happened?'

'Ah, you fainted,' Bert said.

'What's the last thing you remember?' Stevie asked, offering him a sip of water from a plastic cup and sitting down on the floor beside him.

'I . . .' He took the water. What did he remember? *Some strange dream – his dad, a golf course, lots of flowers?* 'Walking onto the green?' Gary said. 'People cheering?'

Stevie raised his eyebrows expectantly. 'Then?'

'Then . . .' He thought hard, but there was nothing. A vague memory of a tickling in his head, a whooshing sound. 'What happened then?'

Stevie bit his lip and bowed his head down. Gary looked up at Bert. 'Bert, what happened?'

Bert coloured. 'Umm, well, it, ye had, ye know, son, ye started having a . . . a wee turn at yourself.'

'Eh?'

Stevie sighed and spoke slowly and clearly. 'You started wanking yourself off in front of everyone. *Then* you fainted.'

Gary looked up at Bert. Bert nodded. Gary swallowed.

'Fuck,' he said finally.

25

LEE IRVINE, SITTING ON THE HOT BONNET OF HIS CAR, lit a Mayfair and turned as he heard the crunch of tyres. The black jeep pulled up beside Lee's Nova in the deserted car park. Alec gestured for him to get in.

'A'right?'

'No bad, Alec, no bad. How's it going?' Lee pulled the hefty door shut behind him. Leather seats. iPod. Satnav. The business.

'Here's how it's fucking going . . .' Alec said, sliding a small green canvas knapsack onto Lee's lap and looking around the park. Empty, save for a pair of joggers on the wooden running track half a mile away.

Lee thought about looking inside, but decided that might be unprofessional. Better to play it cool. The knapsack felt appropriately heavy on his thighs, dense matter, condensed death.

'Cheers,' Lee said with a nonchalance he did not feel.

'It's a revolver.' Alec paused, chewing gum. 'Ye don't want

an automatic jamming oan ye. Fucking nightmare. There's a box o' shells in there too.'

Alec talked slowly, calmly, never turning Lee's way. He kept his eyes on the park around them, constantly scanning. 'Serial number's been filed aff, but don't get smart and figure ye'll keep it and sell it later or whatever. Soon as yer done take a drive doon the harbour and pap it in the fucking water.' Water pronounced in the full Ayrshire – 'Wah-turr'.

'Aye, ah'm no fucking daft, Alec.'

'Ah'm sure yer no, so listen tae this. This job's come straight doon fae the auld boy. He's taking a personal interest. Know whit ah'm saying?'

'Aye.'

The auld boy. Ranta. Lee felt his windpipe tighten.

'So if ye've any doubts aboot this, now's the time tae say. Ye can just gie us the money back and that'll be that. Because after this arrangements will be getting made and ma da'll be giving his word tae the client.' Alec turned to face Lee for the first time. 'And ye wouldnae want ma da tae huv tae go back on his word. Would ye?'

'Course no, Alec. Ah can handle it.'

'Right.' Alec passed him an envelope. 'There's the address and a photo o' the cow. Memorise them and burn them.'

'When's it tae get done?' Lee asked.

'Not for a wee while. Probably be a month or so. There's arrangements tae be made. Alibis and stuff. Give ye time tae dae yer homework. We'll be in touch. When it's aw done ah'll meet ye and square ye up wi' the rest o' the dollar.'

'Aye, right, Alec. Fair enough. Ah –' But Alec was turning the ignition on, indicating that the meeting was over.

Lee watched Alec drive off in a beige cloud of gravel. He got in his car and looked around. Still no one in sight. He opened the knapsack, slid his hand in, and closed his fist around a real gun for the first time in his life. Not an air pistol or a replica. A. Real. Fucking. Gun.

It felt oily and cold, and gripping it tightly did not bring the excitement Lee had thought it might. Only fear. He opened the envelope and took the photo out – a woman, fat, blonde, middle-aged, smiling for the camera, a close head and shoulders shot, taken in a restaurant somewhere. She looked happy. Lee pushed away the thought of how happy she was going to look with a fucking bullet hole in her coupon. He looked at the address written on the back of the photo: *Riverside, 42 The Meadows*. Rich cow then. For some reason this made him feel a little better.

Memorise it.

'42', like four-four-two formation with one of the fours taken off. 'Riverside', the River Ardgirvan that flowed under the shopping mall, on its banks, its sides, the pitch-and-putt course and the putting green.

He pulled his lighter out and set it to the corner of the photograph. He held it out of the car window, watching as it burned, the glossy paper flaming blue and then pink and then orange as Leanne Masterson's face crumpled, smoke wreathing away from Lee on the breeze, the ashes fluttering around him like grey-black snowflakes. Lee remembered something he hadn't thought of in a long time – running down the first fairway at Ravenscroft, him and Gary, throwing their father's ashes into the air from a gold plastic tub.

26

FACING GARY AND PAULINE ACROSS THE DESK IN THE antiseptic consulting room was Dr Robertson and a short, bespectacled man in his forties wearing a beige corduroy jacket. He looked more like a teacher to Pauline than a doctor. 'Yes, congratulations!' Robertson said. 'Sixty-one! I heard you nearly holed a seven-iron at the eighteenth?'

'Yeah.' Gary said. 'From about 170. Fud. Rolled to about three – OW! – inches.'

'My goodness!'

'Yeah. It was –'

'Sorry,' Pauline interrupted, 'can we just . . . ?'

'Yes, sorry, anyway, this is Dr Fuller –' Robertson extended a hand towards him – 'from the neurology department at Glasgow University.'

'Pleased to meet you,' Fuller said cheerfully, leaning across the desk to shake their hands.

'Hello,' Pauline said.

'Hi. Cunt. Speccy cunt, ye,' Gary said.

'Gary!' Pauline said.

'Fascinating,' Fuller said, scribbling a note.

'Sorry!' Gary said.

'Dr Fuller,' Robertson went on, 'has a bit more experience than myself with these kinds of cases.'

'Oh,' Pauline said, 'with the Tourette's, you mean?'

'Not specifically the Tourette's,' Fuller said. 'I'm leading a team researching behavioural abnormalities as a result of head trauma.'

'Oh,' Pauline said.

'Big tits, ya fud ye. Sorry,' Gary said.

'Mr Irvine,' Fuller began.

'Gary's fine,' Gary said, before adding, 'cunt.'

'Gary, is it fair to say that this performance on the golf course was far in excess of your usual capability at the, um, game?'

'Well, my handicap's eighteen. Grr. So yeah,' Gary said.

'Mmmm,' Fuller said, chewing his biro while he reviewed Gary's file. 'I see here that just before you were struck on the head by the golf ball you were, in fact, practising golf. Can you recall exactly what happened before the ball hit you?'

'Umm, I'd been hitting it really badly, shanking them all over the place. And then I – tits – made an absolutely perfect swing. Spunk. Nine-iron. Baws. Hoor. Right out of the socket. I saw it land, it was rolling towards the hole – *rodeyerfucken-mawyacunt* – and then – bang! Goodnight Vienna.'

'I see, I see,' Fuller murmured, scribbling away.

'I'm sorry,' Pauline cut in, having had just about enough of all this, 'but what's all this got to do with what he . . . did the other day?'

'Oh, I'll come to the masturbation,' Fuller said casually, as though it were common or garden enough, 'but as regards the golf performance, what I think might have happened – and I must stress this is only conjecture – is that the trauma of the cerebellum Gary suffered has served to dramatically reinforce the successful performance of a specific physical action.' Fuller got up and went to a chart on the wall – a detailed cross section of the human brain. 'The cerebellum is attached to the stem of the actual brain.' He pointed it out with his pen. 'Among other things it's responsible for orchestrating and fine-tuning movement and is integral in performing intricate actions like, for instance, threading a needle or –'

'Swinging a golf club,' Robertson said.

'Exactly. Any information to be passed to your muscles is passed first through the cerebellum. Now, when a physical action produces a good, successful outcome this sensation is reinforced in the cerebellum. What I think may have happened in your case,' he came back to the desk, genuinely excited now, 'is that the trauma caused by the impact of the golf ball has somehow massively reinforced the sensation you experienced when you struck the shot perfectly, or "right out of the socket", to use your words. Consequently every time you swing the club now, it's possible that your brain is following, well, a burned-in template of how a successful swing should be executed. I've never come across anything quite like it before. There have been instances of head-injury patients suddenly displaying mathematical abilities they never had previously, but this would seem to indicate physical *and* ment—'

'Hang on.' Gary interrupted, unable to quite believe what he was hearing. 'Are you saying that *I can't make a bad swing*?'

'It's possible. What do you think, Dr Robertson?'

'I think,' Robertson said, staring enviously at the fading indented bruise on Gary's temple, thinking about the millions of amateur golfers gnashing and weeping their way around the world's courses every weekend, 'that if we could market this as an operation we'd all be bloody billionaires!'

'Right,' Pauline said, finally losing patience. 'Can we just forget about the bloody golf please? What about the fact that he . . .' What was the right word to use in front of doctors? '. . . interfered with himself in front of all those people?'

'Oh yes,' Fuller said, 'it's very likely that Gary is suffering from a neurological condition called Kluver-Bucy syndrome.' His tone of voice was that of a geologist who had gone from discussing a rare gemstone to talking about coal.

'Klu . . .' Pauline began.

'Kloo-ver-Boo-sey,' Fuller enunciated. 'It was first observed by scientists studying how various degrees of lobotomy-affected –'

'Lobotomy?' Gary said.

'– affected monkeys,' Fuller continued. 'They found that after performing bilateral temporal lobectomies – which, of course, caused separate lesions of the amygdala, uncus and temporal cortices – a startling variety of behavioural changes were observed in the monkeys.'

Pauline and Gary stared at him.

'Although naturally,' he said, looking to clarify, 'it was simply the bilateral amygdalotomies – and the resultant damage to their outflow tracts, the diagonal band of Broca and, um, stria terminalis – that resulted in the clinical picture.'

Christ, Robertson thought. He cut in and explained it simply.

'What kind of "behavioural changes"?' Gary asked.

'Hyperorality, dietary abnormalities, emotional blunting and, of course, hypersexuality.'

'Hang on,' Gary said. 'Bloody monkeys is one thing, but how – sookit – I mean, do humans get this?'

'Oh, it's pretty rare,' Fuller said happily. 'In over twenty years I've witnessed just two or three cases. One of them, a young woman who was involved in an RTA –'

'Road traffic accident,' Robertson said.

'– had a GCS score of 7, rather more severe than yours,' Fuller continued, nodding at Gary. 'She was in a coma for twelve days. When she regained consciousness she displayed a range of Kluver-Bucy behaviour, including the marked hypersexuality.'

'What kind of umm . . . hypersexuality?' Pauline asked.

'Oh, the usual things, attempting to take her clothes off, inappropriate touching – grabbing doctors' genitals – excessive and often public masturbation.'

'Christ,' Pauline said.

'What happened to her?' Gary asked.

'Mmm?'

'The girl. What happened to her?'

'Oh, she died.'

Fuller said this in exactly the same tone he might have used for 'she's fine'. Robertson closed his eyes.

'But, but,' Fuller said, 'there are several documented cases of patients making a full recovery. You see, I think there's a good chance that you may be suffering from a relatively mild form of Kluver-Bucy syndrome known as post-traumatic KBS. There's a good chance you'll make a full recovery.'

'How . . . how long will that take?' Gary asked.

'Oh, the literature records cases resolving themselves in anything from a week or two to a year.'

'A year?' Pauline said. 'He could be like this for a year?'

'Like what?' Robertson asked.

'Like wanking in the bloody high street!' Pauline said.

'Well, it's possible,' Fuller said. 'However, we have found

that the worst incidences of that kind of thing seem to occur when the subject is placed in situations of unusually high stress or tension. So I'd avoid those.'

'I can play golf though, can't I?' Gary asked.

'Oh for goodness' sake –' Pauline said.

'Well, I suppose so. But I –'

'Dick,' Gary said.

'I'd try to –'

'Big dicks.'

'Try to avoid –'

'Strapafuckendicktome.'

'Avoid the kind of high-pressure situation you found yourself in the other day.' Fuller smiled. 'You know, just play for fun!'

Gary and Robertson – the two golfers in the room – looked at each other, both of them thinking; '*Fun?* What the fuck is this boy talking about?'

27

IN SCOTLAND, MAY AND JUNE CAN OFTEN BE THE MOST incredible months. Winter loosens up its long grip and the whole country erupts in a starburst of flora, fauna and T-shirts. Another blessing: in the fields, in the grassy banks along rivers and lochs, in the tall grass beside the ponds on golf courses, the midges still slumber; tiny embryonic grains dreaming of the days soon to come when they will emerge in their billions and feast upon the plump, blood-rich flesh of tourists.

Dr Robertson signed a sick note which entitled the bearer to three months off work and for Gary Irvine the early summer became a torrent, an incredible blur, of golf, marred only by the local newspaper's report of his breaking the course record, which chose to focus on the more unfortunate part of the achievement. Cathy cancelled her lifelong subscription to the *Ardgirvan Gazette* the same day. 'Ah . . . ah cannae believe it,' Cathy sobbed, the copy of the paper spread out on the breakfast bar between her and Gary. There on the cover was the same photo of Gary they'd run when he'd been in hospital.

Sadly, above the photo, was a different headline from the one Cathy had been hoping for ('LOCAL MAN BREAKS COURSE RECORD!'). It simply said: 'MASTURBATED!'

'Bloody journalists. Scum o' the earth so they are.' Cathy sobbed. There was a quote from Senga the barmaid highlighted in bold: *'He got it out and just started doing it right in front of us.'*

'Aye, bloody Senga Syme,' Cathy snorted. 'Sure there's a good few stories ah could tell ye about her bloody family . . .'

Gary didn't care. Rising with the sun just before six (hearing only a soft moan of protest from the sleeping Pauline), he packed water and bananas – pausing only to masturbate in the downstairs toilet, the act itself mechanical and joyless, a physical necessity required so he could jam himself behind the wheel of a car before he motored out to the driving range where he could work on fine-tuning his new gift.

It was a constant process of discovery and amazement. Before the accident, had he made ten attempts to fade the ball with the driver, moving it from left to right in the air, it might have gone like this: three balls would be mega-slices that curved crazily to the right; two would fly absolutely, maddeningly, straight; two or three attempts would start off looking promising before moving dramatically rightwards – fades, becoming cuts, becoming eye-watering slices. One or two shots would be utter mishits with the topped ball rattling along the ground in front of him. Perhaps, on a very good day, one ball out of the ten would do what it was intended to do: rocket upwards on a penetrating trajectory, gracefully sailing from left to right as it descended.

Now? Christ, now he found he could control the *degree* to which the ball moved in the air. He could hit huge booming draws that finished twenty yards to his left. He could punch irons low into the wind or, by placing the ball further forward in his stance, he could produce incredible height: his five- and six-irons landing soft as wedges.

As for the wedges – he found that he could finally do what every amateur golfer dreams of, what they salivate over when they watch Linklater, Spafford or Novotell, what they see themselves doing in their feverish golf dreams. He could create *backspin*. With the sand wedge he could throw the ball a hundred feet in the air and have it plop down, hop forward, pause, and then spin backwards two, three, four yards towards the hole.

Around nine o'clock other golfers would start to appear – some of them gathering to watch in awe as Gary drilled three-irons all the way to the end of the range – and it would be time to head up to the golf course.

On weekdays the course was quiet in the mornings and he would usually play the first round by himself – hitting extra shots, experimenting, trying out different ways of coming at the greens – before having lunch in the clubhouse and then heading out for a second round in the afternoon, often a four ball with Bert and a couple of the retired boys.

Pauline protested. There were rows and fights. If he was well enough to play golf all the time shouldn't he back at work? The old Gary would have capitulated. The new Gary shrugged and headed for the course.

The erections remained near constant. As did the swearing, although usually it was just the odd word bubbling up into a sentence, or quickly added as an afterthought. There was, thankfully, no recurrence of the incident on the eighteenth green. (*'His wee turn'*, Cathy called it.)

Within a couple of weeks a fresh problem became apparent. Given his new-found power (his 300-yard drives, his 140-yard sand wedges), Ravenscroft, with a layout that used to be as humbling and challenging to Gary as St Andrews or Brookline would have been, was no longer any kind of test. The longest hole on the course, the 510-yard par five tenth, was now driver, six-iron for him on a good day.

'Ah think you need tae stretch yer wings a wee bit,' Bert said.

And so they did. Driving south from Ardgirvan they explored the string of great links courses along the Ayrshire coastline: Glasgow and Western Gailes, Kilmarnock Barassie, Old Prestwick, Turnberry . . .

These were not municipal pitch-and-putts. These were real golf courses, with teeth and claws and poisonous spines on their backs. Courses where you stood on the tee and looked out over hundreds of yards of wild scrubland, heather and gorse bushes and burns and sand dunes, to where a red or yellow flag shimmered in the distance, signalling that there was indeed a green out there somewhere, an oasis of calm in this maelstrom of nature.

Then, when you actually got to the green, you found that it was sixty or seventy yards wide and nearly a hundred long. You routinely had eighty-foot putts that went uphill *and* downhill, moving through several breaks across grass like a laminated-wood floor. When the breeze got up you often found yourself having to putt while standing in the mouth of a wind tunnel.

And all this time Gary thought he had been playing golf.

At first he was astonished at how easy, how effortless it was, to make bogey, to make double and triple bogey on these courses. A frown from the Golf Gods – a bad bounce, a few yards extra roll on the fairway – and you were suddenly in your own personal Vietnam: sweating and blooded by thorny gorse bushes, sand in your hair, mouth and eyes as you tried for the second or third time to launch your ball over the sheer face of a bunker that towered seven feet above you. The bunkers, Jesus Christ, some of these bunkers were like hatches to Hades.

But Auld Bert's counsel was wise. 'The key to links gowf, son – stay out of the sand. If ye cannae drive over them, pull an iron and play well short. *Don't just hit the driver and hope for the best.*' Gary quickly found his scores improving – from the low 80s to the mid 70s to par and better.

Meanwhile, back at Ravenscroft, he was setting new kinds of records. He won the Monthly Medal in May and June. Almost every day for six weeks straight he handed in scorecards with scores of 68, 67, 69, 65 or 66. Finally, on a bright, hot Saturday morning towards the end of June, he walked through the locker room and up to the Handicaps Board. He read quickly down the list of names – Hamilton, Howe, Ingram – and there it was. The most beautiful inscription he had ever seen in his life:

Irvine, G: O.4

From 18.7 to 0.4 in a little under six weeks: the fastest anyone in the history of British golf had ever had their handicap cut.

He didn't know how long he'd been standing there staring at the magical combination of words and digits when he heard something behind him. He turned round to see Bert standing there smiling.

'Congratulations, son.'

'Aye. Thanks, Bert. Fuck.'

'Yer a scratch golfer now.'

'I know. Ah – baws, big baws – I can't believe it. I wish ma dad was, y'know . . .'

'Aye.' Bert nodded. He was holding something. 'Well, there's lots of things scratch golfers can do that others cannae . . .' He handed Gary a sheaf of A4 papers: six sheets, black and white, stapled together.

On the top sheet was a picture of the oldest, most famous prize in golf, the Claret Jug, white silhouetted against a black circle.

Beside the jug: 'The Open Championship'.

Below it: 'Royal Troon, 19, 20, 21 and 22 July'.

At the top: 'Entry Form – Regional Qualifying'.

Gary looked at Bert.

'Has to be in by tomorrow,' Bert said.

PART THREE

I'm gonna be a woman, not a news-getting machine. I'm gonna have babies and take care of them! Give 'em cod liver oil and watch their teeth grow!

Hildy Johnson in *His Girl Friday*

'Back With the Killer Again . . .'

The Auteurs

PART THREE

28

'THE OPEN REGIONAL QUALIFIERS?' APRIL TREMBLE spat the words out like they had scalded her mouth. She found they tasted no better the second time.

McIntyre and Devlin both nodded eagerly.

'Good wee story,' said Alan McIntyre, the *Daily Standard*'s editor, his tie thrown over his shoulder as he resumed tucking into his lunch: roast-beef-and-onion sandwiches brought up from the pub on the corner. Two o'clock on a Friday afternoon and he was just starting lunch at his desk. Fucking newspaper business today. At fifty-one Al McIntyre was old enough to remember when Friday-afternoon lunch would have started around noon and continued until the late afternoon: bottles of Bull's Blood in the subs' desk drawers and not a secretary in the building who wouldn't have popped down to the Albany Hotel with you for the night. Not like now, he thought, looking up at the sleek figure of April, her hands on her hips, her head cocked sideways.

April was twenty-six, five nine in the heels she rarely wore (*rarely wore skirts either*, McIntyre reflected), a clear-skinned beauty with bobbed auburn hair and a degree ('*a first-class honours degree*' as she never tired of reminding them) in Journalism from Napier University. She was the first female sports reporter the *Standard* had ever had; an editorial decision designed to refute allegations of entrenched sexism at the paper and, hopefully, to draw a few female readers into opening the sports section before they passed it to their husbands or boyfriends.

'Just a few hundred words, doll,' said Tam Devlin, the sports editor, unwrapping his ham and cheese, 'local interest, stars of the future, you know the sort of thing.'

'Stars of the future? What fucking planet are you two on? I mean, what's it like? Is the atmosphere breathable? You want me to spend the weekend in the middle of nowhere watching a bunch of nobodies trying to break par? Tell me, Tam, who was the last golfing superstar to emerge from the Open Regional Qualifiers?'

'Er . . .' said Devlin.

McIntyre's office was on the top floor of the *Standard* building on the northern bank of the Clyde. Through the long window the dun river snaked away towards the east and lunchtime traffic crawled across the Kingston Bridge.

'Exactly. Come on,' April moved in and perched on the edge of the big desk, 'there's the World Match Play down in Hertfordshire that weekend. *Linklater*'s playing. I could –'

'Donald's covering that,' Devlin said through a mouthful of white bread and plastic cheese.

'Donald! That fucking old wreck! Look at him!' April pointed through the glass panelling that separated McIntyre's office from the rest of the floor, towards where an enormously fat man sat with his feet up on his desk and his back to them.

Donald Lawson, Senior Sports Reporter. 'He's probably asleep right now!' April added.

'Scottish Sports Writer of the Year two years running,' Devlin said.

'Aye, 1977 and 1978. Fucking hell, Tam, what's the point in sending Donald? He'll just sit in the media bar all week, getting pissed, stuffing his face, and then filing copy cribbed from the daily press releases, occasionally wandering out to watch someone sink a putt on the eighteenth. I'd do a good job.'

'Sorry, April,' Devlin said, 'R.H.I.P. Donald has relationships with lots of the players.'

'Aye, on the seniors tour,' April said, turning to McIntyre. 'Come on, Al, don't give me all this "Rank Has Its Privileges" shite. I'm worth more than this.'

'Tam's call,' McIntyre said.

'So that's it, is it?' April stood up, hands back on her hips. 'Jobs for the boys? Business as usual?'

'Jesus, April,' McIntyre sighed. 'Does everything have to be an Emily bloody Pankhurst situation with you? You've only been here a year. All good things to those who wait.'

'Yeah. Like you two'll be waiting until thirty seconds before the paper goes to bed for that alky's miserable, clichéd-rammed fucking copy.'

McIntyre's desk phone started ringing and he squinted at the caller ID. 'Sorry, April. Conference call. We've got to take this. Call transport and they'll sort you out a hire car and a hotel. Enjoy Midlothian. It's a beautiful part of Scotland, you know.'

She looked at them: two fat, middle-aged sexist bastards who probably thought she was angry because she wasn't getting enough.

'You've got mayonnaise on your tie, Tam,' she said, turning on her heel.

'Bastar—' Devlin dabbed at his tie with a napkin and McIntyre picked up his phone as April – not gently – closed the door behind her.

Devlin pulled his mobile from his pocket and hit the red button, terminating the call he had been making to McIntyre's desk phone.

'Thanks, Tam,' McIntyre said, turning the TV on and getting European football on Sky. 'It's a shame, with all the attitude and that. She's actually no a bad wee writer.'

'Aye,' said Devlin. 'And the body on it? Ye'd ride it till the wean pushed ye oot.'

'Chance would be a fine thing.'

'Whit, ye think she's . . . ?' Devlin made an 'O' with the thumb and forefinger of each hand and started banging the two 'O's together.

'Either way,' McIntyre said, turning the volume up with a mustard-smeared thumb, 'she's probably no getting enough . . .'

It had taken a fair bit of thinking. He hadn't wanted it to look too obvious. He thought about attending some carpet conference or convention, but Leanne knew how much he hated those. Or maybe a trip with the lads to see Rangers play away somewhere, but the summer had started and there weren't any suitable games any time soon. Finally he hit upon it.

Leanne found it *slightly* odd that her husband had decided to make a trip up to Glasgow for a night of 'father-and-son bonding', but she was pleased. He spent little enough time with the boy. The university was on holiday but Keith had got a job in Glasgow for the summer, working at some computer games store and keeping his flat on in the west end. Two weeks on Thursday – 17 July – Masterson would drive up to the city, get a hotel room and they'd go out to dinner, maybe see a film. 'You'll be OK on your own?' he asked her.

'Of course ah will,' Leanne said.

Later, Masterson drove into town on the pretext of picking up some beers. Using a payphone in the shopping centre he made one short call.

Ranta hung up on Masterson and made another short call.

Alec hung up on his father and punched a number up on his mobile. He said the date, repeating it very clearly twice.

'A'right,' Lee said. He was going to say more, maybe something reassuring like 'don't worry', or 'leave it to me', but there was just a click as Alec hung up.

'*The Open Regional Qualifiers?*'

Pauline had been using her incredulous tone so much recently that it was beginning to sound normal to her. Every other word seemed to be coming out of her mouth in italics these days. '*Where?*'

'Musselburgh. It's in Midlothian. Up near Edinburgh. Shut up, Ben!' Gary did not look up from the bag he was packing.

'But . . . you . . . you're off work because you're sick.'

'Have you seen my toilet bag? The wee black one?'

'No! Shut up, Ben!'

'Never mind, I'll just –

'No – not the fucking toilet bag, I mean *no*! You're not going off to play in some stupid bloody golf competition. If you're well enough to bugger about playing golf then you're well enough to go back to work. Will you *ever fucking shut up, Ben*!'

Gary stopped packing and turned to her, a pair of black socks in his hand. Ben continued to growl at him, circling around behind Pauline as the argument paused – her enforcer, her praetorian guard.

How many times had he attempted to defy her in the past? There had been that stag night to Dublin he'd wanted to go on, some guy from work, back in '97 . . . an argument about the extension to the house a few years ago. Not much over the years. Pauline looked at him. They were the same eyes, blue and clear. But it wasn't him any more. Something fundamental was different and she felt a sudden unease, as if the rules had been changed without her consent, as if the same opponent she had beaten countless times before had somehow acquired a new technique, a new level of confidence.

Given how things were progressing with Masterson, Pauline was surprised at how angry she was. What did she care if he wanted to waste his life farting about on a golf course? But every relationship has its comfort zones, its normal way of doing things, and Gary was increasingly transgressing the boundaries laid down over the years. His golf was a pleasure Pauline tolerated as long as it was understood that there was to be guilt attached to it, that it was to be fitted in here and there and could be curtailed whenever Pauline saw fit.

Gary placed a hand on her shoulder, guided her to the edge of the bed, and sat down beside her. He began very gently. 'Pauline, listen. Shitc, fud, cunt. You don't understand. Whatever's happened in here –' he tapped his temple, the indented bruise still visible – 'I can do something I've always wanted to do. I can imagine a shot, I can see it in my head, and then I can do it. I can make it happen almost exactly like I see it. Not now and again, or once in a blue moon – paps – But nearly every single time.'

'So what are you saying? You've had a bump on the bloody head and so you're going to pack your job in and go off and become a professional golfer?'

'No. Don't be daft. I just want to . . . take this a bit further. Can't you understand that?'

A car horn sounded from outside.

'That'll be Stevie,' Gary said, getting up. 'He's caddying for me.'

'Do you want to leave me?'

'Leave you? No, God. Of course not.'

'Because if you walk out that door and bugger off to play fucking golf for the weekend –'

'Can't you just let me do this? Can't you be happy for me?'

Pauline tried to picture herself being happy for Gary. Being happy that he was out swinging a golf club in the sunshine, laughing and enjoying himself while she had a party to do: six-year-olds shrieking and screaming and running around crying their eyes out. She felt a sickening rage twisting in the pit of her stomach. 'If you walk out that door I . . .'

He reached out and put a hand on her cheek. This would be the point where the old Gary crumbled. Where he fell apart and said, 'I'm sorry,' or 'OK.' The new Gary smiled softly. 'Och, Pauline,' he said, 'don't be so fucking melodramatic.'

She listened to his feet pounding down the stairs, the metallic clank of his golf bag being picked up, and then the front door was slamming behind him. She heard him exchanging greetings with Stevie, the boot and then the car door slamming and the two of them driving off.

So, it was war, then.

29

THE OPEN WAS PLAYED FOR THE VERY FIRST TIME AT Prestwick Golf Club – a short drive from Ardgirvan – on a cold, drizzly October day in 1860.

Back then Prestwick was a twelve-hole course, the scrubby fairways and greens laid out on common land, land given to the men of Ayrshire by Robert the Bruce in recognition of their fierce services in Scotland's wars of independence. In 1860 a field of eight players, watched by a crowd of wives, families, curious locals and some sheep and cows, played three rounds in one day, competing for a prize fund of precisely zero. The winner, Willie Park Sr, shot a tremendous score of 174 to beat the favourite, Old Tom Morris, and take home a red leather belt ornamented with a silver buckle. Financially, things improved quickly and, a few years later, when Park won his second Open, he walked away with the winner's purse of £6, which he promptly spent entertaining his fellow players in the saloon bar of Prestwick's Red Lion hotel.

A century and a half later a field of 156 golfers – watched

by the tens of thousands of spectators who crammed into the grandstands and lined the fairways of the Old Course at St Andrews, and by millions more watching on television all around the world – competed for a prize fund of £4 million. When Calvin Linklater secured his second Open victory, he took home a winner's cheque for £720,000. He walked off the final green and was swept into a hotel suite where he was told by his management team that – among other things – he had just been offered $10 million to drink a certain brand of cola, $15 million for the exclusive motion picture rights to his life story, and $120 million to consider switching to another brand of golf clubs for the next five years. The Sultan of Brunei had tabled a million in return for a personal round with the champion.

Entry to the first Open had been restricted to professional golfers only. The following year, in an attempt to attract more players, entry was broadened to allow amateurs to compete and it is a tradition that still stands: any amateur golfer who has a certified handicap of 0.4 or less may attempt to secure a place in the Open. However, today, after nearly thirty exemption categories are factored in – the world top fifty golfers, the top twenty money winners, any previous Open champions aged under sixty-five, any winner of a major championship in the last five years, the top ten from the previous year's Open – only twelve spots in the field of 156 players are still open to amateurs, who must compete for the places through the qualifying process.

Twelve out of somewhere between 1,500 and 2,000 hopefuls will get a place in the Open.

Registration in the teeming clubhouse: the golf equivalent of the weigh-in before a boxing match, with the fighters bristling and pushing and eyeing each other up. There was Alan

McFadden from Ayr, the current Scottish amateur champion, a scratch player when he was fourteen, still only twenty-four and an Ayrshire golfing legend for a decade. There, by the front desk, yawning, relaxed, was Angus Green, a lawyer in his forties who had once qualified for the Open at Carnoustie. Just visible through the doors to the lounge, talking over a pot of tea, were Craig Anderson and Paul Trodden, both about Gary's age and the leading lights of Bogview Golf Club, Ardgirvan's other golf club, the posh one. As is the way nowadays, the older players wore chinos or cords in navy or black or varying hues of brown – copper, rust, earth – along with polo shirts and sweaters by Pringle and Lyle and Scott. The younger players were an acid trip of colour and sheen: trousers in atomic pink or fluorescent blue, iridescent tops in citric greens and lemons, white belts with gleaming chrome buckles. And their hair: dyed platinum, streaked with highlights and teased into fins and spikes. Everyone seemed to know each other and greetings and abuse were being freely thrown about. Gary and Stevie – very much the new boys – shuffled along in line. 'Jesus,' Gary whispered, 'they're young, aren't they? Fuckingcuntfuck.'

Stevie threw a suspicious glance around the lobby. 'Looks like a cross between a fucking boy-band convention and a young Conservative dinner-dance.'

'Name and home club please?' the girl behind the desk asked Gary.

'Er, Gary Irvine, Ravenscroft.'

'Irvine . . . Irvine . . .' the girl repeated as she rifled through a stack of cards. The young golf punk at the head of the next queue along turned to Gary. He was wearing a purple diamond-patterned sweater vest, purple trousers with white piping and wrap-around shades. His hair was spiked with gel, tufting up and over a white sun visor.

'Gary Irvine?' the kid said.

'Ah, aye. Ugh. Baws.'

'Are you that Gary Irvine who broke the course record at Ravenscroft?'

'Aye,' Gary smiled bashfully, extending a hand, 'pleased to meet –'

'The same Gary Irvine that started wanking himself aff oan the eighteenth green?'

Gary's face began to burn.

'HO! KEVIN! DAVY!' the kid shouted across the lobby while pointing at Gary. 'Check it oot! This is that guy who wiz pulling the heed aff it in front of every cunt at Ravenscroft!'

'No way, man!' Kevin or Davy shouted.

Everyone looking now, laughter and pointing as the kid produced a mobile phone. 'Here, big man, let us get a photo wi ye, eh? You're a fucking legend so ye ur!'

Stevie caught his wrist as he brought the phone up. The kid was easily a foot taller than Stevie, so when he went to pull his arm free he was surprised to find he couldn't budge it an inch. Stevie leaned in close. 'Ho, listen, ya wee fud – gie the guy a fucking break, eh? Brain injury. Medical condition an aw that. Ye wouldnae like it if you suffered some kind of accident, ye know, something that prevented ye from playing yer best . . .' Stevie tightened his grip, his sausage thumb digging deep into the inside of the kid's forearm.

'Iya! Fuck sake –'

'Noo pit that fucking phone away before ah stuff it up yer Jap's eye and take a fotay o' the inside o' yer fucken baws.'

Stevie released his grip and the kid walked away rubbing his arm.

'Sign here please, Mr Irvine.' The girl was blushing.

'Thanks,' Gary, said, looking at the girl but really talking to Stevie as he signed his name, very much aware of the dozen or so under-the-breath conversations going on around the lobby, most of them accompanied by nods in his direction and the traditional fist-pumping gesture.

Across the packed room April looked over towards where the commotion had been as the official handed over her press pass: the blushing guy with the freckles and the slightly ginger hair, signing his name. She thought he looked sweet. Sweet, but a bit wet. Gary Irvine.

The name sounded familiar and it was on a whim and no more that April thought to herself, *Might as well follow his match as any of the others.*

Fucking Spam Valley, Lee thought to himself, looking around as he locked the Nova and tugged hard on the leash to pull back the straining greyhound. He'd borrowed the dog – Bastard – from his mate wee Malky. *Good idea*, Lee thought. *Just looks like I'm walking the dug.*

The houses of The Meadows loomed around him, large as castles. The street he was walking down now and the one Lee lived on shared the same first two letters and two digits in their postcodes, but there the similarities ended. The houses of The Meadows were all detached, separated from one another by large, leafy gardens with mature trees and shrubs. The oldest, most expensive, properties in the area were the two Victorian sandstone mansions down towards the cemetery. (A phenomenon Lee couldn't understand – why, if you had the money to buy a big hoose like that, would you buy a manky old place instead of a brand-new one?) The majority of the houses were built in the late sixties and early seventies, with a few others being added more recently.

The Mastersons' house was the last one on the street, the

hedge bordering the property giving onto a small field that contained a couple of grazing piebald ponies. (*Fucking rich pricks. Fucking ponies fur their weans.*) The field gave directly onto the thick expanse of Annick woods, and the woods – as Lee knew from bitter experience – wound all the way down the hill to the bypass.

So: in after dark – she'd be alone in the house – tie her up and gag her while he quickly trashed the place to make it look like a robbery, two shots minimum in the head and then off out the back door, through the field, over the fence into the woods and down to the dual carriageway where he'd have left the motor in a lay-by.

Bob's yer uncle and Fanny's yer aunt.

He turned and strolled back towards the car. Glancing left over a low section of hedging he caught a glimpse of her – blonde, fat, beige top; 'the Target', as Lee was trying to think of her – standing at one of the downstairs windows and, for a second, he thought she was staring at him. He made much show of tugging on the lead and calling to the dog until he noticed that she had a phone pressed to her ear and she was talking, so she wasn't really looking at him at all, just staring into space. Lee tried to think of something hard to bolster his nerves, something like, *'Aye, enjoy yer phone call, ya rich hoor. It'll be yer fucking last,'* but it didn't feel right, so he just hurried on back to the car, pulling Bastard along behind him.

30

'I'M REALLY SORRY,' GARY SAID FOR THE THIRD TIME, 'I can't help it. It's a side effect of the accident. I don't even know I'm doing it. Hoor. *Shite!* Sorry!'

'It's OK,' April said. 'To be honest, I work in an environment where someone with Tourette's would fit right in . . .'

By the seventeenth she'd been very glad she'd followed his match. Because this guy Irvine was really something. He had a crazy, untutored eyesore of a swing for sure, but it worked. Chipping and putting lights out too – he'd posted a fairly incredible round of 64. They would have to wait until the scores were in from all the other Open Qualifying courses to see if it would be incredible enough. All the same, April thought, 64? Definitely worth interviewing him. So here they were in a corner of the clubhouse bar, April's Dictaphone on the low table between them along with their glasses and the plate of cheese-and-ham sandwiches Gary was working his way through. He was a little self-conscious at first about talking while the little red light on the machine glowed at him, but he was loosening up. Definitely cute too, April thought. But she was struggling to keep a straight face with the swearing. 'Anyway,' she said, 'what was I saying? Oh yeah, you were an eighteen-handicapper before the accident?'

'Aye, well, eighteen point seven, so nineteen really.'

'So was it a gradual thing? I mean, did you find you were swinging a bit better when you came out of the coma and then you just worked on it until –'

'Not really. The first time I went to the range after the accident I . . . I just couldn't make a bad swing.'

'Really?' April said, reaching for her soda water, trying not to look as excited as she felt, the adrenalin all good reporters feel when a brilliant story falls into their laps kicking in now. 'But your swing . . . it's pretty, um, unorthodox, eh?'

'Yeah. But it's – fucking cocks and baws, sorry – repeatable . . . near enough.' Gary grinned through a mouthful of sandwich and April noticed again that he had nice eyes, blue and clear.

'Can I ask you – I saw you at registration this morning, in the lobby. What was all that stuff about?'

Gary coloured, his freckles standing out as his cheeks flushed. 'It's . . . fuck fuck fuck, another thing, since the accident. I . . . it's called Kluver-Bucy syndrome.'

'How do you spell that?'

'Sorry, can we not talk about it?'

'Sure,' April said, writing *Clue Ver Bucy* in her notebook.

'You're not going to write about that stuff, are you? I mean, my mum reads the *Daily Standard*. My friends, my wife . . .'

April looked at the gold band on his left hand and smiled. 'How long have you been married?'

'Ah, eleven years next month.'

'Wow. You must have been quite young?'

'I suppose so. We'd known each other since school.'

Christ, childhood sweethearts, April thought. They probably still mate for life down in Ayrshire. Like lobsters. Or was it turtles?

'What got you into golf?' Gary asked her.

'My dad,' April said. 'He took me to the Open for the first time when I was eight. 1990 at St Andrews, when Faldo won his second. He shot eighteen under par that year, the lowest winning score since –'

'Tom Watson at Turnberry in '77.' Gary said, finishing the sentence for her. They smiled at each other, Gary thinking how strange it was to be sitting talking golf trivia with a woman, a very pretty woman, her pale skin gradually turning pink in the warmth of the bar. 'That was *my* first Open. My dad took me. I was only two.'

'Wow,' April said, 'imagine if you qual—'

'Yeah. It'd make quite a story, wouldn't it?'

'Heart-warming, as my editor likes to say.'

April signalled the waiter for the bill. 'How come your dad wasn't here cheering you on?'

'He's dead.'

'Oh, I'm sorry.'

'That's OK. It was a long time ago.'

'Well, I'm sure he'd have been very proud watching you out there to –'

'HO!' They both turned to see Stevie, coming into the bar through the doors that led out onto the patio. He had grunted disapprovingly when April introduced herself as a tabloid journalist but now he was beaming. 'Scores are in,' he said.

'No,' Gary said simply.

'Fucking *aye*,' Stevie said. 'You've qualified. We're going to the Open.'

Gary leapt to his feet and he and Stevie started jumping up and down hugging each other. April reached down and turned the Dictaphone off. *Quite a story is right*, she was thinking.

31

LEE WALKED ON PAST THE CLEARINGS WHERE SO recently he had dug frantically, heading deeper into the trees. He came to a large clearing deep in the woods and sat down on a fallen tree trunk. He was breathing hard, a tick-lish rasping in his chest. Fucking fags. He took a half-smoked joint from behind his ear, lit it and swung the knapsack down off his shoulder.

The gun was black with a chequered-wood grip, the wood warm and natural against the palm of his hand, the metal trigger guard icy cold against the back of his forefinger. Lee pushed the release forward with his thumb and the cylinder sprang out – six empty chambers facing him. He sat the weapon on the knapsack and took out the cardboard box. He counted out the bullets, surprised at how heavy they were, and loaded six into the gun, pleased at how snugly the brass cartridges slotted into their individual compartments. He tried to flip the chamber shut with a flick of his wrist, the way you saw them do it in the films. Three of the bullets fell out. Lee picked them up, reloaded and closed the chamber carefully.

He reached back into the knapsack and took out the copy of the *Sun* he'd bought on the way up here. He flipped through and found a full-page photograph of some Hollywood actress, some daft hoor that Lisa liked. Lee tore it out, walked across the clearing, and used his penknife to stick the page to the trunk of a big tree. He walked away from the tree, counted off twenty paces and turned round.

The woods, the gun, target practice: it all reminded him of some film he'd seen once, years ago, with his dad. Some mad cunt trying to assassinate the president of Spain, or some mad fucking place. He shot a melon or something with this mental bullet and the whole thing blew up. What was the name of the film? Fucking memory oan him. No real.

Lee took a last heavy drag on the spliff, raised the gun in his right hand and pulled back the hammer with his thumb. It took a surprising amount of strength. He closed his left eye and squinted down the barrel, over the sight and towards the target. Slowly he squeezed the trigger.

CRACK! Birds flew from the branches overhead and Lee's hand jerked up and back.

The photograph, the entire tree, remained untouched.

Tongue out in concentration now, Lee took the pistol in both hands, crouched down into a shooting stance and fired again.

Coughing through the acrid gunsmoke, sweating, his ears ringing from the concussion, Lee saw that both photograph and tree remained unscathed.

He edged a few paces nearer, stuck the gun out and tugged the trigger angrily. A third bang and still not a mark on the photograph.

'FUCK YOU, YA FUCKING HOOR!' Lee screamed as

he ran up to the tree and fired three times at point-blank range into the photograph, bark splintering everywhere, the girl's face disappearing in scorched newsprint. Lee slumped down at the foot of the tree, panting.

Later, on the drive home, the needle living triumphantly in the top half of the petrol gauge since his meeting with Alec, it back came to him: *The Day of the Jackal*, that was it. That was the bloody film. Lee couldn't be sure, it was a long time ago and his memory wasn't what it was, but he had a feeling it hadn't ended too well for the Jackal cunt. It hadn't been his fucking day at all . . .

'When ah think of all the hours you had tae work to pay for aw the stuff she wanted done tae that bloody house,' Cathy said, busy with the corkscrew, 'and then *she* walks out oan *you*, son . . .'

He'd known something was wrong as soon as he walked in the front door (tired and hung-over, he and Stevie had hit the bars of Musselburgh pretty hard to celebrate his qualification) and there was no barking. He'd put his golf bag down in the hall and walked through to the kitchen. 'Ben?' he'd shouted to the empty house. Then he saw it – the single sheet of A4 notepaper on the kitchen table, covered in Pauline's girlish handwriting. How many hearts have been destroyed in such a fashion? He scanned it quickly, the key words leaping off the page: '*my own space for a while . . . drifting apart . . . unhappy . . .*'

He'd been dying to tell her that he'd got through. That it hadn't been a waste of time.

He went round to see his mum, and here she was, cooking and – in her own fashion – comforting.

'*Her own space for a while*,' Cathy repeated, rereading the letter while she poured them both some wine. 'Me and your father were together nearly thirty years. We never needed oor own bloody "space"! Has she no got enough bloody space? All the money ye spent oan that extension?'

'Things are – fuck, ya cunt ye, sorry, Mum – different nowadays, Mum,' Gary said, not really sure what he meant. Back home with his mum, in the house he'd grown up in. They were eating dinner at the little table at the back of the living room: chicken grilled on Cathy's 'Magic-Griller', a plastic and metal clamp which magically removed all fat from the meat as it cooked it, less magically removing all flavour too. The pale, dry breast came accompanied by peas, potatoes and carrots, all of which Cathy appeared to have been boiling since before decimalisation.

'Where's she gone?' Cathy asked.

'She's staying – HOOR! – with her pal Katrina.'

'Och, that wan's a fine example. Is she no divorced aboot three times herself?'

'Twice, Mum.'

'And have ye tried calling her?'

'Her phone's off. Fucking boots, ya slut. Sorry.'

'Aye,' Cathy sighed, 'it's some state of affairs right enough.' Her eyes misted over as she gazed into the mid-distance. 'Ah'm only glad he's no here to see this. One of you separated from your wife and the other one . . . God only knows what's going to happen tae that boy. Just recently I had to lend him two hundred pounds to pay this loan the two of them took out – to buy that new sofa and that stupid big telly they didnae even need – and that wisnae the first time ah've lent him money recently, let me tell you . . .'

'Mmm,' Gary said, a significant and long-standing creditor of Lee's himself.

'Anyway, last night, naw, night before last it was. He came

in and says he's got some job he's doing. Pays me it back! Two hundred pound in cash. Counts it right oot oan the kitchen table.'

'What kind of – flaps – job? Pishflapsyaboot.'

'Och, he said something to do wi his pal Scooter and that tyre business he's got. Selling a load of tyres tae some place in Glasgow.'

'Well, that's good, isn't it?' Gary said with a positivity he did not feel. 'Christ, Mum, you're worried when he borrows money off you – fucktitsbaws – then you're worried when he pays it back!'

'Ah just . . . ah worry he slips back into his old ways. Starts hanging aboot wi aw they druggies and God knows what again. Ah couldnae take it he had to go . . . away again. See, the nights I lie in ma bed and I think aboot . . .'

And Cathy was off; a torrent of worry, fear and paranoia roped together into a wine-hazed monologue. Gary switched to AutoAye, reading the paper and saying 'Aye' and 'Aye?' while he tried to convince himself that it really was possible that Lee was enjoying fruitful employment in the world of wholesale radial tyres.

Meanwhile, up in Glasgow, in the gathering dusk of the newsroom, April was finishing off her story. A little bit of googling had yielded her the full *Ardgirvan Gazette* story – Gary's 'incident' on the eighteenth green at Ravenscroft. She'd rung the reporter for a few more details, the hick being mightily impressed to have someone from the big leagues calling. She moved the cursor up onto the little disk and clicked to save. She sat back, lit only by the soft grey-white light from the screen and chewed on a ragged thumbnail while she thought. A moment passed and then a grin began spreading across her face, a grin known to subeditors across the world. April quickly typed the headline in above the piece and hit 'Save' again.

Devlin would wet himself.

32

STEVIE INCHED THE CAR ALONG THROUGH THE CROWDS towards the golf course. The week before the Open and the world had descended on the little coastal town of Troon, which swelled from around 10,000 inhabitants to nearer 60,000 during the championship. The competition began on the Thursday morning, but the course was opened to players for practice play on the Sunday before. Already there were throngs of people wandering through the streets, heading to the course for the opportunity to watch the world's most famous golfers getting to grips with the turf and the weather.

There were TV stations from every major nation on earth, with their miles of cabling and their camera towers and their microphones like big furry pills. There were journalists, caterers, course marshals, punters, pundits and, of course, the players and their entourages – their teams of head doctors, swing gurus, putting consiglieres, managers, agents, personal trainers, personal chefs and personal assistants.

The big guns had rented the finest private houses close to

the course. The players a little further down the ladder – the journeymen, the everyday tour pros who performed supporting roles in the superstars' movie – were in the nicer hotels. The few amateurs took their chances in bed and breakfasts.

Gary and Stevie had managed to find a twin room in a tiny B&B on the outskirts of town for the week. He'd be glad to be out of the house. It was strange without Pauline. The place lay dead around him, the rooms silent, no roaring of her hairdryer from the bedroom, no chattering of her electric toothbrush from the bathroom. His things stayed in the sad heaps where he put them until he moved them himself. He felt no impulse to cook for himself, choosing to eat out – or even round at his mum's house – rather than sit in the living room waiting to hear the three icy digital beeps from the microwave, Morse code telling him that now he was going to die alone. He even missed Ben, that eternal engine of pain, with his ceaseless snuffling, growling and whining.

They pulled up at the booth guarding the entrance to the clubhouse car park and a man in a fluorescent yellow security jacket approached them, walkie-talkie crackling. 'Come on, boys, you'll have to move tha—' Stevie calmly held up the orange vehicle pass. 'Oh, sorry,' the guard said, instantly softening. 'Please, just follow the road around towards the clubhouse and park anywhere you like.'

'Thank you,' Stevie said pleasantly, grinning at Gary as he pulled away. Two years ago, when they'd gone up to St Andrews to watch the Open, they'd ended up parking about two miles out of town and walking the rest of the way. Now here they were, pulling up right in front of the clubhouse, in a row of spaces marked 'PLAYER PARKING ONLY'.

Gary got out and looked up at the long, low sandstone

building. Just as he was trying to fully comprehend that he was about to register as a competitor in the Open, he caught the eye of a passing stranger and his world was knocked completely off its axis by five words. The words were 'Hi there, how ya doing?' and the speaker, the passing stranger, was Gram Novotell – two times winner of the US Open. It took a few seconds for Gary to register this, which was just as well because Novotell was swiftly down the steps and had folded his six-foot-three-inch frame into a waiting courtesy car before Gary, his face flushing, had time to splutter his panicked response. 'Ooohyabigcuntye!' he stammered at the boot of the departing car.

'What?' Stevie said over his shoulder, hauling the golf bag from the boot, oblivious to who had just passed them by.

'Shit!' Gary said, clamping his hand over his mouth. *Calm down, get a hold of yourself. Obviously there's going to be famous golfers here. It's the Open for fuck's sake! It's no big deal. They're just guys like you.*

'Are you OK?' Stevie asked, the golf bag over one shoulder, their player registration forms in his free hand.

'Aye, fine.'

Up the stone steps and into the polished wood and thick carpeting of the clubhouse lobby. Stevie strode towards the registration desk set up at the end of the long lobby, Gary following behind, his gaze flickering around, catching faces, faces he knew well.

There was Torsten Lathe (*fucking Nazi wank baws*) talking to Kevin McKerrick (*ooh ya dirty Fenian prick ye*).

It felt like his head was buckling under the nerves and stress, his interior monologue becoming a blur of obscenities, every one horribly shaped to fit with whatever he looked at. He bit his lip and tried to keep his head down. *Just keep following Stevie*. But he couldn't help it. He glanced to his right – Bent Hendricks (*fanny fuck poofy name fuck*) explaining something to commentator Rowland Daventry (*FuckEnglishtitscunt*). Gary began to twitch and had to clamp a hand over his mouth to stifle a yelp. He looked around to see if anyone had noticed and there was Montgomery Hymen (*fuckingbignoseJewFUCK*) laughing at something James Honeydew III (*wankYankwank*) was saying.

Stevie handed Gary's registration documents over to a smiling middle-aged lady. 'Ah yes,' she said, handing over a form. 'Could you fill this in please, Mr Irvine?'

'Ah, aye . . . f—' He was flushed, sweating. Stevie looked at him.

'Are you sure you're OK?'

'Yeah, just . . . hot.' Gary glanced to his left. The world number seven, the black American player Cyrus Cheeks – six and a half feet tall and bald as a schemie's tyre – was checking in next to him. He looked down at Gary and smiled.

That did it.

'OWW!' Gary yelped. The woman behind the desk jumped a little and everyone looked at him.

Oh shit, Stevie thought.

'Are you OK, fella?' Cheeks asked.

'Fuckingprick,' Gary said in a thick, rapid accent. 'Fucking golfprick.'

'Excuse me?' Cheeks said, still smiling uncertainly.

'Sorry,' Stevie said, turning Gary away from him, 'he's just excited. Can,' Stevie said to the woman behind the desk, 'can we just –'

'Big tits,' Gary said.

'*I beg your pardon?*' the woman said.

'Sorry! Fucking big-titted hoor jugs spunk FUCK!'

The woman gasped, everyone in the place looking at them

now. Cheeks leaned in towards them. 'Hey, what's the problem here?'

Gary turned to face Cheeks, a man whose game he'd admired for years, and said, 'Fucking massive darkie ye!' 'Darkie' pronounced 'Dorr-kay' in the full Ayrshire manner and incomprehensible to Cheeks' ears. 'Sorry! Shit! Fucking Malteser-heeded cunt. FUCK! Grrrrrrr!'

'What'd he say?' Cheeks asked Stevie.

'YA FUCKING BLACK B—' Gary began.

Before he could finish the sentence Stevie booted Gary in the balls as hard as he possibly could and he went down growling in agony in front of everyone in the clubhouse lobby.

'Sorry about that, folks,' Stevie said, helping Gary to his feet and towards the door. He turned back to the woman on the desk, her jaw lolling on the table among her passes, badges and forms. 'Thanks for your help. We'll come back and sort it out later.'

The woman watched them go. She recovered her composure and reached for her telephone.

After Pauline moved in with Katrina, in recognition of the fact that their relationship – while still secret – was moving onto a new level, Masterson gave her the loveliest thing he had ever given her, a beautiful artefact that made Pauline's heart leap in her chest: a new credit card. Gary's calls went unanswered on her new mobile (ice blue, slim as her new credit card) and his messages unchecked. When he did cross her mind over those first few days it was in the form of an abstract problem she had yet to fully solve.

As often as he could manage it, Masterson would come over to visit her, arriving after dark and parking a little way along the street. (And Ben's reaction to the first time he observed Masterson defiling Pauline was a super-fury of such ferocity – his snapping jaws inches from Masterson's pale buttocks – that Pauline realised Ben may have *loved* Gary all along.)

'Do we have to live here?' Pauline asked him in bed one night. 'I thought we could maybe move somewhere a bit more . . . cosmopolitan.'

The thought of living anywhere other than Ardgirvan had never crossed Masterson's mind. Where else was there?

'What, like . . . Ayr?' he said cautiously.

'I was thinking maybe Glasgow?'

'Glasgow?' he repeated, managing to make it sound like 'Uzbekistan'.

'Yeah. There's some beautiful new houses being built on the South Side, near Shawlands? Private development. Katrina and I had a wee nosy in the estate agent's the other day.'

'Aye, well. Let's think about it, eh?'

'I'll get them to send the house details for us to have a look at. Maybe we –'

'Jesus Christ, Pauline! Like I've no got enough on my plate the now?'

Silence. The same silence that always arose whenever the subject of Leanne swam near the surface of the conversation. Pauline had not asked exactly what Masterson had decided to do in connection with Leanne, but she knew they weren't getting a divorce.

In the mind of the sociopath, subjects like this are dropped into a box labelled 'UNPLEASANT'. The box itself is then firmly sealed and tucked away in a distant corner of the vast, dark, spider-filled warehouse of the unconscious. The conscious mind is then furnished with a pretty confection that is presented to the world as 'truth', this 'truth' gradually becoming reality in the mind of the sociopath. In Pauline's case this process was already quite far along.

Leanne really was going to have some kind of 'accident'.

'Sorry,' Pauline said. 'I was just trying to think about our new life together.'

'Aye, ah'm sorry too. Ah didnae mean to snap at ye, hen,' he said, pulling her naked body closer to him in the warm bed.

33

BORN FROM THE SOCIETY OF ST ANDREWS GOLFERS AND awarded royal status in 1834 by King William IV himself, the Royal and Ancient Golf Club of St Andrews is the historic and venerable body responsible for overseeing the rules and etiquette surrounding the sport. In its long and distinguished history the R&A has grappled with issues as varied and intricate as the acceptable dimensions of golf balls, the appropriate dress code for players, and the notion of exactly what constitutes excessively slow play on the course. It had never had to deal with an issue like the one now before R&A Chairman Jeremy Park and his four-man disciplinary committee in the small conference room at Royal Troon.

Stevie and Gary sat before the committee like schoolboys in front of the headmaster, Gary twisting his visor in his hands.

Did players swear and indulge in violent displays of temper during competition play? Yes, of course they did. The miscreants were fined and admonished, but such outbursts were regarded as a necessary by-product of a sport that could turn a man from a striding god into a salivating mental patient in the 1.4 seconds it took to swing a golf club. But, a player swearing at an official in the clubhouse? Making lewd and unsavoury sexual comments towards her? Insulting other competitors, making racist comments, and then being physically assaulted by their own caddie? Park had never heard the like.

'I've never heard the like,' he said, turning left and right to look at his fellow committee members. 'And you claim this is a medical condition? Something called . . . Tourette's syndrome?'

'Yes, Mr Park. Sir.' Gary couldn't look him in the eye. 'I, when it happens, I don't even know that I'm doing it. Fffff—' With great effort he stopped himself.

'Extraordinary,' one of the other committee members said. Stevie looked along the line of blazers, ties and grey faces.

'And what,' one of them asked, 'are we to make of this?' He held up a copy of the sports section of that morning's *Daily Standard*: a photo of Gary, raising his club after finishing his round at Musselburgh. Above the photograph the headline screamed: 'HOLE IN WAN-KER!'

He tossed the paper across to them. April had been thorough; the accident, the Tourette's, the Kluver-Bucy, the eighteenth green at Ravenscroft. 'Your pal, the tabloid journalist,' Stevie said as Gary looked at the little photo of April at the top of the page.

'We're very sorry for your . . . afflictions,' Park said, leaning forward and clasping his hands together, 'but we have to think about the risk of an outburst of this sort damaging the reputation of the Open. We have to think of your playing partners too. How might they be affected if, during their backswing, you decided to shout something like – what did you say to Mrs Porter?' Park picked up a sheet of paper, squinted at it and swallowed as he read the words '*big-titted whore jugs spunkfuck*'. 'Yes, I'm afraid we have no option but to disqualify you. I'm really very sorry.'

Gary burst into tears.

Park and the disciplinary committee looked on astonished as he fell to his knees, wringing his hands, the words coming out in gasps between the sobs: *'OH GOD! Oh p-please . . . l-let me . . . p-play!'*

'On what grounds are you disqualifying him?' Stevie said loudly enough to be heard over the sobbing, looking directly at Park, ignoring Gary.

'On the grounds that he might disrupt the competition,' Park replied.

'Might?' Stevie said.

'Well, yes.'

'I don't believe it's legal to punish someone because of what they "might" do. If that was the case half the bloody country would be locked up.'

'Legal?' someone said.

'Also, and correct me if I'm wrong,' Stevie continued, 'but didn't Drew Keel "disrupt the competition" when he smashed a driver in half at Hoylake three years ago? Didn't Calvin Linklater "disrupt the competition" when he told a spectator he was going to "break his fucking nose" for trying to take a photo during his backswing last year? Didn't –'

'Yes, yes,' Park said impatiently, 'but these were all one-off incidents. Completely unforeseeable. In this case there's medical . . . evidence that –'

'There's what?'

'Medical evidence.'

'Tourette's syndrome is not "medical evidence" of anything.

It's a *handicap*. The kind of handicap recognised by the British Medical Association.' Stevie let this sink in for a moment before continuing. 'There's a load of journalists from all the Scottish papers out there.' Stevie jerked a thumb in the direction of the outside world. 'How do you think they'd like a story about the R&A disqualifying a local boy – someone from just along the road who's made it all the way through the qualifying process – just because he suffers from a recognised disability?'

'We . . .' Park began and then stopped.

On the floor Gary had stopped crying. He dried his eyes with his sleeve, looking up at them like a wretched, beaten animal.

'Now,' Stevie crossed his legs and continued in the same even tone, 'if you want to take away a young man's lifelong dream, if you want to tarnish the whole idea of what the "Open" championship is supposed to be about, then go ahead and disqualify him before he's even hit a ball. But make no mistake, my friends – you will be entering a shitstorm of negative press like you wouldn't believe. You'll think that a front-page story implying you're all kiddie fiddlers is a positive development.'

Park exhaled a long breath through his teeth. He tapped his pen on his notepad. He turned to the man on his left and they whispered. He turned to the man on his right and they whispered. He cleared his throat and looked down at Gary, still hunched on the floor.

'One further incident of this nature . . .' Park began.

'That's very kind of you,' Stevie said, extending a hand to help Gary up from the carpet and leading him off towards the door, looking very much like a circus entertainer leading a shambling chimp by the hand. The door closed behind them.

'Extraordinary,' the man on Park's right said.

'Make sure he's off the tee very early for the first two rounds,' Park said. 'Before the TV coverage really starts.'

'And then?' another man said.

'Come on,' Park said, 'the chances of him making the cut are about a thousand to one.'

34

APRIL SCANNED THE BUSY TENT – AGENTS, PRS, PLAYERS and managers all bustling in and out of various suites, glad-handing a combination of journalists, sponsors, TV producers and the like. All strictly B-list, however; the brief appearance of Cyrus Cheeks had aroused the only real flicker of interest in the media centre all morning.

In years gone by the days running up to the opening Thursday of the competition used to be a quiet time for the players: practice rounds in the morning, a little tweaking on the range in the afternoon, dinner and maybe a few drinks with some buddies in the evening, the only real interruption being the traditional pro-am match on the Wednesday. Nowadays, for the top players, there were demands being made upon their time almost every minute of the day: photo opportunities, face time with sponsors and advertisers, people like April clamouring for interviews.

'Hi, doll.' April turned. Donald Lawson, Senior Sports Reporter, *Daily Standard*, stood beaming down at her. All twenty-two stones of him. He had a brimming glass of red wine in one hand and a plateful of sausage rolls in the other.

'Oh. Hi, Donald.'

'I heard you were coming down.' Lawson smiled. 'Got a wee human interest story on the go, have we?'

'Fuck off.'

'Language, dear. No, I think it's nice. Ah'll catch ye in the bar later, eh? Ah've a wee interview with your man Drew Keel to get out the way first.'

'Watch you don't eat him by mistake,' April said, nodding towards the greasy fistful of sausage rolls before turning and walking out of the media tent, trying to look purposeful, as though she really did have somewhere to go. What now though? Maybe swing by the practice range and see if there was anyone interesting about. She turned round and someone walked straight into her. 'Hey! Why don't you – oh.'

'Fuck,' Gary said.

'Hi.'

'Thanks – cunt. Sorry! – Thanks a bunch.'

'Listen, Gary, it's –'

'Yeah, really lovely profile of me. Great. Fannies. Hoor ye. Cheers.'

'Listen, it's just –'

'I should have listened to Stevie. Fat cunt. Ooh ya fat cunt ye,' Gary said, walking off now, jaw twitching.

'Hang on, wait!' April fell into step beside him. 'Look, I'm sorry, OK? It's just the job. It's how you sell papers.'

'*Hole in Wanker*?'

April bit her lip. 'I'm sorry, OK? Look, no one remembers these things –'

'I fucking will!'

'Stop, hang on. Please, Gary.' April put a hand on his arm

and they stood off to the side of the metal walkway they'd been clanking along, people passing by them in all directions. 'I hate to say it but you just weren't enough of a story otherwise. Fucking Donald's covering the tournament itself and I . . . I wanted to get a piece in too. If you do well enough I might get a chance to write something else about you. Something better.'

'Better than "foul-mouthed compulsive masturbator"?'

'Umm . . .' She smiled naughtily. God, she had a nice smile, Gary thought. 'Sorry about that. Got away from me a wee bit.' There was a pause, both of them shuffling awkwardly on the sandy grass. 'Where are you off to now?' April asked.

'Back to the clubhouse for a shower. Slut. Dirty slut tits. Sorry. Been on the range for a while.'

April nodded and they stood in silence for a moment.

'Look, I could lie to you,' she said. 'Tell you some crap about how the subs rewrote the piece behind my back. But I wrote it. I . . . I'm just trying to get my foot in the door.'

Suddenly she looked very young and vulnerable.

'Well, I suppose it'll be – fuck – "lining the budgie cages tomorrow" as my mum says.'

She looked up at him, squinting into the sun, shielding her eyes with her hand, and said, 'Do you fancy coming for walk on the beach?'

Gary thought. 'Off the record?' he asked.

'Off the record.'

It was a fine july morning, the Irish Sea still, green and glittering under a huge sun. April stopped for a moment and grabbed Gary's arm, steadying herself as she slipped off her shoes. Gary looked around, inhaling fresh sea air, conscious of her grip around his elbow, strangely calming to him, the need to yelp and bark and curse fading. 'Ah, that's better,' she said, continuing barefoot through the warm sand, gulls crying overhead and a ferry silhouetted on the blue horizon, edging its way back from Arran.

'You come from around here, don't you?' April said, remembering.

'You see those?' Gary said, pointing. April followed his forefinger north along the shoreline to where, a few miles away, four squat tower blocks stood darkly against the sky.

'Mmm.'

'That's what we call the "high flats". I live not too far from them. You see this pipe just up here?' He pointed again, to where a black iron pipe, the iron stained and pitted orange with rust, ran across the beach and into the sea. 'That's the shite pipe. You don't swim near that. When we were little there was a basking shark – massive thing – washed up on the beach here. Dead. It was there for weeks. Everyone said it had swum too close to the shite pipe and died from inhaling the toxic jobbies of all the bams from Ardgirvan.'

April laughed.

'Who's we?' she asked, one hand behind her back, loosely holding her shoes.

'Eh?'

'You said "when *we* were little"?'

'Oh. Well, me and my brother I suppose I meant.'

'Older or younger?'

'Older. He's . . . Anyway, how about you? Brothers? Sisters?'

'Both. He's a lawyer, she's a doctor. I'm the black sheep, the evil tabloid journalist.'

'I quite fancied university,' Gary said. 'I got an offer from Glasgow.'

'Why didn't you go?'

'Well, I got offered a pretty good job. Pauline wanted – we both wanted – to buy a house, get on the property ladder. You know. Being a student, three or four years with no money . . . it seemed like a long time back then.'

To April the thought was incredible: make a decision about who you were going to spend the rest of your life with while you were still a teenager? Christ, she was twenty-six and she'd only recently decided what her favourite drink was, in the way that she knew automatically what she was going to have in the pub. 'Is she going to be here this week? Cheering you on?'

'Ah, I don't think so. She's moved out for a wee while. Staying with a pal of hers. We've been having some problems.'

'Oh,' April said, embarrassed. 'I'm sorry.'

'It's just, since the accident, with all my . . . stuff and everything. It's been a lot for her to cope with.'

'I'm sure you'll sort it out.'

'Yeah.'

They sat down on the shite pipe and looked out to sea, at the grey mound of Ailsa Craig, an island of rock jutting up in the Firth of Clyde. A few hundred yards along the beach a woman in a pink tracksuit was jogging down the surfline.

'Ailsa Craig,' April said.

'Aye, they'll take ye away tae Ailsa,' Gary said.

'Eh?'

'There used to be a mental hospital in Ayrshire called Ailsa. If you were acting up when you were a kid your mum and dad would say they'd come and take you away to Ailsa . . .'

'You know something?' April said, turning to face him. 'You haven't sworn at all since we've been down here.'

'Well, the doctors said I was less likely to have outbursts in situations I was comfortable with . . .'

'So you're comfortable with this?' April said.

'Yeah, I am,' Gary said, smiling.

Just then the jogging woman slowly passed by them a few yards away, her jog not much more than an exaggerated walk. She was a big girl, the best part of fifteen stones, April reckoned, with a tangled mop of curly brown, sweat-drenched hair. They were the only three people on the stretch of beach and she waved cheerily to them, mouthing the word 'hello'. April smiled and waved back.

'FAT PINK HOOR!' Gary screamed.

He clamped his hand over his mouth. 'Sorry! Christ.' But April was laughing, having already seen the white headphone wires trailing up into the thick nest of the woman's hair.

'You'll get sent to Ailsa,' April said.

PART FOUR
THE OPEN

The attraction of the virtuoso for the public is very like that of the circus for the crowd. There is always the hope that something dangerous will happen.

Claude Debussy

Not being a machine, you simply can't hold onto 'perfect' form at golf for very long. The game is thus a continual balancing act.

Jack Nicklaus

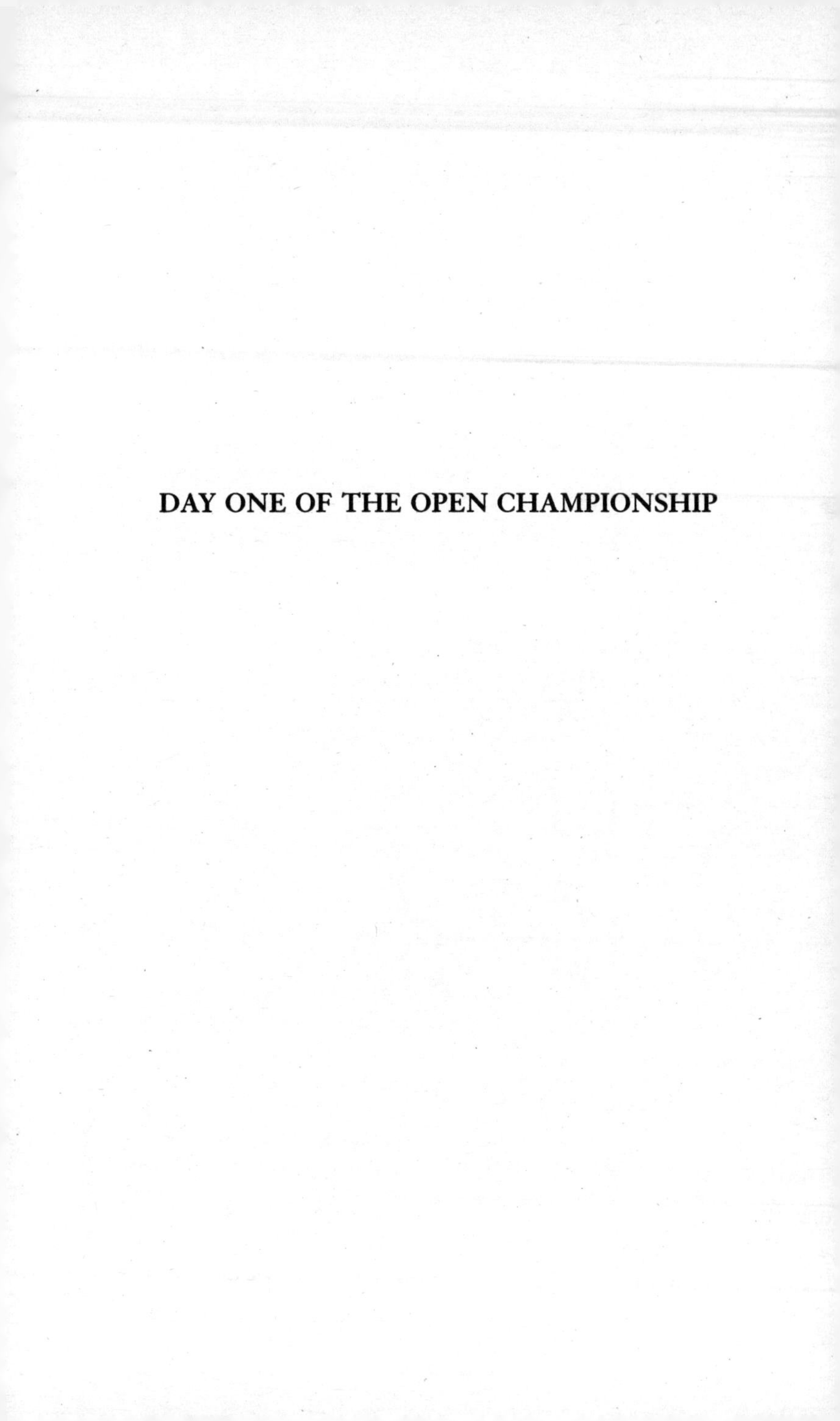

DAY ONE OF THE OPEN CHAMPIONSHIP

35

GARY AWOKE AT 6.15 WITH BLOOD HURRYING THROUGH his veins, a squalling pit of butterflies in his stomach, and a life-threatening erection tenting the sheets. Stevie was already gone from the other twin bed, doubtless downstairs cramming a full English into himself. Briskly, Gary masturbated, showered, shaved and dressed and was sipping coffee down in the lounge when Stevie pulled the car around at exactly 6.45. He went out and threw his clubs into the back seat. 'Are we ready?' Stevie asked, looking at him very seriously as he climbed in.

'We're ready.'

'Are we mean?'

'We're mean.'

'What are we?'

'Eh?'

'Christ – we're mean and ready!'

Stevie whirled the volume knob on the stereo all the way to the right and the opening chords of 'Complete

Control' filled the car at deafening volume as they screeched off.

The roads quiet and the Clash loud as they drove through the Ayrshire summer morning, just the cows yawning in the fields around Troon, a milk float and a fat-bellied jet lumbering in over them on its way to Prestwick.

Through the town, a couple of eager lads already out and coming down the first fairway at Dalry as they came along the road leading towards the seafront, the Royal Troon clubhouse proud on their left as Stevie flashed their pass and pulled into the car park.

'Fuck,' Gary said as they got out the car and looked down towards the sea.

'Jesus Christ,' said Stevie.

Stevie was not one to be often moved by the majesty of nature (and a golf course was not exactly nature either, it was nature shaped and coerced so that a few square miles of it ran parallel with some men's twisted idea of a good time) but, right at that moment, it was as though God Himself had run a gentle hand over this stretch of the Scottish coastline, caressing and finessing what was already beautiful into something incredible. A translucent sheen of dew sparkled over the whole course, broken here and there by the zigzagging tyre tracks of the green staff's vehicles as they crisscrossed the course, making last-minute checks and adjustments, reraking sand and combing tiny stones from the greens. A silver mist hung over the sand dunes that marked the boundary of the course and the beach. The air was cool and still, not even a breath of wind to ruffle the flags.

Their start time was so early that there was a grand total of five spectators gathered around the first tee when they walked onto it. There was Cathy and Aunt Sadie, grinning and thumbs-upping. Next to them, giving Gary a sombre nod, was Auld Bert, attending his first Open since the late seventies. Dr Robertson smiled. He'd taken the time off work to be there. Just in case. And there, next to Robertson, waving with a silver Thermos of coffee, was April. 'Good luck, son!' Cathy shrieked over the thin trickle of applause.

A man walked over and shook Gary's hand in businesslike fashion. He was in his late forties and wore check trousers and a bright red sweater vest, his accent was American, springy and Southern. 'Crawford Koon,' he said simply. Gary placed the name – an old-school journeyman pro. He'd been on the tour since the early 1980s. Never won anything big.

The third member of their three ball was a young English professional who'd come through the qualifying process. Dean Coffey was in his early twenties and decked out in the requisite fluorescent chinos and polo shirt. Like Gary, it was his first Open.

'Awright, mate!' he said, shaking Gary's hand.

'How ye doing?' Gary said.

'Facking shitting meself, mate!' Coffey replied.

'Gentlemen?' the starter said. 'If you're ready . . .'

Stevie handed Gary the driver. 'Nothing fancy, just knock this one up the middle,' he said.

'On the tee now, from Ravenscroft Golf Club, Ardgirvan, amateur competitor, Mr Gary Irvine!'

Whooping and whistling as Gary walked onto the tee. 'You go on yourself, Gary son!' Sadie said. 'Gary! Gary!' his mum chanted. Gary grinned sheepishly at them.

'Got the fan club here, then?' Coffey said.

Gary teed up his ball and everyone fell silent. He took a few loose easy practice swings, feeling for the tempo, and then sighted down the fairway. The first hole at Royal Troon, 'Seal', is a par four that runs away from the clubhouse and doglegs slightly left. The penalties are severe if the tee shot is offline; thick gorse and marram-grassed hillocks abound. With the sea hard by on the player's right, many a round has been wrecked early on with a sliced – or even slightly pushed – drive spiralling into deep trouble. Gary cracked it hard down the right-hand edge of the fairway. They watched as it started to fall to earth drawing slowly to the left.

Too slowly.

It landed on the edge of the fairway, took a crazy bounce to the right and vanished.

'Uh-oh', Stevie said, using the two-syllable golf shorthand for despair for the first time that day. Oh well, Gary thought, so the first shot hadn't gone their way. No big deal . . .

'So, aye,' Masterson was saying, 'Ah've just checked in. We're going tae go fur a walk up around the university this morning. Some buildings up there the boy says. Right fucking . . . old. Ancient an aw that. Then we'll go and see some film and then oot fur something tae eat. The boy fancies this bloody Japanese place so he does. Raw fucking fish. Ah telt him there's no way ah'm eating that pish, but he says they've got chicken and rice and stuff so ah'll get something so ah will. Aye, so, er, yer no going to go out tonight then?' he said.

'No. I told you, Karen's away on holiday,' Leanne said, 'Audrey's not well, I'm just going to get a film out and have a night in by myself.'

'Aye, right enough, hen. Ye did tell me. So ye did. Aye.' Masterson was standing up by the blue-tinted, floor-to-ceiling windows of his suite on the twenty-second floor of the Glasgow Hilton. From the adjacent bedroom he could hear the crashes and bullets of the billion-dollar atrocity his son was watching on Pay TV. Always had to be spending bloody money. Couldnae sit and watch normal telly for an hour. He didnae even like the football. Sometimes Masterson wondered if his son was . . . naw, no way. No fucking danger. 'Well, have a nice night then, doll. Ah'll try and phone ye later.'

'Don't call after eleven,' Leanne said. 'I'm going to have an early night.'

Another one of her early nights. He pictured it – her away over on her side of the bed, her back to him, grunting or tutting if he kept the telly on a minute past eleven o'clock. Christ, Leanne bored him. All the same, this would probably be the last time he ever spoke to her, to this woman he'd once loved. Should he have something profound to say?

'Aye, right, well, bye then, hen.'

'Bye.'

Click. That was that.

Masterson hung up. He badly wanted a drink, a big glug of whisky or something, but it was barely ten o'clock in the morning. He realised there was no way he was going to get through this day sober. Would there be a bar at this cinema? Maybe no. He'd have to make sure this fucking Jap restaurant was licensed. He dialled Pauline's number but it went straight to voicemail. Where was she going today? To look at some house or other? Maybe she was right. Maybe they should move away. Think about Pauline – that was the way to get through this. Think about those breasts, the arse cheeks. All his. Forever. Keep thinking about that. He stood there and pressed his forehead against the cold glass, his temples going numb as he watched the traffic flowing in and out of the city.

* * *

Leanne walked through the big, empty house towards the kitchen, thinking that there had been something weird about the phone call, other than the fact that it was unusual for him ever to call her without a specific reason. 'Just for a chat.' It was a few minutes later, as her hot-cross bun was bouncing up out of the toaster, that she put her finger on it.

Nervous.

He'd sounded nervous.

36

A COUPLE OF HOURS LATER AND *NOTHING* WAS GOING their way. It was unbelievable. Stevie had no idea a golf course could change so much in the one day it took to move from practice play into the first round of competition. From a relatively benign stretch of turf, a difficult yet solvable succession of problems, to a hostile, malicious living thing – a sentient creature hell-bent on your personal destruction – within less than twenty-four hours. They'd made four bogeys in the first six holes and (almost) none of them had really been Gary's fault.

Now they trudged towards the seventh green in silence, four over par. For the first time in the round all three players had found the green in two regulation strokes, but they were all a good distance from the hole on an enormous green baked lightning fast by the weeks of warm weather.

As they walked across the green towards Gary's ball (both of them conscious of the fact that it took thirty-four paces to cover the distance from hole to ball. 1 pace = approx. 1 yard,

1 yard = 3 feet, so a putt of over a hundred feet) Gary noticed the unmanned TV cameras around the green, shrouded in polythene, their eyes black and lifeless and pointed at the ground, ready to be activated as soon as a match worth televising came around the course.

He crouched down behind the ball, trying for a read. It was hopeless: downhill, breaking left to right and then, about two-thirds of the way to the hole, turning uphill and breaking right to left and then – maybe – back the other way again as it got to the hole.

'What do you think?' Gary asked Stevie, who was crouching behind him.

Stevie tried to read the putt, but it was Sanskrit. Hieroglyphics. In lieu of something intelligent to say about the line of the putt he tried to think of something more general and inspirational. What would Martin Luther King have said? What would *Strummer* have said?

'Nice and firm up the middle,' Stevie said.

They both felt like what they were: two chancers who shouldn't have been there.

Gary sighed and settled the putter head behind the ball. Not really caring at this point, he just made a nice easy slap, ignoring the break and sending it straight up the middle. The ball charged at speed downhill, looking like it had been massively overstruck. It started to veer right, looking like it would end up twenty yards offline. It turned left as it began heading uphill, slowing down dramatically now, looking like it would never reach the crest of the incline. But it did, rolling slightly downhill now, gathering pace and changing course a third time as it turned gently towards the hole. At this point, at exactly the same time, Stevie and Gary both said, 'Aye, yer maw.'

The ball hit the cup very hard, hopped three inches into the air above it, and then plopped down into the hole with a satisfying rattle to give Gary his first birdie of the day. His little gallery burst into spontaneous cheering and applause. Stevie and Gary looked at each other and simply burst out laughing.

Suddenly Gary's mind was racing, utterly transformed in the second it took for the ball to drop into the cup. From a hellish four over par to three over in a heartbeat. Three over wasn't so bad. He still had eleven more holes to play. He only had to make three more birdies and he'd be level par – a fresh start from which anything might be possible. And suddenly the eleven holes that still lay before him had been transformed from an ordeal to be survived into a flowering paradise overflowing with birdie opportunities.

This feeling of transcendent power and potential was to last approximately three and a half minutes: the time that elapsed between sinking his putt on the seventh and striking his tee shot on the eighth. The eighth at Royal Troon.

The Postage Stamp.

One of the most famous holes in golf, at just 126 yards long it is the shortest hole on the Open rota and earns its name from the size of its tiny green. The green itself is surrounded by bunkers – deep fearsome maws which have devoured many less than perfectly struck tee shots and wrecked many a man's round and sanity.

A German amateur by the name of Herman Tissies, playing in the 1950 Open Championship, found one of the left-hand bunkers with his tee shot. Five shots later he managed to launch his ball out of the bunker . . . and into another one. Another five shots and he succeeded in dislodging his ball from this bunker, sending it flying back into the original bunker. Tissies managed to get out of this bunker in only three shots and holed out for a card-incinerating 15.

Even Calvin Linklater had once carded a dreadful quintuple bogey nine here.

Incredible that a straight, simple 126-yard par three – just a slap with the sand wedge if the prevailing winds are favourable – could be responsible for so much misery and fury.

Of course, Gary Irvine knew all these stories and more. However, as he climbed the wooden steps to the eighth tee, still basking in the post-birdie glow, he chose to forget them. A slight headwind blowing into his face made his hand wander over the sand wedge and pull out the pitching wedge.

The moment he hit it, he knew he had overstruck it, and he watched, a rising nausea in his chest, as the ball hurtled down towards the back of the green, took one bounce and disappeared.

'Unlucky,' Stevie said.

37

FUCK IT, LEANNE THOUGHT AS SHE ALLOWED THE upended wine bottle to drain into her glass, one of those massive goblets that easily held half a litre. She had long since lost interest in the movie she'd rented – some American romcom thing, the kind of film the wee fat guy who ran the video shop on the high street always made some comment about when you took it up to the counter. Cheeky bastard. But he hadn't been working tonight, so she'd gone ahead and got it anyway.

Using the remote she flipped from DVD to AUX and Dido softly flooded through the speakers. She stretched out on the couch, propped up on the cushions, resting her brimming glass on her stomach (God, she'd have to get back down that gym soon), a bit sleepy now from the wine, alone in the big living room, in the big house, as the summer darkness finally gathered outside. The day had been hot enough to move her to leave windows open all round the place and the chatter of swallows and thrushes darting in and out of the big maples that lined the street intertwined with the music to create a peaceful murmur.

It was lovely to have the place to herself.

Leanne sipped her wine, splashing a little down her front and not really caring and realising that that meant she was drunk.

From the kitchen, a noise. Like something falling over.

She turned the music down and listened. Nothing.

Kitchen. Maybe time to make herself a wee snack. Starving. With some difficulty she levered herself up from the couch and headed down the hall. She stopped in the doorway and peered into the dark room. She thought she could smell something odd, something sweet and fragrant, and, just for a second, she felt a tiny current of fear. Then logic – buffered by a bottle of Chardonnay – kicked in. 'Stupid,' she said out loud as she turned the lights on.

Lee leapt out from behind the island in the middle of the kitchen and Leanne screamed.

He was wearing a black leather jacket and a black balaclava. *Like rapists wear*, her mind just had time to think before he was upon her, his hand slamming over her mouth, silencing her screams, as he wrestled her to the floor, pressing something hard into her side.

'Shut it!' Lee said. 'Shut yer fucking mooth!'

The pressure on her side stopped as he brought something up to her face. It was a gun. 'If ye make a fucking noise ah'll fucking kill ye. Right?'

Leanne was shaking, on the edge of fainting, she could feel the wine churning in her stomach, nausea rising. Her pupils were tiny, her eyes bulging out of her head like golf balls. *Please, God, let me live,* Leanne thought.

Lee got up, keeping the gun pointed at her, and reached into his pocket. He took out a big roll of duct tape and started tearing off a long strip.

38

GARY WAS LYING ON HIS BED IN THEIR ROOM AT THE B&B. Still wet from the shower, a towel wrapped around him as he listened to Stevie, who had taken his place in the shower, tunelessly singing 'What You Do to Me' by Teenage Fanclub.

Eight over par he'd finished. One of the worst rounds of the day and the worst score he'd shot since the accident. How? Apart from the atrocity in the bunker at the eighth he hadn't really felt like he'd done much wrong. A few whiffed putts here and there and a couple of bad bounces – just half a dozen shots, but still the difference between a half-decent round and a living shithouse. The course had played tough, dry and hard, and running fast and unpredictable – like '62 all over again Auld Bert said – with Drew Keel posting the best opening round; a three-under-par 69.

Stevie came padding out of the bathroom, a towel around his waist and another turbaned around his head. 'Christ,' he said, looking the catatonic Gary up and down. 'Ah've left ma razor out on the sink. Just try and not get blood all over the floor when ye slash yer wrists.'

'Eighty, Stevie. Fucking eighty.'

'Ach – we couldnae buy a putt and you were unlucky at the Postage Stamp. That's all.'

'Game over.'

'Over?' Stevie said, lifting his towel and spraying deodorant into his crotch now. 'Did you say over? *Nothing* is over until we decide it's over! Was it over when the Germans bombed Pearl Harbor? No and –'

'Oh shut it. I'm – hoor – finished. We won't even make the cut.'

The Cut: out of the field of 156 players who began the competition only the lowest seventy scores from the Thursday and Friday rounds would qualify for third and fourth rounds on Saturday and Sunday.

'So?' Stevie said.

'Eh?'

'So whit the fuck? What did ye think was going tae happen here this week, pal?' Stevie cracked open a can of beer. 'Did you think ye were going to come here and win it? This is the Open. No the Ravenscroft Monthly Medal. Never mind making the cut, the fact that we're here at all is a miracle. Have ye forgotten something? Two months ago you were celebrating – fucking *celebrating* – when you broke ninety!'

'Aye, but –'

'"But" ma fucking erse. Just you listen to your Uncle Stevie. Now c'mon.' Stevie threw a pair of trousers at him. 'Get dressed and let's go over to the bar and get the pints in.'

'Go out drinking? Surely I should get an early night?'

Stevie sighed. He came over and sat on the edge of Gary's bed. 'Gary, this is what I'm talking about. Listen to me – *you are probably not going to make the cut*. We might very well only have two nights of our lives as player and caddie in the Open Championship and you want to get an early night? The place is hoaching with golf groupies, TV celebrities, professional golfers. Aw manner o' bams ripe for having the utter piss ripped out of them and you want to watch the fucking telly and have an early night?'

They looked at each other.

'Well,' Gary said, 'a couple of pints couldn't hurt . . .'

Lee ran from one bedroom to another, randomly pulling out drawers and emptying them all over the floor. He pocketed the odd bit of jewellery, some cash he found in a bedside cabinet. His heart, amplified by the card-edge of cocaine he'd snuffled up while waiting in the woods, was pounding and his mouth was dry.

He ran into the bathroom – bigger than his fucking living room – and stood there, thinking for a second. He opened the medicine cabinet and ran a gloved hand along the shelves, sending toiletries and medicines clattering into the sink and onto the floor. '*Mrs L. Masterson. Valium 10mg*.' He pocketed it and looked up. On the wall was a family photograph, the hoor from downstairs, her husband and a couple of weans. The husband cunt had a big *Magnum PI*-style tache. He looked vaguely familiar to Lee.

He ran back downstairs, looking at his watch. The whole thing had taken less than ten minutes. Breathing hard, Lee skidded back into the kitchen.

Leanne was duct-taped to a wooden chair he'd dragged in from the dining room. A strip of silver tape across her mouth too. It was a hot night and she was covered with a sheen of sweat. Lee was sweating too under the balaclava as, with trembling hands, he flipped the small revolver open and checked the chamber.

Six bullets – gold nuggets of death the size of peanuts.

Three grand – for him, Lisa and the weans.

One obstacle – squirming in a chair in front of him.

He snapped the gun shut and walked up to Leanne.

'Ah'm sorry about this,' Lee said as he brought the gun up to her forehead. His voice was cracked and broken and his hands were shaking. Leanne was really struggling now, her eyes bulging like mad and muffled, desperate noises coming from beneath the tape as she tried to talk, her cheeks puffing rapidly in and out and her nostrils flaring.

Lee tried to press the stumpy barrel against her forehead but she was writhing and twisting, turning away, trying to shout something, trying to tuck her head into her chest, trying to shrink, to disappear. Lee stepped back and pointed the gun at the crown of her head. He pulled the hammer back with his thumb. He rested his finger on the trigger. An ounce of pressure would do it.

A long moment passed, Leanne crying, Lee's head pounding as he fought to clear it of a barrage of images, one in particular recurring and recurring, impossible to shake.

'I'm really sorry,' Lee said.

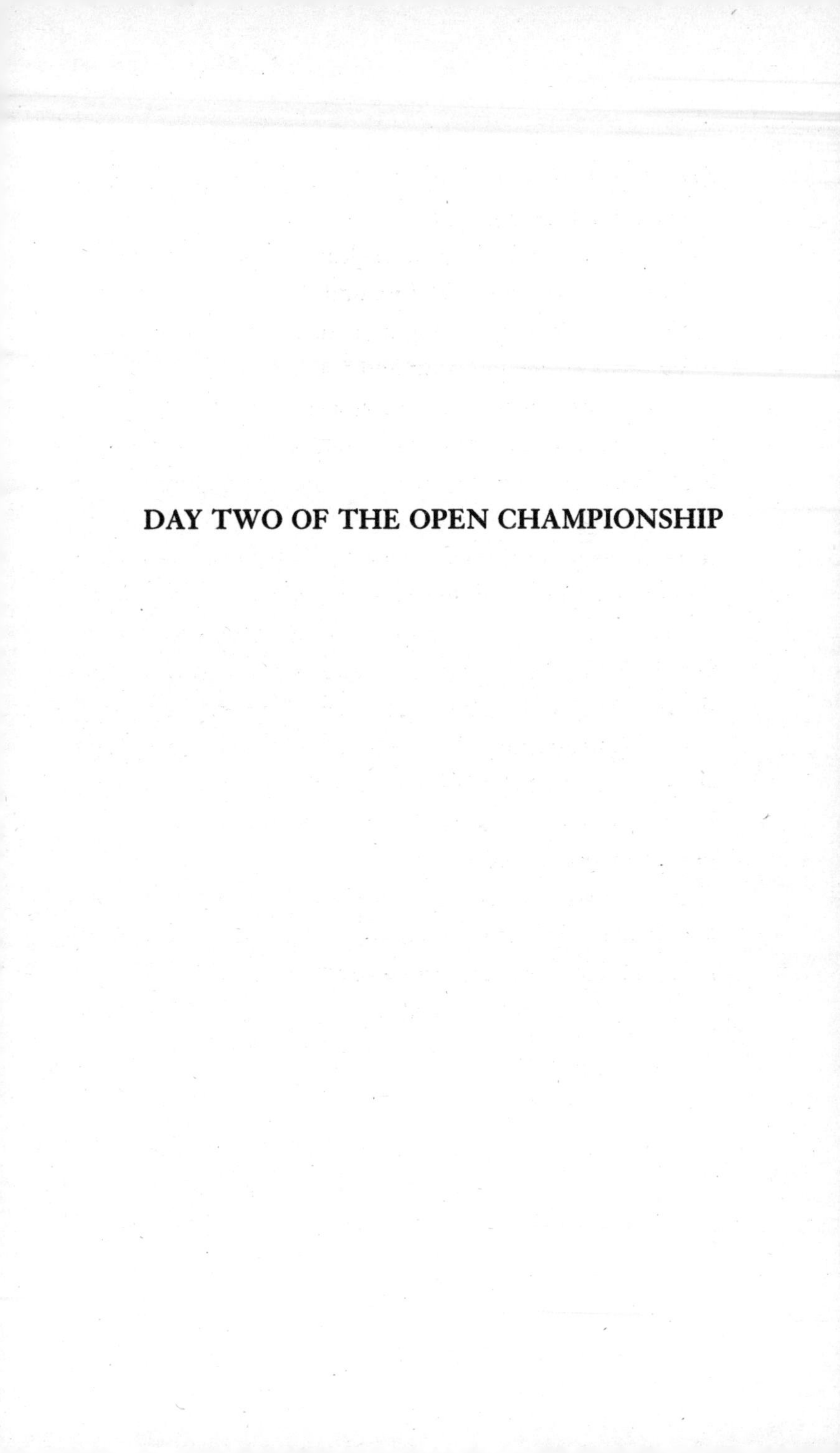

DAY TWO OF THE OPEN CHAMPIONSHIP

39

SOMETIMES IT SEEMS LIKE GOLF JUST DECIDES AND IT has nothing to do with the player. Sometimes you can do all the preparation in the world – hours of practice with every club in the bag, fine-tuning every aspect of swing, body and mind – and you step onto the course and spray the ball all over the place.

Then, on other days, you turn up tired and rusty, stumbling out of bed just in time to make it onto the first tee as your name is called, and the ball goes where you want it to every time. The pitches check where they should and the putts drop.

Today was turning out to be one of those days.

'Christ, look what the facking cat dragged in . . .' Coffey had said as Gary stumbled bleary-eyed onto the tee. He'd been right: a 'couple o' pints' hadn't hurt at all. Neither had the two bottles of wine with dinner in the clubhouse. Nor the whisky and Cokes they'd moved onto afterwards. Nor the tequila slammers . . .

Gary could feel his brain tapping against the inside of his

skull as he moved his head. Make the cut? He only cared about playing the first few holes without fainting. Birdies? He was just thinking about surviving each swing of the club. As anyone who understands the psychological intricacies of golf will tell you, this is just about the perfect mental state in which to play the sport.

He birdied the first, second and third and – just to be different – eagled the par five fourth, hitting a towering 230-yard three-iron onto the green and holing a slippery, downhill thirty-footer.

Five under par for the round after four holes. Down to three over for the tournament. Word got around the course that the local boy was playing some golf and by the time they got to the seventh green, his loyal gallery – Cathy and Sadie, April, Dr Robertson and Bert – had been swollen by a couple of dozen golf fans.

Among them was Nick Parr, one of the BBC's on-course reporters. Parr had been roaming the fairways with his hand-held mike and cameraman, looking for anything interesting happening before the big guns teed off in an hour or so. When Gary's birdie putt on the seventh also smacked straight into the centre of the cup, taking him to six under for the round, Parr looked at the name on the red bib Stevie was wearing. 'IRVINE' it said. He ran a finger down his player sheet. 'Irvine, Gary (A), Ravenscroft G.C. Ardgirvan.' A local boy then.

'Excuse me,' Parr said to the small woman in the blue sweater who was jumping up and down and cheering, 'do you know that lad?'

'That's my son!' Cathy shrieked delightedly. 'That's his fourth birdie so far! And an eagle at the fourth!'

'Really?' Parr said.

As Cathy and Sadie hurried off, following the others

towards the eighth tee, Parr spoke into his headset microphone to his producer Debbie Reynolds, who was in the BBC's mobile studio parked at the media centre. 'Debbie? It's Nick. You might want to have a look at the eighth. Local boy making a bit of a run of it. Six under after the first seven.'

'OK, thanks, Nick.'

As Gary climbed the worn, wooden steps onto the Postage Stamp tee the black lenses of the cameras dotted around the green swivelled up to frame him.

'Rowland? Bob? Have a look at this,' Reynolds said into her microphone.

In the BBC commentary box overlooking the first and eighteenth fairways Rowland Daventry and Bob Torrent, the BBC's stalwart commentators, jotted down a few notes as she filled them in – Gary's score today, the day before, his home club, etc.

'OK, Debbie, got it,' Daventry said.

'Let's go then,' Debbie said. 'Cameras 14, 12 and 21.' The red lights on the cameras around the Postage Stamp lit up and Gary Irvine made his first ever TV appearance.

'Over to the eighth tee now, the famous Postage Stamp,' Daventry purred on-air as a shot of Gary conferring with Stevie over the yardage book filled the screen. 'Claimed many a victim over the years. Bob, you'll remember Herman Tissies, the German player.'

In the control booth Reynolds heard the word 'German' and held her breath, thinking, *don't do the accent, don't do the accent . . .'*

'Oh yes,' Bob said.

'Made a fifteen here, back in 1950 I think it was.'

'That's right. Out of one bunker, back into another . . .'

'Und for him, ze war vas over!' Daventry said.

Reynolds closed her eyes. 'Oh shit,' someone said as the

control-room staff started taking bets on how many calls of complaint there would be – a favourite sport whenever Daventry was live.

'Anyway,' Daventry continued as Gary began teeing his ball up, 'let's see if this young fellow can do better than old Herman the German. Name of Gary Irvine – och aye, good Scottish name that – local lad, one of the very few amateur players who made it through the qualifying process, comes from Ardgirvan just up the road. Some wonderful courses between here and there, Glasgow Gailes, Prestwick . . .'

In his den up in the loft, with the *Racing Post* in his lap and a mug of tea in his hand, Ranta turned the volume up as a shot of Gary lining up his shot filled the huge flat screen.

'. . . real golfing country,' Daventry continued. 'Now, I'm just reading that he made an eight here yesterday, not so good. But he's going great guns this morning. Six under par through seven holes. Let's see if he can keep it up.'

A hush now as Gary settled the clubhead – a nine-iron today, the wind stronger in his face and the pin at the back of the green – behind the ball.

He swung. Hard.

'Smoke ma dobber,' Stevie said, unaware that millions of viewers were hearing him, as the perfectly struck shot rocketed off dead on line. The camera swung up off the tee, tracking Gary's ball as it sailed high into the blue.

'He's given that some,' Daventry said.

The TV coverage cut to a second camera positioned at the side of the green. Two seconds passed and then the ball smacked down twelve feet past and a couple of feet to the right of the hole.

'Sit down!' Gary barked.

The ball bit hard into the turf and spun back and to the

left, the moan of the crowd rising in pitch as it trickled back down towards the hole, tracking, tracking.

'I say,' Daventry said.

'Come oan, come oan, ya fucking . . .' Ranta said, on the edge of his seat now.

'Shit, that's close,' Coffey whispered to Koon.

The ball grazed the hole and curled around it, finally coming to rest an inch from the lip.

'OOH YA FUCKING HOOR YE!' Ranta screamed, fist pumping.

'Well, well, well,' Daventry said as Gary, smiling, picked up his tee peg. 'Must have had his porridge this morning . . .'

Ranta looked at Gary's smiling face on his TV screen and felt a tingle between his shoulder blades, a sensation familiar to all gamblers.

A hunch forming.

Findlay Masterson pulled into his driveway and turned the engine off. 'Right,' he said, breathing in deeply.

He went through his strategy: go in, see the body, run out screaming and hysterical, find one of the neighbours, get them to call the police and take it from there. He'd come home from a trip to Glasgow to visit his son, he'd walked into the house to find that the place had been burgled and his wife had been shot dead. No, how would he know she'd been shot? He just found her lying there in a pool of blood. Don't plan it too much. He had a rock-solid alibi. He'd be fine. Breathe deeply. Breathe deeply.

He got out the car and walked to the front door. He put his key in the lock, his hand shaking badly.

He stepped into the hallway and put his bag down. It was quiet.

He walked slowly down the hall, glancing left into the living room. Nothing there. All neat and tidy. He swallowed, took a deep breath and turned into the kitchen.

There, on a kitchen chair, was his wife.

She was eating a sandwich.

'Hi there,' Leanne said. 'Did ye have a nice time?'

Ranta was putting his jacket on and looking for his car keys when his mobile rang.

'Aye?'

'It didnae happen,' Masterson barked.

'Eh?'

'That thing that was meant tae happen? That thing that cost me fifteen fucking grand? *It didnae fucking happen.*' Masterson punched the roof of his car in frustration.

'Is that right?' Ranta said calmly.

'Aye it's fucking right.'

'Well, I'll have to look into that.'

'You fucking better.'

'Findlay?' Ranta said, very, *very* calm now.

'Whit?'

'Ah'm sensing how upset ye are, and ah'll find out what's happened, but do yourself a favour, eh? Don't forget who you're speaking to here.'

Ranta hung up and dialled Alec. He got voicemail.

'Alec? We've a wee problem. Phone us back on the mobile. Ah'm away over tae Troon tae catch a bit o' the golf. Looks like this boy fae around the corner is playing up a storm.'

40

'AND HOW MANY NIGHTS WILL YOU BE STAYING FOR?'

'Ah, er, jist the wan, hen.'

The receptionist did her thing with the computer and Lee shuffled about uncomfortably. He wasn't used to places like this. The Glasgow Radisson was a big modern hotel with a facade of distressed copper, airy open public spaces, neat, minimalist bedrooms and views over the River Clyde. None of these, however, were factors in Lee's choosing the place. It had simply been the first hotel he'd come upon when he stumbled out of Central Station.

It had been an uncomfortable night for the elder Irvine brother. He'd scrambled his way down through the woods in the dark, tripping and falling and cutting himself many times. He'd got back to his car to find that during one of these falls he'd lost his car keys. Cursing and swearing, his eyes still raw from the crying fit, he'd walked alongside the dual carriageway in the dark – jumping back into the ditch when the odd set of white lights came roaring by in the night – until he got to the big roundabout.

'Newspaper in the morning?' the receptionist was asking.

'Er, naw, hen.'

He'd followed the main road down into town. Avoiding the mall and the town centre, he'd cut along the riverbank and over the old iron bridge, finally arriving at Ardgirvan train station just before dawn. Then a shivering hour in the icy waiting room before the first train to Glasgow pulled in at 5.30 a.m.

'If I could just take an imprint of a credit card?'

'Naw, ah don't . . . ah'll pay cash, hen.' Lee flattened the notes on the counter with filthy, scratched hands.

'You're in 501 on the fifth floor. Just turn left when you come out of the lift. Oh, do you have any bags?'

'Er, naw. Travelling light. Thanks, doll.'

Under the stinging, reviving needles of the shower Lee began to think.

He really was in deep shit now.

Out of the shower, wet, a towel wrapped around him as he smoked a cigarette, he sat down on the edge of the bed, picked up the phone and dialled Lisa's mobile. She answered on the second ring.

'It's me, hen.'

He let her shout and scream and swear for a few seconds. When she paused for breath he said, 'Listen tae me, listen,' but she was off again.

'Ya fucking bastard, where the fuck were ye last night, eh? Ah'm hame maself wi three weans while you're oot doing fuck knows whit and no even a phone call tae l—'

'LISA! FUCKING SHUT IT AND LISTEN TAE ME!' The line went quiet. 'Listen,' Lee continued, 'ah'm in trouble, right? Ah cannae explain now. Naw, just listen. Upstairs, in ma sock drawer, away in the back left-hand corner, there's aboot a grand in there. Take the money and get the weans and go and stay wi your cousin May doon in Galashiels, a'right?'

'*Whit?* Why? Where are ye? Whit's going on?'

'Lisa, please, hen, ye have to do whit ah'm telling ye.'

'Aw God, aw my God, Lee,' she was crying now, 'whit have ye done? Whit have ye done now?'

'Shhh, hen. It's OK. It'll be awright. Ah love ye, doll, so ah dae. And it's no something I've done. It's something I haven't done.'

And, as he said those words, for the first time since he ran from the Mastersons' house into the woods in the early hours of that morning, Lee felt something other than shame, failure and fear. He felt relief. Almost pride.

She'd been looking at him, her eyeballs bulging like mad, struggling against the duct tape, trying to speak. He'd said, 'I'm sorry,' and then, just as his finger tensed on the trigger, an image and a short string of words came to him very clearly. He'd burst into tears, slumped down against the wall and cried for a long time, cried like he hadn't done since he was a wee boy, big convulsing, racking sobs. Crying because of what he had come to, what he'd been about to do, yes, but also crying because he knew now he could never do it. And he'd be in big trouble. And they could have really used the money.

With a trembling hand Lee had reached up and peeled the silver tape gently off her mouth. For some reason, something in her eyes, he knew she wasn't going to scream now. Clearly, very calmly, she said, 'It's my husband, isn't it?'

They had talked for a while, the two of them, Lee sitting on the kitchen floor, Leanne still taped to the chair.

'Shhh, hen, shhh,' Lee said as Lisa sobbed steadily on the other end of the line. 'It'll be OK. Just get the weans ready and go. Ah'll sort everything out and ah'll come and get yese.'

'Aw, Lee,' Lisa sobbed, getting her breathing under control, 'where are ye?'

'Ah'm OK. Ah'm in Glasgow. At a hotel. Get going, hen. Ah'll phone ye at May's, right?'

Lee hung up, feeling better, and lit another cigarette. He walked over to the window and pulled back the net curtain. Just visible over the slate rooftops was the River Clyde and the railway bridge that led into Glasgow from the south, from Ardgirvan.

Lee remembered the family trip to Glasgow on the train, years ago when he and Gary were just wee boys. They'd walked all over the city that day, covering the great length of Sauchiehall Street, into the leafy streets that ran along the River Kelvin, taking turns riding up on their dad's shoulders, squealing with delight as he unexpectedly jumped and jiggled them, or squeezed his strong thumbs into their fleshy calves. They'd gone to a fair in the Kelvin Hall and then ate the picnic they'd brought with them in the park, warm Vimto and the bread of the sandwiches wet from the tomatoes, the crusts dark and bitter. (*'Curls yer hair,'* their dad told them as he ate theirs.) Him and Gary play-fighting with their dad on the grass, climbing over him like he was a mountain. His parents kissing. Walking back to the station in the warm dusk they'd seen a beggar slouched over a grating outside some shops. He was filthy; a long straggly beard, his skin yellow with dirt under several layers of tattered clothing. He had a little tin next to him and a sign that said 'Please Help Me'. It was the first time Lee and Gary had ever seen a beggar. You didn't get them in Ardgirvan. (There was Benny, the town drunk, who famously shat his pants in Shorts the baker's once, but that was different.) Their dad bent down and dropped the change from his pocket into the man's tin. 'Why did you give the man money, Daddy?' Lee had asked him. His father took his hand and squeezed it and said, 'There but for the grace of God go I, son.'

It was those words and that image of his father that had come unbidden into Lee's head as he stood over the Masterson woman in the kitchen of her big house last night. Those words and that image that had stopped him from doing what he'd been going to do.

Lee tossed his cigarette end out the window and watched the glowing tip spiral five floors to the street below. He lay down on the bed, his head swimming.

Just a wee nap.

Alec Campbell, as angry as he'd ever been, drove fast and hard through the winding streets of his housing scheme, calling up the Beast's number on his mobile as he went.

'Frank? It's Alec. Meet me at 15 Burns Crescent in ten minutes.' Alec listened for a moment. 'Good. And Frank? Bring yer kit.'

41

BY CHRIST, THE BOY *WAS* PLAYING WELL, RANTA thought. Gary had been at the eleventh when Ranta arrived, the fearsome par five known as 'Railway', on account of the train tracks that ran parallel to the hole. He'd made par there and all the way through to the sixteenth, which he birdied to go to eight under for the round – currently looking like the best round of the day – and level par for the tournament: safely within the projected cutline of one over par. (Gary's playing partners had been less fortunate: a string of bogeys had taken Coffey to six over par and out of the tournament. Crawford Koon's drive at the eleventh had been pushed too far right, clattering onto the train tracks. Koon triple-bogeyed the hole to go to four over and Goodnight Vienna.)

When Gary's putt dropped for birdie on the sixteenth Ranta was thinking hard, feeling that tingle between the shoulder blades. If he waited until he made the cut Ranta's odds would be drastically reduced. However, if he made the bet now and

Gary didn't make the cut then he'd be out an awful lot of money in the time it took to play two holes of golf.

Ranta called his bookie – Big Malky. He spelled Gary's name out. 'A hundred and eighty to one,' Malky told him. Ranta thought about Masterson's envelope still sitting in his desk drawer. Fuck it – it was found money anyway. There was a long, long pause after Ranta told Malky how much he wanted to bet. Even Malky, long used to Ranta's extreme-danger betting was stunned. 'Jesus fuck,' Malky said. 'Are you sure about this, Ranta?' Ranta was sure. He hung up.

'Just get it on the green somewhere,' Stevie said, handing Gary the five-iron as they walked onto the seventeenth tee: a tough par three, 220-odd yards, wind freshening and coming off the right now. 'Nothing fancy. Two pars and we're done and dusted.'

'Nae bother,' Gary said, feeling as relaxed and confident as he'd ever felt.

A few seconds later he was saying 'Fuck' and feeling his stomach collapsing as he watched his ball sailing horribly offline.

Ranta fought his way back to the front of the ropes, tucking his mobile into his pocket as the crowd began to groan. 'Whit happened?' Ranta whispered to the girl next to him as he strained to catch sight of the ball.

'He's pulled it,' April said.

Ranta felt faint.

Lisa packed quickly. The boys were out, playing at the skate park round the corner with their pals. Wee Amazon was out the back in her sandpit. *Phone a taxi, finish packing and pick the boys up on the way to the station.* She hurried across the bedroom, pulled open a drawer and started throwing underwear into her holdall. The thick roll of fifty-pound notes in the front pocket of her jeans felt hot.

The slam of a car door made her look up and out of the bedroom window: a black jeep in front of the house and two men walking up the garden path.

Alec Campbell.

Jesus Christ, Alec Campbell at their front door. Behind him was a huge man with a deep scar running from one temple to his chin. Lisa swallowed and took a couple of deep breaths before she came running down the stairs as the doorbell started ringing.

'Haud oan!' Lisa said, trying to sound pissed off as she tugged the door open.

'Aye?' she said aggressively.

'Lisa?' Alec said, smiling.

'Alec?' Lisa said, squinting, pretending not to recognise him at first.

'It's been a few years, eh?'

'Aye.'

'We're looking for Lee.'

'You and me both.'

Alec looked past her, into the hallway where the bag she'd packed for the kids lay. 'Off somewhere?' he asked. The other guy was just staring at her.

'Och, ah wis just taking the weans oot for the day.'

Alec smiled. 'Is that right?' he said.

He pushed past her into the house, the Beast following.

'Hey, whit dae ye think yer –' Lisa began, following them into the kitchen, where Alec took a seat at the little breakfast nook. The Beast stood at the back door, looking out into the garden, where Amazon was playing in her little sandpit.

'Lisa hen,' Alec said, 'don't be a fucking erse. Listen tae me now. Lee's been a daft boy. He took a wee job on for me and my dad.' Ranta. The mention of him was enough to make Lisa unsure of her legs. 'And, well, let's just say he's let us down.'

'Alec, ah swear, ah don't know where he is. He didnae come home last night. Ah've been sick worrying about him. Ah –' Alec held up a hand to silence her.

'He went out last night then?'

'Aye. About the back o' nine. Said he'd be home aboot midnight.'

'He hasn't phoned?'

'Naw, Alec, ah swear tae ye. Ah swear oan ma weans' life.'

'Sure and that's the second time we've heard that, eh, Frank?' The Beast opened the kitchen door and walked out into the concrete backyard. 'Christ, when was it I last saw you, Lisa?' Alec went on pleasantly. 'Doon the Metro or somewhere back in the day? Right wee raver back then, weren't you? Loved yer pills.' Lisa didn't answer, she was looking at the Beast, standing over the sandpit talking to Amazon. 'Big Suzie Donald and Karen Henderson you were pals wi, weren't ye?'

Lisa reached into her pocket and took the money out. She held it towards Alec. 'Here, there's nearly a thousand pound there, Alec. Ah don't know how much ye gave him but we'll pay it aw back.'

Alec laughed as he took the money from her. 'Oh aye, raid wan o' yer Swiss bank accounts, will ye?' he said, looking around the tiny, squalid kitchen. 'Anyway, Lisa, it's no even aboot the money any more. It's a question o' professional ethics. Ma family's standing in the community and aw' that.'

The Beast came back in, carrying Amazon. He sat down opposite Alec with the child in his lap. 'Yer wee lassie was showing me her sandcastles, weren't ye, hen?' he said.

Amazon nodded proudly. 'We're going away on holiday!' she said. 'You can't come!' she added, pointing to Alec.

'I'd love to sit here and chat about the old days, Lisa, ah really would.' Alec, getting up now and coming over towards her, putting his hands on her shoulders. 'But ah've got to sort this out. So, why don't ye just tell us where he is, eh? And then we can all get on with our day and Frank here'll no have to carve a pair o' smiley faces into your wee lassie's fucking cheeks.'

Lisa started to cry, her head bowed down, hair covering her face. Over her shoulder Alec saw her mobile phone sitting on the counter next to the sink. He reached out and picked it up. Into 'Received calls' and there was a Glasgow number. Alec had dialled it before Lisa realised what he was doing. She made a grab for the phone, but Alec clamped her wrist with his free hand and easily held her away.

'Mummy!' Amazon said.

'It's OK, doll,' the Beast said, restraining the child. 'They're just playing.'

'Naw,' Lisa sobbed.

'Glasgow Radisson Hotel, Deborah sp—' the girl said before Alec hung up.

'Please, Alec,' Lisa said through tears, 'd-don't hurt him.'

'Cheer up, hen,' Alec said, reaching out and cupping her face, 'you're still a good-looking lassie. Ye can do better than Lee Irvine. Now, ye don't mind if ah leave Frank here for a wee while, do ye? Prevent ye from making any rash phone calls or anything like that.'

The front door slammed behind Alec and Amazon ran over and wrapped her arms around Lisa's leg while the Beast slipped his jacket off and hung it over the back of his chair. 'Be a doll and stick the kettle oan,' he said to Lisa, 'ah'm gasping fur a cuppa tea so ah um.'

42

IT HADN'T BEEN THE WORST PULL IN THE WORLD; HE JUST came in a little heavily with the right hand, coming across it and tugging it a little to the left. However, with the prevailing right-to-left wind, it was enough to send the shot ten yards offline, where it smacked down into the left-hand greenside bunker.

Worse was in store when they got up there. The ball had plugged under the lip, buried down in the fine sand. 'Fuck,' Stevie said.

'Oh shit,' April said, tiptoeing to get a look over the ropes and the heads of the other spectators.

Ranta couldn't believe it. The minute he puts his bet on the cunt makes the first bad swing he's made in six fucking holes?

Gary was thinking. There was no way to play the ball forward. No way back either. About the only shot open to him was to try and blast it out sideways. Get it out close to the green, get up and down for bogey and then try and make birdie down the last. If he . . . Gary stopped himself, derailing the thought process while it was happening.

One shot at a time.

He took the sand wedge from Stevie and dug his feet into the sparkling, powdery sand. Too hard and he might send it flying into the thick rough behind the green. Too soft and he might not clear the bunker. He took a couple of jerky, nervy practice swings, closing the clubface right down to get it to cut into the sand behind the ball. *Just dig the fucker out*. He hovered the club behind the ball and held his breath.

'Come on, Gary,' April whispered.

An explosion of sand and he was brushing grains of it out of his face and hair, coughing as he squinted to see where the ball had gone, noticing how oddly silent the crowd were. Gary looked down. There it was – maybe half an inch from where it had been when he swung the club.

'OK, come on,' he whispered to himself as he retook his stance. He swung again. Another eruption of sand, launching the ball up and forward this time – where it caught the lip of the bunker and bounced back to land in almost exactly the same spot again.

Ranta's face was turning a very alarming colour.

Silence as he swung the club for a third time – not even caring any more – and, incredibly, the ball hopped up and landed in the light rough around the edge of the green, about thirty yards from the hole.

Gary put his hands on his hips and stared at the ground.

There was that fizzing sensation in his skull.

'Easy,' Stevie said.

'Grip. Hoor. Baws. Cunt,' Gary said.

Stevie handed Gary the eight-iron to play his pitch-and-run and tiptoed away from him towards the ropes. Cathy came up behind him. 'Stevie son, is he all right?' she whispered.

'He's fine. Just having a wee turn.'

Gary growled and then made a strange bark.

'He's fine,' Stevie said with a reassurance he did not feel.

Lee Irvine – a real Ayrshireman, an unreconstructed product of the old school – was what his mother affectionately termed a 'plain eater'. Which is to say that he was a thirty-five-year-old man with the palate of a fussy toddler. He would not eat anything in any kind of sauce. Apart from when it came soaked in fat-dripping batter, he had never knowingly eaten fish in his life. Other than potatoes he did not eat vegetables of any description. He liked his meat well done, his cheese orange, his bread white and he was as likely to be found munching on a substantial penis as he was eating a salad.

Consequently, it was with a mixture of trepidation, revulsion and outright fury that he scanned the room-service menu at the Glasgow Radisson. His eyebrows dancing, his lips quivering, his pupils widening: he looked like a devout Muslim reading a very extreme S&M manual. Every dish, even when it contained a central ingredient Lee could tolerate – hamburger, beef, chicken – had been corrupted and perverted by some demonic addition: '*black olives . . . lemon mayonnaise . . . garlic-and-herb crust . . . Jerusalem artichokes . . . fennel*'. Whit in the name o' fuck was fennel when it was at hame? Glossy photographs of the repulsive dishes – marooned in the middle of enormous white plates and brazenly oozing their luminous sauces – further taunted him. Fuck this. Lee was starving. Hank. Fucking Hank Marvin. Lee Marvin.

Lee was Lee.

There was a chippy near the station. He'd seen it on the way here. Black-pudding supper. The auld darkie's walloper and chips. Magic.

He stepped out of the elevator and crossed the sunlit atrium towards the revolving glass doors that led to the street. Lost in hunger he realised too late who was coming swirling through the glass doors.

'A'right, Lee?' Alec Campbell said.

As his knees buckled Lee sensed someone else moving up behind him, then something hard hidden beneath a coat was being pressed between his kidneys and then he was being led towards a car idling at the kerb.

Suddenly he wasn't hungry any more.

The wind had really freshened now as Stevie and Gary walked in silence down the eighteenth fairway towards his drive, a decent strike considering he'd hit it in a numb daze. He'd managed to get up and down in two at the last hole, for a triple bogey six. Three over par. Even a birdie here would most likely leave him missing the cut by a single stroke. He fingered the indent in his temple, aware of the fizzing sensation, the sparkling lemonade in his skull intensifying. 'Oh well,' Stevie said as they reached his ball, 'we gave it a good go, eh?'

'Fudfannyflapsboot,' Gary replied.

They looked down the fairway to where the grandstands surrounded the eighteenth green. It looked like quite a crowd – people already reserving their places for when the likes of Linklater and Keel started to come rolling through in a couple of hours. Stevie consulted the yardage book.

'You've got about 190 to the pin.'

'Pishpishcuntpish,' Gary said, plucking a tuft of grass and

flicking it into the air above their heads. It blew straight over them and back down the fairway towards the tee.

'Five?' Stevie said.

'Spunk. Six. Spunk ya slut.'

Intae this wind? Stevie thought. But what was the point in arguing now? Let him hit what he wanted. Stevie pulled the six-iron from the bag and said, 'Give it a good skelp . . .'

'Fucking cock.'

Gary sighted towards the green, the wind blowing a little from right to left, the pin back left of the green. *Keep it right of the flagstick. In line with the clock above the entrance to the clubhouse.*

He settled the clubhead behind the ball.

Stevie closed his eyes.

Bert looked at the ground.

'Come on, son, stick it close,' Ranta whispered, praying that a birdie and two over might just be good enough.

Cathy looked up to the sky and whispered, *'Come on, you.'*

April was surprised at how much she wanted him to hit a good shot. Surprised at how she felt a little depressed when she allowed her mind to follow the logical chain of events that would be caused by him hitting a bad shot: he misses the cut and goes home and she never sees him again.

A long moment passed before Gary swung the club, whipping through the ball fast and hard, picking it cleanly off the fairway. He pivoted through the shot and came up watching the ball disappear into the sky above the clubhouse.

'Slut,' he said instantly.

'Ye caught that,' Stevie said.

In the crowd, in unison, Auld Bert and Robertson both murmured, 'Gowf shot.'

They lost sight of the ball for a second. Then a cheer went

up from the grandstands as it landed at the front of the green, right in line with the clock, dead centre where Gary had been aiming. It bounced left and disappeared from sight into the heart of the green.

'It's good . . .' Stevie said.

The cheer from the grandstands was still growing, twisting into a kind of *'ooooh hh'*.

'Fud?' Gary said.

The *oooohhh* reached a crescendo and then exploded into a roar as everyone in the grandstands leapt to their feet as one, the clapping and whistling carrying down towards them on the breeze.

'Flaps?' Gary said, numb and confused, his skull boiling.

Stevie turned to him. 'I think you've . . .'

Now everyone – from the people in the grandstands to the spectators all the way along the ropes – was going berserk. The tickling sensation in his skull erupting now as Gary's eyeballs flipped upwards in their sockets.

'Urrr,' he said, as his vision dimmed.

'Hey!' Stevie said, reaching out for him as he went over, clattering into the golf bag on his way down onto the hard, baked turf.

43

HIS DAD WAS ON THE VERANDA AT AUGUSTA NATIONAL, IN the shade, just out of the hot sun. In front of him on the table was a bottle of the Grouse that was famous, an ice bucket, two cans of Sprite, two glasses and a pack of Regal. He was wearing the hat he always wore when he played in hot weather, an old-school Bing Crosby-style trilby in a lightweight blue-and-white-striped fabric, with faint brownish rings visible where his sweat had soaked through. The hat was tilted back at a rakish angle and Gary smiled as he watched his dad mixing himself a whisky and lemonade and thought to himself: After you died I used to stuff my face into that hat so I could still smell you.

But he wasn't dead. Here he was: fresh as the morning and very pleased with himself, laughing like a blocked drain as he torched another Regal.

'Aye, by Christ, you should have seen his face! He's four feet fae the hole – dead set for a birdie – ah'm aff the bloody green. Ye wouldnae believe it – ah chip in and he misses the putt! He whiffs it

and leaves it short! Ah thought Snead was gauny explode so ah did.'

Gary laughed. 'So you won?'

'Aye, three and two. The boys are up at the bar,' his dad said, sipping the whisky. 'By the way, son, that was some shot there. Had to have been two hunner yards.'

'You saw that?'

'Oh aye. Ah see all your shots. Ah see it when ye improve yer lie in the rough, when ye ground the club in the bunker. Everything.'

Gary felt his face going red. 'I don't –'

'Hey, come on. Don't kid a kidder.'

Gary thought he could smell a reeking sulphurous stench. He eyed his father – a man who had, on more than one occasion, found humour in farting in the faces of his wife and children – with suspicion, but the old boy was still talking. 'It's funny, ye'd think it would be more helpful to think of the dead when ye were about to do something that wouldn't *make them proud, eh? Then they could act as a moral corrective. So tae speak.'*

How strange to be sitting here talking philosophy with his father, an electrician by trade.

'What could I do that wouldn't make you proud?'

His dad shook his head. 'You're that self-centred sometimes,' he said. 'What makes you think ah'm talking about you?'

Lee. Where had Lee got that money?

'He's no a bad boy really,' his dad said. 'He's just had a bad run. Anyway,' he started gathering up his cigarettes, his scorecard and pencil, 'I'm away tae play the puggys. We won eighty dollars the other night. Two bells on the left and we nudged the other two up!'

Gary got up and went to follow him through the open doors and into the dark of the clubhouse, where a throng of golfers stood laughing and joking at the bar. Sam Snead was talking to Harry Vardon. Payne Stewart was demonstrating a putting stroke to a baffled Walter Hagen.

'Sorry, son,' his dad said, putting a hand on Gary's shoulder. 'Members only in the clubhouse, ye know that.'

He did know that. He could already feel everything starting to whirl and blur around him as the terrible stench grew stronger, blocking out the pine, magnolia and dogwood.

'Pauline left me, Dad.'

'Oh aye?' his dad said fairly cheerfully.

'You never liked Pauline?'

'Well, ah wis never that keen, son. Ah huv tae say.'

'Why didn't you –'

'Ach, come on now. Giving advice about relationships is like giving advice about club selection. People always end up going with their gut feeling anyway. There's no caddies in love . . .'

As his father said this the smell of pure sulphur hit Gary hard.

Robertson pulled the bottle of smelling salts back from Gary's nose as he sat up coughing and blinking. He was in a tent of some kind, with faces all around him: his mum, Stevie, Dr Robertson, two uniformed St John's ambulancemen, April.

'What happened?' he asked

'You holed it,' Stevie said.

'You made the cut,' April said. She was smiling.

44

PAULINE WALKED THROUGH THE BIG, EMPTY ROOMS alone, her heels echoing on the hardwood floor, the stifling heat pressing in on her. She could hear the estate agent talking on her mobile somewhere far away in the house, but the sound was pleasantly distant, reminding her just how large this place was, how many rooms it contained, how much fun she was going to have filling these rooms with nice new things.

She was in the master bedroom, a space that could contain her and Gary's bedroom three times over. Super-kingsize bed there, she was thinking. Maybe some bookshelves in that alcove in the corner? (Although they would have to get some books first.) An archway led off the bedroom to the en suite bathroom with matching his and hers sinks. Pauline had wanted an en suite bathroom with twin sinks so badly for so long that it almost made her tearful to think that here she was – on the verge of having one.

She walked over to the big bay window and looked outside. There were eleven other homes in the development, all slightly different variations on what the agent called 'classical' architecture: sand-coloured stone with grey slate roofs, two-car garages and conservatories.

Directly below where Pauline stood, French windows led from the living room out into the garden. It was over a hundred yards long, with a raised decking area off to one side. She pictured them having garden parties. Barbecues. Beyond the tall wooden fence at the end of the garden was woodland, the edges of the country park, with Glasgow to the north, somewhere in the distance.

Pauline heard heels clacking towards the room and turned as Mrs McMahon from Bowles, Kinney & Ross entered.

'Sorry about that,' she said, indicating her mobile, 'crazy at the office just now.' McMahon was older than Pauline, late thirties, and well groomed. 'Fabulous garden,' McMahon said, joining Pauline at the window. 'Perfect for children . . .'

'Mmm,' Pauline said.

Right, McMahon thought, quickly adding, '. . . or for entertaining.'

'I know. I was just thinking that.'

'Well, if you're definitely interested, I wouldn't hang about, Pauline. It's the last house left and I've got three more viewings lined up this weekend. I don't think it'll be on the market much longer.'

'I just need to talk to my . . . boyfriend tonight. I'm pretty sure we'll be making an offer.'

Just as she climbed back into her stupid jeep – hopefully soon to be another relic of her past life – her mobile rang. Findlay. Perfect.

'Hi, darling. Listen, I've just been to look at the house again. And –'

Masterson talked. Pauline listened.

'What?' she cut in. 'I thought you said –' She listened some more. 'But the estate agent was just saying –' He cut her off again. 'But we might lose the house! Don't shout at me! Look, I, we'll talk about it when I get back.'

Pauline drove back to Ardgirvan fast and aggressively, at one point seeing the road through a smear of angry tears. He'd said it was all going to be fine. If they lost the bloody house because . . . She flipped the radio on and, punching through the presets, caught a snatch of an oddly familiar voice. Frowning, she punched back until she found it again. It was Radio Ayrshire, the local station she listened to mainly for the traffic reports. She turned the volume up. 'I don't know really,' the voice was saying, 'just try and go out and do the same again tomorrow, I suppose. Try not to think about it too much . . .'

'Great, well, good luck tomorrow,' the interviewer said.

'Aye, er, cheers. No bother.'

'Ardgirvan golfer Gary Irvine,' the studio announcer's voice said, causing Pauline to swerve towards the right-hand lane of the dual carriageway, causing the driver of the car passing her to scrunch his horn angrily, 'who fainted on the eighteenth fairway at Royal Troon earlier this afternoon after becoming the only amateur player to make the cut at this year's Open Championship.'

'But he sounds fine now,' a female voice cut in.

'He does, Joan, he does. Now, tell us what's going on with the weather. Are we in for much more of this heat?'

'We certainly are, Tom, we certainly are . . .'

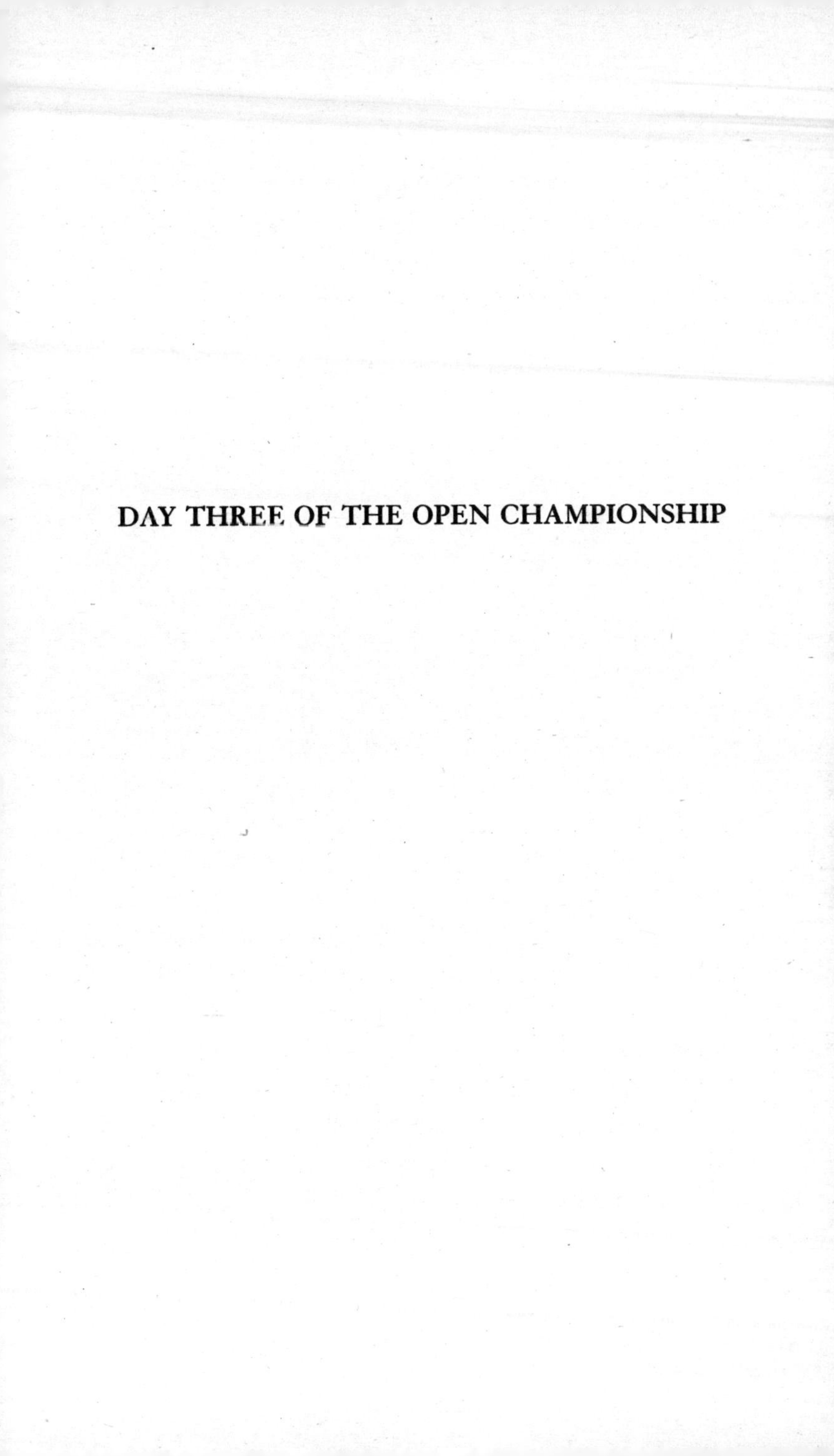

DAY THREE OF THE OPEN CHAMPIONSHIP

45

SATURDAY MORNING: THE TEMPERATURE RISING AND the crowds escalating for the weekend.

Gary and Stevie made their way from the locker room to the first tee – stunned by the change in the process from the previous two days. Where before there had been a handful of friends and family along with the odd knot of curious golf fans lining the path, now there were hundreds of people pressing against the ropes, clapping and cheering. Some of them seemed to know his name. 'Go on, Gary!' a middle-aged woman shrieked and Gary sheepishly tugged his visor in recognition, something he'd seen some of the professionals doing on TV.

When they came round the corner of the clubhouse building the enormity of what was happening really became apparent: the first tee was engulfed by a heaving mass of spectators. Those who couldn't get near the tee box were lining the first hundred yards of the fairway. Cardboard periscopes wavered above the bobbing heads. 'Holy shit,' he whispered to Stevie out of the corner of his mouth.

'It's fine,' Stevie said. 'Be cool.'

They walked up onto the tee box – seeing his mum, April and the rest pressed against the ropes (where was Lee? He might at least have . . .) – and shook hands with the starter and the R&A official who would be following the match. 'Listen, son,' the starter said, leaning in close to Gary's ear and having to raise his voice over the hubbub. 'You just enjoy yourself out there today. You've done a hell of a job just getting this far. Remember that.'

'Aye, thanks,' Gary said.

April jockeyed for position near the ropes behind the tee. After yesterday's miraculous shot her second story about Gary had run in the main paper this morning – not the sports section. If he managed to hang in there near the top until tomorrow she was – as she'd patiently reminded Devlin and McIntyre on the phone last night – sitting on a huge story.

Suddenly, all around them, a massive cheer erupted from the crowd. Gary and Stevie turned and looked back along the path, where a sea of hands was now stretching out, fingers waving, desperately trying for high fives. The ground didn't begin to shake, but it might as well have, as Drew Keel heaved into sight. Drew Keel; the third best golfer in the world, three-time major championship winner, one of the longest hitters on the PGA tour, walking right towards them, pausing here and there to high-five a well-wisher, laughing and joking with the galleries. Keel – a man Gary had only ever seen on television prior to this moment – walking up the steps and onto the tee now, his hand extended towards Gary and a big lopsided grin on his face. Drew Keel saying, 'Hi there. I'm Drew.'

In the commentary booth Rowland Daventry was frantically scanning a sheaf of papers he'd just been handed by an assistant as Reynolds squawked in his earpiece. 'Rowland? *Rowland!* On air in five, four –'

'Yes, I know! Fuck!' Daventry snapped.

'– two and –'

'And over to the first tee now,' Daventry purred smoothly. 'A very interesting pairing this, the world number three alongside Gary Irvine, the only amateur player to make the cut this year. And what a spectacular fashion he did it in, eh, Bob?'

'Indeed,' Torrent said.

On television the screen cut to a replay of Gary's last shot the previous day, the perfectly struck five-iron drifting towards the hole.

'. . . eagling the eighteenth from two hundred yards.'

'And then promptly fainting!' Torrent cut in.

'Yes, poor lad,' Daventry continued as, on television screens all across the country, a shot of Gary's face, biting his top lip in concentration, filled the screen. 'A combination of the heat and the excitement we've been told. However, we've since found out a little more about Mr Irvine. Extraordinary story, which I'm sure some of you will have been reading about in this morning's papers . . .'

Pauline was doing her make-up when Katrina rushed into the bedroom. 'Come and see this,' she said, excited. Pauline followed her into the living room, Ben snorting and snuffling at her heels. 'I was flicking through the channels when . . .' She pointed to the TV: Gary's face, biting his lip in that stupid, goofy way he did when he was concentrating, while Torrent picked up the story. 'He got his handicap cut from around eighteen down to scratch in the space of a couple of months, which I think is a record in itself.' Ben looked at the TV screen and began emitting a low growl.

'I should think so,' Daventry said. 'How long did it take you, Bob?'

'Oh, a good bit longer than that! Every year thousands of amateurs compete for just twelve spots.'

'Yes. Many are called. Few are chosen,' Daventry said solemnly. The banter went on as Pauline and Katrina sat down to watch.

'Well, he made it through and here he is now – playing with Mr Drew Keel.'

'And a question here via email from a Mrs Agnes Kincaid in Dumbarton,' Daventry continued as Gary pushed his tee peg into the ground, 'who asks "What would happen if Mr Irvine found himself in the prize money and he took it?" Well, Agnes, he would of course lose his amateur status and immediately become a professional sportsman. He'd be unable to play in any amateur competitions again. Although, I have to say, if you were a betting man, you'd be a little nervous of sticking your money on him, wouldn't you, Bob? There hasn't been an amateur winner of the Open since the late, great Bobby Jones won at Royal Liverpool back in the glorious summer of 1930.'

'You'll remember that, Rowland,' Torrent said.

In the booth Daventry stuck two fingers up at Torrent while he said, 'Oh yes. Great days.'

Pauline watched the man she already thought of as her ex-husband stand behind his ball and sight down the gun barrel of his extended driver. She felt a curious mixture of emotions: the electric tingle of seeing someone she knew intimately on the television; resentment that, despite the fact that she had no discernible talent, it was Gary and not her who was appearing on TV; and also, and unexpected this, there was a curious rush at seeing the surname which was still hers standing out in white-on-blue lettering in the top right-hand corner of the screen.

'God, doesn't he look fat?' Katrina said while, from the television, there came the swish and crack of the driver as Gary hit his first shot of the day.

'The camera adds ten pounds,' Pauline said. She'd read that somewhere. In one of her magazines. Ben barked twice sharply as on-screen Gary's match walked off the tee and headed down the fairway.

Lee had endured worse nights, but not many. His first night in Saughton had been worse; on his back on the hard bunk in the cold cell, listening to that guy wanking three feet above him, listening to the prison making its prison sounds all around him – pipes clanking, metal gates rattling, distant footsteps on concrete floors, humming machinery. (Prisons, Lee learned, are like hospitals and hotels: insomniac buildings, never silent, never completely asleep.)

But this night, spent handcuffed to a radiator, lying on an oil-stained cement floor with his arms twisted over to the side and his back against the damp breeze-block wall and his jaw aching from the oily rag they'd stuffed in it, this was definitely up there. He could just about move his tongue around the rag, enough for him to probe the tip of it into one of the ragged, salty holes in his bottom gum where two of his molars were missing. One of the small mercies of the rag was that he couldn't run his tongue across the gap where his front teeth used to be; they'd splintered when they'd thrown him headlong and face down onto the floor as they'd dragged him in here.

Through sheer exhaustion, he'd managed to drift off for a little while. When he opened his eyes he saw sunlight filtering in through the cracks around the door on the far side of the room. He could hear children's voices and a dog barking somewhere close by. Somehow these sounds made him more miserable than he'd ever been. Like when you were little and you got sent to bed early on a summer's night for being bad: the worst punishment. You'd hear the sounds from the street, ice cream vans chiming, kids playing; all reminding you that life went on without you.

'Christ knows what's going tae happen to you, boy.'

His father had said this to him more than once, after one or other of his escalating teenage transgressions (the truancy, into shoplifting, into glue-sniffing, into smoking hash, into whatever) had been uncovered. Well, Christ knew now. And Lee knew too, swallowing and tasting coppery blood. He was going to die here, in this windowless concrete room, surrounded by engine parts, oil stains and men who were harder than he was.

46

FOR TWO HOURS GARY AND STEVIE, AND A PRESSING gallery of thousands of spectators, watched in awe as Drew Keel heroically tackled Royal Troon's front nine. He crunched drivers 350 yards. He went for the par fives in two shots every time. He slashed mighty three-irons out of rough most players would have trembled at taking the lob wedge to. He went right at every pin, no matter how riskily they were positioned.

Golf, of course, couldn't care less about heroics and by the time they were walking towards the tenth tee Keel was a horrendous four over par for the round.

Gary drove the ball conservatively, routinely hitting the three-wood and the rescue club. He laid up on par fives, playing for position in the centre of the fairway and leaving himself soft wedges into the greens and comfortable two putts for his pars. After a morning of grinding it out he had made one birdie over nine holes. Level par for the tournament.

Cathy Irvine was once again watching her son lining up his second shot at the treacherous eleventh. He'd pushed his drive a bit, landing in the first cut of rough on the right-hand side of the fairway, just at the corner where it doglegged right. Cathy automatically tilted her eyes up to the sky. '*Come on, you . . .*'

Meanwhile, sixty-odd yards away, Gary was hearing the more corporeal advice of Stevie. 'Fucking fucked fae here, cunty-baws,' Stevie said, surveying the situation.

The eleventh is a shortish par five by modern tour standards, almost a par four for some of the bigger hitters. Keel had creamed his drive and was lying in the middle of the fairway about fifty yards ahead of Gary, who still had over two hundred yards to go, with thick rough and out-of-bounds waiting all along the right and a huge, yawning bunker guarding the left of the green. The sensible shot – the shot Stevie was urging – was something like a seven-iron into the neck of the fairway, leaving a wedge in for a two-putt par.

At the same time . . . he could definitely reach the green and there weren't many two-putt birdie opportunities left out here today. Something else too – he just fancied this. A phenomenon unique to golf: sometimes a straightforward chip can fill the player with unexpected dread while the most ludicrous shot, an arcing draw from a scrubby patch of rough over a terrible canyon, makes the mouth water. Something about the way the wind was blowing, the way his ball was lying – in the rough, but sitting up a little on a springy tuft of grass – conspired to make Gary think he could just muller this one. He reached past Stevie's proffered seven-iron and pulled out the four.

'Ho, bawbag,' Stevie said, 'are you aff yer tits? If ye come up short over this rough it's game over.'

'I can make it.'

'Sayonara.'

'Ball's sitting up nice.'

'Kaput.'

'Wind's helping a wee bit.'

'Goodnight Vienna.'

'Stevie!'

'Sorry. Best o' luck.'

Stevie stepped back and Gary took his stance. Pin back right. Fucking out-of-bounds all over the place. No, don't think about that. Plenty of room.

In the crowd Cathy turned to Bert. 'Whit were they arguing about, Bert?'

'It looks like he's going for the green. Ah think young Stevie wanted him tae lay up. Difficult shot. Tricky hole.'

'Yeah,' April said. 'Didn't Nicklaus make something like a 12 here back in '62?'

Bert looked at the lassie, impressed. 'Thirteen, hen. Thirteen.'

'Aww my God!' Cathy cried as thousands of necks suddenly snapped to the left.

Gary and Stevie held their breath as the ball flew over the right-hand rough, terrifyingly close to the railway tracks. An '*oooh*' from up ahead as his ball came down.

'Is he on the green?' Cathy asked Bert, her hands over her face.

'On the green?' Bert said. 'I reckon he's about three feet fae the bloody pin!'

'Oh thank God for that,' Cathy said as she felt a tugging at her elbow. She turned.

Lisa looked terrible: bloodshot eyes, streaked mascara.

'Lisa hen! Whit is it? Whit's wrang?' Cathy's stomach was tightening.

'Aw Cathy!'

'Aw God, whit's he done, hen?'

Lisa burst into fresh tears.

47

THE ROOM WAS SUDDENLY ILLUMINATED BY A BURST of sunlight as the door was thrown open. Lee squinted up and saw Ranta Campbell floating towards him, perfectly silhouetted, a corona of sunlight burning around him, his long coat flowing out like black smoke and an axe in his hand.

Lee made a sound he'd never made before. He whimpered, like a miserable dog, or a child who knows they have done something very, very bad. Ranta tore the oily rag from Lee's mouth and heard exactly what he had been expecting to hear:

'Rantapleasefucksakeah'llpayyeawthemoneybackah-sweartaefuck'

Lee went on like this for a while, all the time staring straight into Ranta's eyes – an unsettling enough experience in its own right. Ranta listened to the speech in the same way a seasoned judge might listen to an earnest, but inexperienced, barrister, tuning out all the cliché and hyperbole he'd heard countless times before while keeping a weary ear open in case a surprising detail emerged from the babble. After a minute or so of garbled raving Lee gave up and just started crying.

Ranta looked down at him. The boy looked vaguely familiar, but he couldn't place him. Ranta had met a lot of bams over the years, in rooms like this, with a tool, a chib, an equaliser in his hand. Leaning casually on the long-handled axe as a golfer leans on a club when he is waiting for a green to clear, Ranta said, 'Sorry, son, Lee is it? Is that yer name?' Lee nodded miserably. 'Look, ah kin see what happened, Lee. Ye thought ye'd play wi the big boys and when it came doon tae it ye shat yer pants and ran away. Ah see that. Ah'm no a monster. It's just that ah gave ma word that this job would be done. Ah cannae let it get about that any wee fanny in the town can make me look like a total fud whenever he feels like it. Can I?' Lee, crying softly, head bowed, did not answer. 'Look at me, son.'

Lee looked up, blinking away his tears, and saw Ranta was hefting the axe up into his hands now. 'I mean – do you want me to look like a total fud?'

Alec and Frank laughed. The boss was a fucking riot sometimes so he was. Lee shook his head. 'Naw,' Ranta said, still calm and pleasant, 'ah didnae think so . . .'

Frank stepped back as Ranta widened his stance and brought the axe back. He'd seen this before: one time Ranta had almost missed the guy completely, slicing off half his face by mistake – right forehead, tip of the nose and right cheek – and the cunt had thrashed around screaming and spraying blood everywhere before Frank shot him in the face.

Lee looked at Alec. 'Please, Alec.'

'You're a fucking amateur, Lee Irvine,' Alec said as Ranta brought the axe down hard.

Lee shut his eyes.

He felt the breath of air on his face as the blade passed very close to his cheek. Simultaneously he felt the familiar thick, oily spurt into the gusset of his boxer shorts, then the hollow clang of metal hitting cement, his bare forearm tingling as sparks bounced off him. He looked up.

Ranta was standing over him, breathing a little hard from the exertion. The axe had dug a chip of concrete the size of a toffee out of the floor next to Lee's knee. Ranta, his massive hands stinging from the impact, like when he misstruck a long-iron, looked down at Lee and said, 'Irvine? You're no any relation to the boy Gary Irvine who's playing in the Open, are ye?'

48

MASTERSON WAS FINDING IT HARD TO RECOGNISE THE woman sitting across the table from him. He glanced around nervously, hoping none of the other lunching customers could hear Pauline as she repeated herself, this time inserting an expletive between the two words.

'You're fucking joking?'

'Calm down, for fuck's sake,' he whispered.

'Calm down? I've been to see the place twice. I told the estate agent we'd be putting an offer in tomorrow. I found a *sofa*!' Pauline delivered this last sentence with the kind of panicky stress normally heard only in emergency rooms, on battlefields, on the flight decks of failing aircraft.

'It's only a fucking house!' Masterson said. 'We'll just have to live somewhere smaller for a wee while.'

'Smaller?'

'It's just, after the divorce, ah won't have as much spare cash. But, once the boy's finished university and aw that . . .

and Leanne might get remarried sometime. As long as we've got each other, eh?'

'I thought you weren't going to get a divorce. I thought . . .' Pauline wasn't quite sure what she'd thought.

'Well. Change o' plan,' Masterson said. He couldn't go through with it again. That was that.

Pauline let him put his hands over hers but she didn't meet his gaze. She stared at the tablecloth, thinking about the house, the matching his and hers sinks, the garden. Lawyers for neighbours.

'There's just the two of us, eh?' Masterson said enthusiastically. 'A nice wee flat would do us for a bit.'

'Flat?' Pauline said, doing a very good job of making it sound like she had just said 'Aids' or 'cancer'.

49

BERT HAD BEEN WRONG. GARY'S BALL HAD ACTUALLY finished four and a half feet from the pin. He rolled it in for an eagle: two under for the tournament. A few moments later, after Keel had three-putted his way to a par, they were walking towards the twelfth tee when Stevie said, 'Holy shit.'

'What?' Gary asked.

'Look,' Stevie said, pointing. Gary followed his finger towards one of the huge leader boards that dotted the course. It had just been changed. Gary's mouth flapped open as he looked at it. It said:

1st: LINKLATER C – 5
2nd: LATHE T – 4
3rd: RODRIGUEZ J – 3
4th: HONEYDEW III J – 2
4th: IRVINE G (A) – 2

He'd known he was playing well, but he hadn't really been thinking about his score. Now here he was – tied fourth in the Open. Just three shots behind Linklater.

Calvin Fucking Linklater.

Gary felt his chest tightening and he was breathing harder. 'Jesus, Stevie,' he said. 'Jesus fucking fuck.'

'I know, come on, breathe easy now.'

'Aye. Breathe. Cunt. Dug rider. Fuck.'

Oh Christ, not now, Stevie thought as Drew Keel sloped over to them. 'Listen, son,' he said, laying a massive gloved hand on Gary's shoulder, 'don't you even think about that shit. Just keep playing your own game and don't worry what anyone else is doing, OK?

'Aye. Wankyawankye. Wank me aff,' Gary said.

'Sure, son,' Keel said, Gary's Ayrshire accent as foreign and indecipherable to his ears as Chinese. 'No need to thank me. You just hang in there.' He sauntered back towards the tee.

'Oh Christ, Stevie,' Gary whispered, 'ah've got a fucking hard-on.'

'I know. It's exciting. Calm down. Just a few holes to –'

'No!' Gary whispered through gritted teeth, 'I mean I've got an actual hard-on. It's killing me.'

Stevie looked at him. Then at their gallery – thousands of spectators now, lining the fairway, pressed up against the ropes all along the tee box and the paths. 'Look,' Stevie said, 'it cannae be that bad . . .'

'Bad? It's fucking bionic.'

'Jesus.'

Keel and his caddie were already waiting for them on the tee as Stevie walked over to their marshal. 'Umm, sorry tae to be a pain but my player needs a quick . . . comfort break?'

'Christ, son, the match behind is nearly caught up with us.'

'I know, he really needs to . . . go.'

'OK, but make it quick.'

Inside the humid Portaloo, breathing through his mouth against the tangy fug of urine and faeces, it took just forty-five seconds before – cross-eyed, sighing and separated from thousands of spectators by just half an inch of green plastic – Gary felt blessed relief beginning to rumble up from the floor of his testicles. He reached for the toilet paper to find that the box was, of course, empty. Only one thing for it. He grunted as he ejaculated gratefully into his golf glove.

He ran back to the tee box only slightly red-faced. 'Go on, Gary!' someone shouted from behind the ropes. 'You can do it!'

'Thanks, cheers.'

'That was quick,' Stevie said, holding the driver out.

'Aye, give us a new glove out the bag, would ye?'

'Glove?'

'Aye.'

The various sponsors provided an endless supply of free golf junk: balls, tees, gloves, towels, umbrellas and the like, all piled high in the locker room. Stevie knelt down and rummaged through the golf bag.

'Feeling better, kid?' Keel asked.

'Yeah, thanks.'

'Your honour, Mr Irvine,' the official said, gesturing towards the tee.

'Aye, just a sec.'

Stevie came up from the bag. 'Umm, sorry. I forgot to lift some new gloves this morning.'

Gary swallowed.

'Please, Mr Irvine,' the official said. 'I'm going to have to put you on the clock.'

'OK,' Gary said, fishing in his pocket.

He shuddered as he slid his left hand into the cold, glutinous semen-filled glove and walked onto the tee.

Pauline had popped back to the house to pick up some clothes. She knew he was staying in Troon, that the place would be empty. What with the heat and trauma of the day she'd decided to take a cool shower to try and relax. She had the radio on as she leaned into the cold needles, but terrible words kept drifting up to haunt her – *only a house . . . somewhere smaller . . . a flat*. She felt the water tingling into her scalp and held her breath for as long as she could.

She turned the shower off and in the quiet heard that the hourly news bulletin had commenced. '*. . . with the Prime Minister now in close discussion with the rest of the Cabinet. In sporting news, in a dramatic turn of events at the Open Championship in Troon, amateur player Gary Irvine has just birdied the eighteenth hole to take the lead as the penultimate day of play draws to a close. More now from Roger Morton at Royal Troon.*'

Pauline ground a pinkie into her left ear, squeaking out the soapy water.

'*Yes, Angela, dramatic scenes here. All the more so because Gary Irvine really is a local boy, from Ardgirvan just a few miles along the coast and –*'

The doorbell rang. Probably Shona from next door, an avid Radio Ayrshire listener, wanting to tell her that Gary was on the news. Pauline wrapped a towel around herself, turbaned her hair up and ran downstairs.

She opened the front door, the words 'I know, Shona' already forming on her lips.

Pauline was dazzled by a fusillade of light guns.

Reporters were crowded around the doorstep. More were streaming through the garden gate, making their way across the front lawn and along the path, some of them even managing to avoid the various decaying turds Ben had strewn around the place. (And 'strewn' was wrong, for it suggested the random acts of a madman. The satanic beast had, of course, placed the reeking mounds as strategically as a retreating commander would landmine a field.) Pauline felt the heat of a lamp on her face as cameras, microphones and Dictaphones were thrust in her direction. 'Mrs Irvine,' someone was asking her, 'how do you feel about your husband's performance?'

'Do you think he'll go all the way?'

'Was his accident a big factor?'

Faced with such an ambush, many people would crumble. They would stammer and slam the door. Pauline – a veteran of tabloids and celebrity magazines, well versed in doorstep journalism and reality TV – found her answers coming immediate and slick.

'I'm very pleased he's playing so well . . . he works hard at his golf . . . I'm not a doctor so I'm afraid I couldn't say how much his accident affected his playing . . . I think if he keeps playing the way he is he can definitely go all the way!'

Cameras flashed, microphones were thrust closer, more questions were shouted and Pauline began to feel . . . what, exactly?

For so long she had felt like there was a hole somewhere in the centre of her being. A sense that she was missing something, that she was living out the wrong life. That greater, better things had been intended for her. Now, here on her own doorstep, under TV lighting and the strobing of the cameras with the long, heavy lenses, the hole was being filled. The missing part was being found. She was finally slipping into the right life. For the first time in a long time she felt like she was exactly where she was meant to be. She felt alive. She felt *famous*.

Pauline was experiencing nothing less than a rebirth.

'How much would the money change your life?' someone asked.

'The money?' Pauline said.

'The winner's cheque. Seven hundred and fifty thousand pounds.'

Pauline felt her jaw twitch.

'Why weren't you out there cheering him on today?' someone else asked.

'Well . . .' Pauline stammered, trying to regain her composure. 'One of us has to work, you know! But, as a matter of fact, I was just getting ready to head over there right now . . .'

Lee puffed furiously with trembling hands, blood on the filter and the cigarette smoke searing the cuts and holes in his gums. A small portable TV had been turned on, the screen glowing a brilliant green in the dark room, Rowland Daventry's gentle commentary burbling incongruously in this terrible space. Ranta was watching the TV. Alec, the Beast and the others were watching Ranta. Ranta turned from the screen and looked at Lee. Lee shifted uncomfortably, the oil slick in his pants cold and terrible now whenever he moved.

Ranta Campbell – a firm believer in the management philosophy of 'a good plan today is better than a perfect plan tomorrow' – was not much given to confusion. In the world of drug retail and the violence that accompanies it there was usually little grey area: people paid or did not pay. Money was made or lost and reward or retribution followed accordingly. But here he was: confused. No two ways about it.

It may have been a poor choice on Alec's part to hire the quivering bam sitting before him – they'd get into that later – but, no matter. Lee had failed them. Lee would have to pay. However, Ranta was also prone to the myriad superstitions, the juju and voodoo that afflict the chronic gambler. Would he kill the owner, trainer or close relative of a favoured horse on the eve of a big race?

'Son,' Ranta said, 'do you think yer brother can win this fucking thing?'

Lee swallowed a smoke-flavoured blood clot. 'S-see since his accident, Ranta, he . . . he cannae hit a bad shot, so he cannae. Ah swear tae fuck he –'

'Will he no be wondering why you're no over there watching him?'

'Aye, probably.'

'Come tae fuck, Da,' Alec said. 'Let's just do the cunt.'

Ranta drummed his fingers on the tabletop, thinking.

'Fuck sake,' the Beast said. 'Look at this . . .'

Ranta turned back to the screen. The camera was tracking a fast-moving putt as it snaked across a green, zeroing in on the hole. The shot cut back to Gary's face, biting his lip as he watched the ball anxiously. It was the first time Lee had seen his brother on TV. It was an odd sensation. 'That was Gary Irvine for birdie at eighteen a moment ago,' Daventry said as the ball slammed into the hole.

'Ooh ya hoor ye,' Ranta said.

50

GARY SHYLY TWEAKED HIS VISOR AT THE CHEERING crowd. It had been a hell of a putt all right: thirty feet through about three different breaks. All the more impressive because he'd made it with his golf glove superglued with semen to his left hand. He tossed his ball into the crowd – something else he'd seen them do on TV – as Drew Keel came over and shook his ungloved right hand. 'Well played, son. You come have a drink with me later on, ya hear?'

'Thanks, Drew.'

It was unreal. Drew Keel telling him they'd have a drink later, the crowd pressing in, calling his name out, pushing hats and programmes forward for him to sign as the marshals cleared a path towards the marker's hut for him. Gary picked out the grinning faces on his way – Dr Robertson, Aunt Sadie, Bert. Where was his mum?

In the marker's hut he tripled-checked his scorecard. It was true enough. He'd shot 68 – two birdies, an eagle and no bogeys. Not quite his 65 of yesterday, but still one of the best rounds of the tournament so far.

'Well played, son,' the official who ratified his card said. 'Just you watch. This wind keeps getting up and you might be up there on your own before the end of the day.'

Gary walked out of the hut in a daze, right into April. 'Well,' she said, grinning, 'the man of the moment! Right, you, after your press conference you can give me the first exclusive interview.'

'Press conference?' Gary said.

There must have been over a hundred journalists crammed into the media tent. Applause as Gary entered flanked by April and a press officer called Kelly. April looked across the crowded tent and caught Lawson's eye. He was sitting near the back and sweating profusely. She flashed him a benevolent smile and he mouthed the words 'fuck you'. Gary was trembling as he scanned the logos on the TV cameras at the front – BBC, NBC, CBS, the Golf Network. Kelly led him onto the stage. 'Ladies and gentlemen,' she announced into the microphone, 'the current clubhouse leader, amateur entrant, Mr Gary Irvine.'

Fresh applause as Gary sat down. Cameras flashed and microphone booms wavered and jockeyed for position. Beneath the table his knees were clacking. Jesus, this was worse than any downhill putt. He went to lift one of the bottles of mineral water that had been placed in front of him and noticed how badly his hand was trembling. He put it back, dry-swallowed and folded his hands in front of him.

'Gary? James Weston, the *Independent*. How does it feel to be leading the Open?'

'Er, well, I might only be leading it for a wee while. There's still quite a few players out there.'

A man in the front row thrust his hand up. 'Bob Corrigan, the *Telegraph*,' he said. 'How did your nerves hold up out there? You took quite a long comfort break after eleven, were you just steadying yourself?'

'Umm, aye . . . that's right,' Gary said, scratching his still-gloved left hand. That lemonade, trickling through his skull. Fizzing.

'David Tollhouse, the *Guardian*.' Tollhouse stood up. 'Was it intimidating playing alongside someone like Drew Keel?'

'Aye, well, you know, I'd only ever seen Drew on the TV and that, so at first it was a wee bit – baws – aye, but, ye know, after a wee while it was fine. Spunk.' The last word was uttered quietly, like an afterthought, and went unnoticed in the crowded, noisy tent.

Cameras flashed, more hands went up. People shouted his name, the name of their publications.

'Do you think you can be the first amateur winner since Bobby Jones?'

'Will you be turning pro?'

'Did the conditions work in your favour?'

'Was local knowledge a factor?'

April noticed he was starting to twitch a little.

'Are you out of your depth?'

'What clubs do you use?'

'What ball?'

Lawson stood up. 'Donald Lawson, *Daily Standard*. It's possible,' he said, 'that you'll be out with Calvin Linklater tomorrow. How does that make you feel?'

'Obviously it . . . it'd be a great . . .' Gary's head was fizzing now and his hands were shaking, 'fat honour. Fat bastard.

Fuck! Fucking fat cunt ye! AWOOO!' He let out the strange yelp and his hand flew to his mouth as a stunned hush fell over the room. Cameramen looked at each other.

Oh no, April thought, moving fast through the crowd to find Kelly.

Tollhouse from the *Guardian* missed this exchange as he'd been scribbling a note. He looked up smiling and said, 'I understand your mother was here today. She must be very . . .'

He tailed off as he realised Gary had stuffed his fist in his mouth and was turning purple.

'. . . proud.'

'AIEEE!' Gary spat his hand out of his mouth. 'MAW! AH'VE RODE YER FUCKING MAW! Oooh ya hoor ye! Big-nosed bastard! Sorry! Cunt! Fuck!' He was going full tilt; the 'cunt' as involuntary as a sneeze and the 'fuck' in surprise, astonishment and anger at the 'cunt'.

April grabbed Kelly and shouted, 'Get him off!'

'BAWS, TITS, CUNTS YA FUDS!'

Kelly leapt onto the podium. 'Sorry, everyone! No more questions right now!' Still the cameras kept rolling as Gary stumbled to his feet. He was singing now.

'TEGS, BEGS AND HAIRY FEGS!'

Kelly placed a hand on his shoulder. 'Please,' she began.

Gary locked eyes on her cleavage, staring down into her deeply cut blouse. 'Ahhhhh,' he began to moan.

'Let's just get you –' Kelly said.

Gary launched himself at her breasts, screaming with maximum urgency, *'GIE'S A FUCKING DIDDY RIDE, YA BOOT!'*

Kelly screamed as she reeled back and fell off the podium. Pandemonium now, chairs clattering over as people got up, cameramen and photographers clambering to get better shots. Shouting, screaming chaos.

'Ohhh, uhhh,' Gary was saying now as he scrabbled at his flies. April tried to fight her way through the mob towards the stage, shouting, 'Gary! Gary! No!'

Stevie walked into the tent through a flap at the side of the stage in time to see Gary stuffing his hand down the front of his trousers.

He ran full tilt onto the stage and *hurled* himself at him, both of them smashing onto the floor of the podium.

'BASSSTTARRD!' Gary screamed as Stevie began repeatedly punching him in the face as the cameras flashed.

'It's. For. Your. Own.' Stevie was timing each word with a punch. 'Fucking. Good!' Six blows until Gary passed out, his head lolling over to one side. Breathing hard, Stevie looked up at the assembled media of the entire world. He absolutely had to say it.

'OK, folks,' he panted. 'Nothing to see here . . .'

51

GARY WOKE UP WITH A LIGHT HEADACHE – A SOFT, regular throb behind the right eye – and a woozy, washed-out memory of something bad happening; like a nasty hang-over. His jaw hurt. His left eye socket too. He lay there for a moment with his eyes closed, trying to remember what had happened and where he was, gradually becoming aware of another presence in the darkened room, the smell of some-thing familiar, fresh and lemony. He opened his eyes and sat up a little, his headache giving a ticklish throb in the process, and saw that April was sitting on the other bed watching over him. 'Hi,' she said, smiling.

'Where am I?' Gary asked thickly as he tried to sit up.

'They've given you a room here in the Marine. It was nearer. Easy.' April moved over and gently pushed him back onto the bed. 'Don't try to get up. Stevie's gone to get Dr Robertson.'

'Dr Robertson? Why? What – ow!' His jaw ached when he opened his mouth too wide. 'What happened?'

'You don't remember anything?' April said.

'Ah, I was in the media tent answering questions . . .'

'Mmm. Then?'

'Then . . . I woke up here. What happened?'

She told him.

Gary lay there silently.

'Would you like some tea?' April asked gently.

When she got no response she crossed the room and busied herself with the hotel tea things: the plastic mini-kettle in contrasting shades of beige, the plastic pots of milk and cream, the single tea bags on their strings. 'I think we've managed to calm it all down,' April said, her back to him. 'But I wouldn't look at tomorrow's papers if I were you. And I'd steer clear of the Internet for a –' She became aware of a noise above the rattle of the cups and saucers and turned round. Gary was crying.

Crying? He was *destroyed*.

'Hey, come on,' April said, sitting back down beside him on the narrow single bed. 'You can't help it.' She put her arm around him as he continued to sob, his head in his hands.

'I . . . I . . . I . . .' Gary said, trying to start a sentence but, like a five-year-old who has suffered a great injustice, unable to get the words out for the racking sobs. 'I . . . I'M A FREAK!' he blurted through a fresh, hot squirt of tears.

'No you're not. You've got a . . . a neurological condition.'

'I am!'

'Come on,' she cuddled him. 'Deep breaths.'

'At first I . . . I thought it was great. The accident.' He got his breathing under control and began to speak evenly. 'Playing golf the way I could. But now . . . the Tourette's, the fucking Klu-Kluver-Bucy. I mean, April, I tried to wank off in front of hundreds of people!'

Actually, April thought, factoring in live TV feeds and the

footage that was surely being uploaded onto YouTube as they spoke, it was probably more like *millions*. She twisted around so she could look at him. He was lower than her, looking up at her anxiously and expectantly, the way he sometimes looked up into the air after a slightly mistimed swing. April traced her pinkie around the indent in his right temple, beneath it the damaged artery, the bleeding that had brought them both here. She moved her other hand up his spine, placed it on the back of his neck and pulled his face towards her. Their lips met and she kissed him, softly at first, then a little harder, taking his top lip between her teeth. The erection in Gary's pants – which was near constant now – somehow managed to increase in intensity, then, suddenly, he was pulling away from her.

'I can't, April.'

'Eh?' April was surprised at how hard she was breathing.

Gary held up his left hand, the fat gold band.

'It wouldn't be fair to Pauline.'

'But . . . she left you, didn't she?'

'Sorry, I really like you, but . . . I've got to try and make my marriage work.'

Wow. Do they still make you? April wondered.

A sharp knock at the door. 'That'll be Stevie,' April said. 'Here.' She handed him a box of tissues from the bedside table before shouting 'Come in' towards the door.

'Surprise!' Pauline said, beaming as she put her head around the door. Her beaming continued for exactly as long as it took for her to register that there was a girl – a young, attractive girl – sitting on the bed next to Gary.

'Pauline!' Gary said nasally through a wad of tissues.

'Hi!' April said, trying not to get up *too* quickly.

'Hello,' Pauline said, her initial smile now replaced by one that was brittle and terrible to witness.

'This is April,' Gary said. He tried to get up, then he thought better of it. 'She writes for the *Daily Standard*. We were just doing an interview.'

'Pleased to meet you,' April said, coming over and extending her hand. Pauline held it limply for two seconds before letting it drop and moving towards Gary. 'I went to the golf course, they told me what happened, where you were. Darling, are you OK?' She stood over him and put a hand on his brow.

'Aye, ah'm fine. Just a wee headache.'

'Excuse me,' Pauline said, turning round, 'Avril,'

'April.'

'Sorry – April – I really need to talk to my *husband*.'

'Oh, of course,' April said. 'I'd better get on. I have a deadline. I'll see you later, Gary, OK?'

'OK. Thanks, April.'

'Deadline,' Pauline said sourly the second the door was closed. 'She fancies herself, doesn't she?'

'She's nice enough,' Gary said ultra casually. 'Anyway, how come you're –' Just then an enormous groan went up from the golf course across the road.

'What was that?' Pauline asked.

'Sounds like someone just missed a putt,' Gary said.

Pauline sat down on the bed next to him. 'Oh Gary, I've missed you.'

'I've missed you too,' Gary said as Pauline moved closer to him. He felt his blood give an involuntary groinwards lurch. His physical attraction to Pauline had been with him for so long now it was hard-wired. Reflexive. 'But what about all those things you said. What's changed?'

Pauline took his hand before she spoke. 'I have. I think we . . . we'd been together for so long. Since we were kids really, I . . .' She'd worked hard on this speech on the drive over. 'I just felt a wee bit trapped. And I didn't cope very well with your accident. I'm sorry.' She was actually managing to well up.

'Don't be sorry,' Gary said. 'I'm sorry. It's been hard for you.'

'But it's been hard for you too,' she said, sliding in. Kissing him hard now, her hand going to his fly.

'Ah . . .' Gary said as Pauline started to unzip him. He was just about to enjoy the cool air of the room upon the hot, caged beast when suddenly the door was bursting open and a breathless Stevie was standing there. Gary and Pauline sprang apart.

'Hello, Stevie,' Pauline said.

The mortal enemies eyed each other coolly, Pauline thinking, *Yeah, I wonder what you've been saying about me the past couple of weeks? Well, I'm back, pal. So you better get used to the idea*. Stevie, in his turn, was thinking, *Interesting timing, Pauline.*

'Sorry to interrupt this touching reunion,' Stevie said, scoring a quick first point, 'but ah thought ye'd like tae know that Calvin Linklater just bogeyed the eighteenth.'

'What does that mean?' Pauline said.

'It means,' Stevie said, 'that laughing boy here is now tied for the lead with the world number one going into the last day of the Open.'

'But that means –' Gary began.

'Correct,' Stevie said, cutting him off. 'You're playing with him tomorrow.'

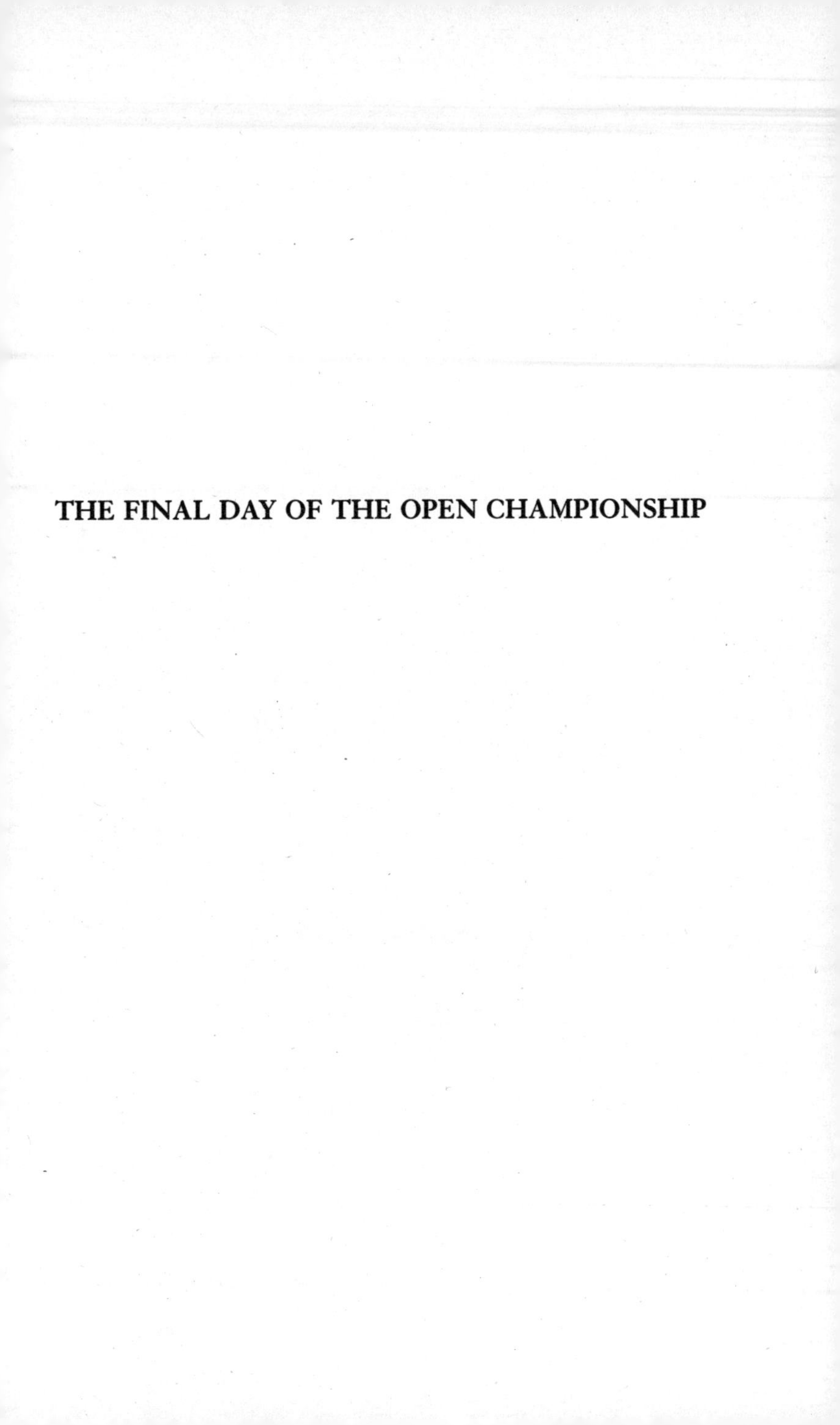

THE FINAL DAY OF THE OPEN CHAMPIONSHIP

52

LEE TOOK THE TICKET RANTA HANDED HIM AND MOVED through the turnstiles, Ranta in front of him, his huge shoulders blocking out the morning sun, and Frank and Alec behind him. The queues to get in were already long: with the fine weather and all the local interest in Gary the R&A were predicating enormous crowds.

Ranta turned when they were all safely onto the course and the four men formed a tight huddle. 'Right,' Ranta said quietly, 'here's the fucking script: you –' he nodded to Lee – 'are gonnae let yer brother know that you're here and that everything's hunky-dory. Frank'll go wi ye.' Ranta looked at his watch. 'We've got a good wee while until he tees off so me and Alec are gonnae go and get some scran intae us. Ah'm fucking Hank so ah um. Now, Lee son, in case ye get any daft ideas aboot maybe slipping aff intae the crowd and daeing a runner oan us, just think for once in yer life. Do ye really want us paying another visit tae yer wife and weans? Or yer maw? Awfy nice woman. Ah was watching yer brother wi her yesterday so ah wis. Would be a shame if she hud a wee accident. Like, fur instance, Frank here cutting her paps aff so ah kin make a set o' fucking earmuffs out o' them. Eh?'

The Beast grinned and Lee nodded miserably.

'Good boy. Right, we'll meet the two of ye at that place that does the steak sandwiches, just next tae the fish and chip stall, OK?'

'Right,' the Beast said, nudging Lee towards the hotel. 'Come on, ya fanny. Let's go and play happy fucking families.'

Breakfast in the hospitality tent. Journalists, guests of players and esteemed corporate clients wandered through the hot waft of frying bacon and grilling sausages. There were devilled kidneys, kedgeree, kippers and eggs poached, fried and scrambled. Pastries and croissants were piled high on silver trays, flanked by huge urns of coffee and tea.

April, who got hungry when she was nervous, was sliding a third sausage onto a plate already groaning with a very full English when she spotted Pauline up ahead at the buffet. It was not yet 7 a.m., April had barely brushed her hair after jumping straight into the same crumpled clothes – jeans and a fleece – she'd been wearing the day before, but Pauline looked like she'd come straight from a weekend at a beauty spa. Perfect hair and make-up, her lips shining a glossy pink in the light of the heat lamps that were warming the food.

'Hi there,' April said, sliding up beside her. 'Sleep well?'

'Oh, hello,' Pauline said, giving her a thin smile. 'Not great, actually. He was a nightmare, up and down the whole night.'

'Well, nerves. Oh.' April turned away from Pauline as Lawson approached. 'Hello, Donald! Peckish?' She nodded down at the plate Lawson was carrying with both hands. It made April's breakfast look like an *amuse-bouche*. In addition to the bacon, sausages, eggs, black pudding, kidneys, grilled tomatoes, mushrooms, beans and potato scones, he'd piled a couple of pastries on the side, perhaps as a kind of dessert, April wondered?

Lawson grunted, ignoring the sarcasm, and asked, 'How's your boy this morning?'

'Actually, Donald, this is his wife.' April gestured to Pauline. 'Pauline Irvine, Donald Lawson.'

'Hi.' Pauline smiled.

'Pleased to meet you. Watch what you tell this one,' he said, continuing on his way.

'Shall we?' April said to Pauline, motioning to a nearby table for two. Pauline hesitated for a second, glancing around the room before realising she knew absolutely no one.

They put their trays down. On hers Pauline had four grapes, a banana and a cup of peppermint tea.

'Not hungry?' April asked.

'Oh, I only ever have fruit in the morning. Maybe some porridge.' Pauline now took in April's tray. 'God, how on earth do you keep your figure?'

'Dunno,' April said, already spearing bacon onto toast and pushing it into the greasy golden heart of one of her eggs. 'I pretty much eat whatever I like. Never seem to put weight on.'

'Wow,' Pauline said, sipping her herbal tea and thinking, *you total fucking cow.*

'So, pretty unbelievable story, isn't it?' April said, chewing.

'What is?'

'Your husband. Amateur player gets hit on the head and wakes up tied for the lead with the world number one on the last day of the Open. Make a great book.'

'Do you think so?'

'Oh yeah. Sporting-triumph books? Sell bucketloads.'

'How . . . I mean, do you know, roughly, how much money you'd get for something like that?'

'Depends,' April said, blowing through a mouthful of hot sausage. 'A lot of money, I should think. If he wins? An awful lot of money.'

'Really?' Pauline said.

'Oh yeah. Then there's all the other stuff.'

'Well, I know the winner gets . . . is it seven hundred and fifty thousand pounds?'

'That's the least of it. Endorsement fees for clubs, balls, clothes and bags. Appearance fees at tournaments, advertising, instructional books, magazine fees . . . I mean, whistles and bells, you're talking millions of pounds.'

'Really?' Pauline said innocently, aware that she was gripping her mug so hard it might splinter apart in her hands.

April looked up, a dot of yolk shining on her bottom lip. 'Are you OK, Pauline?'

'Just a bit . . . nervous.'

Pauline looked over to their right, to where a man was stacking copies of all the morning's newspapers onto a rack on the wall. Her husband's face was on the cover of four of them. April gave a little shriek and ran over and grabbed a copy of the *Standard*. Above a photo of Gary walking off the eighteenth green yesterday was the headline 'HE CAN DO IT!'. Below it was the byline 'by sports reporter April Tremble'.

Her first front-cover byline.

April whistled in Lawson's direction. He turned to see her beaming, holding the paper up by the top corners. Lawson simply nodded and turned back to his food. *Fuck you, fat man*,

April thought, sitting down to read her story. Pauline looked again at the headline.

'Can he?' she asked.

April just smiled.

53

WHILE CALVIN LINKLATER BEGAN HIS FINAL-DAY routine (the stretches and stomach crunches, the silent, high-fibre breakfast) alone in a room that could comfortably have held a party for forty people, Gary's preparations were more hectic. Cathy, Lisa, Aunt Sadie, Stevie, Dr Robertson and Gary were all crammed into the small twin-bedded room. Stevie was packing the golf bag, loading up on gloves, Robertson was shining a penlight into Gary's left eye, and Lisa, Cathy and Sadie were crying.

'Aw God, son, ah'm sorry tae bother ye wi this the noo, ah didnae want tae tell ye yesterday, ye've enough oan yer plate, son, it's jist we . . . we don't know whit he's gone and got himself intae this time. God only knows where he is,' Cathy went on, 'lying . . . lying DEED SOMEWHERE!' She and Lisa burst into fresh peals of tears. It had been a terrible, sleepless, tear-filled night for Cathy and Lisa as they tried to work out what to do. The kind of night Lee specialised in causing.

'By Christ,' Sadie said, snuffling, 'the hertbreak that boy's brought you, hen.'

Robertson stepped back from Gary, snapping off the penlight. 'You seem OK. But the minute you're finished we're going to the hospital for a CAT scan. How's the headache?'

'No too – prick – bad,' Gary said.

'Aww God, Doctor,' Cathy said, 'ah'm sorry you've had tae listen tae all this. You must think we're some family.'

'Not at all.'

'Sh-should,' Cathy stuttered, 'we go tae the police?'

'Mum, listen,' Gary said, taking her trembling hands in his own, 'that might only make things worse. He probably – tits – owes these guys money. We'll just have to pay them back.'

'But, Gary,' Lisa cried, 'he said it wisnae even about the money any more. And whit was this money for anyway?'

'Aww God only knows, hen,' Cathy said, sucking in a deep breath and composing herself. She stared wistfully off, looking out of the window, but not seeing anything through tear-stinging eyes. 'Ah cannae believe that your own brother isnay here the day to see you play. Thank God your father –'

'Look, Cathy,' Stevie cut in, 'ah'm sorry, but we really need tae head down the practice range.'

'Ah know, son. We'll just have to –'

'Shit,' Gary said. 'Maybe you're right. Maybe we should call the police. I mean, if –'

The door opened and Lee Irvine strode into the room.

In terms of effect it was something like Jesus strolling into church at the climax of Sunday's sermon.

Amid the silence Lee was trying for an expression somewhere between defiant and nonchalant, his eyes darting about the walls, not meeting anyone's stunned gaze. His studied nonchalance was undermined by the fact that half his face looked like raw steak and his front teeth were missing. Finally Lee looked at his brother and spoke.

'A'right, bawbag?'

Masterson felt his mobile vibrate twice in his pocket, announcing the arrival of a text message; a seismic event for those engaged in an affair, enough to cause the heart to flex hopefully in the chest. Well covered by the Sunday papers he had spread across the kitchen table, and with Leanne busy at the cooker a good distance across the kitchen, he slipped the mobile out and glanced down at the text. Bastard: just her cousin Gerry, crowing about the Rangers defeat, the dirty Fenian fucker.

'One egg or two?' Leanne was asking him.

'Ah, gies two.'

He lifted his mug and blew on the hot tea. He'd left three messages now. Where was she? He'd tried Katrina's. He'd driven by Pauline's house. Nothing. Maybe he should send her another text? Naw, start to look desperate. She was just a bit upset. Had her heart set on that big house, so she did. He'd make it up to her. After his lawyer served the papers on Leanne and it was all out in the open they'd have a nice wee holiday somewhere. Spain maybe. She'd come round.

He turned the page and there it was in black and white: Pauline on the doorstep, wrapped in a white dressing gown, her hair turbaned up in a towel, smiling as she spoke to someone just to the right of the camera. Gripping the mug tighter in his left hand and the corner of the paper tighter in his right, he scanned the article, eyeballs jerking left to right as various phrases sprung up at him: '*pleased he's playing so well . . . works hard at his golf . . . can definitely go all the way . . .*'

'YA FUCKEN HOOR!' Masterson screamed, boiling tea spilling down his arm.

'Jesus Christ!' Leanne said. 'What is it?'

'I . . . nothing. I just spilt ma tea. Chuck us a cloth for fuck's sake!'

Leanne rinsed a cloth under the cold tap and took it over to him. She watched as he dabbed at his arm, then at the table and the papers crumpled in front of him.

She had surprised herself these past few days.

She was surprised at how equably she was able to behave towards this man who had paid someone to come here in the night and shoot her in the head. (Surprised too at how coolly she had handled her would-be murderer, at how much information he'd told her after he'd finally stopped crying.)

She was surprised at how calmly and diligently she had gone about plotting her revenge: withdrawing funds from the bank account he didn't know she had, the emergency fund she'd squirrelled money into over the past twenty years, five hundred here, a thousand there. It certainly had added up.

She allowed herself a smile as she walked back to the cooker to turn the bacon over.

'Aww, son, yer f-face. Whit happened tae yer face?' Cathy had been crying for a long time now as Sadie rubbed her back. Lisa sobbed softly while she held Lee's hand. Just the four of them in Gary's room now, Lee with his mum and his wife on either side of him on the narrow single bed.

'C'mon, Maw. It's a'right. It looks worse than it is, so it does.'

'Whit have ye got yerself intae now, Lee?' Cathy said for the third or fourth time.

'It's just a misunderstanding wi some boys.'

'My God, Lee,' Sadie said, 'the state o' yer teeth. It makes ma bum go aw fizzy just looking at them so it diz!'

'But, Lee,' Lisa said, 'Alec Campbell? My God.'

'Och, Alec's no that bad,' Lee lied. 'Ye don't want to believe half the shite ye hear in this toon.'

'Ah . . . ah couldnae take it if ye had to go . . . away again, son,' Cathy said. 'It'd put me a pine box so it would.'

Cathy's departure from the family home ensconced in a pine box had been a regular threat when Lee and Gary had misbehaved as children – 'Aye, see how ye feel when they're carrying me oot that door in a pine box.' Lee flashed briefly on the pine box that had contained his father. He'd helped carry it into the crematorium and he remembered how nice the grain of the cool wood had felt against his cheek: he'd drunk half a bottle of Buckfast and taken a phenomenal amount of temazepam. The big, old-school jellies. Eggs. Couldn't get them any more. Fucking brilliant gear. He wished he had some now.

He lifted his mother's head up and held her face tenderly as he spoke softly. A strange experience, to see Lee Irvine holding tenderly, speaking softly: like seeing a heavyweight fighter painting a watercolour, the brush daintily inserted in the boxing glove.

'Maw, listen tae me. Everything's fine. Ah'm no going anywhere. Ah've learned ma lesson. Come on now, we'll go and get some breakfast, eh?'

While the women dried their tears and began gathering their things, Lee moved to the window and pulled the net curtains aside. Hundreds of people were making their way through the sunny streets of Troon towards the golf course, windcheaters and sweaters tied around their waists. Shielding his eyes against the sun's glare Lee looked west, towards the sea, towards the course, the towering camera cranes and the scaffolding of the grandstands in their green netting. He looked back at the street and caught the sun straight in his eyes. So it was through a shimmering haze of pink and yellow sunspots that he saw the Beast standing across the road waiting for him. He was smoking a cigarette and looking straight up at the window, grinning a cold, frightening grin.

For fuck's sake, Gary, Lee thought, *make some fucking birdies today, pal.*

54

BY 2.30, THE TIME THE FINAL PAIRING – LINKLATER, C. and IRVINE, G. (A) – was due to tee off, the gates had long been closed to the public and officials were estimating the crowd at over 50,000: a final-day record. Most of the 50,000 seemed to be crammed around the first tee, spilling onto the road behind, into the car park and onto the flower beds in front of the clubhouse. Marshals struggled to keep people behind the ropes and off the walkways designated for players only. Half the county, from school kids to pensioners, seemed to have turned out to watch one of Scotland's own do battle with the world's best golfer. Children perched on the shoulders of adults, the cardboard periscopes bristled and bobbed. Many faces were painted with the saltire, or daubed crazily with blue in *Braveheart* fashion.

Preceded by a clutch of R&A officials, two policemen, his personal security guards and, finally, his caddie, Snakes, Calvin Linklater strode out of the clubhouse. The crowd went berserk: screaming, cheering, whistling, hands and children thrust out in an attempt to make contact. Linklater acknowledged the reception with a smile, a nod and a tweak of his visor but, really, he wasn't there. The pandemonium was already as distant to him as the waves breaking on the beach a few hundred yards away.

Stevie and Gary – late – were half jogging round the side of the clubhouse when they heard the roar for Linklater. They looked at each other. 'Fuck,' Gary said. 'Easy,' Stevie said as they turned the corner. As soon as they came into view a roar went up that made Linklater's greeting sound muted. Individual cries pierced through the din, some more sporting than others.

'GO ON YERSELF, GARY!'

'C'MON, BIG MAN!'

'FUCK IT INTAE THAT YANK BASTARD!'

'YA FUCKING DANCER YE!'

'FREEEEEDOM!'

Stevie was helping officials push people back behind the ropes, which were straining, threatening to break.

Up high in the commentary booth, Rowland Daventry said, 'And here he is. He seems to have recovered from a rather unfortunate incident in the press tent yesterday, which I'm sure many of you read about in today's papers.' On screen: a close-up of Gary's face, his jaw working silently as he muttered to himself. 'And what,' Daventry asked, 'can be going through this young man's head right now?'

'Fuck,' Gary was saying. 'Bigtittedhooryespunkfuck.' He came through the crowd and stepped up onto the tee. There, dressed in a powder-blue polo shirt and dark chinos, was Calvin Linklater. He was taller and even more powerfully built than Gary had expected, the cords running down the inside of his arms seemed to suggest that thick hydraulic cables rather than veins were buried beneath his tanned skin. Calvin Fucking Linklater. He was extending a hand towards Gary.

'Hi, I'm Calvin.'

'Aye.' Gary looked like he had been punched in the face. He was beginning to hyperventilate.

'Gary,' Stevie shot in. 'This is Gary.'

They shook hands and Linklater walked back to the far side of the tee box, a boxer returning to his own side of the ring. 'Baws,' Gary said to Stevie. 'Baws and flaps.'

'Ye can say that again,' Stevie said, pulling the three-wood out of the bag.

'*Sook it*,' Gary added with some urgency.

'LADIES AND GENTLEMAN,' the starter said. Incredibly, the crowd instantly fell silent. 'Can you please ensure all mobile telephones are switched off and be aware that no photography is permitted during play. The final pairing of the afternoon, on the tee, from Ravenscroft Golf Club, Ardgirvan –' an enormous cheer – 'Mr Gary Irvine.'

A jubilant explosion of noise went on for nearly thirty seconds. Cathy was jumping up and down, screaming herself hoarse. Lee looked across the tee and made perfect eye contact with Ranta. Ranta did not smile.

The crowd fell completely silent as Gary walked up behind his ball. As soon as his brain engaged the activity of calculating the shot, factoring in wind and pin position, the swearing roar of voices in his head fell away and the tic in his jaw stopped. *Nice and safe*, he thought as, with a low, punchy sweep, he brought the three-wood down. An enormous roar, the ball flying straight down the middle, Gary picking up his tee peg, not even needing to look, and Linklater was already behind him, looking for where he was going to tee up.

'And the battle was joined,' Daventry said to the millions watching around the planet.

Three things became apparent during the first few holes.

One, and in stark contrast to yesterday's round with Drew Keel: Team Linklater did not invite conversation. After Stevie had made a couple of innocuous opening gambits – How did they like Scotland? What an honour it was to be playing with the great man – only to be met with one-word answers – 'Great' and 'Thanks' – Snakes took him aside. 'Listen, kid,' he whispered out of the side of his mouth, 'ya all seem like nice folks and maybe later we'll grab a beer. But this is the last round of a major championship. So, no offence, but we don't do chit-chat.'

Two: in between shots Gary's Tourette's had become constant and low-grade, a ceaseless mantra of soft, breakneck swearing peppered here and there with actual conversation relating to what was going on around him. A sample conversation from the third hole went like this:

Stevie: 'I reckon you're probably looking at seven-iron. Maybe even a six.'

Gary: 'Titscuntfuckbawsyahoor. Wind. Pishflaps. Fuck! Sorry! Smokemafuckindobber. Probably make it – cuntcuntfucktitsflapsfannyflaps – with a seven. Hoor.'

Three: Gary was playing like a dream.

A lob wedge from the side of the first green so perfectly struck that when the ball spun towards the hole it was like watching a piece of film being played backwards. A stinging four-iron at the second that appeared to brake in mid-air before dropping softly to within ten feet of the flag. And he was sinking every putt in sight.

Three birdies in the first four holes.

Linklater – perhaps figuring that as long he kept within striking distance then Gary was bound to fall apart under the pressure sooner or later – wasn't trying anything spectacular and made four safe solid pars. The net result: here they were on the fifth with Gary three strokes ahead of the world number one.

'And I don't think anyone was expecting this,' Daventry said as the TV showed the two players sizing up their shots.

'No, Rowland,' Torrent agreed, 'I think the consensus was that the pressure would be far too much and that this young man's incredible streak of, well, you don't want to call it luck – he's playing some incredible golf – but whatever you want to call it, I think a lot of people thought that today would probably be where it ran out. Not so.'

'And let's not forget that there's still a lot of other players out there,' Daventry said. 'You've got Rodriguez and Torsten Lathe both on a couple under. Honeydew III there or thereabouts. It's by no means a two-horse race yet.'

'Absolutely not,' Torrent agreed, 'but I think, as far as the people here are concerned, this is the only match on the course.'

'The only game in town,' Daventry said enigmatically.

'Eh?'

'Solitaire. You know the old song?'

'Sing it for us then, Rowland.'

'I'll sing it for you later. In the bar. After we've had a wee drink. A few wee drams.' Blood all over Scotland came to the boil as Daventry went into his terrible faux-Glaswegian accent.

Meanwhile, down in the crowd, Gary's gallery could not believe their good fortune. 'Aww God, hen,' Cathy said to

April, 'ah cannae believe he's playing so well with all these folk watching, so ah cannae.'

'I know,' April said. She was beginning, for the first time, to allow herself to believe that he could win. Although, watching from a distance of nearly a hundred yards, she was worried about him. Apart from when he was actually swinging the club his mouth was now constantly in motion.

Ranta was watching Gary – taking a few lazy practice swings with his pitching wedge now – with the pure current unique to the inveterate gambler crackling through his veins. He was making calculations. If he won the fucking thing? At the odds Ranta had got? He'd be taking Frank and maybe Big Benny with him when he went to collect his winnings, that was for fucking sure. 'Come tae fuck, son,' Ranta whispered as Gary assumed his stance.

Pauline was making calculations too. The winner's cheque, plus the endorsements, plus the appearance fees, plus the book deals, advertising . . . although she was worried about the constant, demented mantra he seemed to be emitting. How long could she put up with that? Well, she reasoned, it only takes money to make money. A couple of million well invested? You could probably double it in a few years. She could live with some swearing, gibbering lunatic for a few years. Maybe it wouldn't be too . . .

She broke out of her reverie as the crowd gasped and craned her neck to try and follow the ball. A moment where it was invisible, white lost against white somewhere high in the air, then – whump! There it was, bouncing slap in the middle of the green again as the crowd went bananas, everyone cheering and jumping up and down, thousands of Scottish voices singing 'here we go here we go here we go' as Gary waved shyly, wiping his clubhead against the sole of his shoe as he continued to mutter whatever he was muttering.

Pauline found herself hugging Cathy, April even, all of them laughing and jumping up and down. 'Go on, son!' Cathy shouted as they started trying to move off, their little group being sucked along in the slipstream of the great crowd. Suddenly Pauline felt a sharp tugging at her sleeve. She spun round and found herself eyeball to eyeball with Findlay Masterson. His face was scratched, his shirt was ripped and he had sand in his hair. Even though his jaws were clamped so ferociously together that it looked like his teeth might explode in a glassy shower, Pauline could smell the whisky on his breath.

He looked deranged.

'Fin—' she began.

55

HE'D STORMED OUT OF THE HOUSE – TELLING LEANNE he had to go into the office – and driven straight to the Hospitality Inn, scene of so many pleasantly obscene memories. He started on the pints of heavy, his rage increasing as he leafed through the complimentary Sunday papers spread out on one of the coffee tables.

Gary, Pauline, Gary's mum, Pauline, Gary.

He upgraded to single malt as the barman turned the TV on and together they watched the coverage from Troon: the enormous crowds, Calvin Linklater and Pauline's fucking husband. 'No real, eh?' the barman said pleasantly. 'The boy lives just round the corner.'

'Aye,' Masterson said, gagging as he knocked back his double and signalled for another.

The whisky was still burning in his throat when he peeled out of the car park and pointed the nose of the Mercedes towards Troon.

By this time the whole town was basically an NCP and the

closest he could get was the seaside hamlet of Barassie, a few miles along the coast. He parked there and – pausing only to pick up a four-pack of vagrant-strength lager from a newsagent's – walked furiously back into Troon, drinking all the way.

On arrival at the golf course he was told very politely that the course was filled to capacity and no further admissions were possible. Masterson produced his wallet and offered the clown on the gate one hundred pounds in cash. When this was declined he increased it to five hundred. This too was declined. Masterson unbuckled his Rolex and added it to the negotiations. He used the expression 'come tae fuck, ya cunt'.

Realising that alcohol rather than golf fanaticism was at work here, the clown called over two security guards and a few seconds later Masterson was trudging away from the course back towards Barassie. After paying another visit to the same newsagent's he found himself stumbling along the beach, uncapping another golden tube of loony soup and finding that they were starting to go down surprisingly well. He discarded his jacket, basking in the hot sun as he slouched through the sand towards the golf course once more. He was certainly feeling no pain when he scrambled up through the high dunes, cutting his face and hands on the sharp-edged, clawing grass. Very little pain as he crawled under the barbed-wire fence separating the course from the beach, ripping his shirt open in the process and finally stumbling hiccuping onto the outer perimeter of the course.

Masterson had now walked nearly ten miles in the summer heat while consuming roughly thirty-two units of alcohol.

* * *

Thankfully the press of the crowd was so great that Pauline and Masterson were quickly yards away from everyone else, over by some gorse bushes, off the heaving pathway.

'Fin—' Pauline tried again.

'Shut it, ya fucking hoor,' Masterson said, cutting her off. 'So this is yer fucking game, is it? The minute ye think he might be ontae the big time suddenly he's no such a bad deal and auld muggins here can get himself tae fuck, eh? Eh, ya fucking boot, ye?' Masterson had only ever put a little money between himself and the animal that grew up on Wilton Terrace. It had just taken a few drinks and the right circumstances for the animal to come snarling back.

'Please keep your voice down!' Pauline hissed. Everyone passing by was looking at the dishevelled, drunken madman shouting at the attractive, well-dressed woman. 'It's not like that at all.'

'Oh aye, whit's it fucking like then?'

'I just thought . . .' Pauline said, thinking, whispering now, 'if he won, I might, um, get some of it in the divorce. For us.'

'Oh aye?'

'Yes.'

Masterson thought for a minute. Or rather, lager-spangled voices shouted at each other in his head for a minute. Finally he spoke.

'YOU'RE A LYING FUCKING HOOR!' he screamed, spraying beery flecks of saliva all over her. 'AFTER WHIT A WIS GAUNY DAE FUR YOU! FOR US! I –'

Pauline slapped him.

It took Masterson a couple of seconds to fully register this outrage, but, when he had, he grabbed her by the lapels and reared back to headbutt Pauline in the face.

Someone grabbed his hair from behind, stopping his forehead from beginning its forward-and-down trajectory, and suddenly a face was very close to his. 'Findlay,' a voice said quietly in his ear as the fist gripped the hair at the nape of his neck harder, 'there's no need for this now, is there?'

56

A FEW HUNDRED YARDS AWAY, ON THE SIXTH GREEN, Stevie was worried. Not about the putt – the approach shot had landed in exactly the right spot, leaving them a pretty straight, nicely uphill putt – but about the escalation in volume Gary seemed to be undergoing. The occasional word was now leaping out of the bubbling mantra at considerably more than a whisper. They were standing off to the side of the green while Linklater lined up his putt, a tricky, thirty-foot, left-to-right number.

'Aye, putt, ya cunt,' Gary said. 'Bawsbawsfudspunkhoor-ERSE!-flapsfuck! OW!' Linklater and Snakes glared over, then resumed examining the line of the putt.

'Easy,' Stevie whispered.

'Ah cannae – fuckcunts – ow! – help it – cunt – Stevie.' Gary was stuffing his fist in his mouth, biting down hard on his knuckles. But it was no use. He spat his fist out and screamed 'PRICK!' at Linklater. People gasped. Linklater threw his arms up in the air, abandoned his putt and approached the marshal. Stevie put his head in his hands.

'Well,' Rowland Daventry said on-air, 'we can't hear it from up here, but it seems that Mr Irvine, I'm not quite sure, but . . . Linklater is speaking to an official. Extraordinary.'

Two R&A officials were walking towards them now; a tall, thin Englishman called Dawkins and a short, fat Scotsman called Morton. 'Just keep your mouth shut,' Stevie said. 'Unnghh,' Gary said, chewing on knuckles.

'Mr Irvine,' Dawkins said, 'we simply cannot tolerate this behaviour. We cannot allow a competitor to insult another player during his pre-shot routine.'

'He's not insulting him specifically. It's just an aspect of his condition,' Stevie said.

Across the green Linklater stood with hands on hips. Thousands of spectators looked on.

'If,' Dawkins said, addressing Gary directly, 'there are any further outbursts of this nature I am afraid we will have no choice but to disqualify you. Do you understand?'

'Urrr . . . aye,' Gary said, before quickly adding, 'prick! ooh ya cunt! Fuck! Sorry! Skinny English prick ye. Sorry!'

'Are you telling me,' Morton said to Stevie, 'that isn't specific?'

'It's an aspect of his –' Stevie began.

'Prick. Wank. Sorry! Cunt fat wank. Sorry! AIEEE!'

'Condition.' Stevie clamped a hand over Gary's mouth. 'It won't happen again.'

'Mmmff. Uhnn,' Gary said.

Dawkins and Morton marched off and Stevie took Gary over to the side of the green. 'Right, listen, please calm down for fuck's sake. Just try and control yourself for five minutes. I've got an idea.'

Gary nodded miserably, fist stuffed back in his mouth,

while Linklater got on with his putt. Stevie ran over to one of the BBC camera positions. 'Sorry, mate,' he said to the cameraman, 'I've a wee bit of an emergency. You wouldn't be able to help me out with something, would you?'

Ranta let Masterson go. People were looking. 'I mean, there's a golf game going on here, Findlay,' he said.

'Fuck your fucking game. If you hadnae fucked things up ah widnae be in this mess. Where's ma fucking money?'

'What money?' Pauline said.

Ranta sighed and stepped towards Masterson. 'Seeing as we go back a long way, Findlay, ah'm gonnae do ye a favour and have Frank here drive ye home. And ah told ye – you'll get yer money back, right? But if ah wis you ah'd be very careful about what ah said in future.'

'Fuck off. Do ye think ah'm scared o' –'

The Beast's massive hand fell on Masterson's shoulder.

'Come on, pal,' he said, 'ye can sleep it aff in the car . . .'

'See you later, Findlay,' Ranta said. He turned and jogged up the path, fighting his way back into the crowd, towards where wild cheering was indicating that something important had just happened.

57

LINKLATER STRODE ON AHEAD TO THE NEXT TEE, HEAD down, ignoring the outstretched hands of the fans behind the ropes, furious that his birdie putt had lipped out. Snakes followed him, then, bringing up the rear, Gary and Stevie. While Gary was not unhappy with his performance on the last green – his uphill ten-footer for birdie had rattled straight into the middle of the cup, taking him to a four-stroke lead – he too, and for very different reasons, was trying to ignore the smiles, shouts and stares of the fans.

He had a large strip of silver tape plastered across his mouth.

Stevie had used a golf tee to punch four small holes along the middle of the strip of tape, where his lips met, so Gary could breath through his mouth, but he could make no sound beyond muffled 'mmmgghhs' and 'unhhhhs'.

'Well,' Daventry said, 'I've seen it all now.'

'Mmmmfff,' Gary grunted as they walked onto the next tee – straight into Dawkins and Morton. Dawkins had his hands on his hips and was shaking his head slowly from side to side. He looked very angry. Morton was thumbing frantically through a copy of *The Rules of Golf*. 'He can't play like that!' Dawkins said.

'Why not?' Stevie said.

'Because . . .' Dawkins turned to Morton.

'It's . . .' Morton said.

'Mnnngggh,' Gary said.

'It's a bit of tape,' Stevie said. 'And there's absolutely nothing in that book that says anything about not being allowed to have a bit of tape over your face.'

'Ah!' Morton said, stopping triumphantly at a page. 'It constitutes a distraction to other players.'

'Does it fuck,' Stevie said reasonably.

'Piss off!' came a shout from the crowd.

'Leave him alone!' came another.

'Mr Linklater,' Dawkins said, turning away, ignoring the voices as Linklater walked over from the other side of the tee, 'if you deem . . . *this* –' he pronounced the word with maximum distaste as he gestured to Gary – 'distracting . . .'

Linklater looked at Gary, at the fat strip of tape, at his lowered, shameful eyes, the eyes of Ben after he had expansively urinated on the living-room carpet. A long moment of silence then Linklater started to grin. 'Hell,' he said, 'long as you're not shouting at me, you wear what you like.' The crowd around the tee box burst into applause and cheering.

'B-but . . . surely . . .' Dawkins said.

'Come on, let's play some golf,' Linklater said, gesturing towards the tee box. 'Your honour.'

'Mnngghh. Uhnnnn,' Gary said.

'He says thank you,' Stevie said as he passed Gary the driver.

Pauline rejoined the huddle just in time to see Gary hit a perfect drive. 'Wha . . . what's that on his face?' she asked beneath the roar of approval that followed the shot.

'Stevie did it, it's tae help wi his . . . Turret's syndrome,' Cathy said.

'Christ,' Pauline said, 'he looks ridiculous.'

Lee turned round in front of them and Pauline smiled at him. Lee did not smile back. As soon he'd seen her arguing with that guy with the massive tache, he'd figured it all out.

The tache guy was that carpet guy whose adverts were on the telly.

The same guy from the family photo in the bathroom the other night.

Pauline – the fucking dirty hoor.

A little way off in the crowd, Ranta's hands were beginning to shake. He had to fight hard to keep from visualising his winnings. Cannae be doing that yet. Fucking jinx it.

His mobile began to vibrate in his pocket. Jesus fuck – *whit now*? He slipped it out and looked at the screen – 'FINDLAY HOME'. Christ, Frank must have got the foot down if he was home already. Probably starting to sober up, calling to apologise. Ranta thumbed the button. 'Aye?' he said gruffly.

'Mr Campbell?' a woman's voice said. 'Mr Ranta Campbell?'

'Er, aye. Who's this?'

'It's Leanne Masterson.'

Ranta moved away from the ropes, deeper into the crowd, his eyebrows going up as he listened, pressing the phone harder against his ear.

At the thirteenth, a par four of just over 465 yards, the match turned into the wind as the run of homeward-bound holes began. Both players had smashed their drives into the middle of the undulating fairway and still found themselves facing

200-yard approach shots, with Linklater's ball slightly behind Gary's.

Linklater rubbed his chin. The pin was on the back of an elevated green, a club more than usual in normal circumstances. With this wind getting up? Two clubs? Maybe more.

'What we got to the flag?' he asked.

'Two hundred and five to the stick,' Snakes said. 'What you thinking?'

'I'm thinking we need birdie putts every hole from here on in or this thing is over.'

'You got that right.' Snakes looked over to where Gary and Stevie stood, the silver tape on Gary's mouth glinting in the sunlight.

'Gimme the four,' Linklater said, hitching up his sleeve.

'Dial in, boss,' Snakes said, passing him the club.

Linklater would later say it was one of the purest golf shots he ever hit: a long, low, stinging four-iron into a stiff wind, the ball bouncing once in front of the green, again right in the middle of the green's elevated bank, the second bounce killing the ball's energy and allowing it to roll the last forty feet, curling up eleven feet from the hole. The champion acknowledged the cheers of the crowd with a raised, gloved hand, head down as he passed the club back to Snakes. 'Follow that in,' Snakes said quietly as the spotlight shifted over to Gary.

Communication between Gary and Stevie was now being conducted with grunting and pointing. Gary grunted and pointed at the five-iron. Stevie shook his head and proffered the four. Gary grunted and reached for the five.

'Are you aff yer fucking heed?' Stevie said. 'Two-hundred-odd yards? Intae this wind? Elevated green? Pin at the back? The big man just hit a four for fuck's sake.'

'Mnnghh!'

'Your funeral.' Stevie passed him the five-iron and stepped back.

Gary had never felt so pumped up in his life. It was as though the gag was stoppering up all the energy that would normally have been released by the Tourette's. As if every fuck, cunt, balls, hoor, flaps, wank, tits, spunk and fanny that should have been coming out of his mouth was now being channelled through his veins and into his muscles, like his body was literally being supercharged by the unreleased expletives. Ominously, that strange sensation in his head returning; a tingling of the scalp, not completely unpleasant, as though the excess adrenalin was bubbling up through the top of his skull.

He swung the club so hard he nearly fell off his feet, but the connection was good, the ball coming down right at the green. It bounced once right in the middle of the elevated bank and hopped forward, stopping quicker than any five-iron had a right to, finishing perhaps a foot behind Linklater's ball.

The crowd went berserk.

'Jesus,' Snakes said as they headed off towards the green. 'What you gotta do to beat this guy?'

There was something inevitable about what happened next. Gary's putt slammed into the cup for his *sixth* birdie of the day while Linklater's grazed the lip and curled around the hole before coming to rest above ground. *'Fuck it,'* Linklater growled through gritted teeth as he walked forward to tap in, frustration beginning to show now.

'Go on, bro!' Lee shouted.

'My Gawd . . . oh my Gawd!' Cathy was shrieking. 'He's gonnae do it. He's gonnae win!'

Ranta was hyperventilating. Still reeling from Leanne's

phone call, he was watching the golf equivalent of a race where his horse was twenty furlongs ahead of the field with five furlongs left to go. Still, Ranta had gambled long and viciously enough to know that horses had lost races from such positions. So, with an eye on the finances and the worst-case scenario (and business was business after all), he decided to cover his bet.

The Beast was enjoying being on the bypass, getting the foot down. It had taken forever to get out of Troon. He glanced at Masterson in the passenger seat; out cold, paralytic, his head against the window, his hair greasing up the glass. The reek of bevvy aff the cunt. Maybe he should give him a slap, tell him to sit up. Naw, he wis an auld pal of the boss's. Better play the white man.

The Beast's mobile trilled into life. 'Ho,' he said.

'Where are ye?' Ranta asked.

'Oan the bypass. Took fucking ages tae get aff the course and oot the toon so it did.'

'How's oor friend?'

'Cunt's lying here spark out, boss. Fucking steamboats so he was. We'll be at his place in about ten minutes.'

'Might be a wee change o' plan . . .' Ranta said.

58

FRUSTRATED, PUSHING TOO HARD TO MAKE SOMETHING happen, Linklater overhit his tee shot at the fourteenth – the par-three Alton – and wound up scrambling to make par. Both players parred the fifteenth. Gary birdied the sixteenth while Linklater notched up another par. They walked towards the seventeenth tee, the crowds ecstatic now, some singing 'Flower of Scotland', impromptu celebrations breaking out, Gary's victory seeming assured, inevitable. So far Stevie and Gary had managed to avoid looking at a single leader board. Finally they looked up at one of the towering yellow walls. It said:

IRVINE G (A) – 11
LINKLATER C – 4
RODRIGUEZ J – 2
LATHE T – 2

They looked at each other. Gary pointed at the strip of tape, at his mouth. Stevie looked around. They were at a safe distance from the spectators. Linklater and Snakes were ahead of them, upwind and out of earshot, Dawkins and Morton safely behind them. Stevie nodded and Gary stripped the tape from his mouth.

'FuckjesusfuckyacuntoohSteviefatbastardweefatbastardye!'

'Easy, nearly home. Nearly there.'

'Stevie-fuckcuntstits-ma-hoormasterflapspishbaws-head's-ersemawrodeyermaw-sore.'

'Your head's sore?'

Gary nodded, rubbing the crown of his head – a gallon of boiling lemonade in there now.

'Oh fuck,' Stevie said.

'And ah cannae – oohyacuntyefuckingblackbastard – stop it'

'Stop what? The swearing?'

'Aye – fuck. OW! Prick. Big pricks. Baws ya fat cunt ye. Slutboothoornail.'

'Shit. Look, it's just two holes tae go. Do ye think ye can keep it together that long?'

Gary took a deep breath and nodded. 'But, Stevie?'

'Aye?' Stevie noticed that he looked very scared.

'Whit if – fuckingslutyacuntsookmabawsgrrrBASTARD! – ah'm like this – PRRRRRRICK! – forever?'

'It . . . it's probably just the stress. This is a pretty fucking unusual situation here. Try and relax. But, in the meantime –' Stevie glanced towards the pathway, where Dawkins and Morton were waiting for them, Morton looking at his watch – 'there's no sense in us getting disqualified this close to finishing, eh? Sorry, pal, no be long now.' He reaffixed the makeshift gag firmly across his friend's mouth.

* * *

'This is just a fucking nightmare now, so it is,' Alec said to Ranta. The crush and press of the enormous crowd was so great that it was impossible to get anywhere near the action. All they'd seen the last couple of holes had been the odd club-head popping up above the sea of people, then the crack of metal on ball, followed by heads turning as one to follow the shot.

'Aye, right enough,' Ranta agreed. 'Come on and we'll go and watch the last couple o' holes on the big screen in the bar. Get a pint.' He was rubbing his hands briskly together. 'The boy's got this in the bag anyway. Seven shots ahead wi two tae play? Ho ho!'

'Whit aboot laughing boy?' Alec said, nodding towards where Lee was standing with Lisa, cheering as Gary and Linklater passed by.

Ranta, a man who was capable of feeling more affection for a winning racehorse than he was for certain family members, looked over at Lee, thinking. He smiled.

'Ach, fuck it. We'll let this wan go. Let the boy stay and watch his brother. We all make mistakes, eh?'

'Christ, how much did you put on this cunt?'

Ranta tapped the side of his nose and winked conspiratorially. 'You just leave it tae yer auld da, son. He'll see ye right. Come on, ah'm gasping fur a bevvy so ah um.'

'Another fine pair of tee shots,' Daventry said as, on television, Gary and Linklater walked up to the seventeenth green. 'Both players on the green at this very demanding par three. But, you'd have to say, Bob, it looks like it's all over bar the shouting.'

'And I'll tell you something,' Torrent added, as the screen filled with a shot of Gary, walking along, head hung, mouth taped, 'there's going to be some shouting in a minute for this lad . . .'

Gary had made the front of the green and was still looking at a putt of nearly seventy feet. Linklater was closer, with maybe a fifty-footer for birdie.

Stevie chewed his nails nervously as he watched Gary line his putt up. They were no longer conferring on putts. Gary's mind seemed to be reading them with superhuman intuition. Although his swearing was inaudible now, the muffled words hammering against the tape were coming thick and furious, in a near-constant stream. He was red-faced and sweating and seemed to be developing a slight tremor, a flicker, in his right eye, the eye beneath the indentation on his temple where the ball struck him. It seemed to Stevie like his golf was reaching a crescendo of perfection along with the swearing. As the round had progressed he'd swung more easily and relaxed almost in direct proportion to the magnitude that the swearing had increased by. Stevie wished he knew more about the human brain, about what could be happening in there, what fusing and rewiring of cortex and cerebellum had happened, how one thing might be affecting the other.

The crowd fell silent as Gary assumed his putting stance. Seventy-three feet, left-to-right. He aimed a foot and a half left of the hole and pulled the trigger. The ball snaked across the green, curving slightly right as it reached the halfway point, turning towards the hole. It was so sweetly struck, on such perfect line, that it looked like the ball was running along a little channel dug into the green, leading directly into the cup and seen only by Gary.

'Shit,' Linklater said, crouching by the side of the green.

'Aye, yer fucking maw,' Stevie said.

'I say,' Daventry said as the moan of the crowd began to escalate and sharpen in pitch.

'AYE! AYE! AYE! AYE!' Ranta was shouting, up on a table in the beer tent now.

Golf fanatics all around the world were yelling all of these things and more at their television sets in over seventy different languages.

The ball broke a final few inches to the right, bang on line but slowing, slowing, slowing. It reached the lip and stopped, half of the ball teetering over the cool dark below, half of it somehow remaining on the grass.

'GO OAN, YA FUCKING TOTAL HOOR YE!' Ranta screamed.

The ball dropped into the cup and the crowd erupted. Even Linklater was smiling now, shaking his head in what-can-you-do? fashion.

'My goodness,' Daventry said.

Gary ran into the middle of the green and ripped the gag off. 'AAGGHHHH!' he screamed. 'YA FUCKING DIRTY BIKE BOOT SLUT YE OOHH YA CUNT FUCKING BASTARD HOOR BAWS SPUNK SHITE SHITE SHITE! COCKS YA FUCKING PRICKS!'

The astonished crowd gradually stopped cheering. As the silence fell, Gary's volume increased, or rather it became much more apparent, and his outburst became more rapid. He was now atop a greenside bunker, screaming right into the faces of the crowd.

'FUCK FUCK FUCKING TITS FANNY PISH FLAPS . . . BENDERS! FUCKING GOBBLING DUGS!'

People's jaws falling.

Parents covering children's ears.

'CUNT . . . CUNT SUCKING ON THE TEATS OF A HOOOORRR!'

On television they quickly cut to footage of dogs scampering on the nearby beach while Daventry improvised. 'And, er, there seems to be something of an . . . unusual celebration going on there. I'm sure we'll come back to it when things have . . . umm . . . calmed down a wee bit.'

Back on the green: 'SOOK IT SOOK IT! HONK MA FUCKING BOBO, SMOKE MA DOBBER! BITE MA BANGER! BITE IT, BITE IT . . .' Gary was scrabbling at his trousers now, unbuckling, unzipping, just feet away from a horrified knot of pensioners.

Stevie started sprinting across the green.

'BITE IT, YA FUCKING CUNNNNNTSSSS!'

An old woman fainting.

Stevie was almost upon him when Gary turned, one hand down the front of his trousers, clamped around the root of his titanium erection, about to haul it out.

'BITE IT –'

He stopped in mid-sentence, a strange expression on his face, as if he'd just remembered something important. A trickle of blood ran from his right nostril. Stevie stopped.

'Gary?' he said.

Gary's eyes were screwed shut, like he was about to sneeze.

Something burst in the middle of his head.

A thick spurt of blood sprayed out of his nose, gushing down his chin and across his shirt. The crowd gasped.

'SON!' Cathy screamed.

Gary toppled backwards into the bunker, everything going milky, then black, as the screaming and shouting of the crowd faded away, and soon there was nothing at all.

59

HE KNEW WHERE HE WAS THE MOMENT HE INHALED. HE opened his eyes and looked up into the trees, listening to water splashing over stone, to the crickets thrumming. A bee – body as big as a grape – lurched drunkenly overhead. Amen Corner: the eleventh, twelfth and thirteenth at Augusta National, one of the most challenging stretches of holes in golf. And one of the most beautiful: Rae's Creek runs through it, burbling around the greens and across the fairways, the green water caressed by the weeping blossoms of golden bells. He became aware of another sound; the rhythmic swish and click of well-struck golf balls.

He followed the sound along the gravel path through the trees and, rounding a huge reddish-pink rhododendron bush, he saw his father alone on the twelfth tee, the short par three. He was hitting balls over the creek and onto the green. There was a bag of balls at his feet and a pale blue plastic cooler nearby. He watched as his father pulled another ball towards him with the toe of the club.

Swish click.

The ball floated gracefully up into the sky. It looked good for a moment, but, as it came down, it drifted, splashing into the water, short and left of the green.

'Bastard!'

'You pulled it, Dad.'

'Dae ye think?' his father said sarcastically, his back still to Gary. He hit another shot, smoother, straighter. 'That's mair like it,' his father purred to himself as he watched it. He turned round and pushed his hat back on his head. He was sweating. 'Morning, son, some day, eh?'

Gary stepped up onto the tee, his dad lighting a Regal now, and together they looked downhill, along the fairway, striped with bars of the morning sun, and across the creek onto the velvet grass of the immaculate green.

'No half,' Gary said.

'Here, ye thirsty?' his dad said. 'There's some cans o' juice in there. Come on and we'll get a wee seat.'

They sat down on a wooden bench at the back of the tee. The Coke was cold and sweet and they sat there quietly, savouring their drinks in the shade. After a while Gary said, 'Dad?'

'Mmmm?'

The 'Dad?/Mmmm?' exchange, one he had heard thousands, millions, of times in childhood. One that seemed as routine and dull as it was possible for something to be, but which now sounded as delicious to Gary's ears as the sweetest poetry.

'Am I a member here now?'

'Well, you're damn sure going the right way about it.'

Silence. Bees and crickets.

'Dad?'

'Mmmm?'

'Did you love me more than Lee?'

'Naw. If anything it was more the other way.'

'What?'

'Hey, you asked! You're not allowed tae lie up here. Ye get barred.'

'But –'

'Look.' He sighed. 'You were always a sensible wee boy. Worked hard at school. Got a good job. We always knew you'd be fine. Do you no understand, son? Love goes where it's needed.'

Gary thought for a moment. 'Maybe I should see him more.'

'Well, that would be a start.' His dad took a long swallow of Coke and burped happily.

'Do you know how much Mum misses you?'

His dad smiled.

'Ah watch over your mother every day. Every night ah float down above her bed and smell her hair and kiss her cheek as she falls asleep. She thinks she's daft. Thinks she's dreaming it, so she does.' A frown crossed his dad's face. 'But listen, tell her tae get that boiler in the bedroom cupboard looked at, would ye? It's making an awfy noise in the middle o' the night.'

'Do ye regret anything, Dad?'

'Ah wish we'd had more children. Ah'd have liked a wee girl. And ah'd have taken better care o' ma teeth. But everyone says that.'

'What's God like?'

'He looks a bit like George Raft, ye remember him? Yank actor. Bit before your time, ah suppose. Well.' He looked at his watch. 'Looks like it's about that time.' His dad stood up. 'Come here, son . . .'

They embraced, Gary drinking in the Dad smell: golf-sweat and Old Spice and Regal and the faint perfume of the Grouse that was famous, the blending scents bringing on a slide show, fragments of his whole childhood wheeling in front of his eyes: running on Ardgirvan beach, a football game in the back garden, him and Lee staring in the shop window at the Airfix models and their mum buying them unasked, a cinema – their dad cackling so hard at the film, their mum crying when they broke the portable telly, the menus for the Christmas dinner their mum got them to write ('prawn coktail . . . fish in white sawce . . . turrkey with al the trimmings'), a snowball fight – their dad's snowballs packed hard and flying fast as bullets, the same Airfix models built and waiting for them on the living-room table in the morning, Saturday night, waiting for their dad to come home from the golf – steak and onion rings and mushrooms and chips, their dad singing 'My Brother Sylvest' ('He's got a row of forty medals on his chest – BIG CHEST!') and all of them laughing, going somewhere in the car in the summer, their parents young and dark-haired and in love and him and Lee in the back, play-fighting on warm leather seats.

Gary crying now.

His dad saying, 'Go on. Shhhh. That's enough. There's only one thing the dead have tae say to ye.' Whispering now, close to his ear. 'Live, son. Live.'

60

'GET BACK A BIT, PLEASE. GIVE THE BOY SOME AIR.' Gary opened his eyes. Faces: Robertson, Pauline, Stevie, Lee, Lisa, April, a couple of old boys he didn't recognise, and someone who looked very much like Calvin Linklater. Gary realised he was lying on the grass in the shade of a huge grandstand. He looked down and saw his shirt was covered in blood. 'Oh, son. Oh God,' someone was saying, 'are ye OK?'

He looked up. Cathy was kneeling beside him, her face slick with tears. 'Mum?'

'Aye, son, it's me.' She stroked his forehead, the way she had done countless times through childhood illnesses, her hand and her voice trembling. 'Ah thought we'd lost ye there. How dae ye feel?'

'I'm . . .'

Apart from the thick, rusted taste of blood in his throat Gary felt like he had just awoken from the deepest, most refreshing sleep he had ever had. His head felt clear, like someone had drained off the boiling lemonade and replaced it with cool water. For the first time in a long time he also experienced the sensation of awakening without a painful erection digging into him. He sat up.

He recognised the two old boys now – Morton and Daw-something. From the R&A. In that moment it all came back: the match. That *was* Calvin Linklater.

'Mr Linklater. I'm so sorry about . . .'

'Hey, don't worry about it. You rest up there.'

'There's an ambulance on its way,' Robertson said.

'Ambulance? But what about the match?'

'I think we'll have to forfeit, pal,' Stevie said.

'Forfeit? No chance. Come on. Is there a clean shirt in the bag?'

'I don't know if we can allow that,' Dawkins said.

'What – you're disqualifying me because I had a . . . nosebleed?'

'I think it might have been a bit more than that,' Robertson said.

'We're not disqualifying you,' Morton said. 'It's just, medically, under the circumstances . . .'

'The circumstances,' Gary said, getting up now, 'are that I am leading the Open by eight strokes with one hole left to play. Is that right?' He felt fine, better than he'd felt in months.

'Yes, but –'

'So the only way you're getting me off this golf course is if you carry me off in a bloody straitjacket.'

Ranta was going mental.

Not just regular mental.

Absolutely triple-bonkers, pull-your-own-teeth-out-with-pliers mental.

He'd tried to charge out of the tent and head back up to

the seventeenth green to see what the fuck was going on. He couldn't even get out of the bar because everyone was pouring in to try and find out what was happening from the TV. The coverage on the giant TV screen for the past ten minutes had just been shots of crowds and wildlife and that fucking auld fossil Rowland Daventry talking utter pish. A rumour was flying around that Gary was dead.

But, if he was alive, and somehow able to continue, then the match would move onto the eighteenth. They might stand a chance of muscling their way onto the grandstand there.

'Come on,' he said to Alec. 'Ah'm gonnae try and get over tae the eighteenth. Just in case. You go and find that wee prick . . .'

Ranta's good mood had evaporated much quicker than it had built up.

A huge cheer as Gary emerged from beneath the grandstand, blinking in the sunlight. He wore one of Linklater's fresh, powder-blue shirts and waved to the crowd. 'Can you believe this?' he said to Stevie, as though he was noticing all the attention for the first time. He stopped by the ropes on the pathway connecting the seventeenth green to the eighteenth tee and shook many of the hundreds of outstretched hands that were thrust at him. He apologised to people for his outburst.

'You're the boy!'

'Well done, pal!'

'GARY! GARY! GARY!'

'Aye, cheers, nae bother, thanks,' Gary said.

'Stevie,' he whispered as they hurried off along the path, 'have you noticed?'

Stevie nodded.

'I think,' Gary said, 'it's gone. It's all gone.'

They grinned at each other.

It was still his honour. He walked onto the eighteenth tee to cheers audible in Glasgow nearly thirty miles away. Eight strokes clear with one hole left to play.

The first amateur to win the Open in seventy-nine years.

The first Scotsman to win the Open in over a decade.

The only Scottish amateur to have *ever* won the Open.

History.

Gary pulled out the driver. Four hundred and fifty-three yards to the green. Behind the green stood the red sandstone clubhouse and, somewhere within the clubhouse, at that very moment, the Claret Jug and the engraver, practising the words 'Gary Irvine (Am)'.

He took a couple of practice swings and settled the club-head behind the ball. He took it back, slowly coiling up, and then pulled the trigger.

'FORE!' Stevie screamed the second the ball was struck.

'My goodness,' said Rowland Daventry.

61

RANTA WAS IN LUCK. THERE WAS A LONG QUEUE TO get onto the grandstand overlooking the eighteenth green, but the security guard manning the steps was, like many of the temporary staff on the course, an Ardgirvan boy. He swallowed as Ranta strolled up to the head of the queue.

'Hey!' a man shouted. 'I've been waiting half an hour!'

'VIP,' the guard said solemnly, holding back the rope.

Ranta took his front-row seat just in time to hear the gasp rippling its way down the fairway from the distant tee. He could just make out Gary, still cocked in his finishing position. 'Where's the ball gone?' Ranta said to the man next to him, who was squinting through a pair of binoculars.

'Oblivion,' the man said.

It was lucky no one was killed. The ball had rocketed diagonally right at a 45-degree angle, barely skimming over the heads of the gallery all along the right-hand side of the fairway, and disappearing into the thick, thick rough.

'Umm,' Gary said. He looked at the clubhead, as if some strange malfunction had occurred, but . . . he knew.

Something felt different.

'I think you'd best play a provisional, Mr Irvine,' Dawkins advised. 'It's very thick over there.'

'Aye, right enough,' Gary said. 'Sorry about that. Don't know what happened there!' Stevie handed him another ball. With the penalty strokes if his ball was lost he was now hitting his third shot.

'Watch your heads over there!' Gary joked to the crowd as he again assumed his stance.

He swung a little gentler this time. KE-KLANG!

Linklater winced.

The new ball rattled off a wooden advertising hoarding at the side of the tee box and flew straight up in the air before plopping down in the rough, less than a hundred yards in front of them. Stevie felt his face beginning to burn.

Gary would play the second ball. The first one has not been found to this day.

Linklater nailed another perfect swing straight up the middle and they began the embarrassingly short walk towards Gary's ball.

'Jesus Christ,' Lee said.

'What's happened?' Pauline said. 'Why is he doing that?'

'It looks like he's . . . he's lost his swing,' April said, whispering the word with all the reverence, fear and dread that it merited.

'Calm down,' Stevie said as they got to his second ball. 'Breathe easy.'

'I'm fine, Stevie. It's just . . . whatever happened in here –' Gary tapped his temple – 'I think it's kind of sorted itself out now. So the swearing and everything's gone but –'

'So has the swing?' Stevie said.

The two friends stood there for a moment, the realisation dawning: an eighteen-handicap club golfer was going to have to play the final hole in the final round of the Open, against the best golfer in the world, in front of tens of thousands of on-course spectators and millions of TV viewers, *with the shanks*.

Stevie put his hand on Gary's shoulder and said solemnly: 'I was a mongo who dreamt he was a professional golfer –'

'But now the dream is over,' Gary said, finishing the quote from *The Fly*, 'and the mongo is here.'

'It's good tae have ye back. Now,' Stevie nodded down at the ball, 'we still have over three hundred yards to the green. You've already hit three and I'll bet ye Linklater's no going tae make worse than a par. So, the question is, can you, playing as Gary Irvine, eighteen-handicap golf spastic, make no worse than eleven on this hole?'

They looked towards the green. It looked a long, long way away. Whereas before they had been travelling the third of a mile or so between tees and greens by supersonic jet, it now felt like they were about to make the trip by horse and cart.

'Let's find out,' Gary said, grinning as he pulled the five-iron from the bag.

Findlay Masterson woke up; his eyes still closed, his head pounding and his mouth feeling like it was made of baked cotton. Christ, some session, he thought. Then he began to remember – the golf course, Pauline, Ranta. Shit. He could smell oil. He opened his eyes. It was dark. He tried to stand up and found he couldn't.

He was chained to a radiator.

'Why are they laughing?' Pauline said, pointing to Gary and Stevie. 'Did he want to hit the ball there? Was it, like, a tactic?'

Jesus Christ, April thought.

'Mind,' Cathy said thoughtfully, gazing at her son, 'he looks a bit back to his old self again.'

'Whit, duffing it all over the place?' Lee said sourly as Gary swung again. Thousands of heads snapped round, trying to see the ball dotted against the sky. After a second or two thousands of heads slowly swivelled back towards Gary, who was peering down into the rough at his feet. The ball had moved perhaps two inches, burying itself even deeper in the rough.

'Oh dear,' Daventry said.

'Head up,' Stevie said, offering one of the oldest, most pointless tips in golf.

To the untrained eye Gary wasn't really doing very much different. But, to the professional, his swing had suddenly, inexplicably, changed beyond recognition: his takeaway becoming shallower, the clubhead drifting dangerously in-to-out on the way back. Tiny changes, but success in golf is measured in millimetres.

'Shit,' Linklater whispered to Snakes, 'what the hell's going on over there?' He had to fight the urge to run over and give Gary a quick lesson.

'Right,' Gary said. 'Come on.'

Incredibly, however, he felt no anger. He felt clear, calm and relaxed. A day at the beach. It really was a beautiful afternoon. He was fighting hard not to laugh.

He swung again. Much better this time – the ball spurted forward at least three yards, coming to rest in a more open patch of light rough.

The crowd gasped. People had their hands over their mouths. 'Oh dear, oh dear, oh dear,' Daventry said. 'What on earth is going on out there?'

'Seems to be having a bit of a breakdown,' Torrent suggested.

Hardly pausing to aim, Gary took a casual swipe at the ball and – incredibly – actually connected quite well. It rocketed out of the spinach and flew low and straight for about a hundred yards. A few wags in the crowd burst into joking applause and cheers and Gary raised his arms in the air in mock triumph. He was on the fairway!

In six shots.

And still short of Linklater's drive.

April started to laugh.

'What's so funny?' Pauline said.

Ranta wasn't laughing. He was twisting and crushing a plastic lager glass in his hands while he stared at the scoreboard. He pulled out his mobile and dialled the Beast's number.

'Frank? Fuck it. Do it.'

He hung up.

Gary's next shot was a mega-shank of such colossal proportions that it caused Rowland Daventry to swear on-air for the first time in his broadcasting career – a hissed 'Shit!' as the ball ricocheted off the hosel of the club, heading diagonally right and low, bulleting into the crowd at gut level, where it hit a fat man in a yellow cagoule squarely in the stomach, sending him to his knees, doubled up and gasping for air.

Gary and Stevie ran the short distance over there. Luckily the man was not seriously hurt – 'Plenty o' padding here, son!' he said, cheerfully patting his stomach – and the softening impact of his belly had dropped Gary's ball in a decent lie on the edge of the fairway. Gary changed tactics, taking a six-iron and going down the grip to try a wristy punch shot with a shortened backswing. He succeeded in hitting a sort of a thinned duck hook that skittered across the fairway into the rough on the opposite side.

He had now hit eight shots to Linklater's one. He still had about 140 yards left to the green.

In the crowd, Pauline was furious now. People were openly laughing. 'What's he doing?' she said to everyone and no one. 'Why doesn't he just hit it properly?'

April sighed. 'He's lost his swing.'

Lee felt a hand on his shoulder. He turned.

Alec Campbell, smiling.

Frank stepped out of the sunshine and into the cool dark of the lock-up. As soon as he entered Masterson started kicking around and making the usual noises – 'mmmff' and 'unnghhhh' and 'nnrrrr' and stuff. He maybe sounded a little angrier than they normally did, Frank thought as he ripped the gag off.

'Whit the fuck do ye think yer doing, ya cunt! Do ye know who ah fucking am? Yer boss is going tae fucking kill ye fur this!'

'Aye, well, ah'm no so sure about that . . .' Frank said. Masterson watched as he placed a black, plastic toolbox on the table and ran a hand over it.

62

SHUFFLING ALONG LIKE A CONDEMNED MAN, LEE followed Alec towards the eighteenth green, the grandstand towering over him like a scaffold. Just then a huge collective groan went up, followed by a gasp, followed by laughter, followed by cheering and applause. Lee and Alec hurried up, running by the TV screen positioned behind the hospitality bar. On the screen a shot of Gary, laughing and shaking his head, and Rowland Daventry's voice saying, 'Have you ever, in all your days, seen anything like that?'

Gary's approach shot – his ninth strike at the ball – had definitely been an improvement. Rather than shank it again, he'd simply hit a very, very bad slice. He and Stevie and the rest of the world watched the ball heading for the deep rough to the right of the green. They watched in amazement as it struck a little hillock, created that very morning by a burrowing rabbit, and ricocheted back at a crazy angle, coming to rest just on the edge of the putting surface.

'Someone up there likes him,' Daventry said.

Linklater was safely on the green in two, with a birdie putt of about thirty-five feet. An outside shot. But he'd almost certainly make par.

Assuming Linklater *didn't* sink the birdie putt, Gary would have to get up and down in two shots from about sixty feet to win by one clear stroke.

If he took three it would mean a play-off between the two of them.

A very short play-off.

Lee sat wedged between Ranta and Alec in the stand. Ranta had stopped speaking. He simply sat staring down at Gary as he walked around the green below them, a seven-iron in his hand as he lined up a chip-and-run. Ranta just had a single phrase running on a loop through his head now, the Ranta Mantra: *cometaefuck, cometaefuck, cometaefuck, cometaefuck*.

'Fucking nine shots and no even oan the green,' Alec laughed hollowly, shaking his head. 'Fucking family o' losers.'

'He could get up and doon fae here,' Lee said.

'Aye, right,' Alec snorted. 'An ah –'

'Hey, you two?' Ranta said, not turning to look at them. 'Shut yer fucking mooths.'

Cometaefuck, cometaefuck, cometaefuck . . .

Linklater had seen many opponents crumble down the final stretch when faced with his relentless, grinding staying power – but he'd never seen anything like this. The guy hadn't crumbled so much as . . . exploded. *Steady on*, he thought, *we might still have to make a putt to win this sucker.*

Gary rehearsed his backswing – a short punchy scoop, the kind of bump-and-run shot indigenous to this part of the world – over and over. For the first time this week he was aware of the thousands of spectators, of the TV cameras. His hands were shaking as he moved the club behind the ball. He held his breath – the whole of Ayrshire held its breath – and swung a little harder than he meant to, his head coming up too soon, jerking the blade of the club into the middle of the ball rather than under it. The horribly thinned chip flew across the green towards the hole, on line, but travelling much, much too fast. The crowd in the grandstands gasped in horror.

Then came a hollow clank as the ball hit the flagstick and rocketed off, finishing six feet downhill from the hole. Had it not hit the flag it might well have been off the green.

Ranta opened his eyes when he heard Alec saying, 'Ya fluky bastard!'

Gary marked his ball and Linklater stepped up; an uphill putt, breaking right-to-left, a little at first, then sharply towards the end.

'Easy money, boss,' Snakes whispered.

It was in all the way – perfectly struck, breaking exactly as he'd visualised, slowing, slowing as it reached the hole . . .

The crowd noises were a strange jumble of strangulated cheers and moans: the crowd schizophrenic, many of them huge Linklater fans, many wanting to cheer a huge putt dropping, but more of them still praying that Gary might be allowed the chance to win the thing.

The ball slowing, slowing, inches from the cup now.

Linklater on his knees, out of character, game face gone. '*Come on, baby, come on, baby*,' Linklater whispered.

His third Open title in a row: the first player to do so in over half a century, since the great Australian Peter Thomson won in '54, '55 and '56.

Slowing, slowing . . .

Stopped.

And still – somehow – quite clearly above ground.

'Goddamnit!' Linklater muttered. He put his hands on his hips and shook his head.

'How on earth did that stay out?' Daventry wondered as Linklater walked up to tap in, being careful not to run over the ten seconds he was allowed to wait for the ball to drop. He barely had to touch the silver face of the putter against the ball for it to clink into the cup.

Incredible cheers and applause all around him as the full extent of reality dawned on Gary.

It was the stuff of golf dreams and nightmares.

He had a six-foot putt to win the Open.

'Ah cannae take it,' Cathy said.

April put an arm around her.

Come on, you stupid, useless bastard, Pauline was thinking. How hard could it be to tap the ball into that wee hole? She could probably bloody do it.

Ranta turned and stared at Lee, his black eyes had no bottom to them. Lee nearly fainted.

'Any last-minute advice?' Gary whispered to Stevie.

'It's uphill now. Don't be short.'

Stevie had committed one of the most grievous sins in the caddie's handbook: he had used a negative in a motivational statement. Stevie said: 'Don't be short.' Gary heard: 'Hit it very hard.'

Total silence. On TV Daventry whispered, 'This for the history books.'

Gary smacked the ball straight past the hole.

The crowd gasped.

'Oh dear,' Daventry said for the umpteenth time.

A muffled cry came from somewhere in the grandstand.

Stevie shut his eyes as Gary walked straight round to his ball. Now he had a very slippery downhill four-footer to tie Linklater.

He lined it up.

'This for the play-off,' Daventry whispered.

It didn't even graze the hole, slipping by a few inches on the left-hand side and dribbling on, coming to rest in almost exactly the same spot as his first putt had been made from.

Linklater had just won his third consecutive Open.

Gary walked back round and immediately assumed his putting stance.

'Putting for second place now,' Torrent said numbly.

'Easy now,' Stevie said. Gary's brain heard 'easy' and translated it to 'barely touch it'. The ball dribbled forward, coming to rest with a little over two and a half feet still to go.

'Good lord,' Daventry said.

A strange noise from the grandstand as Ranta emitted a high-pitched squeal, somewhere between a train whistle and a piglet being butchered.

'This for *fourteen* and third place,' Daventry said.

Completely beyond caring now, Gary just brushed the ball with the putter.

It climbed towards the hole.

It stopped on the lip, trembling.

It dropped in.

For a moment, out of perhaps ten thousand people crowded around the green and filling the grandstand, only two people went berserk.

'YES!' Gary screamed, sinking to his knees, putter raised over his head in triumph.

In the grandstand Ranta leapt to his feet, screaming, 'YES! YES! YES! YA FUCKING DANCER YE! BASSTTTT-TAARRRDD!'

Alec and Lee looked at Ranta astonished as the rest of the crowd began to come to life, gradually clapping and cheering. Ranta stopped dancing a jig, leaned down and planted a kiss on Lee's lips.

'EACH-WAY! FUCKING EACH-WAY, YA CUNTS!'

With his ten grand each-way bet at 180 to one he had just won a little over a million pounds for a top-three finish.

'Ah'll tell ye whit, son,' Ranta said to Lee, 'if that last putt hadnae dropped you'd be in the boot o' ma motor the now. Getting fitted fur a set o' fucking concrete Nature Treks. Anyway –' he threw an arm around Lee – 'c'mon and we'll go tae the bar and get a drink. Boy's a'right, Alec. Ye hear me?'

Alec glowered at Lee.

'Aye, cheers, Ranta,' Lee said, 'ah'll see ye in there. Ah'm just gonnae go and see ma brother first.'

As they made their way out of the packed grandstand Ranta remembered something.

The beast picked up his chirruping mobile. 'A' right, boss?'

'Aye. Magic, big man. Fucking magic,' Ranta said. 'Listen, ah wis just thinking, maybe ah wis a wee bit hasty earlier. Let's just leave the boy Findlay alone, eh?'

'Ah . . .' Frank looked down at Masterson. 'Maybe a wee bit late for that, boss,' he said, stepping away from the spreading puddle of blood.

Ranta thought for a moment. 'He's definitely deed?'

'Well, ah cut the cunt's fucking throat. That normally sorts them oot like.'

Ranta thought some more. Ach – fuck it.

'Ach, fuck it. Do us a favour then, swing by 42 The Meadows up in Riverside. Woman called Leanne. She'll have a wee envelope fur ye tae pick up. Then get yer arse over here when you're done. Ah'm getting the drinks in.'

'Nae bother, see ye in a bit.'

Frank hung up and started whistling as he walked over to the wall and began uncoiling the hose, his shape reflected in Findlay Masterson's dead, open eyes.

63

DOWN ON THE GREEN, IN FRONT OF THOUSANDS OF cheering fans, Gary and Stevie were embracing when Linklater walked over, his hand extended. 'Well,' he said, 'I guess I gotta ask you what everyone else is going to – what the hell happened?'

Gary grinned, shaking hands as he said, 'I was a mongo who dreamt he was a professional golfer. But now the dream is over.'

'And the mongo is here,' Stevie said, clapping a hand on Gary's shoulder.

'Ah, right . . .' Linklater said.

On TV screens all over the world, viewers saw Gary and Linklater talking. Daventry supplied the sound; 'I should think Calvin will be saying, "Thanks very much for handing me that, chum!" Dear oh dear oh dear. Not since poor old Jean Van De Velde at Carnoustie back in '99 have we seen someone throw it all away so dramatically.'

'He doesn't look too bothered though,' Torrent said.

'It's been a real honour to play with you,' Gary was saying to Linklater. 'A dream come true and all that.' It felt so good to be in control of what came out of his mouth again, to have no crippling erection burrowing into his thigh. It was gone, all gone.

'If you ever get to Florida gimme a call,' Linklater said. 'I think I can help you with that shanking.'

'Really?'

'Yeah. You're probably just standing too close to the ball.'

They started to make their way off the green, towards the marker's hut to turn in their scorecards, thousands of people cheering in the grandstands above them, hundreds more pressing against the ropes lining the pathway, policemen holding them back as the sky began to darken for what felt like the first time in weeks. In a group right at the front of the ropes he saw his family – his mum, his Aunt Sadie and Uncle Danny, his sister-in-law, his nephews and niece. Bert and Dr Robertson too.

His mum had tears streaming down her face as he pulled her through the ropes towards him. 'Aww, son,' Cathy said, 'I'm that p-proud o' ye.'

'Mum, listen, has the boiler in your bedroom been making a funny noise recently?'

'Eh? Ma boiler? Er, aye, a bit. Sometimes in the night.'

'Maybe we should get it looked at, eh?'

He hugged her to him, smiling as he looked up into the darkening sky. Then, above the roar of the crowd, he heard Lee's voice, the words 'ma brother' and 'ya fucken prick'.

'It's OK,' Gary said to the policeman. Lee stepped through the ropes and the two brothers embraced, Lee smelling sweat and blood, Gary smelling the sweetish hint of cannabis.

'Fuck sake, bro,' Lee began, 'that was some –'

'I'm sorry, Lee.'

'Eh?'

'Listen, do you want to get a round in next week? Me and you? Up at Ravenscroft?'

'Er, aye, sure. That'd be magic so it wid.'

People on all sides calling Gary's name out. Flashbulbs popping, cameras on him, microphones and tape recorders thrust towards him and now Pauline appearing through the crowd, holding her player's guest pass imperiously in the face of the policemen.

'Gary,' a man next to him said, extending a microphone towards him. 'Nick Parr from the BBC. Can we have a quick word?'

'Aye, sure,' Gary said as Pauline pushed through and slipped her arm around him, taking her place beside him in front of the cameras.

'Here with Gary Irvine,' Parr said through the microphone to the crowd, to the television audience at home, 'who has just become the highest finishing amateur entrant in the Open for nearly eighty years. But what could have been. Gary, you threw away an *enormous* lead. I hope you don't mind me asking – what happened on the last hole there? Was it the pressure?'

'Ach, you know golf, Nick. It's a funny game.'

Everyone laughed. Pauline giggled and gazed at him adoringly.

'I'm sure everyone knows your story by now, but tell us – what's it like to go from being a club golfer just a few months ago to playing with the world number one in the final round of the Open?'

'Ah, it was fine, Nick. Brilliant. I just hope I didn't put Calvin off too much!' More laughter.

'As I say, you came so close to winning, but the third-place cheque for nearly three hundred thousand pounds should be some compensation, I would think.'

'Ah, no, not really. I'm not going to take it, Nick. I don't want to lose my amateur status.'

Those close enough in the crowd and the millions watching on TV saw Pauline's face change.

She was still smiling, but the corners of her mouth were quivering, fighting not to turn down as she turned to look at him. Gary smiled back at her.

'He's just kidding,' Pauline said to more laughter.

'Pauline?' Gary said. 'Fuck off.'

He briskly shook Parr's hand – 'Thanks, Nick' – untangled himself from Pauline's embrace, and stepped out of shot and into the crowd.

Pauline stood alone in front of the cameras for a long, agonising, silent moment.

It was the most beautiful thing Stevie had ever seen.

Then a roar went up as Linklater emerged from the marker's hut and Parr, the camera crews and the crowd were all surging towards him.

Pauline turned round, speechless, to find herself face to face with a very angry Lee.

'Listen, ya dirty fucking boot,' he whispered through grinding teeth, 'ah ken fine well you've been riding that fucking carpet guy. Tom fucking Sellick right up ye. Just do us aw a favour and get yourself tae fuck before ah panel yer daft fucking coupon in.'

Lee shouldered his way off into the crowd, leaving Pauline blinking back tears, her jaw working strangely.

Gary pushed on through the crush – people slapping him on the back, trying to shake his hand – until he found her.

As April watched him coming towards her she noticed that there was still a tiny fleck of dried blood on his cheek. She wet her thumb and reached out and wiped it off. 'So what happened to "I've got to try and make my marriage work"?' she said, smiling.

'Well, God loves a trier . . .' Gary said as he leaned into her.

They kissed, oblivious to the cheering fans, to the TV cameras and the flashbulbs, to the officials trying to get Gary into the marker's hut to return his card, and to the cool rain that had finally started to fall softly, sweeping in from the Irish Sea, heading inland, moving eastwards across Ayrshire, covering the dry fields and the baking roads and making them sizzle gently, making everything smell fresh and sweet and new.

Epilogue

Gary Irvine resigned from Henderson's and attended Strathclyde University as a mature student. He graduated with a 2.1 in History and is now a teacher. He recently got his handicap down to sixteen.

April Tremble became Sports Editor of the *Daily Standard*. *The Amateur*, her account of Gary's accident and performance in the Open, was a surprise best-seller. She and Gary live in Glasgow with their two young children.

Pauline Irvine was declared bankrupt after Kiddiewinks finally went into liquidation. She still lives in Ardgirvan, with her friend Katrina, where she works part-time as an escort.

Findlay Masterson's body was never found and no one was charged in connection with his murder. After she banked the insurance money **Leanne Masterson** sold the carpet business and retired to the Caribbean.

Lee Irvine received a substantial cheque from an anonymous benefactor and has invested in several diverse business opportunities. He and Lisa have since had a third son – Ganges. He regularly plays golf with his brother.

Stevie Burns finally sold Target Video to Silver Screen for a six-figure sum. He donated half of this to the Ardgirvan branch of the Socialist Workers Party. He and Gary still argue about the second Stones Roses album.

Ranta and **Alec Campbell** were gunned down in a gangland shooting. Ranta alone suffered sixteen separate gunshot wounds. Despite this he survived while Alec died in intensive care.

Ben lived to be twenty-one years old, earning himself a half-page feature in the *Daily Standard*. ('Scotland's oldest dog!') When finally put down he attempted to bite the hand of the vet administering the injection.

Much later **Cathy Irvine** passed away quietly in her sleep. She loves to walk the manicured fairways of Augusta National with her husband, her leg no longer stretching out into the empty side of the bed.

Author's note

For the sake of narrative I took a few small liberties with the process of qualifying for the Open. I hope those familiar with the procedure will forgive me. I'd like to thank Dr. Fintan Sheerin for his generous, insightful help with all questions neurological. Also, and most importantly, a big thank you to all those kind and foolish enough to regularly tee it up with me. The Charlie Hodge Invitational boys: Stewart the Bull Garden, Peter McSween, Allen Reid, Graham Fagen (am I 4 up G?), Paolo Righetti, Andy Daly and Martin Murphy; Barry, Joe and Robin at Royal Beaconsfield; Fin and Eamonn at Ashridge; Russell Brown, Ron Fernandez and Danny at Little Hay; and Andy at Princes Risborough. I'll take this opportunity to apologise for every tortured profanity over the years.

Also a very special thank you to my editor, Jason Arthur at William Heinemann. Lastly, but certainly not leastly, as Jessica Lange would say, enormous and ongoing gratitude to my wonderful agent, Clare Conville at Conville & Walsh.